I0722640

BORRELIA

Praise for Millicent Eidson

"Millicent Eidson's unparalleled talent shines through in this remarkable work, ensuring a thrilling reading experience. I confidently predict that this offering will be warmly embraced by the literary world, solidifying Millicent Eidson's place among the most esteemed authors of our time."—Midwest Book Review, ***Anthracis: A Microbial Mystery***

"Dr. Eidson's medical thriller serves up unique and carefully drawn characters, fascinating and chillingly realistic threats, and enough Happily For Now resolutions to satisfy any women's fiction or romantic suspense fan. You won't want to miss this new entrant into the genre. I hope the author is busy writing the next book in this engaging series."—Reviewer, ***Anthracis: A Microbial Mystery***

"This 2nd book in the Maya Maguire series follows the intrepid CDC veterinary detective as she tries to track down the mysterious tick microbes causing Borrelia infections. Her travels lead her from her home in New Mexico to the European sites of other outbreaks. Meanwhile, Maya is dealing with her own professional and romantic issues. This is a fascinating insider's look at the increasingly menacing diseases arising from animal microbes worldwide."—Reviewer, ***Borrelia: A Microbial Mystery***

"The author's background as a scientist working for the CDC gives you an insider's view of this public-health agency at a time of crisis. I recommend Corona to all fans of medical mysteries."—Reviewer, **Corona: A Microbial Mystery**

"The mystery, the characters, the setting, and the uncanny timing of this book make it a compelling read. I would recommend it to anyone who loves medical thrillers, mysteries set in Hawaii, mysteries with diverse characters, books with a strong female protagonist, and fictional tales related to climate change."—A.M. Reade, USA Today Bestselling Author, **Dengue: A Microbial Mystery**

Also by Millicent Eidson

Series Titles
Microbial Mysteries: A Story Collection (Book 0)
Anthracis: A Microbial Mystery (Book 1)
Corona: A Microbial Mystery (Book 3)
Dengue: A Microbial Mystery (Book 4)

Short Works
Monuments: A Ten-Minute Play
Red Thread
Pariah

BORRELIA

A MICROBIAL MYSTERY

Millicent Eidson

Maya Maguire Media - Vermont

DEDICATION

Epidemic Intelligence Service (EIS) Officers

UPWARDLY MOBILE

Disease vector—such a vague and mathematical term for transmission of death. Antagonist, villain, criminal? Those are more powerful labels.

Soft-bodied ticks are bloodsucking external parasites that ascend from the soil or animal nests in a voracious search for fulfillment. They're arachnids but not spiders, and attractive with a mottled black and tan shell, like a softshell turtle. Upon feeding, after the meal satisfies, the tick's flexible shell swells and brightens.

Across all lifeforms, mothers are revered, honored and protected. She's only trying to nurture her eggs and survive as a species. The real culprits that kill are the spirochete bacteria, mere squiggles under the microscope, which infect within thirty seconds of the bite.

ONE

The naked swollen belly glowed under fluorescent lights as the pregnant woman knocked aside her gown and scraped the widespread rash. When her mother tried to restrain the frantic arm, low moans floated through the clammy intensive care room of the Albuquerque Indian Health Center.

Dr. Maya Maguire stood frozen, frustrated that as a veterinarian, there was nothing she could do to help the barely conscious patient. Despite the woman's critical condition, Maya couldn't control a twinge of envy. Giving birth was her only chance for a biological relationship, having been adopted as an infant from China by Irish American parents.

With her gloved hand, Maya touched the gowned shoulder of the middle-aged woman with streaks of gray in a long dark ponytail. "Mrs. Lucero, your daughter has a beautiful name. Bina—does it have special meaning?"

The woman lifted her eyes. "It refers to music."

In the challenging first year of her Centers for Disease Control and Prevention training, Maya had learned to reach people on a personal level before plowing ahead with her disease investigations. "I dabble at the piano. Does Bina play an instrument?"

"Guitar. Her four-year-old loves silly songs."

Maya's innate hyperfocus kicked into gear and she whipped out a small notebook from her blazer pocket. Last year, she would have held back, waiting for a physician to take the lead. But not anymore.

She gestured to the angry rash on Mrs. Lucero's forehead. "The

Dulce clinic called yesterday about your family's illness. I'm based at the New Mexico health department, but help out the Indian Health Service as needed."

Maya put a hand on a chair, one of her coping mechanisms with moments of weakness. Despite the master's in public health after the veterinary medical degree, she felt self-conscious whether she was accepted as an equal partner to physician epidemiologists. In all her previous visits to IHS hospitals, Dr. Manolo Miranda, an infectious disease specialist, had hosted her. With his incapacitation from anthrax, she was on her own.

Notes checked, she continued. "Bina is current on her immunizations, plus measles and chickenpox were ruled out by the lab. So I need to track down more unusual rash-illness exposures."

Maya had no idea where to go next on her interview. As a brief flash of panic clouded her eyesight, she took several deep breaths, annoyed that insecurity could intrude on the job. Epidemic Intelligence Service Officers were the front line federal disease detectives—no room for distractions or mistakes.

Mrs. Lucero's voice was tentative. "I need to focus on Bina. My family went to find something to eat. Can you talk to them?"

"I'll do everything possible to find out how this happened." After Maya left the room, she deposited her gown, mask, and gloves in the bin outside the door. At the central computer station, she recognized Ron Blake, the gray-haired ob/gyn who had approved her visit. "Any updates on Bina's condition?" she asked.

"We're not sure, it might be JHR."

Maya's brow furrowed. "I never heard of it, but human clinical medicine is not my expertise."

"Jarisch-Herxheimer reaction is a rare adverse response to antibiotics. Bina has cognitive impairment, low blood pressure, and appears to be in a lot of pain. She's in labor at twenty-four weeks."

He ran wrinkled hands across eyelids sagging over pale blue eyes. "I'm researching treatment options—never had this before."

"Which antibiotic?"

"Doxycycline. Listen, I assume you're here to find out what

caused all this, but I need to check on my patient. The family's in the cafeteria."

"Of course, Bina should be your priority." After heading out into a hallway through orange carved arches, Maya pulled out her iPhone to call Santa Fe.

"Dr. Grinwold, I have an update on the family from last night. Hope I didn't interrupt anything."

"I was on the phone with Nancy. We watch *CBS Sunday Morning* together from our different state capitals and chat."

Maya was surprised by the personal detail from the gruff State Epidemiologist. Dr. Nancy Bingham was his counterpart in Arizona, and Maya's temporary boss when tackling anthrax last year.

"I'm following up on the Apache family with fever, headaches, and rash."

"I had one beer last night—I wasn't too drunk to remember your call."

That was the grumpy Fred Grinwold Maya feared. His voice often triggered weak muscles, but three months of cognitive therapy and the prescription Klonopin kicked in.

"One patient was flown here to the Indian Hospital in Albuquerque. She's six months pregnant, and they diagnosed JHR."

"Syphilis should be ruled out. When antibiotics kill the bacteria, cytokines are released, causing a lot of damage."

Maya kneaded her arm as goose bumps rose with the air conditioning despite her black blazer. "But all the family members are symptomatic, so I don't think the organism was sexually transmitted."

"Then it could be TBRF, from *Borrelia* infection. We had some cases in Colfax and San Juan counties."

Tick-borne relapsing fever, she dredged up from veterinary school in Colorado. *Borrelia* were helically coiled bacteria called spirochetes, transmitted through tick bites.

"I'm on my way to check with the family. I'll keep you posted."

After several minutes wandering the halls of the multistory complex, Maya spotted a family who matched the Dulce clinic's description—two senior citizens, a man in his forties, and a dancing preschooler.

"Hello." Her voice was hushed. Although she gained confidence during her first year of training, her instincts tended toward reserve with new people. "Are you the Lucero family?"

Looking up, the middle-aged man answered, "I'm Mangas. These are my parents and granddaughter. My wife and daughter are in the ICU."

"Yes, I'm sorry to see Bina so ill—you must be very worried."

She showed him her identification. "The IHS requested my help. Your symptoms, when did they start?"

The child scratched at scabs on her arms and started fresh bleeding. "Amacita, stop it." Mr. Lucero picked her up and positioned her back on the cafeteria chair. "She's too young to understand the threat to Bina and the baby, but the long drive, this new environment—it's all a bit much. What was your question?"

Red bumps on his right forearm caught Maya's attention. "Your rashes, how long have you had them?"

He shrugged and pulled down his sleeve. "Close to a week."

After lowering to a chair next to Amacita, Maya scribbled a quick sketch of a plump black cat on her notepad and tore off the page for the gleeful child. "This is my Grandma's kitty, named Hypatia. She's cuddly and purrs." Then she directed her attention back to Mangas. "My supervisor suggested I ask you about ticks. He's seen other rash illnesses after their bites."

"You mean like Lyme disease?" His face scrunched in confusion. "But that's not a risk out here."

"Although we haven't found Lyme-infected hard ticks in New Mexico, we have human cases, probably from travel. But tiny soft shell ticks don't stay latched as long, so people aren't aware of the bites."

The white-haired couple grimaced and moved closer together. Maya hurried on. "It sounds barbaric, but female ticks are larger and drink the most."

At their expressions, she pinched her arm and shut her mouth, reminded that scientific information fascinating to epidemiologists was gruesome to the public.

"Mr. Lucero," a young nurse called out as she rushed into the cafeteria. "Bina's taken a turn for the worse—she has fluid in her lungs and difficulty breathing."

The older couple said they would remain with their great-granddaughter while Maya hurried after Mr. Lucero. "I can work with environmental services to look for rodents and ticks. Do I have permission to check out your home?"

In her notebook, he scribbled the address where they went on a fishing trip to celebrate Bina's twenty-sixth birthday. They were almost the same age, with Maya's birthday three months earlier on Feb. 14.

She noticed the ob/gyn in the corridor as Mr. Lucero turned the corner. "Dr. Blake, if you're busy with Bina, I can swing back later."

"Not a problem, Dr. Maguire." He sat in the waiting room chair and indicated for Maya to do the same. "The pulmonologist is in charge with the lung changes. Her pregnancy is stable at the moment."

"Our State Epidemiologist, Dr. Fred Grinwold, wondered about relapsing fever from *Borrelia* infection. The family was all together at a cabin. Their symptoms are nonspecific but similar, except Bina's reaction to the antibiotic. Coming down with the same thing in the same time period, it makes me think of point-source, possibly ticks."

"I never had *Borrelia* cases before but I'll make sure the lab tests for it."

"Can your lab run blood samples for the other family members? If they need any assistance, our CDC labs in Ft. Collins or Atlanta can help."

When Dr. Blake stood up, Maya followed. "I'll work with the Jicarilla Nation looking for soft ticks on their property. We'll also check for hard ticks, which transmit Rocky Mountain Spotted Fever. Your lab should rule that out, as well."

He shook her hand. "Thanks, we appreciate working with CDC on this. It's important for Bina and the family to figure out where this came from."

. . .

When the Bernalillo exit sign popped up north of Albuquerque on her drive back to Santa Fe, Maya made an impulsive decision and turned off the interstate. She hadn't visited her colleague since February. As the federal Area Veterinarian in Charge, Dr. Dave Schwartz had been her partner on the anthrax medical detective team. Would he know anything about *Borrelia*?

Peering through the windshield into the afternoon sun while driving west, she adjusted her Yankees cap, a gift from Manolo Miranda's father. Since Manolo's neurologic damage, Sebastian Miranda had stayed in Phoenix to help with physical therapy that allowed his son to get around with a wheelchair and feed himself, even if he couldn't speak.

She could use a cowboy hug from Dave and wondered whether to pull off the two-lane highway to give him a call. But even if he wasn't home, the soothing nature of a greening bosque along the swift-flowing Rio Grande with the melting winter snows would justify a detour.

When she pulled up to the adobe ranch and hopped out of the Prius, the family's black lab Bo raced over, barking and wagging his tail in friendly greeting. Maya crouched to play with him, then fell onto her backside as she wrestled with the dog. Just the medicine veterinarians would order—a tumble with a lovable dog. No vet should ever be without a pet, but her two years of training with CDC were too unpredictable to manage one.

"Hey, girl, long time no see." Dave burst through the front door and reached down to help her up. At thirty-one, he'd suddenly developed gray highlights in his brown hair and deep wrinkles around his eyes.

"Come around to the back," he invited in his Texas drawl. "My ladies are all in the corral."

With the warm spring air, Maya reclined on the outside bench after greeting his wife Emilia and the girls, who trotted their ponies under their mother's tutelage.

"Any summer plans?" Maya asked.

"Not really, we're occupied with work and kindergarten. Emilia says we should drive up to see my new family members in northern Arizona. If we show up, what are they going to do, kick us out?"

In the shade of the overhead thatch, she removed her cap and set it on the bench. "I agree with her—you should try. And if they refuse to acknowledge your relationship, you still have her parents here in Albuquerque."

"I guess." He looked cautious, not like the aggressive cowboy she'd become close to. "Speaking of taking chances, any news about you and our favorite IHS doc?"

"Yesterday when they visited from Phoenix, Sebastian left us alone while he explored Santa Fe. I drove Manolo up to Taos Pueblo. On the Rio Grande Gorge Bridge, he made the 'I Love You' sign with his hand." She pulled the ponytail loose and fluffed her hair. "But he didn't appear to know me when they left this morning."

"Be patient, his brain needs time to rewire. Hey, I'm gonna grab a beer, want one?"

Despite her refusal, he came back with two. Dave never drank in the early afternoon. Perhaps he forgot she took anti-anxiety meds, which wasn't a safe combo with alcohol. And maybe his stress was more severe than he was showing.

When her iPhone rang with a call from the hospital, she hastened for privacy to the barbed wire fence line. It was Dr. Blake.

"Dr. Maguire, I want to let you know in case it influences your field investigation. We lost Bina. She became more unstable, and then had cardiac arrest. We couldn't save her baby boy, either."

Loss of their daughter and her infant—Maya couldn't imagine the depth of the Lucero family grief. All the anthrax cases came flooding back, including the death of the first patient, a teenage Hopi sheepherder.

Bina was another Native American death mocking her medical

detective skills—not unusual with the number of tribes in the Four Corners region.

"We sent sera to the state lab for antibodies." Dr. Blake's voice brought her back to the present. "And a specimen went to CDC—results should be available within a few days."

In front of Maya's eyes, daffodils bobbed their yellow heads in the spring breeze ruffling the greening grass. But her mind was sucked back to the deadening autumn when *Bacillus anthracis* spores spread in mysterious ways. Her knees began to give way, and Bo ran up for playtime. She fended him off and spoke into the phone.

"Thanks for calling, and let the Luceros know how sorry I am for their loss. Reassure them we'll get their cabin checked out tomorrow. They should go to their primary home and stay away from the cabin until I clear it."

"I'll pass that along. The IHS is grateful to you and your boss for the idea about relapsing fever. At your recommendation, we looked at Bina's peripheral blood smear and found a heavy spirochete load. So you might be right about the *Borrelia*. I never knew it could kill."

TWO

For once, Dave didn't come to her rescue as Maya dropped the phone in her pocket and sank to the pebbled dirt next to the corral. Emilia, almost as tall as her six-foot husband, raised up Maya's shorter frame.

"Hermanita, are you okay? Did anything happen with Manolo?"

The prickles on Maya's arms increased. Sebastian had promised to call during a planned break with her parents for a Flagstaff lunch.

"They're driving home to Phoenix."

She pushed aside the statistics on the high rate of New Mexico and Arizona traffic fatalities—it was a curse to know so much about the ways to die.

"They should have touched base by now, but that's not my main problem. I have another new disease and a deceased case. I think I'm in the wrong line of work."

Emilia lifted Maya's chin and their dark eyes met. "But you're good at it. And you mourn for patients you don't know—that shows how much you care."

"You give me too much credit, but I appreciate it." Maya hugged her, the only friend who wasn't a colleague. "I didn't anticipate a state assignment would be so difficult. Should have asked for an Atlanta CDC placement at a computer."

Emilia's gaze shifted to the porch where Dave kicked back, cowboy hat pulled down over his eyes.

"I don't think either of you would be happy tied to a desk. My family and long-time restaurant coworkers make me comforted and sane. You and Dave, you're adrenaline junkies, and you want to make a difference."

Honks of Canada geese filtered through the cover of bright green ash and duller Russian olives hugging the creek, reminding Maya of spring's fresh start. Both women leaned on the corral upper rail, attuned to the peals of laughter from the four- and five-year-old girls chasing each other around the ring on their pinto ponies.

"We'll leave mi esposo to his midday nap. Newly-discovered relatives in a Latter-day Saints polygamist sect creeps him out." Emilia paused, then added, "He might be drinking too much."

Maya leaned her shoulder into Emilia's. "Your family has been turned upside down—he's lucky to have you." But with her anti-anxiety meds to cope with Manolo's near-death, both she and Dave might be chemically dependent.

Her iPhone rang again. "Hola, Maya, ¿cómo te va?" Sebastian's Puerto Rican accent was stronger than Manolo's. She waved at Emilia and stepped away from the fence.

"Are you at lunch in Flag? Can I say hi to Manolo?"

"Go ahead, I'll hold the phone to his ear."

She was at a loss for words in their one-sided conversation. Manolo had been so ebullient, he often dominated their time together. His current lack of feedback made interaction miserable. If she was a chatterbox, she could plunge on, but that ability was not in her wheelhouse.

He had seduced her with Spanish endearments, simplified for her rudimentary level of school classes. She could repeat one from their intense courtship. "¿Qué tal, mi amor?"

Going through the motions, not expecting an answer, she hastened to continue. "I miss you already, Mano. It's wonderful your dad could bring you to Santa Fe for the weekend. I'll fly to Phoenix when I'm done with a rash investigation. Your ideas on this would be invaluable."

She exhaled, embarrassed that she might make him feel inadequate because he couldn't respond. "Talking over these medical mysteries—that will come with time. Neither of us has ever been patient enough."

Sebastian came back on the line. "Hey, he grinned. I think he recognized your voice."

Small blessings. "Thank you, Sebastian, for driving to Santa Fe for the weekend. And for everything you do to help us stay close. Are you with Mom and Dad at their favorite restaurant?"

"Yes, I'll turn the phone over."

Her mom's strong Catholic beliefs had not supported Maya losing her virginity at Christmas to a recently divorced man. So Maya was relieved it was her dad's steady, engineer-calm voice on the line.

"Hi, sweetheart. This was a smart idea to meet, thank you. Manolo looks great—you must have had a good visit."

"We drove to Taos. The time alone was rejuvenating."

"Your tone isn't as bright as those words. What's wrong?"

Maya's arms flushed red. She was too obvious to those whom she loved, even voice-only. "Another outbreak—it's a new disease for me and a pregnant woman died. Life and death, happens every day. I'm a vet and not responsible for it."

His voice lowered. "Sounds like cognitive therapy talk—is that still helpful for you?"

"Sure." Her brief answer reflected hesitance about her treatment. The lifelong nightmares since the childhood bicycle accident were vivid and the lack of sleep left her exhausted, a challenge when driving around the state. The doc advised adding a sleeping pill, but Maya didn't want to complicate any potential side effects from the combination.

She hadn't told her parents about the medication worries, and wanted to shove those issues out of her mind. "Dad, my job is 24/7—you know that. Tell Mom sorry, I've got to go. I'll check in sometime next week." Clicking off the call, she regretted her short temper, increased since Manolo's hospitalization.

She always struggled with her parental relationships. Her dad thought she was too young and immature for the frequent jumps in grade pushed by her brilliant astronomy assistant mom, allowing her to complete three college degrees by the age of twenty-five. Most of the other trainees in her CDC class were at least five years older.

Turning to Emilia, her heart pounded. "I always dread that steep La Bajada Hill between here and Santa Fe. Even with a crawl lane to the right, sharing it with the big rigs is my worst nightmare. Not that I need to worry—failing brakes would be an issue coming down to Albuquerque, not going up."

Emilia tossed her dark braids, a puzzled expression on her face. Maya realized today was a first—she had never confided fears to her colleague's wife before. They really were becoming friends. Maya gave her a quick hug and wandered back to the porch, kicking at Dave's boots. He awoke with a start and knocked his hat to the ground.

"Warm sun was nice," he said, although the light didn't reach the bench under the covered portal. "I'll walk you to your car."

As she climbed into the Prius driver's seat, he smiled. "Thanks for stopping in. I'm back to diseases without human risk, so we might not work together. We're developing surveillance for rabbit hemorrhagic disease. There were die-offs last year in Canadian feral rabbits, and then pets in Ohio."

She took his weather-beaten hand through the open window. "Last thing we need are thousands of dead rabbits, with people scared it's plague or tularemia threatening their families. Keep me posted."

Should she say anything about the two beers not long after noon? Emilia had looked concerned—it could be her duty as a friend to butt in. But she kept her worries to herself. Dave was the epitome of a hardened Texas rancher. Her interference could be counterproductive.

· · ·

Maya leapt up Monday morning to wash away a ghastly dream. Manolo had been a cold, dead fish, a tail instead of legs and a dorsal fin replacing arms. Glassy eyes stared without blinking and thin fish lips gaped. His dark hair curled on his forehead, and the fish chin had the goatee she loved when he wasn't working. In the shower, she scrubbed to remove fish slime on her naked flesh, then peeked out at the empty bed to verify she only imagined it.

Remembrance of the teenager's truck smashing her five-year-old body had generated years of nightmares, then the anthrax attacks added mounds of bleeding carcasses. She wasn't thrilled by a creative imagination that developed new ways to haunt. And where in heck had a fish image come from? The Luceros mentioned their fishing camp on Jicarilla land—perhaps the germ of the vision.

After pulling herself together and driving to work, she passed Stephanie's graying head bent over a folder at her desk. At Maya's greeting, the secretary popped up with a spontaneous squeal. "You drove to Taos with Manolo—how was it?"

Maya gazed down at the older woman. In the face of a new medical mystery, the Saturday visit seemed a lifetime ago. With a successful marriage before becoming a widow, Stephanie supported Maya's relationship with Manolo. But the office support hadn't been universal. Erika, their disease surveillance coordinator, was skeptical of the timing for Manolo's divorce.

Secretly separated from his east coast wife, Manolo forced through the final paperwork. Erika's attitude came around when he promised Maya more transparency. Stephanie's enthusiasm for their bond never faltered. After the epic romantic camping to the ancient ruins in Chaco Canyon, they'd shared posole on a snowy Christmas day with Stephanie, listening to humorous stories about her husband.

As a fan of their pairing, Stephanie lived vicariously through their story. "Does Manolo show any sign of improvement?"

Maya led the way down the hall to her small office with the tiny eastern windows filtering the morning's light, then Stephanie plopped into the second chair.

"We took the High Road to Taos," Maya said, "with those curvy mountain roads through the ponderosa pines, and finished at the Rio Grande Gorge Bridge. The view was spectacular, several hundred feet down through the black volcanic rock to the river sparkling below."

Stephanie nodded with enthusiasm. "Incredible area, but I thought you hated heights. Didn't you get dizzy at the Grand Canyon when you two visited in November?"

That trip had been one of her first dates with Manolo, stopping at all the South Rim overlooks. "I hoped that re-enacting our Grand Canyon trip might jog something in Manolo's mind. And it worked. You know how to say 'I Love You' with your hand? He formed the letters I, L, and Y all at the same time, like this. Then I kissed him— maybe he kissed back." Maya's expression begged for supportive joy from her friend.

But Stephanie frowned. "How intimate have you been since his illness? You were so much in love. I realize he's cognitively impaired, but maybe re-establishing that physical closeness would help trigger memories."

Maya swept her notebook from the desk to the floor in frustration. "Damn it, Stephanie, I don't need a reminder it's been so long—I feel guilty enough." Then she spun away in the chair and lowered her head. Tears leaked from her eyes and she exhaled quiet gasps. Stephanie's grip guided her back around.

"Sorry, Maya, I don't mean to criticize. Maybe you could benefit from more time together, without his father."

"No, I'm the one who should apologize for yelling when you're only trying to help."

She reached over to hold her friend's hands, hoping to make her understand. "My emotions are on a knife edge. There was a sign at the Bridge warning people not to jump. For a half-second, ending my despair and confusion flitted through my mind. But I wouldn't do anything with him right there."

Stephanie handed her a tissue from the box on the desk. "Promise to tell me if you ever have impulses like that. After Tony died, I had a few of those feelings. Are you still seeing a psychiatrist?"

Maya wiped her face and glanced at the door. The last thing

she needed was Dr. Grinwold bursting in. "With Dr. Kim's therapy and meds, I've been working hard to function despite Manolo's disabilities."

"You've had no downtime—working like crazy on your presentation to the CDC conference, plus all the mini-outbreaks." Stephanie patted Maya's arm. "You only got that Atlanta talk behind you a couple weeks ago. It must drive you crazy that you don't have more time to join Manolo in Phoenix."

After pulling away to rub her throbbing back, Maya stood to stretch. Tension always worsened the chronic pain in her pelvis and right thigh from the permanent metal holding the bones in place after her childhood injury.

"Manolo and I never made any commitments—our relationship was too new. But in the hospital, his family told me he intended to propose marriage. I was on the slow track and didn't say I loved him until he was unconscious. So there's no obligation, and I can't stay in Phoenix for him. Most of the time, he doesn't recognize me, and he's comfortable with his father's care."

Stephanie stood and opened the door. "You're right, I'm pushing too hard, just a romantic. I'm a Manolo Miranda-Maya Maguire fan, the M&Ms."

Giving Stephanie the slip of paper with the Lucero cabin address, Maya asked for help, another thing she wasn't accustomed to. "Can someone from the Jicarilla Apache Nation meet me today at the Dulce clinic so we can investigate this location? We've got a rash illness outbreak, including one death. That's how I spent yesterday."

"Of course, anything you need, no wonder you're on edge."

After Stephanie headed back to her desk, Maya found her boss in his office at the early hour. "Dr. Grinwold, our lab might have confirmation later today on the *Borrelia*. The hospital spotted spirochetes yesterday on the blood smear."

"I was spitballing with the TBRF guess, but those earlier cases came to mind."

"I researched it last night." Flatter the boss, one of those bureaucratic skills she tried to work on. "Your years of experience are wonderful. Could we do a Star Trek mind meld so all your knowledge would flow to my brain?"

He smiled—an uncommon reaction. "It'll come with time. When I'm old and in the nursing home, you'll sit in my chair."

She was shocked by his rare compliment and speculated whether his positive mood was for an upcoming rendezvous with his Arizona counterpart. He had mentioned chatting with Nancy Bingham over a TV show, but neither ever confirmed a relationship.

"Stephanie's making arrangements for me to visit the cabin where the family stayed during the incubation period. If she works that out, I'll head up to Dulce."

"Good plan. Remember tribal sovereignty—they're in the driver's seat. Be deferential, don't step on toes."

She nodded, hoping her jangled nerves didn't interfere with carrying out the directive.

THREE

Greening valley, sensuous piñon-dotted ocher hills, creamy jagged cliffs—Maya understood why famed artist Georgia O'Keeffe settled in the Abiquiu area. Relaxing outside Ghost Ranch, the home converted into an education and retreat center, she was tempted by the tours, curious about the local perspective on O'Keeffe's landscapes with their rounded naked female forms and vulvas in opening flowers.

Stephanie was right—she should have forced the issue with Sebastian about sleeping with Manolo. If Manolo had stayed with her for the weekend, they wouldn't have needed a motel, because his father could have used her foldout couch. She should have tried—Sebastian might have agreed. She and Manolo had been inseparable for two magical weeks after consummating their love in his blue tent during the Chaco camping trip. But his current neurologic function was unclear, and sleeping in the same bed could confuse him.

When had he told his sister Ramona about his proposal plans? Maybe on New Year's after Maya flew home to New Mexico. Not long before then, the passion during weeks of Spanish endearments, gentle touches, and electric hugs burst into flame in a glorious high desert not far from this one. His secret eight-year marriage had some benefits—he knew all the possible moves of lovemaking, although her inexperience left her with no comparison.

She stepped out of the car for a stretch and a drink from her water bottle. Obsessing about their future was insane. Good thing her vibrator for chronic back pain was doing double duty, with infrequent success. Maybe it could benefit him, if they were ever alone again. Fuck—stupid, stupid, stupid to think about it. Focus on the Luceros—they were grieving and she needed to be in Dulce within two hours.

. . .

Edward Newton, Maya's guide from the Jicarilla Nation Environmental Protection Office, loaded supplies in his four-wheel-drive outside the Dulce health clinic. "Our Nation's President Yazzie sends his greetings. We don't have to consult with CDC very often, but don't mind your being here today."

Not the warmest of welcomes, but adequate. Her gaze wandered to the mountain looming over the small town of adobe-colored ranch homes.

"Archuleta Mesa," he said. "Ring any bells?"

She shook her head. "I spent my childhood in Flagstaff before my family moved to Denver during high school. I've only lived in New Mexico since July."

"Some of our citizens saw a spaceship and aliens. Rumor got around about a secret human and alien base inside the mesa, perhaps the cause of mutilated cattle. Bigfoot sightings, too. Anyways, the town capitalized on the publicity and had a Dulce Base UFO conference here at the casino."

Maya smiled. "Should I ask whether you're a believer?"

He scoffed. "Gives everyone another reason to talk about us. Before that, Apache only conjured up Geronimo. He was a different band, down south, but it's all anyone knows."

"I used to get bothered when people were confused by my Irish last name and Chinese heritage, but now I'm leaning into it. They probably won't forget me."

His dark eyes crinkled and she flashed to August when she met Manolo—she was a sucker for swarthy good looks.

"Ma'am, I don't think anyone will forget you."

She blushed, ill at ease with compliments, especially from someone twice her age. She understood she was reasonably attractive. A grad school classmate, trying to keep in touch after their spring 2018 graduation, called her a young Rachel Chu, lead character in *Crazy Rich Asians*. An engagement ring from Manolo could head off flirtation like this, if he ever recovered enough to offer it. But her guide seemed laid-back and friendly—she shouldn't overinterpret.

"Do you know the Luceros?"

"Only a few thousand live near Dulce, so we're well-acquainted. I can't believe the news about Bina's death, and they were so excited for a new boy in the family. The docs asked them to stay another day in Albuquerque for evaluation. Mangas called and said we can check out the fishing cabin."

"If the roads are reasonable to Stone Lake, I prefer to follow you and head south this evening, rather than double back up here."

"Sounds fine to me, let's get going."

· · ·

An afternoon storm blustered east across the small blue lake swollen by winter runoff. Except for two years at grad school in Manhattan, she never lived close to an ocean, but was transported there by the crash of white-tipped waves on the lakeshore.

Even after Mr. Newton closed the roughhewn door behind them, her face cooled as air whistled through cracks between cabin logs. She pulled her navy sweater tighter and appreciated the last minute decision to wear jeans rather than a more professional skirt or dress pants.

The wind carried the odor of decaying fish, evidence that the Lucero's trip was successful, although at a terrible cost.

"I'm sorry we haven't confirmed what we're dealing with yet. Our State Epidemiologist is guessing *Borrelia hermsii* due to similar outbreaks at high altitudes. The bacteria are transmitted by *Ornithodoros hermsi* soft ticks, which are associated primarily with squirrels and chipmunks."

"I'm not familiar with this disease. Why are they narrowing in on that, if the results aren't in?"

She pulled on latex gloves and knelt, looking for rodent nesting material under a queen bed in the corner. "They smeared a sample of Bina's blood on a slide and looked at it with a microscope. In between the usual red and white blood cells, there were long narrow squiggles. These bacteria are called spirochetes because of the spiral shape. But there are lots of other diseases caused by spirochetes."

For confidentiality, she left out syphilis. No one had mentioned Bina's husband or partner.

"Should we check out their regular home after the cabin?" He opened the front of the small wood stove.

"Mr. Lucero said they were here for two weeks. The incubation period—the time between a tick bite and signs of illness—is anywhere from four to eighteen days. Some other cases have been cabin-associated. The ticks leave rodent nests in the middle of the night and seek blood meals from humans."

He grimaced. "My job is indoor air—mold and radon. I'm not comfortable with these critters and might not sleep soundly in a cabin again. Should we split up the rooms and attic?"

"Collect any materials that may have been used by rodents. You likely won't spot any ticks—the nymphs are tiny and the lab can look for them. We'll mark on each bag where the nest was found."

After an hour and a half, they met again near the front door. Multiple gallon bags held torn paper, twigs, dry grasses, and dead leaves collected from under dressers in the bedrooms, the attic, and inside the kitchen cabinet with the sink. She brought in a cooler from her trunk for the bags, firmly locking the latch.

"I'll drop them in Albuquerque tomorrow," she offered, "if that works for you."

He nodded, but no longer smiled. "We receive the results first. You and the state don't do any public announcements."

"Agreed. I'm your guest, and appreciate working together on this." As she grasped the doorknob, a tiny furry creature scampered into the bathroom. They raced after but it was gone, vanished under a floorboard.

Maya, on her knees looking for the animal's escape route, rapped her knuckles on the floor in frustration. "Looked like a young rock squirrel. I've got some traps in my car."

Together they unfolded the first flattened steel cage. Maya spread peanut butter on a small paper plate and placed it in the end opposite the opening. A squirrel heading in for the treat triggered the door drop to humanely live trap it.

After spreading the cages out, she gave her final requests. "Check these rodent traps first thing in the morning. Before anyone uses the cabin again, do tick treatment. Over-the-counter foggers will work, one for each room, four hours. Of course, don't leave anyone inside after setting them off."

He loaded the chest of samples in her Prius. "Thanks for your advice. Drive carefully on your way over to Tierra Amarilla. It's a desolate road—help might be awhile if you break down."

The clouds had lowered and looked angry, ready to spit. Long drives three days in a row settled on her shoulders and she longed to be home with her heating pad.

After reaching for a warmer jacket from the back seat, she brushed dirt off her jeans and opened the driver's side door. "Our humane protocols prohibit leaving the animals enclosed for too long. If you capture anything, give me a call. I'll draw blood before releasing them away from the cabin. We could test for antibodies, then decide on additional steps. Some studies found infected owls and bluebirds."

His expression was skeptical. "The more you look, the more you find. Remember, you're on Jicarilla land here. This is our ballgame."

. . .

At Heron Lake, she pulled off the narrow, two-lane highway to the parking area at the earthfill dam and forced open the vehicle door. She was too busy at Stone Lake to play tourist, and didn't want to let another vista pass her by. To the north, the dark green expanse of water was churned by whitecaps as the wind stirred dust at her feet. She snapped a cell photo and crossed the highway for one of the Rio Chama. But the sun had dropped behind the pine-covered mesa, and there was barely enough light to be worth the effort.

Like an electric charge, sense memories of a terrifying encounter years earlier with the same river weakened her arms. Her head spun around, looking for landmarks. But it had been downstream in late August, on a float trip between towering sandstone cliffs, majestic cottonwoods, and willows sparkling the water's surface with tiny gold flakes.

Her dad had suggested the excursion as a distraction on the momentous childhood move from Flagstaff to Denver. Her heart had pounded as she climbed into the raft and agonized over entering tenth grade in a new state at only thirteen. As a rare Asian kid in the mountain west, the new big-city school might make her feel even more isolated.

Like other passengers, she had straddled a side rubber tube and hung onto a metal ring as the raft bucked like a bronco in the whitewater. She soon traded spots with her dad and moved up front, whooping with the spray in her face and hair. But when the boat plunged into a pit at the bottom of a class three wave, she flipped over the front into the turbid water, barely hanging onto the ring. The guide leapt forward and dragged her out before she broke her spine on the rocks, or drowned.

More than a decade later, she'd never been rafting again, but Chama whitewater glistening in the deepening shadows ramped up apprehension.

She snapped a final photo to overwrite the traumatic memories with a different river panorama, then slipped the cell into her jeans pocket. The storm clouds let loose, and more than rain pelted her face.

As she rushed for the car, tiny pieces of white ice carpeted the soil. Hail, in mid-May. But she was at high altitude near the southern tail of the Rocky Mountains. Weird weather from climate change warmed the earth, but also triggered extremes.

The wind hampered her popping open the Prius hatchback to grab her raincoat. After verifying the refrigerated chest and its sealed specimen bags were intact, she calmed her involuntary sensation of tiny ticks migrating up to the front seat to feast on her blood.

Heading east on the deserted highway, she fantasized about dinner, unable to remember the restaurants in Tierra Amarilla, Rio Arriba County seat. Manolo was a history buff and inspired an interest in her new home area. T.A.'s claim to fame was a violent raid on the courthouse in the nineteen-sixties, led by a local preacher demanding rights to Spanish land grants. Based on her vague recall, hostages had been taken.

The incident inspired the Chicano movement. Native Americans, Hispanics, and Anglos still fought over who belonged in the region. Where did that leave her, as an Asian immigrant adoptee? Sometimes it felt like nowhere, when work-demand panic and personal despair descended.

Her mental meanderings were interrupted by the snap of hail on the windshield, and she groped for the wipers. Then a loud thump, and the vehicle shook. She slammed the brakes and swerved off the road. As she zipped up her jacket and stepped out, nothing caught her eye in the sleet through the headlights. Then turning back to her left and the darkened highway, she glimpsed a large bundle.

A friend once had a night-time collision with a deer, but even in the pelting gloom, this looked nothing like an animal. The flashlight was in the glove compartment. Despite pulling up the jacket hood, ice slashed her face, so she prioritized a rapid investigation over illumination. After jogging along the unbroken center line toward the small bridge, she bent down to a humped cloth blanket. Tugging up a corner exposed a booted foot.

"Oh my God, my God." She collapsed on the pavement, withdrawing more of the fabric from an elderly man's dark face and white hair. It was too foggy to detect breathing, but she grabbed his wrist. Twisting her fingers, she couldn't feel a beat. Reaching for his throat, she pressed in his neck area. With no pulse found, she howled like a wild coyote, as the lights from an oncoming vehicle danced over their bodies and brakes squealed, the truck halting a foot away.

FOUR

"Shit, lady, are you all right?" A petrified male voice filtered through Maya's fading moans but her throat failed to form an answer.

"Sheriff, there's an accident. We're off the rez, so I called you. It's on NM 95 where it crosses the Rio Chama, west of US 64."

There was a moment of silence except for the crunch of gravel from the young man's pacing booted feet. Maya swallowed her cries and tried to take him in through the slashing hail. As the rain streaked his smooth, round face, he pulled a dark windbreaker up higher to shield the hand holding a phone to his ear.

His voice started up again, shaky. "Two people, both might need an ambulance."

In the glare of truck headlights, the man, maybe only a teenager, turned for his vehicle and cursed. Icy drizzle pelted Maya's scalp, and she refocused on the victim as a dark pool of liquid spread from the back of his head to her feet.

With terror and weakened muscles, her eyes closed, but her hand stayed pressed to the elder's neck for interminable minutes as she willed the body to wake up.

Flashing lights penetrated her eyelids and a door slammed. Thick fingers shoved hers aside on the victim's neck.

"I'm Deputy Cedillo. Ambulances from Tierra Amarilla will be here shortly. Can you tell me what happened?"

"Sorry, not sure." The younger voice groveled before Maya could form any words.

"Everything was like this when I stopped and called. She seems out of it, and he looks dead."

"Kid, I've already determined that. So you had nothing to do with this?"

"I swear, I promise. My dad's gonna kill me if I'm arrested."

The frantic tone from the young man matched Maya's internal screams. The voices were clear but panic and weather fogged her visual perceptions.

As the deputy grunted and moved away, his instructions were faint. "I'll deal with you later—give me your driver's license and keys. Last thing I need is you fleeing the scene."

Then he knelt next to her again and rested a heavy hand on her shoulder. "Ma'am, are you hurt? Can you stand? Were you hit by this truck?"

Her body vibrated with deep chills—the shaking made any response impossible. Ambulance sirens blared as she gave into the weakness, slipping to the asphalt.

"Take them both to the Española ER." The deputy's voice floated from a distance.

Hands on either side of her body began to lift, and her eyes opened to see medical gloves. One set of arms cradled her back and another lifted her legs to a gurney.

"Do what's needed, but give me one second to look at the vehicles—don't leave until I talk to you again."

The movements were rapid and jolting as they shoved the gurney into the ambulance. She tried to keep her eyes open. Blankets draped her body and monitoring equipment was hooked up.

"Ma'am, can you tell me your name and if you're hurt anywhere?" This time it was a female voice.

Maya leaned her head to see blonde braids dangling over a white shirt. She attempted to talk but nothing came out and her eyes closed.

"Prius has damage to front bumper and skid marks behind it." The deputy again. "Her license says Maya Maguire of Santa Fe. I collected health department and federal IDs, plus a pill container with Klonopin. No alcohol that I could find—did you detect any on her breath?"

"None," said the female voice to her left. "Initial exam finds no injuries—nothing substantial except rapid heart rate and breathing. Probably panic. Speaking of alcohol, the other team mentioned a broken beer bottle on the highway under the guy's body. Figured you wanted it as evidence."

"Damn straight. Is she up to a standardized field sobriety test?"

Maya could barely follow their conversation but understood that things were getting complicated, despite the safety and warmth of the ambulance.

"She can't stand at all."

He grunted and slammed the wall of the vehicle. "She's breathing so hard and fast, not sure how to interpret a breathalyzer. Take a sample for blood alcohol now but ask the hospital if they can test for benzos. Sheriff Baca's a Drug Recognition Expert—he'll meet you there. I'm staying with the kid to verify his role in this."

Limbs jerked with ambulance acceleration, then the motion lulled her into drifting away, body and mind overwhelmed.

. . .

Maya's eyes fluttered open with bumps of the gurney under the fluorescent lights of a hospital entrance bay. A bandage pinched inside her elbow—she guessed a blood specimen had been taken.

Darkness filtered from the side of the building. Sunset at the dam had been around eight o'clock, so it still must be Monday. The crisp smell of rain-washed pavement wafted in but no sleet swept under the shelter of the overhang.

The ER nurse changed Maya's damp clothes to a hospital gown. Involuntary shakes started again with cool air on her flesh, so staff dropped freshly heated blankets over the bed.

After checking Maya's vital signs, an older nurse peered over half-glasses. "When was the last time you had any food or fluid, dear?"

Maya tried to remember. She sipped from her bottle at Ghost

Ranch in the late morning, then a brief stop for a sandwich before meeting Edward Newton at the Dulce clinic. "Not for a while." Her first words. An ambulance snooze, the distance from the devastating scene, and slow breaths practiced in cognitive therapy all paid off. Back to functioning, sort of.

"Initial evaluation indicates you're stable. I'll get the resident in as soon as possible. In the meantime, the sheriff has some questions."

The nurse pushed open the curtain for a heavy-set middle-aged man with a gold badge pinned to the upper left of his tan uniform.

"Ms. Maguire, or is it Doctor? I'm Sheriff Baca with Rio Arriba County," he said with a high, friendly timbre.

Her wallet was open in his hand. "You're a veterinarian for the government, correct?"

She inclined her head in a nod.

He dragged a chair close to the bed. "Give me your version of how the accident happened."

In a raspy voice, she reviewed everything after the brief photo break at Heron lake—the bad weather, poor road conditions, her immediate stop after feeling the bump and rushing to the victim's side, the truck arrival and its driver's phone call.

Both of her hands kneaded her forehead. "I can't think of what I should have done differently. Maybe use my own phone to call 9-1-1. But the kid arrived moments later and I was overwhelmed when I couldn't feel the man's pulse."

"We towed your car to our lot in Tierra Amarilla. What's that cooler and bags in the back?"

After running her tongue over parched lips, she answered. "Specimens from a Stone Lake cabin, part of my disease investigation with the Jicarilla Apache nation."

"Lucky for you, the accident occurred in my territory. Things get more complicated on Nation land, including the FBI."

Her throat constricted as she remembered the FBI investigation last year. "Can I have a drink?"

The sheriff filled a cup from the sink and handed it to her. "Let's finish the interview. How much were you drinking tonight?"

Prickles spread from her arms to her legs. "None. No beer or wine since February, no mixed drinks, nothing."

His eyes widened. "Very specific timetable. On the wagon?"

"I've never drunk much alcohol. My boyfriend was hospitalized in January and I started therapy for stress in February. The doctor prescribed Klonopin and I didn't want any interaction."

"The deputy found it in your pack. When's the last time you took a dose?"

A niggling concern crept in. "None since morning. I held off on the evening dose because I didn't want to feel tired." As soon as the words slipped out, she wanted to pull them back. Had her medication side effects reduced her alertness when driving?

He kicked back in the chair. "Hmm, well, a beer at sunset is always great. You mentioned the break at the lake."

Where did his comment come from? Tears brimmed and she blurted, "The older man in the road, did I . . . kill him?"

The sheriff removed his cap and ran fingers through his gray-streaked hair. "Dead at the scene, and yes, we think you did it. He had no ID, so we're trying to track him down. We have blood alcohol concentration pending on both of you."

She hadn't been drinking and breathed a sigh of relief. But he was dead, and she had run him over. No matter how hard she tried to be on top of everything, her imperfections had a catastrophic result.

"Benzos are the second leading cause of DWI. It's legal to drive when taking them, but if I have any reason to believe you were impaired, you have a big problem. We've got a team assessing distances, tread marks, and damage to your vehicle. I'm not filing charges tonight, but that may change, depending on his autopsy and other information."

No longer in the hospital to investigate a family with *Borrelia*, she was the nasty germ killing people. She slid lower on the bed and pulled the blanket tighter to her chin. Fear flooded back from December when the FBI labeled her a 'person of interest' with Dave. Firefighters are sometimes the arsonists, they said. For someone so scrupulous about doing the right thing, getting in legal trouble twice in less than a year was extraordinary.

"Can I call someone on my cell?"

"Sorry, gotta check if you were texting. The kid apparently arrived too late to see anything, so we need to reconstruct the facts. Was there anything distracting you before you hit the old man?"

"The weather was bad, with poor visibility from sleet and hail."

A tiny hint of reassurance lit the sheriff's face. "I skidded pulling out from my in-laws after dinner." Then he resumed the official stern demeanor. "Tell me your password so I can unlock the phone."

Unsure whether to comply, she wondered about reaching her attorney. But she was accustomed to cooperating with governmental authorities. Confident his review would put her in the clear, she wanted everything over. After unlocking the phone, Sheriff Baca checked emails, texts, and calls, then handed it back.

"Nothing incoming or outgoing around the time of the incident."

She relaxed into the pillows. Thank God no one tried to reach her while driving.

"But I'm retaining your pills for chemical analysis. If you need more, talk to the doctors."

The nurse pulled open the curtain, and Baca invited her in. "We're not pressing charges at the moment, so you can release her when ready. Dr. Maguire, we know how to find you."

As he exited, a young female resident entered and completed a rapid physical exam. Maya eyed the remaining water in the cup on the table. "The sheriff took my Klonopin. Can I get a dose from you?"

The doctor's brown eyes squinted. "You're not exhibiting clinical signs of a panic attack now and we prefer you connect with your own physician." Then she handed over the iPhone from the stainless counter.

Stephanie was the logical one to call. As the office secretary, she arranged the Dulce trip and put Maya up in December when the FBI tore apart her apartment for traces of anthrax. Definitely not Dr. Grinwold—dealing with him at the office would be soon enough.

"Stephanie? This is Maya. I screwed up again and need your help. Can you pick me up from the Española ER? I'll fill you in later."

. . .

In the waiting room, Stephanie's face was lined with worry when Maya came out around midnight, back in her damp, muddy clothes. Once settled in the old Chevy, Maya filled her friend in on the horrific events. She sank into the seat and hugged her knees.

"I still don't understand what happened," Maya said. "Was he lying in the road, or walking across it? They mentioned a beer bottle—what does that mean?"

"New Mexico highways are lined with broken bottles."

"If only there had been a way to prevent it. I was tired from drives to Taos and Albuquerque, but didn't doze off—I was looking forward to a late dinner."

Stephanie started her engine. "You've got a lot on your plate, but no one is more cautious. Let's go home. Depending on what's in your refrigerator, I'll whip up something for you to eat."

It was after one a.m. when Stephanie rinsed the dishes from scrambled eggs and herbal tea. "Wish I could stay, but Quetzy is upset if he's alone too long."

The hyacinth macaw was Stephanie's close companion for two decades, almost like a child after her husband's death. Maya accepted Stephanie's maternal embrace. "I'll visit that rascal soon. Thanks for all your help. I pulled you away from home in the middle of the night and you came to my rescue—you're my guardian angel."

"Call your attorney, he did a good job for you last fall."

After Maya said goodnight and closed the door, visions of the accident scene shoved in. She ransacked her pack for the Klonopin in hopes of relaxing her racing heart and heading off nightmares, until she remembered Sheriff Baca kept the pills.

The automated greeting at Dr. Kim's number advised calling 9-1-1 in an emergency but allowed her to leave a message. After a glass of warm milk, she flipped through the iPhone Broadway show tunes.

Her *Hamilton* favorite might not be advisable with death as its culmination, so she chose *In the Heights* after climbing between the sheets. Maybe the lively songs could distract her restless brain and slow her thrashing legs. Stopping anti-anxiety meds cold turkey after killing someone on a rural New Mexico highway—the remaining hours of the night would reveal her level of dependence.

FIVE

Maya's right leg twitched as she pressed her foot again and again to the brakes in the blinding blizzard, until a streak of Santa Fe sunlight lasered her eyelids and she awoke from the dream. Rebound anxiety with the single missed dose of the confiscated meds had overpowered her ability to achieve a deep sleep. The accident was surreal, like something in a movie. How did it happen? Her friends joked that she drove like an old lady.

The health department was quiet as a funeral home when she arrived by cab at seven o'clock. Her attorney's office opened at nine, then she'd try Dr. Kim again when the receptionist was reachable at ten. Recover her car and specimens which needed delivery to Albuquerque. Arrange for blood draws if Mr. Newton caught any animals. The logistics were daunting.

As a boulder settled in her stomach when she considered how to tell Dr. Grinwold, he burst open her door, veins visible on his forehead. "Dr. Maguire, what the hell have you done this time? You KILLED one of the Jicarilla revered elders?"

Tears flooded from her eyes and she gasped for air. "I was waiting here for you . . ."

"You're off the investigation. Pam in Vector Control will retrieve the specimens from your vehicle. Mr. Newton caught some squirrels but won't take samples—they don't want any of us on Nation land."

"But I . . ."

"Did I say something about being deferential? You may have

torpedoed our health department's access to native nations for decades to come."

After he removed his wire-rim glasses and pulled out a handkerchief to wipe his face, his voice volume lowered.

"This is too big for you to juggle while meeting work demands, so you should go home and focus on your personal situation. I'm calling Atlanta for advice on handling this." Walls vibrated as the door slammed on his way out.

She started to follow and protest, then locked the door and crumpled on the carpet, muscles flaccid as noodles. He was right— she was too fuckin' weak and screwed up to function with the stress. Being smart did no good when her emotions were a hydrogen bomb. There was only one thing to control—staying out of the hospital for panic. Even if she had to lock herself in a bathroom and never come out, she would not let anyone see her like this again.

A light tap on the other side of the door interrupted the raging inner storm. She tried to lift her arm, but it drooped. The tap came again with greater vigor and Erika's voice penetrated the door jamb. "Unlock it now."

Her friend's words offered motivation to try again. On her knees, she opened the door. Erika helped Maya to her feet, then steadied her with a bracing hug. "You can't get a break, but it will work out. After I bring you home, Pam and I will get the cooler and she'll drop the specimens at the lab. If the sheriff releases your car, I'll drive it back here."

Maya stood frozen, but managed to eke out a response. "You and Stephanie are my rocks. What would I do without you?"

After slipping blonde strands behind her ears, Erika leaned over the desk for Maya's purse and handed it to her. "I need to finish all that by three because Kyle's afterschool program was cancelled, something about a water leak."

Erika held open the outer glass door. "They confirmed *Borrelia* in the Luceros. A single positive antibody titer in most of them, so we'll need a second with the four-fold rise for confirmation of recent infection. I'll contact providers to look for similar cases, but the Jicarillas have a tight lid on everything."

She was so matter-of-fact, Maya couldn't tell if she was angry like their boss. "His name," Maya asked as they reached Erika's minivan. "Did you hear his name?"

"Dr. Grinwold didn't say."

Maya climbed into the front and clicked the seat belt. Erika turned and touched her shoulder. "New Mexico has the highest rate of pedestrian fatalities in the country. Trust me, I manage the data. Too many long distances, changeable weather, and people disregarding traffic laws—walking across streets outside of crosswalks, wandering the deserted backways. And alcohol, way too much alcohol."

Erika's comment brought back a flood of hazy memories from the emergency room. Impairment, that was the sheriff's insinuation. Could it be true? She hadn't taken the evening dose, but maybe the pill in the morning reinforced exhaustion after three days of long drives. And beer at the scene—he implied it was hers.

When arriving at her apartment, Maya waved goodbye to Erika. Plopping on the couch, she felt the studs from the Navajo bear claw earrings she wore daily as a reminder of Manolo. While stretching out, she struggled to organize her thoughts. So many calls to make, and she dreaded all of them, except for the one to Dr. Kim. She let her eyelids close, suddenly leaden after the night's missed sleep.

. . .

Ringing, ringing, what was that ringing? Maya scrubbed her eyes, then reached for the iPhone. Nope. More chimes, somewhere nearby. The doorbell. After stumbling on stiff legs to the door, she yanked it open.

Framed against the purple, red, and gold of a New Mexican sunset, a dark-haired woman with tiny streaks of gray approached an old sedan in the parking lot. At the noise of the door, she turned, and Maya recognized her friend.

"So you're home," Stephanie said. "Hope you got some rest. I slept in, so stayed late at work."

Maya examined her iPhone. The ringer was off, her frequent practice in the office to avoid interruptions by personal business. Chagrined that she forgot to turn it back on before falling asleep, she scrolled through multiple missed calls. "Thanks for checking on me so I didn't sleep the entire day away."

"With all you're going through, I think you need it."

Maya perched on a kitchen chair. "Let me check this message from Dr. Kim. I called her earlier this morning after you left, hoping to get my meds and an appointment."

The brief voicemail asked her to stop by at five o'clock. But she was three hours too late. Her heart raced, another day without the Klonopin. Maybe withdrawal was why she felt like jumping off a cliff. But she was okay, her friends were helping her, and Dr. Kim could squeeze her in again tomorrow. One more night without an anti-anxiety pill should be bearable—she couldn't be addicted.

"Have to call her again in the morning. I'm letting everyone down, including myself." She tossed the phone in the wastebasket.

"Erika and Pam took care of things but your car is still impounded. When I saw Dr. Grinwold stomping around, I poked my head in and shared what I knew from your perspective. Possibly he cooled down afterward."

Maya leaned over for a long hug. "I'm grateful that you all crossed a few things off my list."

Stephanie's eyes misted. "Hija, you're the daughter I never had. When I welcomed you to New Mexico last summer, I encouraged you to make good memories. Not sure that's been working out."

"On Saturday, I was on top of the world when Manolo visited. It's hard to believe that was only a few days ago."

In the kitchen, Stephanie opened a cupboard door. "Here's a can of ravioli. Want it heated up?"

"Thanks, I'll knock off some of these missed messages."

Maya retrieved the phone from the garbage, grateful it hadn't sunk into something gross. In the bedroom, she cocooned under the comforter. The call from the Arizona State Epidemiologist couldn't be a coincidence. She might have some advice on how to deal with Dr. Grinwold. He'd softened in recent months with Manolo's impairment, so his explosive outburst was unexpected.

Nancy's sympathetic voice came on the line. "I'm glad you got back to me—Fred unloaded his frustration."

The Arizona public health physician was Maya's greatest comfort at the Phoenix Indian Medical Center when Manolo was hospitalized. "You must be devastated and Fred can't see that right now. His mind is clouded from losing years to get New Mexico allowed on tribal disease investigations. As a federal representative, you had an inside connection, but that's messed up now."

Maya pulled the pillow over her head, but kept the phone to her ear. "Have I ruined my entire career, in addition to taking this man's life?"

"Don't jump the gun. Talk to your attorney and check in with CDC headquarters. On a happier subject, Enzo Russo will be out this weekend, arranging housing for August when he's done with the Atlanta training course."

Arizona had gone seven years without an Epidemic Intelligence Service Officer and Nancy was delighted to match with the Harvard internal med doc for the two-year assignment. Plus Dr. Grinwold was relieved that Arizona wouldn't need to borrow his own EIS Officer.

Maya's feelings were mixed. Relief that Arizona's disease problems wouldn't fall into her lap with the need to satisfy two State Epidemiologists, and more free time to enjoy New Mexico. But Manolo and her family were all in Arizona—a tight leash to her home state.

When she met Dr. Russo at the annual May conference, his excessive confidence had her flustered. But Nancy could benefit from someone who was Maya's extreme opposite, brimming with optimistic talent. And Maya's initial reaction to Enzo didn't matter. If there were few cross-state outbreaks, their work together would be minimal.

Nancy interrupted Maya's reflection. "I know you come on weekends to visit Manolo in Phoenix. Can I take you to brunch with Enzo before he flies back to Boston?"

"I haven't planned my next trip."

"Talk to Dr. Jaworski in Atlanta about your work status. Fred's got a massive temper, but he'll simmer down."

As the call ended, Maya heard Stephanie's voice through the bedroom door. "Ravioli zapped and ready."

Maya left another message on Dr. Kim's line, apologizing for the missed appointment and requesting a new one as soon as possible. Then she pulled out a kitchen table chair. "Can you join me?"

"If I don't feed Quetzy on time, he'll upset the neighbor on the other side of our common wall with 'Hello food' screeches."

Her friend's humor about the macaw had a calming effect, and Maya tried to refocus on work. "I'll check with the lab tomorrow to see if they found infected soft ticks in my squirrel nest specimens."

"Hmm, I wouldn't do that. Remember, Dr. Grinwold took you off the case. Focus on yourself, not work. Dr. Kim and your attorney should be your top priorities." The warning reminded Maya that a compulsion to be thorough could get her in trouble when her involvement wasn't welcome. It was hard to accept that her efforts could be tainted by the accident.

Stephanie opened the front door and turned back to Maya. "Did you call your family yet?"

Maya flushed, ashamed to admit another major setback to her parents. They had disagreed over Maya's rapid advancement through the educational system, leading to heavy work expectations at a young age. "I will, but need to talk to my attorney first. My mom has a tendency to leap into action, and we need a coordinated response."

After her friend left, Maya changed to pajamas and crawled into bed for a FaceTime videochat with Manolo and his father. Brushing fingers through her hair to look presentable, she decided against broaching the accident until her level of criminal risk was more clear.

"I tried to reach you with great news." It had been a long time since Sebastian appeared so excited.

"Tell me, please, I'd love to hear what's going on."

"Remember when Manolo wrote your name on a scrap of paper a while back?"

She couldn't forget—it was tucked in her nightstand drawer. Whenever there was a dark night of the soul, she took it out and read it, imagining that the bad things in the past were erased, or could be rewound.

"He wrote this last night." As he held up a napkin, Maya saw the words *I love her* in blue marker.

Sebastian's laugh lines were accentuated. She could only hope that Manolo was as handsome when he was sixty.

"I assume that means me?" Maya's tone dropped with a twinge of doubt.

"You know there isn't anyone else. We have an appointment with the neurologist tomorrow. Mano's communication skills might be leaping forward, like the improvements in his motor function."

A tear trickled and she brushed it away with her sleeve. There couldn't be any better news, especially if she flew to Phoenix for the weekend. But instead of sharing Sebastian's joy, she demanded, "Put him on," then worried she sounded too abrupt. Unstable—she wasn't sure if it was worse on the medication or without it.

"No problem, hija. He's in bed but I'll set the phone on the end table and leave the room. When you're done, hang up."

Manolo's eyes squinted as he lay on his side in bed, like her. Then he smiled, not quite the flirtatious grin from last fall, but the reaction was in response to her image, she hoped.

"Manolo, I miss you so much. I'm still thinking about our day in Taos. We should have more like that. Your dad showed me what you wrote . . . I'm overwhelmed. Can you understand what I'm saying?"

Then she held her fingers in front of the phone, forming the I-L-Y like he'd done at the bridge. "I love you," she said out loud, first time in months. Way overdue.

SIX

"An EIS Officer never killed anyone while on duty." In the first phone call next morning, the stark declaration came from Dr. Suzanne Jaworski in Atlanta. The CDC supervisor continued. "Last fall, you were a bioterrorism suspect until cleared when you spotted the real one. Now, vehicular homicide. You keep our lawyers hopping here in Georgia."

Maya stayed silent. With a fuzzy brain after another restless night with minimal sleep, she had no idea how to respond.

"Take vacation time this week until things are resolved. Although you were transporting scientific samples for a CDC investigation, I don't think our legal department can help."

Before saying goodbye, Maya assured her headquarters boss that she'd seek legal representation. Then she gasped in hyperventilation and tried to refocus on the sun-streaked peaks of the purple Sangre de Cristo mountains visible through the kitchen window. Maybe the caffeine rush from hot green tea to counteract a woozy brain was a bad idea.

Her schedule was totally off kilter, sleeping most of yesterday on the couch and then up all night, trying to distract with old movies. With a later office opening time than her attorney, the psychiatrist would be the second priority. Only six-thirty, several hours to wait.

Near the coat closet, the old bicycle beckoned, one of her first Santa Fe purchases with a steady income. Red and rusting from its life with a prior owner, it was all tuned up at the bike shop. Between weather, Manolo, and work commitments, she never used it. Exercise reduced depression—maybe it would help with anxiety too. At a minimum, a ride would kill time until the attorney and psychiatrist offices were open.

As she navigated the pavement of the Santa Fe Trail out of the neighborhood, adjusting to the sensation of balance, an overpowering lilac scent floated from huge clusters of purple and pink blossoms draped over adobe walls. Yellow daffodils and blood red tulips brightened the dirt on either side of the path.

With a gap in stuccoed houses and trees along the railroad tracks, the sky opened up, streaked with high white clouds. She braked suddenly to avoid hitting a prairie dog darting from the gray-green chamisa shrubs. The fresh air was invigorating, but thoughts continued to haunt. Did she deserve a refreshing day in the Land of Enchantment after taking someone's life?

When the trail changed to dirt and gravel under the highway trestles bearing commuter traffic on I-85, she turned around. In her parking lot, she waved to a neighbor backing out of his spot. He knew her as the quiet veterinarian who kept odd hours, not someone who killed another person the day before yesterday.

In the shower as she rinsed soap from her eyes, the iPhone next to the sink rang. In a rush to grab a towel and answer it, she didn't verify where the call was from.

"Ma'am? This is the *Rio Grande Sun*." The voice was male and energetic. "We'd like to talk about Waylon Otole."

She headed to the bedroom. "Who?"

"I'm a reporter, Española, following up on the report about Mr. Otole's death Monday night. How did it happen?"

Nobody warned her about the press. "I'm sorry, I can't . . ." Her thumb disconnected the call and she searched her phone contacts. Eight o'clock, maybe she could reach someone early in her attorney's office.

After Maya explained the situation, the receptionist scheduled an appointment for nine-thirty and promised a ride.

. . .

Professionally pulled together in a navy blazer and skirt with a white blouse, Maya paced below the metal roof of her front porch. When a black Lincoln Navigator slowed next to her, she was surprised at the sight of Mr. Zielinski behind the steering wheel.

She smiled in gratitude and scrambled up into the plush leather seat. He grinned back as he doffed a Stetson above crisp black hair and adjusted the seatbelt across the thickness of his belly, drawing attention to the silver buckle of his belt. Wearing leather gloves, he leaned over to shake her hand as braided loops dangled below a saguaro cactus pendant anchoring the bolo tie under his shirt collar.

"Sorry you had to make this stop for me." She glanced over as he navigated the narrow streets of Santa Fe's Plaza to his hidden parking space. "I thought you might send a law clerk."

"You were on the way from my Pecos ranch. Supposed to break a hundred today in Phoenix. I bless my stars to escape the Arizona office for northern New Mexico during the warmer months."

Before exiting the Navigator, he reached behind for two forearm crutches which he didn't use when she saw him in December. "Horse threw me and needed fusion for a spinal fracture."

Her lower back and right upper thigh tightened with a memory of the acute phase of injury. "I'm so sorry—I broke my pelvis and leg as a child, so I sympathize."

"Pendejo rattlesnake came out during a warm stretch and spooked Tessie. Docs not sure yet how long I'll have to wear my lumbar brace and use these. It's damned awkward to get around."

She admired how he flipped the crutch forward to punch the electronic door opener before she had a chance to help. New normal, adjust to what life throws at you—admirable qualities out of reach in her current state of mind.

He guided her into his spacious office with the patterned ceiling of pine vigas and herringbone latillas, a couch of plush leather, and a desk carved with a Zia sun symbol like the state flag. His body braced on the arm of the couch as he lowered next to her, while a secretary with a laptop joined them and perched on an equipale leather chair.

"Katrina gave me the gist of your story. Unfortunate you have to go through this." He turned formal with his deep actor-quality voice. "This is all too common here in New Mexico. Homicide by vehicle carries stiff penalties with lengthy sentences and huge fines. You never had a prior DWI, correct?"

Maya nodded. Alcohol never was a problem except for one drunken party in college.

"We'll check on the BAC levels, blood alcohol concentration, for you and the victim. Do you have his name?"

"A reporter with the *Rio Grande Sun* said it was Waylon Otole."

"I hope you didn't talk to them. That newspaper takes pride in their obituary section and crime reports. Someone even made a documentary movie about them."

She had enough publicity with anthrax to last a lifetime. "My boss said he was a respected Jicarilla elder." She shivered and rebuttoned her blazer.

"If on the rez, the tribal police would have showed up." He cast an eye to the secretary. "Verify it."

After reviewing his notes, he continued. "You told Katrina on the phone about a prescription for Klonopin. Not that I'm criticizing—I rely on pills for pain control."

She lowered her eyes. Her always-had-their-shit-together parents were vocally opposed to the medication. "When Dr. Miranda almost died, the psychiatrist thought it would help me, in combination with counseling."

"As I said—not judging. But it may be problematic. Did they take a urine sample or saliva swab?"

"I don't think so. I dozed off on the ambulance ride. That's when they took the blood specimen."

"Those other samples can detect Klonopin for up to five days, so it's good news they settled for the blood." He reached over to pat her hand. "If they ask for more tests, we'll head them off. Have you restarted the medication?"

"They took it away but I'm trying to get a refill."

"Holding off would be advisable in case they insist on more

testing. For benzos, lab results alone aren't sufficient to cause a problem, unlike with alcohol. Courts require them to make the case you were impaired by your medication."

"My doctor said she prescribed the minimum dose. I feel different on the meds, but I'd never drive my car if I couldn't function fully."

He smiled again. "We got well-acquainted during your anthrax defense, and I know how conscientious you are. I'll check with the FBI to determine if they maintained any records on you after that investigation. Don't want anyone trying to use those for a pattern of problematic behavior."

His elbows shifted to his knees as he leaned closer. "Did the sheriff or hospital do any behavioral evaluations?"

"No, I was too incapacitated with panic." She scratched behind her ear, realizing how it sounded. "Can they hold that against me?"

Both hands kneaded his back as he tried to straighten, a move she was too familiar with. After a brief grimace, he grinned. "We won't let them. Katrina, give Dr. Maguire a ride home. I will follow up with the sheriff's office, Jicarilla nation, and the hospital. Don't talk to anyone. We'll recover your car as soon as possible."

"There's one more thing I need your advice on." Maya pulled out blue stationary. "I wrote Mr. Otole's family a letter this morning. Can I mail it?"

He mopped his face and sighed. "Give it to me." In a quiet voice, he read it out loud. *To the loved ones of Mr. Waylon Otole, No words can convey how I feel about the passing of your beloved family member. You must have treasured the many moments you shared with him. It is beyond my understanding how I became involved in his death, and it's my deepest sorrow. I can never make up for your loss—all I can do is extend my genuine regrets and wish that I could turn back time. If it would help for me to provide my condolences in person, I will return to Dulce to hear what you want to say. I would do anything to make amends, although I realize that's not really possible. Sincerely, Maya Maguire.*

He folded the letter and slipped it in his file. "I won't rip this up because it's your property, but you cannot send it. This is an admission of guilt when the investigation is ongoing. I admire your sentiments, but you need to heed my counsel on this."

As her eyes teared, she wiped them with a tissue pulled from her purse. "I'll follow your advice."

The secretary guided her to the reception area, then stopped behind the front desk. "Should I send the bill to your parents again?"

Maya gulped—she needed to call them and admit what she had done. "I'll get back to you." Although CDC salaries were lower for veterinarians than physicians, she was frugal and should be able to pay Mr. Zielinski's fee. But then she remembered the total cost of the previous consultation—it might be worse this time.

. . .

The cheery blue skies during her early morning bike ride had disappeared. Late morning gloom and drizzle dulled her attitude as she settled back with a full mug of caffeinated tea. Her mood was too tied to the weather, too labile—the term her psychiatrist used. Dr. Kim's office said they'd squeeze her into the end of the day, and she set a phone alarm to make sure she didn't miss it.

She dreaded the call to her parents. They were finally free of work obligations and debt, in the mountain community of Flagstaff where they created a home after meeting as college students in Tucson. With Maya's first job in the state next door, they were thrilled. But her travails with anthrax dominated their lives since summer. If she didn't loop them in, they'd be hurt beyond recovery. Too much pressure on their relationship, after they'd gone around the world to adopt their only child.

"Mom, can Dad join you on the speaker phone?" She crossed her fingers and prayed. Compared to her placid father, her mom was volatile even while emphasizing self-control and achievement for her daughter. Maya was afraid of her reaction—reviewing the situation without her dad's support would be impossible.

"He's in the backyard, hang on a minute."

Maya drummed her fingers on the end table, stomach churning, debating how to break the news.

"What's up?" Her dad's steady pitch calmed her restless hand.

"I, uh, had a car accident. I'm fine but a pedestrian was killed." She determined to keep despair from her voice.

"Maya, this can't be true, not after everything else." Her mom's voice was loud, strident.

"It was dark, awful weather, and I didn't see him."

Her father's voice faded. "Barbara, lie down here, let me figure this out." A minute later, he came back on. "Are you in trouble?"

"I wasn't arrested—they took me to the hospital for a panic attack. And I saw Mr. Zielinski this morning. He was in a bad accident himself, thrown from a horse, but he can take my case."

"Is he back to work, is he capable of something like this?" Her dad's question gave her second thoughts, but she bristled with defensiveness. Disability didn't rule him out for coordinating a legal argument. That's why she never told anyone about the childhood accident and PTSD—they'd assume she was unqualified for a high-pressure job like a CDC EIS Officer.

"He's fine, driving and walking, and he has a sizeable staff to help." She had to think of something or her mom would spend hours finding another attorney. "If you recall, he's slick. He can use his crutches to gain sympathy with the jury. Remember the Michael J. Fox attorney on that TV show *The Good Wife*?"

"That's fiction and this is real. How can we help? We'll pay the bill again, of course. Should we drive over to Santa Fe?"

She snapped. "Dad, I'm twenty-six, don't treat me like a child." A pattern of inappropriate responses that seemed to increase with the medication. "Sorry, Dad, I've hardly slept and I'm feeling super anxious. Can you hold the phone closer to Mom?"

"Yes, we're both here," he answered.

"Things are in control. I'll handle the attorney and I have an appointment with my doctor. But I appreciate your looking out for me."

The job in jeopardy didn't need to be mentioned—it would be resolved before anyone else had to know.

SEVEN

After sprinting through the late afternoon spring shower, Maya joined Erika in the front seat of her Honda Odyssey.

"You should've brought an umbrella," Erika said.

"And get struck by lightning while holding it? No thanks. We have the highest rate of lightning deaths in the country."

"Good thing you're seeing the psychiatrist. You're paranoid."

"Hey there, Kyle." Maya turned to the back seat. "I heard you're turning six soon. Maybe you can invite me to your party?"

The blond boy smiled and sucked on the straw in his juice box as Erika turned out of the apartment complex. "I'm relieved Dr. Kim can squeeze you in. The sheriff's made no effort to return your medication or car?"

"My attorney's handling all that." Maya averted her gaze out the foggy window to the sparsely-treed hills. "Am I the talk of the office?"

"Everyone thinks you're working on an outbreak or on vacation. Dr. Grinwold, to his credit, hasn't said anything."

The tension in Maya's spine released. "I don't know when I can come back; maybe if the legal case is resolved." Wiping the window with her hand to clear condensation, she remembered the reporter's call. "The *Rio Grande Sun*—when does it publish?"

Erika flipped the windshield wipers to high as she made a left turn into the Rancho Viejo subdivision southeast of Santa Fe. "Last time we sent them a public health announcement, the publication date was a Thursday. So they might run something tomorrow."

The tan stuccoed office loomed ahead, peeking through low hanging clouds when Erika slowed. "Are you still happy with Dr. Kim?"

"It was great she fit me in. I wanted to stop my prescription after the CDC conference, but she wouldn't agree. She may be right—I've been jumpy as hell without it for a couple of days."

Erika cut the engine. "I thought you two might hit it off, her being Korean. She'd relate to your feeling out of place here with such a small Asian population."

"Her parents were immigrants. She gets the same questions I do, like where I'm from." For one of the few times since the accident, Maya smiled. "I just answer Flagstaff."

"Dealing with that asshole who kept coming onto me at work—she's been great for that." Erika ducked a quick look behind her. "Sorry, sweetie, Mommy said a bad word." She turned back to the front passenger seat. "I hope Dr. Kim is helpful to you. Pick you up after?"

Maya wrinkled her forehead. "No worries—I'll work it out."

. . .

She entered the empty waiting room, shivering in damp clothes. After lowering to the well-worn couch, she Googled her victim. There was nothing about Waylon Otole's death, but she learned more about his life. Born in 1928, he lied about his age to enlist at sixteen to fight at the end of World War II, and was a hero in the South Pacific.

More than twenty years after he single-handedly charged a Japanese machine gun nest to save his platoon at Okinawa, President Lyndon Johnson awarded him the Medal of Honor following decades of Jicarilla lobbying.

Waylon Otole was ninety-one when his life ended on a northern New Mexico highway. He should have died in bed of old age, surrounded by loved ones.

Dr. Kim came into the lobby. "Sorry to keep you waiting, my last session ran long."

As Maya glanced up with moistened eyes, the doctor offered a hand. "At this time of day, I can't give you a full appointment."

After they sat across from each other at the desk, the psychiatrist clicked on the computer keys, then smoothed the low bun at the back of her neck. "The receptionist noted your Klonopin was taken away. Can you tell me why?"

Maya extended her arm with the phone to show the Googled article. "He was a hero for his people and our country. Then Monday night, I ran him over and killed him."

Dr. Kim handed her a tissue and leaned forward in the chair, her face a frozen professional mask. "You told me before that driving is occasionally a panic trigger, but you're super careful and never had an accident, just a racing heart in some situations like driving over bridges. 'Don't freeze up and drive off the road' was the advice I gave. When you have a panic episode, ignore the feeling like you're going to die and keep going straight."

Maya dropped the iPhone into her purse. Her voice shook. "I had just crossed a small highway bridge over the Rio Chama. But the panic didn't hit until after the accident, when I found his body. It was night and bad weather, even worse than right now."

"Your reaction is understandable in the circumstances. I assume the police are involved?"

With both hands, Maya scraped her head from front to back. "They confiscated my pills. My body feels out of control, like it wants to find the Empire State Building and jump off. I read on the internet that stopping Klonopin can cause withdrawal."

"You're at the lowest possible dose—that shouldn't be an issue. But panic after what happened isn't surprising with your persistent anxiety disorder. The accident was an extreme stress event. When you mention jumping off a building—are you truly having suicidal feelings?"

Maya shook her head no.

A musical alarm emanated from the doctor's cell phone. "I'd prefer to keep talking but unfortunately I have a conflict which can't be changed. What's your legal situation?"

"My attorney's on top of it."

"I'll contact your pharmacy to renew the Klonopin, same dose as before. Call the receptionist to fit you in for a longer session with me ASAP. Also, we're considering a new group. I'll keep you in the loop."

Dr. Kim's hands shifted to the chair as if she intended to stand, but Maya's wave stopped her.

"I won't keep you after-hours but I have one more question. The side-effects—maybe I have too many of them. Tired, dizzy, a few headaches. Difficulty concentrating, short-tempered."

"On the Klonopin, before it was taken away?"

Maya nodded.

"Those are non-specific, and you're under tremendous stress with Dr. Miranda and your recent talk at the CDC conference— public speaking is a major fear trigger for you. But I can switch you to Xanax. People vary in their tolerance to different benzodiazepines."

"I think it's less complicated to renew what I've been on, and evaluate."

Dr. Kim held the door open. "Then that's what we'll do."

Maya hesitated—last chance to admit her haunting torment. "Panic didn't cause the accident, but I worry whether the medication did."

Shaking her head, Dr. Kim handed Maya a card. "Impossible at that dose, but keep this phone number handy. Although you said you're not suicidal, this is a 24-hour hotline if you have low moments and I'm not available."

. . .

Concerns about benzo side effects were pushed aside Thursday morning after a night's sleep and second dose of Klonopin. Maya hummed *It's Quiet Uptown* from *Hamilton* while checking phone messages. A missed call was registered from Sheriff Baca, and she notified her attorney's office.

Erika had mentioned the accident might be in the *Rio Grande Sun*—maybe it was time to scoot out of town. Mr. Zielinski called back approving a weekend visit to see Manolo in Arizona but warned her to keep in touch. The county sheriff had said they might have initial assessments of the case within the next week. Dr. Kim's office scheduled a longer appointment for Monday.

Maya dialed the Arizona State Epidemiologist. "Nancy, does that invitation to brunch with your new EIS Officer still stand?"

"Enzo's flying in tomorrow and we can meet up Saturday. Anything new with your situation?"

Maya's brain wanted it all to vanish. "I'll update you later."

"It's ironic. Janey Johnson at Pima County is investigating relapsing fever."

Flooded with relief at the chance to get back on a scientific footing, Maya searched for a notepad and pen. "*Borrelia hermsii*? I guess it's not surprising because tick activity increases with warmer temps."

"No, she's got *Borrelia turicatae*, found at lower altitudes. She could benefit from your experience."

"It's great to have a focus while I wait on the sheriff. I'm off-duty but should still make sure it's okay. Can you email your request to Dr. Grinwold and Dr. Jaworski in Atlanta?"

Escaping her problems—not the recommended way to overcome them, according to Dr. Kim. But things could go south very quickly with the press and legal charges. This might be her last chance at freedom if Mr. Zielinski's dire warnings about prison time came true. A weekend in Arizona during a forced vacation—she should take advantage of it.

Searching for a flight, she vacillated. Although it seemed longer with the trauma of the week, it was only a few days since she saw the Mirandas. Stephanie said Maya should insist on alone time with Manolo. But whether it was fear of failure or the pills, her libido had vanished. She wanted to stay locked on those December memories of sex in the shower, when he was suave but gentle. This time she'd have to take the lead with communication challenges hampering their choices.

She clicked on Janey's number. "Hi, how are you? It's Maya. I'm meeting Dr. Bingham on Saturday in Phoenix and she mentioned your relapsing fever case."

Janey's voice was eager. "I heard you had cases, too. Maybe the outbreaks have common factors. If you're in Tucson, I'd appreciate your help."

Maya weighed her options and prioritized the disease mystery. "I'd love to work with you. Can you pick me up after I fly in?"

. . .

As Janey drove her Civic northeast from Tucson's airport, skirting the foothills of the Rincon Mountains and Saguaro National Park, Maya sneezed at ragweed pollen floating through the open window. Three months earlier when she was in southern Arizona for her February 14 birthday, snow had dusted the saguaro cacti.

"It's been years since I've seen the desert in springtime." Towering above them on both sides of the road, saguaros were topped with large white flowers. On the shorter cacti, a few blossoms bent to the side to show off fuzzy yellow centers of the state flower. The once-a-year blooming drew Maya back into golden childhood memories of visits to her grandmother, and she smiled in anticipation of spending the night with her.

Janey tilted her head. "Glad the early flight allows you to see the blossoms before they fade in the afternoon. Are you hungry? I got lunch at the office, but don't mind a quick stop if you need a bite."

"I ate in the airport—tell me more about your *Borrelia*." She resolved to keep her troubles to herself and focus on the excitement of a new disease investigation.

"One young couple, late twenties. They're married, with multiple common sources. Both women work together at a local landmark, El Corral restaurant, over on River Road. I'm getting to be a foodie because my boyfriend owns a restaurant here."

Light-headed, Maya brushed fingers over her eyebrows—probably changing air pressures on the flight. She shifted her focus away from the beauty of the landscape. "Signs and symptoms?"

"Similar onset time, about a week ago, fever, chills, muscle pain.

Both had scattered bug bites. One had headache and nausea bad enough to seek medical attention."

"What made the doctor consider *Borrelia*?"

Janey navigated a rutted dirt road, then stopped at a small pullover. "Let me complete the story in a few minutes."

The heat knocked Maya back as she exited the car. She'd worn a long-sleeved shirt and jeans as Janey suggested for the fieldwork, but the heavy clothing prevented her skin picking up any brief whiffs of a breeze. She lifted the water bottle to her lips. "You wouldn't believe that I drove through hail on Monday."

Janey pulled her brown hair into a knot and laughed. "Today's a cold snap—only ninety-one. Good thing you didn't visit yesterday when we almost hit a hundred."

Maya fanned her hat to stir the air next to her neck. "Years ago I visited my grandmother often, before we moved from Arizona to Colorado. The weather was more comfortable then."

"Yeah, global warming is hard in cities as they're paved over. Tucson's one of the fastest warming. But I'm a native, so it's easier to take."

After pulling a large pack out of the trunk and handing a second heavy one to Maya, Janey led them down a barely discernible path through the desert scrabble. Thin green ocotillo stems waved red banners of blossoms.

"What's that scent?" Maya asked.

"Like a melon? The bats and other wildlife love the saguaro blossoms."

Maya's leg brushed close to yellow, pink, and red flowers springing from the low, pancake-like prickly pear paddles. Similar colors clustered on different species of squat barrel cacti. Sharp spines reinforced Janey's warning to wear long pants.

"God's country," Janey smiled.

Maya paused and squatted, leaning her pack against a rock while swigging water from her bottle. "Sorry, I should be fine with more oxygen at the lower altitude. But the heat takes some adjusting."

"We'll be cooler soon—we're heading to an old mine shaft."

At the hillside dotted with black-trunked mesquite and green-trunked palo verde trees, a dark opening loomed, framed by rotting wooden timbers. A bold white sign nailed to one of them barked **DANGER** in bright red letters and **UNSAFE MINE, STAY OUT—STAY SAFE** in black letters underneath.

The alarming signs triggered a splash of anxiety through Maya's nerves, but Janey sank to a boulder and pulled out two snack bars. "Southern Arizona is dotted with natural caves, like Colossal Cave and Kartchner nearby, and a long history of mining. Remember anthrax in the Tohono O'odham patient? They were the first to mine the area, for hematite as war paint."

"I knew that's why I liked you," Maya joked. "We're both fanatic about our research."

"My uncle drilled and blasted in the Dragoons and Dos Cabezas Mountains. They were after beryllium for light aluminum alloys in helicopters and satellites. But he died in his fifties from lung cancer, they think from the toxic dust."

"It must have been hard to lose him so young. So this area is associated with your *Borrelia* patients?"

Janey leaned for her bag to pull out supplies. "The sicker one had spirochetes on the blood smear, similar to your Dulce case. Initial serum samples went to your CDC lab in Fort Collins, and they found antibodies. We'll recheck in several weeks for confirmation."

"Same with us."

"Treatment is doxycycline—we have our fingers crossed they won't have a bad reaction like your patient."

Maya gestured to the pitch-black void. "What's the mine or cave connection?"

"Our records show an old outbreak of *Borrelia turicatae* associated with *Ornithodoros turicata* ticks in a mine. These two ladies are big spelunkers and explored this area two weeks ago."

Maya's eyes flicked to the forbidding opening and her voice was tentative. "We're not getting into anything hazardous?"

"Of course not. I appreciate your company and any suggestions you have for the investigation."

After taking deep breaths, Maya arched her back to relax. Anything beyond the entrance was impenetrable to her vision.

"I assume you're not claustrophobic," Janey said.

Maya's throat slipped a nervous giggle. "Do I pass out in tight spaces?" She had offered her help to reorient her brain, postponing the possible dire outcomes in New Mexico. But trepidation kicked in, despite the medication. "Not much chance before now to find out. What are you planning?"

"Live traps for small rodents and blood draws. Did your lab find any ticks in the nests you collected at the Jicarilla cabin?"

"Yes, and they were positive for *Borrelia.*"

"We'll collect nesting material and might find soft ticks attached to the wooden structures."

After donning a helmet and gloves, Maya helped Janey assemble the traps and reorganize supplies in their daypacks. Even through her mask, the acrid odor of bat guano assaulted her nostrils at the mine entrance. She shined her flashlight upward and caught the dark jostling bodies clustered together, hanging from the ceiling in small groups. "What species?"

"Let me take a photo. Cave bats are in Kartchner, and big colonies of Mexican free-tail bats are under Tucson bridges. The bats just returned from Mexico last month. But there are others in the area."

Maya kept up with her rabies vaccination and assumed Janey did too. Aerosol transmission of rabies virus had been alleged with tiny Texas caves. This mine cavity was big enough for them to walk upright. As long as they stayed alert and weren't bitten, they would be fine.

"How far are we going in?" Maya's voice remained steady to counteract fear.

Janey pulled out a crumpled piece of paper. "The two patients drew this map from memory of their route. They wanted to do that cave thing—reach an area with no daylight and turn off the flashlights, experiencing what happens to your eyes in total darkness."

Maya's feet dragged over the rocky floor and her breathing became rough, with a smothering sensation in her lungs. The bare skin of her face detected increased humidity.

"Janey, maybe I do have claustrophobia." It was a difficult admission to a colleague only a few years older. But Janey always appeared so calm and confident. "I was clammy with full protective equipment last year during the initial anthrax case and autopsy—similar sensations now."

"You can set traps at the cave entrance, then look for nest materials and ticks in the wooden beams. I'll tackle the interior."

Maya felt a flush of embarrassment at settling for the easier job. She was the CDC expert—public health had a pecking order. But a calmer disposition won out in leadership of this investigation. Besides, it was officially Pima County turf—she wasn't really a coward. "Are you sure? Is it safe for you to go deeper alone?"

"It's my hobby and my job, so don't worry about it." Janey vanished into the inky black.

With the sun reaching its peak heat, Maya hid small rodent traps under bushes in the shade, baiting them with peanut butter like at the Jicarilla cabin. The pants and long-sleeved shirt were cloying except when she thought of tick bites, unlikely in daytime, but somehow they'd bitten the two women.

Other traps went inside the mine behind vertical wooden braces. Then with plastic bags, she collected rodent waste. The thick piles of bat droppings gave off a rancid, ammonia smell that left her dizzy, and the stench increased as her steps sunk in and turned the guano to dust. So she hastened back to the shaft opening for a breath of fresh air. Histoplasmosis, that was the other disease to imagine creeping into her lungs—a dangerous fungus that loved bat feces. A problem in the Midwest, but she couldn't remember if it was a risk in Arizona.

Maya glanced at her phone. "Fuck!" Janey had been gone over an hour, and didn't pick up when Maya thumbed her number. Probably no reception. Force herself into the mine to find her friend, or call for help?

EIGHT

Maya used a hollowed cholla branch to brush an olive-green cactus segment off her bare forearm. Mistake to have rolled up her sleeves. In her anxiety, the cactus forest crowded like an invading army. Her flesh puckered and pinked as the barbs dislodged.

After grabbing a flashlight from the supplies, she forced her feet to step into the gloom. When a bat flapped by her ear and Janey didn't respond to her shouts, she dashed outside and dialed 9-1-1. Then she tried the second corridor to the left, fingers slipping along the slimy wall. Irritating guano chemicals burned her lungs every time she took a deep breath to calm her panic. Despite her raw throat, she called her friend's name over and over.

A bump on her head with the lowering ceiling height forced a course correction, and she headed down a third path. In pitch blackness when the flashlight went out, she gripped for a support timber and cursed her haste in forgetting a second light or backup batteries. She shook the light in frustration and it sputtered back to a dim beam. Within minutes of searching the new corridor, she spotted Janey's body crumpled on the damp floor.

"Damn it, Janey, can you hear me?"

Fear changed to joy when Janey's head pivoted toward her.

"About time you showed up." Janey's face was tight like a death mask. "I'm relieved you did, considering how you hate caves."

"You're plenty of motivation. How badly are you hurt?"

"Did something to my leg. Pain's intense, can't hop or crawl."

The blare of a siren was faint. "Janey, I hate to leave but I need to direct them here to carry you out. Can I do anything to make you more comfortable?"

"No, just get me the hell out of here."

Maya opened Janey's pack to grab a new light and raced back out through the dust dancing in her beam, until the bright rectangle of the mine entrance beckoned her to the safety of the outside world. Within fifteen minutes, EMTs carried Janey out on a stretcher. "I was starting to think you forgot about me."

Maya willed her heart to slow down. "I'd never do that—got distracted by the work and then couldn't locate you." She looked at the EMT. "Where are you taking her?"

"Tucson Medical Center."

"Janey, I can collect the equipment and drive your car to TMC."

"Same hospital where we first met." Janey dug into her pocket and handed Maya the key fob. "Leave the rodent traps out—I'll get someone to check them tomorrow."

. . .

After stopping at the front desk, Maya followed instructions to the cubicle where her colleague was enveloped by an attractive dark-haired man in his late thirties perched on the edge of the bed.

Janey's face glowed and Maya knew it couldn't be sunburn. Her friend's expression was too cheerful for someone who'd been trapped in a mine, waiting for Maya to remember her. "This is Óscar Hernández. He's the owner of our local Salvadoran restaurant."

His narrowed eyes and tight lips didn't radiate positive vibes. Maya handed him the car key. "Sorry I didn't locate her sooner. My first time spelunking."

He kissed Janey on the top of her head and turned on a thousand-watt smile. "I'm amazed by her gumption. Her work takes her to strange situations."

A nurse bustled in. "Ms. Johnson, time for your x-ray."

Janey encircled Óscar's neck with her arms. "Can you run Maya to wherever she needs to be?"

She reached for her phone and angled it toward Maya. "This is one of the *Borrelia* patients who explored the cave. Tell her we got the rodent traps set."

"Let's get this over so I can get back." Óscar's intonation was a command.

Maya added the name and number to her phone, then ducked her eyes. Her assertiveness had taken a back seat when she hit the elderly man Monday evening. "My grandmother's nearby—should only take a few minutes."

He walked briskly to the parking lot with Maya hurrying to keep up. At the tricked out Hummer, courtesy apparently overruled displeasure and he held the door. They were silent on the drive to the ground level apartment near the Catholic high school where her grandmother had taught math for decades.

After Maya rang the doorbell, her grandmother opened the door. "Sweetheart, I'm tickled pink you called this morning but I thought you were done with Arizona work."

Hypatia, the overweight black cat at her ankles, meowed a friendly hello. Maya bent to hug the diminutive ninety-year-old, then cradled the purring cat like a baby in her arms. The older woman fidgeted with her hearing aid and pressed her ear to the cat's belly.

"Grandma, I'll take any excuse to see you. Sorry not to give much notice."

"More than I usually get." The no-nonsense teacher's face reproached, then softened into a pillowy cushion of wrinkles. "But any visit is wonderful for me."

Maya gazed into the heavily-lidded eyes of the woman who rarely found fault in her only grandchild. Had her parents said anything about the car accident? Too many knew about it already if the weekly newspaper published a story.

"Grandma, you keep watching TV. After a quick call, I'll whip up some dinner. You know I'm not a cook, but I'll do my best not to kill you." The attempt at humor was morose, especially if her parents had clued her grandmother in on the latest crisis.

Maya headed into the bedroom and dialed the number Janey had provided. "Ms. Garibaldi? This is Dr. Maguire. Janey Johnson ran into some trouble and asked me to call on her behalf. How are you doing?"

The voice was thready. "Can't shake the fever and headaches. So many blood samples, then a CAT scan. The worst was sticking a needle in my back to look at fluid in my spine. All for nothing—useless motherfuckers. Did you find anything at the mine?"

Maya sympathized with her frustration, remembering all the tests Manolo went through. "I found one soft tick near the mine entrance. We collected nesting material and set out rodent traps to be checked in the morning. Hang in there—Janey is incredibly thorough and will figure this out for you."

She cooked a tuna noodle casserole and slipped fish bits to Hypatia. A shower followed dinner and she rejoined her grandmother in the living room where *The Best Exotic Marigold Hotel* streamed on one of the cable channels. They were enchanted by romance among an appealing group of senior citizens in India and a young couple starting out. As the movie ended, tears slid along Maya's nose to her lips.

Her grandmother reached both arms to hug her. "Why the sad face, dear? It was a happy ending, for most of them."

"Personal and work stressors are hitting all at once. Sorry, Grandma, don't want to be a downer." Sudden death, lost chances for connection—too many reminders of her own gremlins.

. . .

In the morning, after a quick breakfast, she called Janey. "I'm getting the shuttle van to Phoenix but wanted to stop in first."

"Come on by—I have the day at home for recuperation."

After catching a cab to the northwest apartment, Maya knocked on the screen, main door gaping open. "Janey, can I come in?"

"Sure, it's unlocked."

Janey sprawled on the couch with her leg in a cast propped on a pile of cushions. Three cats snuggled next to her legs and a terrier curled under her arm.

"Óscar spent the night, he just left."

Maya settled in a rocking chair nearby. "I don't think he's one of my biggest fans."

Janey chuckled. "He doesn't understand why you weren't with me."

"I'm kicking myself about that—I need to absorb your confidence."

"Don't sell yourself short. You were at the top of your game with anthrax, and it was challenging."

Maya gestured to the cast. "What's the diagnosis?"

"Fractured fibula, try saying that fast five times. Should heal in place with bones immobilized." Janey lifted her glass. "Update me on my *Borrelia* patient after you get me more juice."

When Maya returned, she detailed the phone call and Janey promised to follow up.

"I hope Óscar wasn't intimidating. He's macho, aggressive, and impulsive—used to being the boss. His parents and siblings were massacred by the Salvadoran army. An aunt escaped with her children and Óscar to the U.S., where they got asylum. Rough start."

Maya was grateful her own immigration story wasn't as violent. "That's a terrible legacy."

"His background has formed a conservative, pull-yourself-up-by-the-bootstraps entrepreneurial attitude. We butt heads a lot. But I give as good as I get, so we have a fun time."

"Sounds like you've worked things out."

Janey grinned. "So far. How's Dr. Miranda doing?"

"Making progress." Maya scratched at the peeling floral iPhone case. Not the time to confide her balance-beam wobble over a request for intimacy, or the pending vehicular homicide charges. "Are you sure you don't need me to check traps at the mine?"

"County staffer's on his way." Janey reached out her hand. "You've seemed a bit down during your visit here to Tucson."

Maya forced a smile. "You're the one with a serious injury that might not have happened if I'd gone inside the mine. I'll call tomorrow from Phoenix to check how you and your *Borrelia* investigation are doing."

After phoning Sebastian during the shuttle ride north on I-10, she met him at the curb of the Sky Harbor arrivals area. His lined face lit up. "You're spoiling us, Maya, coming out so often. Was there an outbreak in Tucson?"

"Let's wait for Manolo. With his progress, I'm curious to see if he recognizes the disease."

Inside his apartment, Maya found Manolo in his wheelchair and bent to give him a hug. For the first time in five months since his hospitalization, his arms lifted up around her back.

"Manolo, it's wonderful to see you looking so well. Sebastian said you had a productive week."

She lowered her mouth and his lips molded to hers. Tears leaked from the corners of his eyes, and she kissed them. After she settled on the couch next to the wheelchair, still holding Manolo's hand, Sebastian cleared his throat.

"Hijo, Maya is here because she had work in Tucson." His eyes moved to her. "Want to tell us about it?"

Just the safe, investigation facts. "Sunday after you left, I drove to the Albuquerque Indian Health Center to meet a family with tick-borne disease. Now Tucson has a couple who also became infected with a similar organism. Both are *Borrelia.*"

Manolo reached for a small notepad on the end table. "We're trying more words with the therapist this week," Sebastian said.

With a slow scrawl, Manolo wrote *LYME?*

Maya's head jerked back with her first full laugh in months—his brain was working. She hugged Manolo again and stroked the dark curl on his forehead.

"Of course you'd ask that. It would be big news to have a Southwest cluster."

She glanced at Sebastian. "Lyme disease is caused by the best-known *Borrelia.*" To Manolo, she added, "But this was TBRF—Tick-borne relapsing fever."

Sebastian walked into the kitchen. "Okay, let's postpone any gruesome details. Manolo has physical therapy in the pool. I've got sandwiches for lunch before we head over there."

An unexpected benefit of being ordered off work and traveling to Arizona on a weekday. She stood and reached for the wheelchair handles. "Can't wait to finally play a role in his rehabilitation."

. . .

Wearing the red tankini she kept rolled in a corner of her suitcase for the rare opportunity of recreation on the road, Maya perched on a chair at the edge of the indoor pool with Sebastian. The therapist completed thirty minutes of exercises, including Manolo jogging in place holding a swim noodle, slow flutter kicks at the side of the pool, and floating on his back.

As Manolo was maneuvered to the top step, Maya spoke up. "If you're done, I'd like to join him in the water."

"Okay, stay here in the shallow end on the step."

He passed Manolo's arm over and she wrapped hers around Manolo's back in a supporting embrace. The therapist met Sebastian at a table in the corner near the deep end.

"Want more exercise?" she asked Manolo, her face close to his own.

He craned his neck toward her and she pulled him tight to her torso. They kissed, lips caressing and tongues dancing. As his arms circled her shoulders, she felt pressure at her waist. After a quick glance to verify no one looking in their direction, she slipped her free hand between them to enhance his excitement. Electric pulsations shot through her nerves at his response. Too many months since such an intimate touch.

"Next week, same time?" Sebastian's voice floated to her ears. She loosened her grip, and the therapist brought the wheelchair to the edge before joining them in the pool. With Manolo's loose swim trunks, she hoped his arousal wasn't obvious to the others.

. . .

They shared pizza that Sebastian ordered for delivery. "Mano's doing better with his chewing and swallowing, no chance of choking now, right, hijo?"

Then Maya stretched out on the sofa with Manolo nestled

between her legs. His head lay on her chest, and she breathed in the clean, slightly chlorinated scent of his hair. Like a butterfly on a cool morning, his eyelids fluttered in slow pulses as they watched *Hamilton's America* on *Great Performances.*

"You still look like Lin-Manuel to me, except better," she whispered, squeezing his chest. "I'm happy your dad's helping you keep this goatee." She stroked his chin.

Show over, Sebastian helped Manolo back to the wheelchair. "Maya, you stay in the guestroom again. I'll take the couch."

If she slept with Manolo, Sebastian wouldn't be so inconvenienced. "Every weekend I'm here, you're kicked out of your room. Could I—?" Her eyes darted to Manolo, chin resting on his chest, already asleep. Sebastian pushed him down the hall without answering.

She remembered the Espanola newspaper's weekly publication schedule and the likely accident press announcement. Curled up on the clean sheets Sebastian provided for every visit, she checked messages. Erika had texted the *Rio Grande Sun* link, which Maya clicked open to a photo and article.

Honored Jicarilla Veteran Killed Near Rio Chama

A Jicarilla member was struck and killed by a Toyota Prius May 13 on NM 95 one-half mile west of US 84 near the Rio Chama bridge. Killed was Waylon Otole, 91, Dulce, according to a report by Rio Arriba Sheriff Rudy Baca. He was struck by the Prius driven by Maya Maguire, 26, of Santa Fe, the report states. The accident occurred about 8:32 p.m. and there were no witnesses. Otole was transported to Española Hospital emergency room where he was pronounced dead. Maguire was also transported to Española Hospital where she was treated and released. No citations were issued. The accident is still under investigation. Mr. Otole served in World War II and was awarded the Medal of Honor, highest U.S. military award that can be bestowed on an individual. After intercession of family and legislators to President Johnson, the recognition was given twenty years after his service.

Maya pulled two pillows over her head and sobbed, attempting to keep the sounds from the Miranda men in the next rooms.

NINE

As the new EIS Officer for Arizona entered the Mexican-Asian fusion restaurant, his haunting amber eyes pierced Maya. A movie buff, Maya recalled actor Bill Skarsgård. Dr. Enzo Russo's similar confident strut mesmerized. In grad school, she'd caught a trailer for the movie *It* where the actor played creepy clown Pennywise. But the horror preview spooked her too much to join her classmates at the film.

When no longer able to meet Enzo's leer, her eyes dropped to the plump mid-fifties woman leading him in.

Only a few weeks had passed since Maya saw Enzo and Dr. Bingham at the annual EIS Conference in Atlanta, and so much had changed. Nancy pulled Maya to her feet in a bear hug, the older woman's reading glasses dangling from her neck between them.

"Still off the clock, dear?" Nancy dropped to the opposite seat and Enzo lowered himself next to Maya.

"Playing hooky for a few days." Maya attempted a light tone but Nancy knew about the imposed vacation pending the investigation of Mr. Otole's death.

Her rational mind understood she wasn't one of the kids in Maine about to be terrorized by a demonic clown. That horror character had no relation to this Harvard-trained internist dedicated to public health and it wasn't fair to judge someone by their looks. She of all people should have learned that lesson.

With his long legs stretched under the table, Maya noted his height. He was taller than Dave, who at six feet dwarfed her during their fieldwork. Probably closer to Ben Smith, the ag department's State Veterinarian who'd been pressured to play college basketball and chose a science career instead. But Enzo had none of Dr. Smith's heft—he was marathoner thin.

Recalling his abrasive arrogance at the May meeting, she accepted his cool hand with reluctance.

Nancy handed over the menus. "I thought Enzo would be familiar with Asian food from Cambridge, but might enjoy this introduction to Mexican. They have share plates."

Maya's stomach was queasy after a groggy night of tears from reading the newspaper report of Waylon Otole's death. So she picked at the egg rolls, churro waffle, chalupa de salmon and pozole verde as Nancy and Enzo chatted about housing choices. Although Manolo's apartment complex was an option, she kept silent, not wanting Enzo so close.

His shoulder bumped hers as they reached across for samples from the rotating platter in the table's center. Then his thigh, which started out at a respectful distance on the seat, nudged and she shifted away.

Why did Enzo raise her hackles? Dave and Ben, her closest vet colleagues, were tall, confident men with strong personalities, but only made her apprehensive when they argued about Arizona politics and immigration.

Her name in the newspaper and uncertain status with Manolo must have triggered her defense mechanisms. Enzo's imperious question about plague and hantavirus during the conference had reminded her she didn't know everything yet.

"Maya, did you help Pima County with *Borrelia*?" Nancy asked.

"We found nesting material in an abandoned mine, and one *Ornithodoros* tick embedded in a wooden pillar. But Janey fell and broke her leg."

"Oh my goodness, thanks for letting me know. I'll call later to check on her."

Enzo jumped in, his voice intimidating. "What rodent species did you capture in your Apache investigation?"

Maya's palms were sweaty. "The Jicarilla staff handled it." She left out the release of the animals without blood collection because she wasn't allowed to help after the car accident.

"I was surprised you didn't include serosurvey samples from coyotes trapped in the USDA Wildlife Control program."

"Evaluating antibody levels from sentinel animals can be valuable in *some* cases." She attempted an even-toned response despite her resentment over his stepping into her jurisdiction.

Nancy cleared her throat. "Enzo, we're excited you're joining the Arizona team. It's been a difficult year with Maya overloaded working in two states."

After Nancy paid the bill and they exited to the sidewalk, Enzo extended his hand a second time and Maya responded with a friendly squeeze to counteract her previous irritation.

"You'll love it here, Enzo, if you can adjust to the heat. Nancy's the best boss ever."

Nancy leaned in for an affectionate farewell embrace. "Maya's right, we have a great health department. Need a ride?"

"No thanks, I already texted Sebastian." It was worth the wait so Enzo didn't know where she lived when in Phoenix. Leaning against a concrete pillar after they drove away, she slipped the Yankees cap on her head and checked messages. The most important was a voicemail from her attorney.

"Maya, the sheriff wants to meet Monday in their Tierra Amarilla office. I'll pick you up from your apartment at eight." Unsteady, she stabilized with a hand on the flower box. Could they lock her up right away? No time for a pre-interrogation appointment with her psychiatrist. But if she avoided incarceration, seeing Dr. Kim afterward would help.

Beads of moisture trickled down her back. Damned Phoenix heat. The purr of Manolo's Corvette interrupted her worries, and she pulled open the passenger door.

A smile of greeting creased Sebastian's weathered face. "Mano's taking his early afternoon nap."

At the apartment, she joined Sebastian working on a *New York*

Times crossword puzzle. "You turned your life upside down to move from NYC for Manolo. Thank you."

"You know how close I am with my kids after losing my wife to cancer. Ramona wants us together back east. With Manolo's military benefits, we could replicate his care there."

Maya's eyes squeezed shut. She wasn't ready for this shocking news.

"His apartment lease is up midsummer." Sebastian appeared to notice her crestfallen face. "Of course, he'd want to be here with you if he could restart his job. But he loves kids—it would be great for him to see his nephew on a daily basis."

She forced out the words. "Didn't they all fly here at Easter?"

"Johnny was frightened to see his uncle in a wheelchair, and for Mano, Johnny's reaction was distressing. Abdi took Johnny for go-kart rides. Focused time with his dad helped counteract the unexpected behavior of his tío."

Turning her back to hide brimming tears, Maya poured a glass of water at the sink. She wiped her eyes and sat down at the table. "I feel so guilty I can't help you more."

"No, Maya, you've got your own life, and no commitment. I'm sorry Ramona told you of his marriage plans. The relationship was new and he hadn't asked you yet. We overstepped our bounds."

If Manolo was moving back to NYC, it was now or never to broach the subject of sleeping with him again. Sebastian was an artist and involved in progressive causes. Perhaps his attitudes toward sexuality were liberal, too.

"This is uncomfortable for me to say, but I want to spend the night with him. Of course, only if he wants it too."

Sebastian looked away, then rose for another cup of coffee.

"Mano recognizes me now." She rushed on, talking to Sebastian's back, somehow easier than looking into the dark eyes that were so like those of his son. "With the work issues I have, I'm not sure when I can visit again."

When he turned around, his brow was furrowed but he nodded.

With a racing heart, Maya collected Sebastian's sheets from the couch and her own from the guestroom for a load of laundry.

. . .

After Manolo woke up from the nap, Sebastian handed her the Corvette keys. With the convertible top down, Maya and Manolo headed up Summit Road through blooming saguaros and pale green palo verdes to South Mountain Park. In sharp turns, her hair blew in the breeze and caressed Manolo's face. He kissed her ear and she squeezed his hand in return.

At more than a thousand feet above the vast expanse of city and suburbs below, her head was in the clouds. Colorful streaks stretched from the Superstition Mountains in the east to the Estrella Mountains in the west.

Sebastian had wedged the wheelchair in the backseat, and she yanked it next to the car along with a folding chair. With an arm around Manolo's waist, she helped him step out, then leaned her head on his shoulder as they settled in for the sunset.

Screaming kids chased each other to a stone structure built at the edge of the mountain. Maya and Manolo remained in the parking lot, admiring the multi-limbed saguaros that loomed twenty feet above with red ocotillo banners waving almost as high. Barrel cacti with multicolored blooms dotted the tan desertscape, an unwelcome reminder of the Tucson mine.

As the air cooled with the setting sun, she snuggled closer to Manolo. Millions of white city lights flickered like fireflies below the purple and red-streaked sky. Their minds melded, lost in the view, until she remembered the hazardous road, even more challenging in the dark.

She glanced at Manolo. With his age, experience, and exuberance, he always took the lead in their relationship, and maybe female deferring to male. But since his affliction, their roles were reversed. She had to suppress the tragic nighttime car accident or she'd shake too much on the drive down the mountain. With any luck, bicyclists were off the road.

"Mano, we need to head back, and I'm flying to New Mexico tomorrow. Can I sleep with you tonight?"

He nodded, then struggled to pull his notebook and pencil out of his jeans pocket. With slow methodical letters, he wrote PLEASE.

The Corvette's powerful V8 engine and lightweight fiberglass body tried to slide out as she white-knuckled the downstream curves. The brakes held but emitted a noxious burning odor by the time they reached the flats. Safe at Manolo's apartment, she shuddered in relief before helping him to the front door.

With anxious eyes, Sebastian jumped up when they entered. "I started to worry."

But Manolo smiled and Maya answered. "Sorry, we couldn't take our eyes off the view."

Sebastian heated dumplings in the microwave and they ate quickly. Then he pushed Manolo's wheelchair to the bathroom as Maya followed. "Need us to provide any help?" Sebastian asked.

Manolo shook his head no. Maya regretted his answer—showers had been one of their favorite times together. But maybe he wanted some privacy. She shifted her suitcase to his bedroom while he cleaned up. When Sebastian's door clicked shut, she changed her mind and tiptoed to the bathroom, finding the door unlocked.

After she eased inside, Manolo's body was outlined through the frosted glass. Clothes rapidly joined his on the floor and she tugged on the shower door handle as he glanced up from a white plastic stool. She dropped to her knees under the warm rain shower spray and wrapped her arms around his slippery body. Her lips moved from his chest to his neck and ears and eyes. His hands encircled her breasts and she gasped, tears mixing with the rainwater droplets.

His knees spread apart and she pressed more closely, squirting shampoo into her palm to provide a sensuous massage to his scalp. Feeling his erection against her belly, like in the pool, this time she bent and used her mouth. After he exploded in satisfaction, she bathed every inch of her skin and his with the washcloth. He stroked his fingers inside her but no tingles reached her brain—out of practice or the benzo side-effects?

As their skin started to prune, the water cooled even though she cranked it to high. "Let's adjourn to the bedroom," she breathed in his ear, "and keep this going there."

Once out of the shower, she lingered while toweling him dry, pausing to caress random body parts with her tongue. After helping him into the robe that hung on the hook behind the door, she wrapped one of the towels around her body and guided him to his bedroom. When she turned to retrieve their clothes from the bathroom floor, the door was closed, muffling the sound of a faucet running.

Sebastian might guess what happened but they were all grownups, no matter how awkward it was to think of family members getting intimate. When she pivoted back to Manolo, he had successfully dropped the robe and slipped between the white cotton sheets. Maya remembered how soft they were—high Egyptian thread count. They both valued smooth sensations on their bare skin.

She crawled in after him and spooned from behind. Nuzzling her lips to his ear, she whispered, "Te amo, Manolo." But he didn't move—he was already asleep.

TEN

Maya awoke to spring birdsong and light sifting along the edges of Manolo's curtains. His limbs encircled hers from behind. His earthy smell and warm breath on her neck brought back memories from a cold and gloomy New Year's Day, the last time they slept together. The weather that day had reflected their mood as she prepared to return home to Santa Fe. The next day, they received anthrax-contaminated reindeer jewelry, and Manolo almost died.

But he was healing. She pressed his hands tighter on her breasts and shifted her hips back to his pelvis. His breath quickened, and his teeth tugged on an earlobe. Then his fingers slipped lower, rhythmic strokes alternating pressure and speed. She wandered closer and closer to the edge of an emotional waterfall, yet unable to crash over—not his fault. His hands were strong and coordinated from months of physical therapy.

With a sigh, she squashed the effort. After stretching to reach a condom from her purse, she rotated to face him. He kissed the small flat mole near her left eye and traced her cheekbone with his fingernails, becoming more aroused with her awkward application of protection. With no sound, his lips formed 'I love you,' and he plunged into her. It was done too quickly, but so many months overdue. She held him close as he continued to vibrate, then grasped his head with both hands, thumbs feathering his brow.

"Manolo, I'm unsure if you heard me other times. So I want to make it clear. I love you, too. Do you understand?"

He nodded, and her laughter burst out with such loud, trilling notes that she slipped a hand over her mouth and raised up, looking with chagrin across to the common wall with Sebastian's bedroom. "Another shower together, before your dad wakes up?"

Again he nodded and tugged his arms into the robe. In the bathroom, she moved the plastic stool and they supported each other, standing. Slippery, gliding hands and warm washcloths caressed every curve. His hand fingered the soap bar hard and smooth against her, but she still couldn't climax. Fuckin' benzos.

After dressing, she wheeled Manolo to the living room where she turned the TV to a Sunday talk show. Mouthing the words for *Say No to This* from *Hamilton*, she scrambled up a panful of eggs, swinging her hips in time with the beat. The song was about uncontrollable sexual attraction, forbidden. Hers wasn't forbidden, just frustrated.

. . .

At Sky Harbor, she whispered 'amante' in Manolo's ear before climbing out of the Corvette's rear seat. Sebastian set her suitcase on the departure curb and she hugged him goodbye. "Please don't make a decision about moving to New York before we talk again."

In Albuquerque, she was tempted to stop by Dave's ranch. Reassurance from her friend that she wasn't negligent in the car accident would be wonderful. But he was also a colleague, and she needed him to respect her as competent.

At the Santa Fe terminus of the shuttle stop, the headline on the Sunday *New Mexican* blared **HONORED VET KILLED BY FED**. Her name was in the first line, along with her CDC and New Mexico health department affiliations. She folded the copy into her pack and rang Stephanie, who picked her up within minutes.

"Glad you got away to Arizona. Everyone thinks you're on vacation with Manolo."

Maya pulled out the newspaper. "Their opinion of me may change."

In front of Maya's apartment, Stephanie scanned the article. "Only thing different from the *Rio Grande Sun* is a family interview."

"He was a hero." Maya cringed as she read aloud. "He deserved a hero's death, not flattened on a highway."

Stephanie walked Maya to the door. Once inside, Maya crawled into bed with her clothes on and checked the phone. Tackle a call from Nancy Bingham before reading the newspaper article again.

The older woman's voice was cheerful. In Phoenix, she wouldn't be aware of New Mexico press. "Maya, thanks for joining us at brunch. Enzo found a sizeable apartment in Tempe—might intend to be here long-term, even after his two-year assignment. Our smaller states struggle to attract public health physicians."

Maya tried to match the mood. "Tempe, why there?"

"Arizona State—he wants to take classes. He doesn't have a graduate degree like you, but he's brilliant, and ASU has a Global Health doctoral program. I can't spare him for course work initially, but they're renowned for online classes."

"Nancy, he sounds energetic, I hope it works out for you."

The tone changed. "You were a bit testy with him yesterday."

Had she treated him poorly because she couldn't keep up with his scientific questions, or because he vaguely resembled an actor in a scary movie? "I apologize. It's been an exhausting week."

"I forgot about your car accident. But I want you and Enzo to work well together on joint investigations, like Fred and me."

Maya squirmed. She couldn't mean that Maya and Enzo should establish the kind of relationship Nancy had with Dr. Grinwold. Nancy supported Maya's bond with Manolo.

After promising to keep in touch, Maya scrutinized the *New Mexican*. Waylon Otole's mourning family included the principal of the high school who was a granddaughter. Maya's name and positions were mentioned only briefly, with no additional information about the accident or criminal charges. Although burial arrangements were private, a mass celebrating his life was scheduled for two o'clock at the Catholic church.

Too late to go there, and she wouldn't have been welcome. It might assuage her guilt to pay respect, but would be a stark reminder to the family of her role in their beloved's passing.

No messages from Dr. Grinwold and CDC, but that might change when they saw this newspaper article—not a positive reflection on their public health commitment. The agencies' missions were to prevent death, not cause it.

. . .

In front of her apartment building, the butterfly-painted umbrella sheltered her from Monday's bleary rain as she paced, wracked with worry about meeting the sheriff. With the uncomfortable squishiness of wet loafers, she regretted not waiting inside her living room. But Mr. Zielinski's Navigator pulled up on time and she jerked open the door.

"Thanks for the ride. Last time I drove in bad weather, it didn't end well. I'm so nervous about the sheriff throwing me in jail, I couldn't focus on the road."

He removed his Stetson and tossed it to the back seat. "Guess I don't need this for the glare. I hope your remark was sardonic, not gloomy like our unusual weather. Let's keep an optimistic attitude."

As they passed Native American casinos on the highway north of town, she was reminded of the political implications associated with the man she hit. The newspaper headlines were respectful, but during her years growing up in the Southwest, Maya had heard disparaging remarks about drunk Indians stumbling along the roads. Her rational mind recalled similar incidents for other ethnicities, but the Jicarilla frustration would be understandable when they couldn't control the legal investigation.

Dr. Grinwold had emphasized the need for deference and diplomacy in recognizing tribal jurisdiction. Too often, native peoples had been overrun by the interests of others. She couldn't have had a worse car accident while heading home from the fieldwork.

Mr. Zielinski tried to distract her on the hour-and-a-half drive with stories of his home near the Pecos Wilderness. Because he ran sheep, they debated guard dogs like the Great Pyrenees with their plume tails versus the Komondors with long white corded coats.

"Grandpa and Dad loved to work with the Pyrenees but they're harder to train. Now that I'm boss, we have Komondors—they're friendly with our other animals but fiercely protective against intruders."

Maya's muscles relaxed with the diverting discussion. "And for herders, what do you use?"

"Our family had Border Collies, but on an Australian visit, I fell in love with Blue Heelers. The breed's so energetic, they nip at the heels of running kids. But I have an empty nest, so no one small is at risk of a dog bite."

Maya adjusted the barrette keeping her hair corralled in a bun, and flattened a wrinkle in her navy skirt with a wetted thumb. "I'd love to see your dogs at work, if I'm not locked up at the State Pen."

He slapped the console between them. "Gal, what did I tell you about a positive attitude? I'd hardly be rich and famous without a good track record of getting my clients off the hook."

The crinkles around his eyes and lips let her in on the joke. Good-humored optimism—she needed to embrace that upbeat perspective.

. . .

In the tin-roofed stuccoed building, Sheriff Baca invited them to join him at the lunchroom table. Maya was relieved they were alone, without Jicarilla officers or the gruff deputy from the accident scene.

When Baca offered coffee, she declined. She never acquired the taste for it, and caffeine would be deadly to her nerves.

"Just letting you know that the Jicarillas wanted their own investigator at this meeting, but we refused. Given the evidence, we don't think it's appropriate at this time."

Maya glanced at Mr. Zielinski, who smiled.

Sheriff Baca flipped through his file. "Not all the test results are in but enough to make an initial determination."

"What about the BAC?" her attorney asked.

"Negative for her, 0.32 for him."

Zielinski's hand slammed the table. "Coma level blood alcohol. Do you have any information why Otole was in the road?"

"He was fishing the Rio Chama, with a lot of success for rainbow and brown trout. His family admitted he liked to celebrate, a beer for each fish. At the age of ninety-one, they figured he had the right to enjoy himself. We retrieved seven empties near the river and up to the road, three others in the truck, and one smashed under his body, with his fingerprints. We think he was crossing back to his vehicle."

Zielinski's expression was triumphant. "So he was at fault, intoxicated in the highway at night."

"The Medical Examiner found he died of a massive heart attack before the accident." Maya's agony floated away like pollen in a spring breeze.

"Hypothermia may have played a role. In the afternoon before the weather turned bad, the road surface would be warm, and perhaps he curled up with his blanket when he was unable to make it to his vehicle."

Mr. Zielinski's ample jowls relaxed. "So to make it clear . . ."

"Based on blood from the skull fracture and testimony from others who drove the road earlier in the afternoon without spotting him, he likely died a half hour or so before the accident."

Maya's legs shook under the table and her hands lowered to calm them. In the catastrophic event of a man's death, she wouldn't let her relief break out. She stared fixedly at Mr. Zielinski's eyes, attempting to take his cue.

Reaching across the table, the sheriff pushed her Prius key fob toward her. "You can take it back—we have all the photos we need. The damage is so minor, you wouldn't need to repair it." With his face breaking into a smile, he added, "But you might want to."

Mr. Zielinski put his hand on hers. "So Dr. Maguire is in the clear?"

Baca shrugged. "I would have preferred an assessment of her impairment at the scene. Theoretically, things could be re-evaluated if pending drug tests find a problem. The Jicarillas are livid; I called their Chief this morning. But these things happen. Alcohol and our highways are a deadly combination."

As they pushed through the door to the parking lot, Mr. Zielinski released his grip on one crutch and draped his arm over her shoulder. "Maya, are you up for the drive?"

Her lips parted in a celebratory grin. "It will be great to get my own car. I need to stop by the office and give my boss the good news."

. . .

Dr. Grinwold lowered his pen to the desktop when Maya knocked. "Atlanta didn't authorize your return." His tone was serious, but he didn't raise his voice.

She remained frozen at the door. "I didn't call them, I wanted to talk to you first. My attorney brought me to see the sheriff this morning. I've been exonerated. They believe Mr. Otole was already dead from a heart attack, related to intoxication and hypothermia. My car gave his body a glancing blow." She shuddered again to use the words—any association with the man's death was repellent.

His eyes widened. "And the Jicarillas are satisfied?"

"Sheriff said their anger will take time to dissipate."

"I'll consult with Dr. Jaworski. Take the rest of the afternoon to decompress, but come back bright and early tomorrow."

He twirled in his chair and gazed out the window, then turned back. "This week's been rough, and I didn't help by yelling. In a few days, I'll call the Nation and determine if things are settled down. I don't want this incident to hamper your work with them in the future."

As Maya passed the front entrance desk, she greeted her two closest colleagues who were huddled over Stephanie's computer screen. "Dr. Grinwold's letting me come in tomorrow, pending CDC approval. Sheriff says Mr. Otole was deceased before the accident."

Erika jumped up from the chair. "Fantastic news—it's not been the same this week without you."

Maya wasn't sure she could let go of the accident's trauma quickly. Regardless of her fault, a man had died. But she pulled both women into a group hug. "I can't wait for a return to normal life." Time to show gratitude for the support of her friends, find a way to get back in her agencies' good graces, and focus on Manolo's recovery.

GO WIDE

Specialists may achieve, but not survive. Multiple talents, multiple species, multiply. Keep them guessing.

Geography doesn't matter, but human incursions help. Vector and disease agent collaborate and multitask, equal opportunity providers.

Any species immune? Apparently not. Favorite organs to attack? Not picky.

ELEVEN

Maya twisted in restless impatience on the chair of the iconic Route 66 restaurant in Albuquerque. Before driving south from Santa Fe, she left a phone message with Dave. "Hey, it's been several weeks since we touched base. I'm giving a noontime bubonic plague talk at UNM. Can we do a one-thirty lunch at the Frontier Restaurant?" His text answer a half hour later was brief—*OK*.

The presentation went fine. Handling more plague infections than the rest of the country, she'd become an expert. She still needed to work on a snappy retort to the question about where she was from, asked by the pimply pre-med student in the first row. Her Flagstaff answer just confused him.

As the usual lecture-associated heart rate and dizziness began to subside, her appetite kicked in. Dave was running late.

To read the menu above the central counter, she strolled past walls covered with Native American rugs and John Wayne paintings. Red chile ristra strands framed a massive set of bull horns and an old rifle.

"Ma'am, would you like to order?"

The college-age student with a pumpkin spice pompadour forced her indecision.

"Yes, I'll go with—." A hand slapped her back and she spun. Dave.

His eyes were bloodshot as he braced a hand on the counter. The alcohol on his breath knocked her back.

"What have you been up to?" She studied his droopy posture.

"Let's order and I'll tell you the whole sordid story." The words slurred like someone with a stroke.

She carried her taco salad and he juggled his carne adovada burrito back to a booth in the corner. Turning to head for the counter and her homemade lemonade, she asked, "Can I buy you a Café Mocha? You look like you could use the caffeine." He squinted, then nodded.

Returning with the drinks, she found his long legs stretched out under the table and his head on his arms.

"Asleep at this hour?" She knocked his booted feet to the side and slid into the opposite bench.

"Oh-h-h-h." He groaned and propped his head between his hands. Fresh cuts on his knuckles were scabbing over.

"Tussle with someone, or is that ranch damage?"

"I followed your and Emilia's advice—drove to Arizona for the holiday weekend. Tried to see my mom, but it was no go. Don't know if it was her decision. Her current husband barred the door, and we exchanged words. Well, more than words."

"I'm sorry you went through that. Perhaps she knew you were there."

"I got loud and kids in the front yard scattered. Some could be related to me. Then the God Squad showed up and I skedaddled."

"God Squad?"

"Local militia that enforces the Prophet's edicts."

"Absolutely petrifying." Her advice to visit his family had backfired. She adjusted her position on the bench, hoping to redirect. "We received calls at the health department about VS— your vesicular stomatitis. Those blisters around the horses' mouths can be dramatic, and neighbors fear the virus blowing over from infected farms."

He leaned back against the seat. "Shit. You told them it's not usually zoonotic?"

"Dave, their worry about catching it from the horses is understandable with the virus in the same family as rabies. We tell them it's not airborne. Human cases are rare, mostly in lab workers.

We connect them up to your USDA website and advise them to be careful handling infected animals."

He took a large gulp from the specialty coffee. "Ranches in Bernalillo County are still in quarantine. Outbreak is kinda unusual—we didn't have any infected horses in May last year. Maybe it's climate change again. That reminds me, I promised to check with my Texas counterpart about their cases." His fingers struggled to pry the phone from his tight jeans pocket.

Maya scooted out from the booth. "Go ahead, I'm looking at desserts."

When she returned, he asked, "What's that?"

"Frontier sweet rolls to bring by the office tomorrow morning—sweeten up the boss, and thank the staff for their support."

With those words, she recalled that Dave knew nothing about her car accident. The news didn't seem to penetrate outside northern New Mexico, and follow-up stories exonerated her. Some of Mr. Otole's family members were still upset. But with no new *Borrelia* cases in the past week, she didn't need to contact them when emotions were raw.

"Texas has something interesting besides a few counties with VS."

She opened up the package and offered him one of the sticky treats. "Tell me."

"One of the mares on a quarantined ranch aborted. They submitted multiple samples to the lab. The mare had a low antibody titer for equine herpesvirus."

She took another bite. "That's another virus without evidence of human transmission."

He held out his phone. "Here's a photomicrograph. Notice the slender, spiral bacteria in placental tissue and fetal specimens."

"Looks similar to the deceased Jicarilla woman's blood smear."

"DNA in a fetal liver specimen indicated *Borrelia*."

From her literature search, Maya didn't recall horses being infected. "Same type as my Jicarilla cases, *B. hermsii*?"

"No, they isolated two different types, *turicatae* and *parkeri*."

"From the same horse fetus? That's unusual. *Turicatae* was found in two women who explored a mine shaft, and an *Ornithodoris turicata* tick from there was also positive."

He closed the cell photo and typed a note to his calendar. "We should check for common factors. Are you involved in those cases?"

"I helped out Janey Johnson near Tucson." Uncertain how much to confide, she added, "After that field investigation, I stopped by Phoenix. Enzo Russo is Arizona's new EIS Officer, so I had brunch with him and Dr. Bingham."

He dipped a napkin in his water glass to wipe his eyes, then yawned. "Will I enjoy working with him as much as you?"

Shrugging her shoulders, she wrapped up her treats. "You don't suffer fools gladly and he's kinda brash. Don't want to prejudice you ahead of time, but I'm guessing you'll butt heads."

"Can't wait," he answered in a deadpan voice.

"Speaking of butting heads, you may not appreciate my next suggestion, but I'm worried about you. That was a long weekend drive and you look wasted. Let me give you a ride home on my way to Santa Fe. You can rescue your truck when you're feeling better."

"Saying I'm incompetent isn't something I'd take lightly from anyone else." Then he beamed his lopsided grin. "But from you . . ."

She paid their bill. "My treat—you distracted me from an obsessive re-enactment of my plague talk." Looping her arm through his, she guided him to the Prius, and they headed north.

. . .

Dave's snores echoed through the quiet car as they arrived at his ranch. When he didn't awaken with the noise of windows rolling down and Bo barking a greeting, she left him in the car and jogged up to the house.

"Hermana, I'm surprised to see you." Emilia pulled open the front door. "Dave's still at work."

"No, he's not." Maya stepped back and gestured to her vehicle. When Emilia peered out around the door jamb, she shook her head, whipping her dark braids.

"Hombre estúpido. I told him to take the day off and recover from the Arizona trip. Other people make Memorial Day a four-day weekend." She lowered to a rickety worn bench under the portal. "How did you end up with him?"

Maya sniffed the pink double blossoms of a crab apple drooping over the adobe wall, and caught the flash of a red-winged blackbird startled to the next tree. The distant sound of a woodpecker resonated with no traffic noise filtering to the hidden paradise.

How much to say? She sat next to Emilia and patted Bo's dark head as he panted in the warm day, pink tongue lolling.

"We caught up on work at lunch. I was down here for a lecture. He's clearly exhausted and upset over the failed effort to talk with his mother."

Emilia sighed. "I should have left the girls with my parents and gone on the trip. But with his responsibility for New Mexico and Arizona, he drives all over for work, and the long trips never wiped him out before."

"I think this was more emotional." Maya hesitated before continuing. "Seems like he had a couple of drinks before the restaurant. In all those months tracking anthrax, he'd have a drink with dinner, but never to this level during a workday."

"Mierda. I'll kill him, drinking and driving."

"Don't beat up on him too much, Emilia. He accepted my offer of a ride home. He's still a conscientious veterinarian with some of those practical Texas rancher brain cells."

"The FBI didn't broadcast that the bioterrorist was his half-brother, but it still got out somehow. He's ashamed, afraid of cyberbullying on social media when the girls are older."

"Something bigger will come along." Maya took Emilia's hand. "I know some guys are too macho, but have you talked to him about therapy? I'm seeing a psychiatrist and taking anti-anxiety medication—it really helped me cope."

She left out the car accident, medication side-effects, and the depth of her own despair over Manolo. Emilia had enough to handle.

But she was also perceptive. "How's your beau doing?"

Maya brightened. "Much better. I was there a week ago." Her skin tingled as she remembered his touch. "He's writing a few words."

"You must be over the moon. Speaking of our men, I'm knocking some sense into mine."

. . .

On Wednesday morning as Maya dropped the sticky pastries on the conference room table, Stephanie looked up from the coffeemaker. "Maya, I'm thinking about Ten Thousand Waves for a soak in their hot tubs after work." She handed over a colorful brochure. "Interested?"

Water too blue to be real contrasted with warm wooden panels and rust-colored tile floors. "I've never been there—we're not required to be naked, are we?"

Stephanie's small round face wrinkled in laughter. "Suits are optional, but we can pick a private tub and keep ours on. I agree with you—nobody needs to see this middle-aged flab."

Maya rubbed the constant pain of her lower back. "A relaxing soak and your company—how can I pass it up? I'll let you know later today."

"The spa is hidden in the trees off the road to the ski area. It's heavenly."

Maya dropped one of her rolls onto a paper plate and knocked on Erika's door. It flung open and Erika's pale face popped into view, distorted with horror.

Maya's anxiety jumped as Erika yanked her into the office and slammed the door. Only a catastrophe with her son could generate that expression.

"Did something happen with Kyle?"

Erika shook her head, and Maya sucked in a deep sigh of relief, picturing the sweet almost-six-year-old. There must be no greater terror, and joy, than having a child.

Erika pointed to a document on her desk, which Maya picked

up and scanned. She blanched at the computer-printed snuff story. **Blood streamed from the brutalized blonde's face as he slammed his penis into her dead body.**

The words plummeted like weights from her eyes to her queasy stomach. "Where did you find this?"

"Under the door," Erika said in a strangled whisper. "I keep it locked when I'm not here to protect our older hard copy case files."

"You mentioned sexual harassment last year from someone in Chronic Diseases. Did he ever do anything like this?"

After tossing the document into the wastebasket, Erika dropped to her computer chair. "No, just uninvited smarmy words and touches. He implied he could help with a promotion if I met him in the unisex restroom."

Maya retrieved the printout. "Could be retaliation. You said he was ordered to stay away from you. This should be kept as evidence. They might be able to identify the printer, and check his computer."

Erika shoved blonde hair behind her ears. "He wouldn't be stupid enough to leave it on a work computer. It could be somebody else—I told you it doesn't pay to be attractive around these cowboys."

"Erika, they're not all that way." Her mind flashed to Dave. He had some conservative western values, and they included treating women with respect.

Maya's back stiffened. She was happy to help her friend, not just rely on Erika's support as she matured in handling her own work and personal challenges.

"Let me take care of it, after all you've done for me. Head home, and I'll talk to Dr. Grinwold. We'll get to the bottom of this."

TWELVE

As the sky darkened to a deeper blue and clouds crimsoned over the rolling hills, the three friends strolled in their swimsuits and flip-flops along the lighted pathway to the Japanese pagoda. Orange poppies spilled over the stone walls, and beyond the fence, magenta-flowered cholla cacti and spindly five-petaled blue flax played hide-and-seek with the piñons and junipers. They opened the carved pine door and set their clothes on the bench, then lowered themselves into purple lit bubbly water.

"Oh lord, this is wonderful." To avoid obsessing about the keloid scar on her right thigh, Maya gazed through the partition at the ponderosa pines towering above. Her dark overgrowth of skin was common in Chinese people, and risk increased if other first-degree blood relatives had them. With no biological family history, she couldn't predict future outcomes, but was grateful the disfigurement wasn't visible to most people.

"We'll come again next winter," Stephanie said. "Snow coating the tiles and trees is beautiful. And the temperature contrast will really get your juices flowing."

"Did you spot those orange koi fish on our way in?" Erika adjusted the alligator clip corralling the thin strands at the top of her head, and her legs stretched almost the length of the pool.

Maya was relieved the mood seemed to distract Erika from the past week. Her tormenter from Chronic Diseases deleted the porn story created on his computer but forgot systems backup, so the technology nerds nailed him. The building was abuzz that Dr.

Grinwold, although not the employee's direct supervisor, insisted that the Commissioner fire him. Shortly before the friends headed to the spa, the staffer cleared out his desk under supervision of Human Resources.

"How are you doing with everything?" Maya asked.

"Fine, now that fucker's out on his tail. Never have to see him again."

White cottonwood fluff punctuated gray streaks in Stephanie's dark hair, and she sneezed. "He picked the wrong chica to mess with."

Draping her arms over the rounded edge, Maya let her toes float. "You're handling this so well. Sorry to be a downer, but are you afraid he might retaliate?"

Erika snickered. "Nah, he's a wimp—didn't even fight his termination. He deserved what he got." But she rubbed her eyes and turned aside.

"In my day, we sucked it up," Stephanie said, "the price of employment. As a widow, I might not mind a little flirtation, but they never notice us past forty."

Maya's jaw dropped. "Stephanie, there's a big difference between flirting and what Erika went through."

"Of course, just trying to make light of a bad situation. I envy you guys having good men in your lives."

Maya rolled over to her stomach and stretched her legs behind. "I'm in awe of you, so involved in the community."

Erika kicked her feet at Stephanie. "Some in the office think Dr. Grinwold is fond of you—the only one he's never yelled at."

Stephanie snorted. "He couldn't keep his head on straight without me."

"I'm almost certain he's committed to Nancy Bingham in Arizona," Maya said. "He's sometimes a jerk, but I can't imagine him two-timing her. I don't think she'd tolerate it."

"When the cat's away . . ." Erika splashed Maya. "Working in bordering states all these years with a long-distance relationship— too weird."

Maya pushed herself out to sit on the hot tub edge. "Whew, I'm a frog for dinner who doesn't recognize the slow boil. Look, Dr. Grinwold and Dr. Bingham are well-respected State Epidemiologists. Can you imagine either giving that up to live together? Maybe when they retire."

"What's the latest with Manolo?" Stephanie asked.

"Speech therapy's going well and he's writing more words. No more doubt he remembers me." She felt hotter with the memory of him kissing her scar. "But CDC has me teaching at the July training for new EIS officers in Atlanta. So I won't see Mano all month."

Erika joined her at the edge, fluttering her feet through the water. "Quite an honor. I don't remember our previous EIS officers getting that invite. Dr. Grinwold okay with you being gone?"

"It reflects well on him that I have the epi and stats skills to help, and he's pleased Arizona won't pull me away when their new officer starts."

From her perch on the underwater bench, Stephanie asked, "Have you met your Arizona counterpart?"

Maya pursed her lips and nodded without smiling. "Enzo Russo—he's from Hahvahd."

"A little Columbia University rivalry?" Erika teased.

Stephanie splashed water in Maya's direction. "I heard about that elite college snobbery."

"My vet school epi instructor recommended Columbia, but I was fine with getting my Master's degree anywhere." She lowered herself back into the tub. "The interaction with Enzo has been minimal, but he seems full of himself. People out here don't like arrogant easterners."

"You're considerably less shy than last summer," Stephanie said, "and I'm sure you'll get along fine with him."

. . .

The next morning, Maya stopped by Dr. Kim's office on her way to work. "We need to talk about my Klonopin."

Like one of the ponderosas at the spa, her back was a ramrod to counter wobbly nerves. A low animal whine directed her attention to a crate with a fluffy red nose poking the wire door.

"My new therapy Irish Setter. Named him Psy after one of those K-pop stars. Remember GangNam style?"

Maya shrugged, noticing for the first time the Korean calligraphy and mountain scene on the opposite wall. Maybe she should consider homeland art for her apartment's bare white walls. "I'm more into Broadway show tunes, like Sandy, the dog in Annie."

"Psy's still an adolescent, but I'm getting him used to strangers. Dogs can be wonderful therapeutic aids with nursing homes, kids in hospitals, and autistic patients. Okay for me to let him out?"

After Maya nodded, she stroked the feathery red silk of Psy's ears and controlled her breathing rate. She had mentioned stopping the meds before, and Dr. Kim always opposed it.

"I'm concerned about addiction. Some of my side-effects match what I find online."

"Who's the psychiatrist here? You need to trust that I know what I'm doing. The Internet is a curse." Dr. Kim called Psy over.

Epidemiologists and veterinarians were trained to interpret the medical literature, but Maya ducked a direct confrontation over credentials.

"If not on the medication, I might have spotted Mr. Otole in time to avoid hitting his body. My car didn't cause him to die, but it was still a nightmare. If he wasn't already dead, I'd be responsible."

"Remind me again of the symptoms you're concerned about."

"Anxiety makes me hyperalert and never sleepy at the wheel. Since the Klonopin, I'm more tired and drowsy. More relaxed, but almost too much. At other times, I'm more irritable. I say things before thinking, which I've rarely done before."

Dr. Kim held up a hand. "Your panic episodes, feeling like you might black out and crash your car, or jump off a building. Are those reduced on the clonazepam? Sorry for the generic name, I mean Klonopin?"

"Yes, I understand there are tradeoffs with medication. But it's been three weeks since any extreme stressor like the car accident. I can manage panic with the cognitive behavioral therapy techniques we've worked on."

"Anything else?"

Like a meerkat spotting an eagle, Maya yearned for a burrow. "Um, I'm having more difficulty with sexual satisfaction, I mean, orgasm." She blushed. "Not that I'm active, but I tried once with my boyfriend, and multiple times with my vibrator. I can't climax."

"I understand he's injured, so adjustments are inevitable."

Maya tried again—she had to speak up for herself. "No, I used to be very sensitive, able to have multiple orgasms. But not now."

Dr. Kim closed her laptop and reached out to scratch Psy's belly. "If there's no more anxiety from deadly pathogens at work, go ahead and stop."

Not expecting immediate agreement, Maya stumbled over her words. "When the sheriff took the pills, the panic was awful."

"Your stress was extreme then. Nothing like that now?"

"I'm off to Atlanta at the end of the month to help with a training conference. Public speaking's got me freaked." She wiggled her arms to reduce muscle tension and smiled. "Maybe I'll pretend the audience is naked."

"All the more reason to transition and get stabilized with group therapy."

"Should I wean myself slowly, rather than cold-turkey? Like one pill a day instead of two, or every other day?"

"You're on the lowest dose they make. You can't be addicted at this point. Just stop it, keep up our appointments, and we'll get you ready for Hotlanta."

. . .

Erika tugged Maya into her office before lunch. "Rolf's home with Kyle who caught a cold at daycare."

"Kyle's doing okay?"

"Yes, just the sniffles. But when Rolf checked the mailbox, there was a small unlabeled package. Child's superhero figure, something cheap, like from a fast food restaurant."

Maya's hair on the back of her arms tickled, but she wanted to assure her friend. "Probably another neighborhood kid. Kyle's popular."

"You're right—it was just spooky. Never happened before."

At home after work, Manolo's face filled Maya's FaceTime screen as she settled to the couch. Sebastian poked his head in, too. "Therapists are working with Mano on keyboarding. He typed a note with their help. I'll email it from his laptop while you chat."

After he disappeared from the screen, Maya tried for a response from Manolo.

"I love seeing you again. At Dr. Kim's office, I met her therapy Irish Setter and last week, I played with Dave's black lab. At Christmas, you mentioned your childhood pets."

He nodded and looked down. A few moments later, he displayed his notepad with a blue-scrawled *PERRITO*.

She laughed. "Little dog—I remember. I wish you were here to help me practice Spanish."

He gestured a thumbs up.

"After work, I went with the girls to Ten Thousand Waves for a soothing hot tub." She wondered if Sebastian could hear them. "There's couples massage, too. Next time you visit, we'll have to try it."

He nodded with vigor. Did she imagine a wink?

Sebastian popped back in. "I just sent Manolo's note. Can you access it without disconnecting?"

MAYA, I LUV U. VISIT SOON? She grinned and scrolled back to FaceTime. "I can check for my usual Friday night flight. Mano, te quiero. Sebastian, I'll text you the details."

After hanging up, she remembered the July training in Atlanta. Flying back and forth on weekends would be impossible, and Sebastian said they might move to New York when Manolo's lease was up.

Fog clouded her brain, maybe a side-effect of the missed dinner Klonopin dose. But with Dr. Kim's permission to stop, she put the pill bottle in the drawer.

As she tapped over to music on the iPhone, she keyed up *Hamilton*, a favorite memory of Thanksgiving in NYC with Manolo.

Renee Elise Goldsberry's soaring *Helpless* lyrics pounded as she laid her head on the bed pillow, cuddling a second one to her chest. Heart fluttering from the skipped dose? She turned up the iPhone volume to drown out nasty microbes and accidents of fate.

THIRTEEN

During Friday's Grand Rounds reviewing cases and outbreaks of the week, Dr. Grinwold leaned forward at the conference room table.

"Erika, send the last decade's hepatitis A data to the Public Information Officer so she can answer the reporter's request. Maya, check with the lab on the diarrheal outbreak at that restaurant in Hobbs."

Maya attempted to write herself a note. "We had a babies consult call today."

"You mean rabies."

She nodded, unhinged by his monstrous bug eyes staring her down. "It came in at two a.m."

"On the after-hours line?"

Shaking her head no, she was emphatic. "I was here. You saw me." Her tongue was dry and rough like sandpaper, and she began to smack her lips.

Erika jumped up to offer a cup of water and Maya knocked it down, liquid pooling. She had to reach the bathroom but her legs were too stiff. Gripping the top of the table, she tried to push up.

"Here, let me help you." Erika reached out a hand.

"Fuck off," Maya snarled, then twisted and tipped over toward the floor face first.

Her arms flipped forward in an attempt to brace but she couldn't move fast enough, and hit her head hard. A cut on her forehead started to bleed.

Dr. Grinwold knelt and pressed a handkerchief to Maya's wound with one hand, cradling her head with the other. "Erika, call 9-1-1."

. . .

Try as she might, Maya couldn't force her eyes open. Waving her right arm, she collided with a tangle of tubes. Someone squeezed her left hand. "Maya, calm down, it's Erika, I'm right here."

"Mrs. Anders, thanks for letting us know about the medication stopping suddenly. We have a call into Dr. Kim." A hand touched her upper arm, and the male voice continued, louder. "Dr. Maguire, can you open your eyes?"

She tried again, but her lids were glued shut. All of her senses and muscles submerged in a gently rocking forest of kelp.

"In addition to the fluids, have you given her anything else?"

"Yes, lorazepam, also called Ativan. We've diagnosed benzodiazepine withdrawal-induced catatonia."

"Would that explain her collapse, mumbling and confused?"

Maya tried to accelerate for the surface, yearning for the clear air of a summer evening at the shore. Her family had spent a week's vacation in San Diego as a high school graduation present. Was she snorkeling again? She twisted and the voices increased in clarity.

"Rapid breathing, flushing, and sweating fits the diagnosis," the male voice answered. "Muscle rigidity and grimacing are now reduced compared to admission, so she's responding to the benzodiazepine."

Gentle fingers brushed hair from her forehead. "With the head injury, could she have a concussion?"

"No evidence so far, but we'll monitor it overnight."

Maya tried to move her right arm to her head, but couldn't coordinate it. The cord from the underwater camera pinched tight against the inside of her elbow and the camera body smacked her forehead with every whoosh of a new wave.

"She's been on several field investigations for *Borrelia* in the last few weeks. Should you rule that out?"

The cord from Maya's camera tethered her arm to a kelp stalk and kept her bobbing in place. Running out of air, she kicked hard to the surface for a blessed deep breath of briny water and oxygen.

A scraping sound of movement and the male voice floated away. "She's more animated, so that's a promising sign. But none of this fits with Lyme disease."

"No." Erika sounded impatient. "Relapsing fever."

"Not a disease we diagnose often, and she doesn't have fever or rash."

A loud grunt came from Erika's side of the bed. "And how often do you handle this reaction to benzo withdrawal? I'm not leaving until someone else she knows can spell me." Erika's voice blared closer to her ear. "Nod if you can understand me, Maya."

With every ounce of will, she dipped her chin and floated on her back as the waves rocked her into relaxation.

"Good. I called your family and Sebastian. Dr. Grinwold and Stephanie are outside."

With assurance she wasn't alone, Maya let go—sleep, heavenly sleep. Her body descended into the cocoon of cool ocean depths.

. . .

A heavy weight pressed on Maya's pillow and she turned to identify it. With squinted eyes and gauzy vision, she stretched her hand up to touch the dark, slightly wavy hair. The head lifted and a beaming smile woke up her brain cells. Manolo.

Shuffling noises emerged from the corner and her mom hovered into view. "Maya, it's early Saturday, around sunup. We drove over from Flag—I'm happy you got some sleep."

Manolo pushed up from the wheelchair and leaned over to brush her lips with his own. Fingertips gliding through his soft curls, she drew him closer to deepen the kiss.

Her dad's voice drifted over. "I talked to Erika before she went home. She said Dr. Kim wants you on your medication again and scheduled an appointment Monday morning."

"Ummm," Maya muttered before slipping away, secure in the comfort of Manolo's arms strengthened by physical therapy.

Late evening at the hospital, her parents noted the lack of sleeping options at Maya's apartment and headed to a hotel. Sebastian and Manolo drove her home in their rental car.

"Let's get you cozy." Sebastian maneuvered her into the bedroom. Manolo followed in the wheelchair, confidently pushing himself, no longer needing a guide. At the nearside of the bedframe, he stood with hands on the mattress and kicked the wheelchair back, then climbed in next to her. Sebastian adjusted a double set of pillows behind each of them.

Maya tugged off her socks and pulled the bedspread up. She hated Sebastian waiting on them hand and foot. But her mind and limbs felt too weak for an argument.

"I'll whip up mac and cheese." His hovering was uncomfortably like her mother's. She leaned her head on Manolo's chest and luxuriated in his protective embrace, relieved to be back in the real world. But eyelids drooped and time smoothed out with the underwater illusion, a peaceful oscillation.

"Love you," filtered into her ear, a breathy sigh muted by the deep sea. She opened her eyes and caught his own.

"Mano, are you talking?" Her question elicited a proud smile and head nod in return.

Steaming noodles wafted the scent of comforting cheese as Sebastian bustled in. "Everyone's excited—he's managing a few words."

Now fully awake on solid ground, tiny locomotives raced up and down inside her limbs. She wanted to do a celebratory dance, but couldn't separate from his arms. "I've never heard better news."

That wasn't quite true. When the hospital restarted his heart in January—nothing compared to that. And unsteady walking and a few words didn't qualify him to practice medicine again.

"You're so accomplished." She picked up some shell mac with a fork. "Can I offer a bite?"

He smiled and opened his lips. She gently smoothed the creamy warmth over them before his tongue accepted the offering. Then he returned the favor.

Within a half hour, Sebastian removed their dishes. "Sleep well." Manolo reached over to unbutton her shirt.

· · ·

In the morning after an energetic shower with Manolo, Maya pushed him down the hall to the kitchen. Spotting Sebastian flipping pancakes while her dad mixed batter, she swallowed the impulse to chase them all out. The foreplay with Manolo had been wonderful, but she was still too weak to make love. More uninterrupted time to focus on their relationship would have been welcome.

Her mother lowered the volume on the radio program. "Your larder was bare so we stopped at the store."

"We used your dad's secret ingredient." Sebastian scooped pancakes on plates for Maya and Manolo.

With the implied compliment, Tom Maguire's chest puffed. "Buckwheat flour, gives them heft."

"Like it." The words slipped out from Manolo's throat after his first bite, and they turned to him in jubilation.

"I told you he was talking," Sebastian bragged.

With this game-changing development, Maya broached the looming subject. "You mentioned last month moving home to NYC. But Manolo is doing so well. Maybe you'll stay?"

"What do you think, hijo, do you want to keep working with your Phoenix therapists?"

Manolo slapped the table. "Yes."

After his welcome answer, Maya stammered. "In full disclosure, I'm heading to Atlanta in a few weeks to help CDC with a July course."

Her mother leapt up from the couch. "This episode in the hospital was terrifying. You're not up for travel so far away."

"Dr. Kim restarted my medication and I have time to recover."

Sebastian rested his hands on Manolo's and Maya's shoulders. "Your work in Atlanta might be an ideal time for us to escape Phoenix heat. Ramona begged us to fly home for a visit. We could find replacement therapists for that month in New York."

"Firewalks," Manolo said.

"The Fourth of July display in the Hudson River is spectacular. Maya, did you enjoy them when attending Columbia?"

"Yes, during my internship with Faye Simpson, the public health veterinarian. Manolo, do you remember I visited her the day after Thanksgiving?"

Manolo nodded and Sebastian asked, "Can you hop up from Atlanta to join us for another holiday?"

Flashing back to her orientation last year, she reluctantly shook her head. "In assistant teacher role, I don't think I could make it work."

"Don't push yourself," her dad warned.

"Manolo has a full slate of therapy appointments this week, so we need to fly back to Phoenix today."

Cut off more loving whispers? But on the phone, they could be in touch. As Maya carried dishes to the sink, she bent for a quick kiss on the top of Manolo's head. "I'll try to visit one more time before Atlanta."

Sebastian rose to join her. "Good plan, hija."

. . .

Her parents stayed in Santa Fe Sunday night after the Mirandas left, taking Maya to dinner and sharing breakfast the next morning. Before they headed out for the six-hour road trip to Flagstaff, she assured them she was capable of the drive to her doctor's office.

The waiting room was empty and she checked text messages until the psychiatrist greeted her. "Dr. Maguire, I'm pleased you're doing better so quickly. You've certainly offered me quite the conundrum."

Maya set her phone on the desk and collapsed into the guest chair. Why did she feel guilty for requesting a stop to the pills? She hadn't known there was a risk of such a severe reaction. "I asked if there was another way besides cold turkey."

The aquiline nose wrinkled with the confrontational statement. "Your hospitalization indicates you need to stay on them. We're not all wired the same. If your body needs a very low dose, there's no shame in that. You want to function at your maximum, correct?"

Maya's lips pressed tight in agreement. Nothing was more paramount than achieving at work—her public health mission against the microbiological enemy was all-consuming. Then she remembered her failed attempts to achieve an orgasm with Manolo. "I understand, but the side effects—"

"Are not important enough to risk catatonia again. There are patients with repeat episodes."

Maya slumped—she was ashamed to be so inadequate. And achieving sexual satisfaction with Manolo was moot with the upcoming separation. "I know you're the expert, and my Atlanta conference will be stressful. I'll keep taking it."

. . .

In the health department office, Dr. Kim's smug expression lingered in Maya's mind. Of course she didn't want her authority questioned—Maya didn't appreciate others disrespecting her expertise, either. Everyone had strengths that needed to be valued.

She dialed Pima County. "Janey, how are you doing?"

"On the road to recovery—very nimble on crutches."

"I want to apologize again for my part in your accident. If only I'd gone into the mine shaft with you at the beginning, maybe you wouldn't have fallen or I could have called for help sooner."

"My clumsiness had nothing to do with you. Doc says two more weeks until my cast comes off and I can line dance with Óscar."

Maya appreciated Janey's forgiving attitude, but her guilt still festered. "Have your two *Borrelia* patients recovered?"

"Not completely. Ms. Garibaldi noticed a floater and blurry vision in her left eye. On Friday, a retinal expert diagnosed inflammation. They're restarting her doxycycline."

"Did you ever figure out how they became infected?"

"Well, you know the ticks tend to feed at night. Turns out the ladies were in the mine later than they originally admitted." Janey sounded like she was suppressing a laugh. "They brought blankets for a midnight picnic and a few other activities, if you know what I mean. Not the most romantic setting but they can chalk that off their bucket list."

"Sounds like what I need looking forward, a bucket list." Maya's mind flashed with an idea. "I haven't eased back into Dr. Grinwold's good graces but there's something that might work."

She paused, remembering that Janey didn't know the reason for Maya's falling out with her boss. But the car accident was over. "Have you prepared one of the CDC Epi-X reports on outbreaks? Ask Dr. Bingham if Arizona would like my assistance. We could combine the southern Arizona and northern New Mexico cases."

"That's a great idea—I prefer fieldwork to being slumped over a computer writing."

Within minutes of Maya saying goodbye to Janey, a text message flashed from Dave on her cell. They hadn't touched base since he showed up intoxicated to their Albuquerque lunch. She picked up the phone to read it: **3 dogs *Borrelia,* want 2 help?**

FOURTEEN

Skeletons gyrated on the sidewalk next to alien heads on lampposts as they drove past the UFO museum. At the end of the block, Maya asked Dave to stop at the Mexican restaurant.

"I didn't appreciate the distance to Roswell." She kneaded her back as he held the café door.

He grinned. "Lady, you weren't doing the driving."

In the booth, she peeked at him over the plastic menu. His hazel eyes were clear with no evidence of drinking, but he deserved a break. "Been on my butt for too long. Want me to take over driving?"

He removed the feedstore cap and shook his head. "Not necessary. The ranch is on the southeast side of town."

Dave's friendly mood indicated he didn't hold a grudge over her taking him home two weeks earlier. After setting aside her Yankees cap, Maya pushed heavy hair back from her face.

"What did you do to yourself?" He stopped her fingers as she struggled to hide the hairline wound.

"Oh, that, I took a tumble at work." Was this the moment to compare their substance issues? But she was under doctor's orders to continue her meds. He wasn't.

He squinted. "You hardly said a word during the last three hours."

"Same for you." Her words snapped like a whip.

But he was right—on the shiny June day, her brain was a kaleidoscope of images. Bright visions of sex with Manolo were swamped by fatal *Borrelia* cases, the car accident, panic, and medication problems. Hospitalized twice in one month. Life was brimming over and she hadn't shared much. But today was their first joint field investigation since December, and she couldn't allow time for sinking into a personal pit.

"Tell me about these perros." She balanced an overfull taco between her fingers.

"Last week, a pit bull was brought to a clinic here. Diarrhea, anorexia, and lethargy for two weeks. Initial tests identified clinical anemia."

"Blood loss would fit with ticks. Is *Borrelia* presumptive or confirmed?"

"Dog's recheck was Friday. Vet saw inflammation in one eye and shipped more samples overnight to the diagnostic lab. Found spirochetes on the blood smear."

"I helped Arizona with a *Borrelia* investigation related to an abandoned mine."

He frowned. "You told me when we had lunch in Albuquerque. Forgetful in your old age?"

She flushed—with the discussion slipping her mind, she couldn't criticize him for being impaired during their previous restaurant meal. After rubbing her skull to re-energize, she winced as the movement stretched her incision. "Better order a second fully loaded Coke to top off my brain. So do the aliens have anything to do with *Borrelia*?"

Fork floating over his flautas, he raised his eyebrows. "What the heck are you talking about?"

"Well, the UFO crash in the forties put Roswell on the map. An Army nurse reported bodies in the wreckage, and a press release went out about a flying disc—later retracted. Official answer is weather balloon."

"What does that have to do with relapsing fever?"

She leaned forward. "In Dulce where I had that family with *Borrelia*, there's an alien base in the mountain. Coincidental, don't you think? These spirochetes are so weird, maybe they came from another planet."

"Kid, what have you been smokin'?"

"And in Tucson, the aliens might hide out in all the caves and mines."

When he shook his head, she swatted his arm and laughed. "Gotcha going, didn't I?"

"For a minute. Started to wonder how hard you hit your head. Let's get back to real life and check on the canids."

. . .

Huge mechanical arms spun in circles to irrigate thousands of corn stalks reaching for the cloudless sky. "Those machines look alien." She waved her cap toward the windshield as Dave raced along the razor-straight gravel road.

"Give me a break," he growled.

She smiled. "Can I help you find the ranch?"

"GPS doesn't work well out here, with everyone using P.O. boxes. Wait, this is it—the guy said to turn left at the corner with white three-tiered fences anchored by stone walls."

A black gate stretched across the driveway, metal images of a horse and coyotes mounted to the lower rail. When they parked, a Hound of the Baskervilles raced up to the other side of the fence, barking and growling. Maya's limbs weakened—a vet shouldn't be afraid of animals, but dogs like this one were a major trigger.

They waited outside the hardscrabble yard surrounding a dark ranch home with a gray metal roof. A wiry man sauntered over, white hair poking out from a crumpled straw hat.

"Hey, Brutus, quit yer yapping." Clouded mud-brown eyes swung to Maya. "Whatcha want, dearie?"

Dave stretched his arm across the chain link and shook the homeowner's hand. "Mr. Jackson, I'm Dave Schwartz and this is Maya Maguire. Did your vet tell you we'd stop by?"

A gummy gap replaced the man's top central incisors and he spit tobacco juice to the yard. "Sure, let me corral 'im. Wouldn't want him takin' a chunk outta you, pretty lady."

He hooked the pit bull's collar to a thick chain rusting in a multicolored glistening puddle on the carport concrete floor, then slid open the gate. Brutus's deep howl was choked off as the steel links ended a mighty lunge.

"Cut it out, you muthafucka." The owner kicked at Brutus, who whimpered and settled down.

She remembered a vet school warning that abuse of animals often indicated similar tendencies toward people. "Mr. Jackson, could I throw some dirt over that oily patch? Ethylene glycol in antifreeze can damage the kidneys, even kill dogs."

His overly friendly tone turned sour. "Lady, I ain't changing antifreeze in June."

Dave circled the dog at a safe distance. "His skin is raw."

"Yeah, he's long in the tooth like me. Vet's been giving him steroids to make him more comfortable."

Dave nodded. "Have you seen any ticks?"

"Just retired this winter for more hunting in the National Forest. Used to be an oil field worker in Lovington, then they removed a golf ball of cancer from my brain. Even the drinking water smells of oil down there."

Maya wondered if his labored speech reflected the brain cancer, and the way he handled Brutus indicated a need for social services. "That sounds like too much to handle on your own. Do you need help managing everything, including Brutus?"

Gappy grin reappearing, he tipped his hat. "Thanks, dearie. We all gotta go sometime. I did pull some of those ticks outta his ears."

"Hard ticks can transmit Lyme disease but we've never documented it in this area," Dave said.

"Have you noticed any bull's-eye shaped rash on your own skin, Mr. Jackson?" Maya asked.

He scuffed his boot in the dirt. "My wife died five years ago of breast cancer so I don't got anyone checking my backside."

She blushed, hoping he wasn't misinterpreting her offer of help. "You're having a run of bad luck. Do you have a health care provider in Roswell? Any family in the area?"

"I got my Medicare."

"Good to hear. Did your vet give Brutus any other medications?"

He reached into his jeans and pulled out a pill bottle. Maya took it from his age-spotted hand. **Doxycycline 300 mg by mouth 2 x day.** "Does Brutus let you give him pills?"

"Not stupid enough to stick my hand down his throat, but mixed up in his food, he wolfs it right down."

"Mr. Jackson, the bacteria can infect people, so call your doctor if you get a fever and rash."

"Other dogs in this area have a similar problem," Dave added. "We want to find out what's going on. Can we put out rodent traps?"

"Go ahead. Guess I should keep Brutus inside so he won't destroy your traps."

"Yes, we use peanut butter to bait them." She smiled. "Will he tolerate being indoors?"

"He's getting old and spends most of the winter curled up on the couch."

After Mr. Jackson dragged Brutus inside the patio door, Dave hauled the steel cages out of his truck. "Based on your recent work, Maya, tell me where you want 'em."

"Third *Borrelia* cluster in a month," she reminded him as they distributed the traps. "Kinda strange to have so many in a short period."

He stopped for a swig of water. "After anthrax, you think all outbreaks have a human hand."

She punched his shoulder. "Still could be aliens."

. . .

Along the gravel road, Dave slowed for a lone Hereford calf stumbling through the brush. In the distance, cows in shades from tan to umber grazed.

"Should we notify anyone?" Maya asked.

"Mom's over there, this young'un is just exploring."

"How come they're not fenced in?"

"Oh, they are, but fences get knocked down. Never-ending job to keep them intact."

The road dead ended at a white trailer. Two midsized mutts yapped as they ran along the tires before Dave parked. Noting the wagging tails, Maya descended from the truck. Unlike the previous property, no gate barred their entrance, so they strolled up to the aluminum door and knocked. A young woman answered, legs swaddled by a small child in swim trunks dotted with grinning red Elmo faces.

"Mrs. Garcia? I'm Dr. Schwartz and this is Dr. Maguire. I talked to your husband last night about stopping by."

"He's still at the co-op, picking up grain."

The boy pushed out the screen door and chased his pets through the yard. "Rudy, get them inside."

She stepped to the refrigerator and poured two tall glasses of ice tea. "He named the pups after his favorite Sesame Street characters. All three spend the entire summer in the wading pool."

Dave turned to Maya. "Lab said they found *Borrelia turicatae*."

"Same as your Texas horse and the two Tucson women," Maya said. "All southern, warmer, climates."

"Bert—is he the skinny one?" Dave asked the owner. "The vet said he lost weight, had a fever."

"He's had ticks. Both dogs love to chase rabbits near the river."

Maya handed the woman a brochure about tick prevention. "Found any ticks on your family members?"

"No, but we got the dogs covered. The vet gives us those chew treats for prevention and now a pill with antibiotics."

Dave nodded with a supportive smile. "Glad to hear you're on top of it. Your vet said he's also on the alert for any problems with your livestock. By the way, let your husband know you've got a hole in the fence and a calf wandering."

The screen door slammed open to fill the small kitchen with boy and dog energy. Maya dropped a knee to stroke the right rear leg of the heavier dog.

"Does Ernie have any Husky in him? He's limping—joint problems are increased in the breed."

"Only acted sore the past week. He's too young for arthritis."

"Lameness could fit with his *Borrelia* infection," Maya said. "Can we catch some rodents to see if they have the bacteria?"

"The dogs'll be inside—they won't bother you."

Placing traps on the property and along the Pecos River floodplain took several hours, and a pizza sign in Roswell lured them to pull over. Small box of Hawaiian warming her hand, Maya stopped at the motel lobby entrance. "I'll die without a shower. Then I need to call Manolo."

His nose wrinkled. "Good thing he's not here—he'd want to give you a wide berth."

"Thanks, Dave, your crudeness is impressive."

Shaking dirt from the folds of his tee-shirt, he bent over in a formal bow. "You're correct, ma'am. I need to clean up before calling home—wife's got me on a short leash. I'll knock on your door at seven for breakfast, then we'll collect rodent specimens and the traps before heading back north."

They'd grown so close last winter when he revealed his newly-discovered family members. Part of her longed to share her joys and challenges of the past month, but not late evening when both were exhausted and needed to reconnect with loved ones. There were the long hours of driving home, but the topics were too heavy when he needed to focus on the highway. And maybe a male work colleague wasn't the best confidante for all her inner turmoil.

FIFTEEN

Adobe walls glowing purple in the slanting morning sun, the Santa Fe restaurant patio hosted nine veterinarians clustered around two glass tables.

Maya completed her relapsing fever report and Dave politely waited to bite into his smoked trout hash. The waiter elbowed through the sky-blue painted doors with Maya's chorizo burrito dripping black beans and green chiles, sweet smoky aroma tweaking her nose.

"Our only animal cases have been from Roswell." Dave warmed his fingers on his coffee cup and continued. "From rodents trapped near the two dogs, we found *Borrelia turicatae* in a fox squirrel at the Pecos River. Mice devoured the peanut butter bait and evaded capture, so the trapping wasn't as productive as we hoped."

Maya took a sip of her pear smoothie and joined in. "We also struck out in finding any soft or hard ticks, but I'll reinforce statewide messages of tick bite prevention, early detection, and reporting rashes."

Dave resumed his summary. "Other than one Texas horse, we're not seeing much relapsing fever in livestock. *Ixodes* ticks could increase with climate change, causing more locally-acquired Lyme. Signs of *Borrelia* in animals are hard to recognize. In horses, we could see weight loss, eye inflammation, and neurologic problems. Cattle can have swollen joints, decreased milk production, and fetal loss."

A vet specializing in large animals took a bite of her torta. "Are you working with the Cooperative Extension offices to reach out to livestock owners?"

He nodded. "If tick-borne disease risk increases with the warmer temperatures, we'll increase our surveillance. Maya and I will work with the Roswell vets to write up the canine cases and get the details distributed to you."

An older vet next to Dave said, "Some dogs test positive for Lyme but the state never confirms it's here. What's up with that?"

Maya hesitated, realizing the issue was controversial. She leaned her foot on Dave's, hoping he'd take the hint to answer.

His deep-set hazel eyes crinkled in apparent amusement. "With dogs not a major focus for ag agencies, I'll turn it over to Maya."

She ducked her chin to gather her thoughts, then practiced diplomacy. "You have the same problem as human clinicians. Animals without confirmed tick exposures can have symptoms and test positive. In public health, we only systematically monitor human cases. Without finding *Borrelia* in local ticks, we can't be certain what's happening."

The president of the local association checked her cell phone. "Well, I need to get to work. Thanks for stopping by our meeting. This is a good government-private sector partnership."

Waiting to pay her bill near the restaurant window filled with painted hand-crafted folk art animals, Maya glanced at the time. "Dave, it's good to finally see you in my neck of the woods. Thanks for driving up so early to join me."

"Sometimes I'm in enforcement mode with animal owners and their vets. I need all chances to overcome that."

As he headed out the door, Maya dropped thirty dollars on the counter with "Keep the change" and answered a call.

"Sebastian, good timing. Can I fly to Phoenix for one more visit before my Atlanta trip?"

"Ramona's been after us about Johnny's fourth birthday on Sunday." His voice sounded apologetic. "So we're headed to NYC tomorrow."

Maya leaned against the building's stuccoed exterior and sighed.

"I understand—it's been several months since you've seen them."

"Why don't you visit us there on your way southeast?"

The acceleration of their schedule hit her like a bullet. Her eyes watered and she patted them, hoping they didn't redden. "I can't pull that off. It's not on my way to Atlanta, and Dr. Grinwold's displeased I'll be gone for the whole month."

"We'll ring you up tonight so you can say goodbye while I pack."

Maya forced the separation out of her mind on the two-block drive to the Runnels Building.

As she locked the Prius in the parking lot, she recognized Erika's blonde locks bouncing off her shoulders as she weaved toward the front entrance.

"Hey, amiga," Maya called out.

Erika stopped and turned, a tissue scrubbing her cheeks. The tears in her glistening eyes matched Maya's mood as she touched Erika's forearm to comfort. "What's wrong?"

"Another toy this morning when I put a letter in our mailbox. Freaks me out."

"Kyle's friend again."

Erika shrugged. "Hope so—I'll check with the parents at his birthday party on Saturday."

Maya locked their arms together as they headed to the double entrance door. "My plans to visit Manolo got derailed by his nephew's party in NYC."

Erika's expression was hopeful. "Please come to ours. You can experience a herd of kindergarten kids, in case you and Manolo get around to having your own."

. . .

On the videochat after dinner, Manolo looked puppy-dog sad. "Maya." Then his lips pursed and he stuttered. "Lo si-en-to."

"Don't be sorry, cariño. I'm amazed at your speech progress. Wish Happy Birthday to Johnny for me. Erika's son Kyle is turning six. At his party, I'll be thinking of you guys."

His fingers touched his lips and reached forward to the screen. Maya pretended to catch the kiss and throw it back to him.

"We'll talk often." She briefly flashed to the idea of phone sex, but didn't know how it would work. Could she be assured of privacy on his end? And if she was unable to have an orgasm when making love in person, it would still be one-sided on the phone.

First step was pressing Dr. Kim about her medication. "When I see you in August, you can show me all your progress. I love you."

. . .

Maya walked her bike through the front door and brushed sweat from her forehead. After lowering the kickstand, she dropped to a kitchen chair and swiped the phone screen to answer a call.

"The party is a disaster," Erika cried.

"What happened?"

"Rolf decorated the backyard last night, but everything's destroyed this morning." Except for the porn story under the office door, nothing else had ever made Erika so distraught.

Maya wiped gritty dust from her cheeks with a paper towel run under the faucet. "Did he set up the party too early? But I didn't hear wind or rain last night."

"Even heavy stuff like the bean bag board was upended."

"Your backyard is fenced."

The sound of Erika slamming a cupboard door came through the iPhone. "Dammit, don't remind me we were stupid. We didn't lock it."

Maya sprinted down the hall to the bathroom. "Don't cancel the party. I'll jump in the shower and come over to help."

Several hours later, kids raced around the lawn with glee. Rolf, dressed as a genial clown, twisted balloons into animal shapes. Maya nibbled on a handful of pecans she bought at a Roswell roadstand and wrapped her arm around Erika's waist. "Your husband has hidden talents."

Erika smiled. "He always comes through in a pinch. Thanks for running to the store for more crepe paper."

"No problem." In mock horror, Maya put her hands over her ears. "But can you adjust the kid volume?"

"Kyle's friends are a huge relief after my yard destruction."

"It's terrifying how this happened while you were sleeping." Maya shivered. "Shouldn't you call the police?"

"Not sure what they can do. Might have been an animal."

After pulling Erika into one of the lawn chairs under the shade of the back porch, Maya continued. "Did you ask parents about the mailbox toys?"

Erika nodded. "None of them admitted it. I'd been hoping someone would fess up to a crush on Kyle. But that wouldn't explain the yard. It's awful to think of someone creeping outside my bedroom windows. "

"Lock the gate. What about security cameras? I think they're affordable for self-installation."

"Vandalism occasionally occurs in this neighborhood. Teens, sometimes. Do you and Manolo really want kids someday? They grow up into wolves."

Maya took a slow sip of her diet cola. "Just make sure the pranks don't escalate."

. . .

Using previous reports on her computer for the format, Maya typed a summary of all three *Borrelia* incidents. Her mind drifted to the FaceTime call where Manolo and his family shared Johnny's Happy Birthday song. She'd never forget holding Johnny in November when the gorillas appeared in the Bronx Zoo exhibit. The warmth of a child's arms hugging her neck—few things were as wonderful.

Erika knocked on the partially open door and burst in without waiting for Maya's answer. "Thanks again for your help—the party was a big success. Rolf got a lock and cameras installed yesterday."

"Return a favor? Dr. Grinwold asked for my draft *Borrelia* report before I fly to Atlanta. Can you pull together lab test details, including the vet diagnostic lab?"

After Erika agreed, Maya called Phoenix. "Nancy, Pima County is fine with combining their *Borrelia* cases with ours in the same summary."

The older woman's voice was enthusiastic. "Great idea. When Enzo gets here, he'll have an example to follow. Cases are rare, so he might not get to investigate one soon."

"I'll copy you on my first draft to Dr. Grinwold."

Nancy's voice became tentative. "I know you're an introvert, but could you take Enzo out to lunch or dinner in Atlanta? Give me your insights about him."

Maya's fingers toyed with the hardware on her desk drawer. "I'll try. Most of the meals might be groups."

"Without another public health physician, I worry about succession with my retirement. If I can last until Enzo completes his training, he might be ready for my position."

"Nancy, I can't imagine you retiring." She was silent for a second, concerned about getting too personal with the senior physician. "Are you having health problems?"

"Some residual issues related to a Chagas infection I got decades ago. Time to focus on travel and my relationships."

Maya stood up to stretch tight muscles from several hours at the computer. "I'll try to ease Enzo's transition and make sure he's up to snuff."

"You're a gem. If Fred didn't need you so much, I would have stolen you away."

. . .

Dr. Grinwold stopped Maya outside the conference room after Friday's Grand Rounds on *Salmonella* from pig ear dog treats. "These pet snacks are popular—dog and human infections could accelerate. Hate to lose you if this gets bigger."

"New Mexico's epi staff have been impressive long before I arrived. But I'll fit in anything you need, even from Atlanta."

He nodded. "A second-year officer being asked to help teach— that's something special. Do us proud."

"I'll try. I emailed the draft *Borrelia* report before rounds. Do you think it's weird we found it in such different locations in a relatively short time?"

"Getting paranoid?" His wide face broke into a smile. "Tick activity increases in warmer weather, and more people are outside. Plus each cluster enhances awareness and reporting."

"That makes sense. Besides, how many bioterrorists can we face down in a lifetime?" Grateful for the civil conversation and travel approval, she leaned forward for a goodbye hug. It would have been automatic with Nancy if she was on duty in Arizona. But with Dr. Grinwold, despite a year of working closely together, she thought better of it.

SIXTEEN

The gaping maw of the massive sea creature opened toward Maya, and the spotted back glistened with reflections from the water surface above. Its belly was creamy, looking soft enough to stroke. Children crowded the thick acrylic glass, screaming cries of surprise and ecstasy.

When a dark-suited diver in long pigtails hovered for a slow wave, a blond boy yanked on a tiny woman's arm. "Momma, I see Abby, can I swim too?"

The woman glided a baby carriage back and forth to shush a bawling infant. "Jason, the Georgia Aquarium requires you to be twelve and trained in scuba."

Maya turned away from the stranger drama to her taller muscled colleague with the helmet of auburn frizz. "Living in California, have you ever done that?"

Lila's painted red lips turned up in a smile and kohl-outlined hazel eyes flashed behind blue-framed glasses. "Off Cabo San Lucas. Whale sharks are the pinnacle of scuba diving."

Recalling an episode of *The Crown* from flight entertainment, Maya bent one knee and tilted her head forward in a bow of honor. "I'm in awe. NYC Marathon, climbing Denali in Alaska. You're braver than me."

Lila hugged Maya's shoulder. "What can I say? ER docs are addicted to excitement."

Maya checked her cell phone. "Museum's closing, what's next on our Fourth of July agenda?"

"Let's find a café to grab dinner before fireworks." Lila parted the sea of reveler-crowded sidewalks with Maya close behind until they spotted a table next to the window of a busy sandwich bar.

"Save these seats while I order," Lila said. "If you know what you want, I'll pick it up for you at the counter."

"Thanks. Chicken or tuna salad on dark bread and unsweetened ice tea."

She watched Lila negotiate the jammed café. Although they'd worked together last year, she still didn't know much about her colleague.

When Lila returned with the tray, Maya snagged a sandwich and chewed quickly as her chair was bumped by impatient milling customers.

"Slow down before you choke." Lila laughed. "We can take a few minutes to relax. I got this teaching gig because of my disaster planning emphasis. How about you?"

"Stats nerd. I did the biostats comprehensive exam for a PhD, but CDC seemed more exciting than additional classroom years."

"Yeah, you veterinarians have an advantage with your extra requirement of graduate training in epi methods. Well, if we're going to be torn away from the beautiful Southwest, we're doing it together."

Like Manolo before anthrax shut him down, Lila's assuredness encouraged Maya's transition from professional to personal. "Where did you grow up?"

"Connecticut. My dad's Jewish and my mom Palestinian, both from Nablus in the West Bank. There wasn't much local enthusiasm for their relationship, so they emigrated. Dad's a professor at Yale in Judaic Studies and Mom's an activist headquartered in NYC."

"Were you born overseas like me?"

Lila shook her head. "No, but we visited a few times. The West Bank looks a bit like southern California, but life is challenging under Israeli occupation. Israel's border checkpoints are such a hassle that people travel from Jordan rather than the nearest airport in Israel."

"My family took me back to China when I was twelve, to visit the orphanage. We walked on the porch step where I was found and visited the baby room."

Maya paused for another bite. "Experiencing my heritage at the Great Wall and Terracotta soldiers was incredible. Everyone looked like me. But I still stood out—not speaking Chinese well, American ways of moving, even smiling."

"My strongest sense memory of the West Bank is food. I could kill for Kanafeh."

"What's that?"

"A Nabulsi sweet with pastry noodles and honey-sweetened cheese, dyed orange and sprinkled with crushed pistachios. If I could locate it here, the smell would take me back to a magical childhood before I realized how much we're supposed to hate the other."

Maya's hand covered her friend's. "Sounds like we've had some similar experiences. I'm sorry this was our first chance to reconnect. I've been editing my *Borrelia* report. CDC hopes to release it to the other states next week."

"We've had occasional *Borrelia* cases in one of our coastal counties north of San Francisco. The strain appears to be *miyamotoi*, from hard ticks. Did you say your cases were soft ticks?"

Maya pulled out her pocket notebook and jotted down the organism. "There's an alphabet soup of *Borrelia* in different vector species—it's challenging to keep them all straight. I'm fascinated with these spirochetes. It's good to get my head wrapped around anything besides anthrax, which ate me alive last year."

Lila collected their paper waste and pushed her chair back. "Let's knock our socks off dancing in the park. Roll with the music and the rocket's red glare."

Maya twisted her hair up, recalling her dance lessons as a kid before the bicycle accident. She needed someone like Lila to push her boundaries.

. . .

On Friday after the holiday celebration, Maya sat around a table at the Emory University campus with ten new EIS Officers. "For anyone I didn't meet at the spring conference, I'm Maya Maguire, assigned to New Mexico. I hope the lectures about your Summer Course Outbreak Response Exercises were helpful. My role is to help my five teams finalize SCORE questionnaires so you can use them door-to-door on Monday."

"Ready and willing, ma'am." In his white uniform, Enzo snapped a smart salute. "All three sections—demographics, clinical history, and exposures."

She nodded in his direction. "Good to hear. Do you have the list of *Salmonella* cases from the lab?"

"Sporadic cases were reported in earlier years," Enzo said, "but started to pick up last fall. So we're using one year for the case definition, July 2018 to June 2019."

"What's the downside of excluding earlier years?" She pivoted to one of the female trainees, but before the woman answered, Enzo's voice pushed in.

"Lower statistical power to detect a possible association with the pig ear dog treats."

Maya didn't want to reinforce his rudeness but admired his gumption. "Correct, Dr. Russo. You were paying attention."

He smirked and high-fived one of the other male officers.

She turned and called on the new ob/gyn assigned to Birth Defects. "Ginnie, if we include *Salmonella* from earlier years to increase statistical power, are there any issues?"

Enzo started to open his mouth and Maya raised her hand in a signal for him to wait.

"Too many cases," Ginnie said. "*Salmonella* is a common gastroenteric infection."

"You're right, we need to consider what size investigation we can pull off. Any other problems?"

Enzo waved his hand but didn't wait for Maya's nod. "If illnesses are garden-variety *Salmonella*, unrelated to our nationwide outbreak, they would wash out the effect."

Once again, he had answered before another officer could comment. But she would keep her promise to Nancy of motivating him. "Correct. If earlier cases are not the population at risk for this problem, we have background noise, like comparing apples and oranges. All investigations should define a specific time period for the case definition."

Ginnie opened her laptop and showed the screen to Maya. "There's different serotypes. Should we include all of them?"

"It's a long list." Maya scrolled the screen. "What do the rest of you think?"

"If we keep multiple serotypes, aren't we comparing apples and oranges, like you said?" Enzo asked.

Ginnie's hand went up, tentatively, and Maya signaled her to respond. "I heard the manufacturers in South America had some problems with multiple serotypes."

Enzo kicked his long legs out from under the table and strolled over to Ginnie's computer, then jabbed the screen. "I think we should pick the leading one."

Seeing the frowns from the rest of the officers, Maya's heart pounded. As their group leader, she strove to reduce Enzo's domination and encourage more input from others.

A shorter, male officer raised a hand. Similar to Maya, he wasn't dressed in a Public Health Service uniform. She recognized him as Keegan Williams, the African American PhD epidemiologist assigned to Vector-Borne Diseases in Ft. Collins.

"Go ahead, Keegan," Maya said, happy to get more of the trainees engaged.

"Let's keep all serotypes for the past year. We should collect pig ear dog treats and try to match serotypes with human cases."

Maya clapped her hands in agreement. "Sounds like a plan. Finish logistical details for your teams so we can hit the ground running."

. . .

Maya exited the campus building into moist heat that seared

her lungs. As she ripped off her black blazer, Enzo's hand on her forearm made her jump. "I'll take you to dinner in thanks for helping me prepare for Arizona."

The promise to Nancy flashed. "Do you have a place in mind?"

"Wear something nice and be ready for me at seven-thirty."

"I'll do my best," she said in her most sarcastic tone. Was he making a move? But this was the start of a long-standing working relationship, and she stayed focused on her pledge to Dr. Bingham.

Once showered and dressed in a sleeveless black sheath with no jewelry, she waited in the hotel's glassed lobby to avoid the hothouse outside. He pulled up in a red Tesla fifteen minutes late.

"Do you like this all-electric?" She climbed into the front passenger seat. "My boyfriend has an old red Corvette."

"Yeah, Nancy mentioned you dated a doc from the Indian Health Service. Sorry to hear about his condition."

His condition? She rotated the air conditioner to high as she flared with anger. "Manolo is recovering quickly now."

Within twenty minutes, Enzo pulled into a downtown garage and led her to the restaurant door. He slipped the concierge a fifty-dollar bill and they were seated next to a huge western window. Maya fingered the white linen tablecloth and studied the menu. "A bit fancy for a working dinner. I'm not prepared for the prices."

"My treat. I'm debt-free from med school and can afford it. Besides, I need the lowdown on Arizona and *Borrelia*, plus Dr. Bingham."

If he wanted to flaunt his status, she'd splurge on scallops. He ordered beef tenderloin and a French Bordeaux, then tilted the bottle. "Sure I can't interest you?"

She shook her head and waved a hand toward magenta streaks above the tree line. "This view is incredible, but Arizona sunsets are like impressionist paintings."

He sipped his wine, gaze focused on her. "I never spent much time in Atlanta or Arizona. My family vacationed in Europe."

Maya tried not to roll her eyes. "Which were your favorite countries?"

"Nothing can beat Paris, even if they're snobs. My French accent is excellent—they thought I was European."

"I took some semesters of Spanish and Chinese in school, but only remember a few phrases."

"You look like Constance Wu but you're not funny like her."

She leaned back. "Do you mean her comedic role in *Fresh Off the Boat?* A friend said I resemble her in *Crazy Rich Asians.* I have to agree, a sense of humor isn't my strong point, but I'm working on it."

His pale eyes narrowed. "It felt like you were putting me down today."

The rapid changes of subject were as challenging as one of Sebastian's crossword puzzles. She scrambled for a diplomatic response. "As your instructor, I was encouraging a lively discussion. Methodologic issues are fascinating. This neighborhood exercise next week isn't the biggest investigation but I want to get it right."

Should she add that he monopolized the workshop, barely allowing other officers a word? Tame a bear with honey. "Dr. Bingham values your intelligence and training."

"Should be quite an adventure working in such a limited state."

"Limited?"

"You know what I mean. You did an internship with New York City, right? The northeastern city and state health departments have considerably more resources and better trained personnel."

"Depends on what you want. In the Southwest, we can be big fishes in a small pond."

"Exactly. I want to make my mark."

Seeking the same, she couldn't disagree. But they might be looking at that in different ways.

He poured another glass. "Tell me about *Borrelia* in both our states."

A lively discussion of the spirochete dominated the dinner. Not an appetizing conversational subject for most, but their interests were unique. Nancy's mentoring assignment became more tolerable, and his genius-level intelligence was intriguing.

After he extended the meal long enough, she feigned exhaustion and he paid the bill. When the elevator door reopened at the lowest level, the garage was dark and musty with southern heat. She'd show him a sense of humor. "I'm hotter than a firecracker, but spooky shivering. What's that from?"

He burned both of her shoulders in a rapid rub. "Our fascinating evening has me energized. Want to continue in my room? A Riesling is chilling in the refrigerator, and some key lime pie."

"No thanks." She took a step back. "I try to call Manolo nightly."

He shrugged and held the car door. "As you wish—maybe another time."

Once inside her hotel room, door double-locked, she nestled into her robe and sank into the chair by the desk. She lowered her head into her hands. Why did she feel like a DUI roadkill without drinking a drop? Enzo's twists and turns were disorienting. She had inserted the mention of Manolo again to put him off but didn't have energy for the NYC call. The chat with Manolo could wait until morning.

SEVENTEEN

Fluorescent blue flashed as a butterfly tickled Maya's bare arm, and a black one splashed with red clung to Lila's wiry hair.

Maya giggled. "This is fantastic. Thanks for bringing me to Callaway Gardens."

Lila drew Maya over to one of the stone seats in the Butterfly Center, and Maya snapped a photo of her friend posing with the decorative insect.

She inhaled steam bath air and luxuriated in the rainforest flora. But Lila flitted off down the winding path to the next corner of the multistory structure. Maya hung back at a glass enclosure where a monarch broke free from its chrysalis and pumped its wings before flying to the wire top.

Lila joined her in awe at the butterfly birth. "Dr. Jaworski suggested this when she heard I rented a car. We come to Atlanta so often for meetings but forget to explore the local color."

Maya pulled an elastic from her wrist and corralled her hair high off her moist neck. "Sometimes I combine business and pleasure, but I'm not the adventurer you are."

"Is your group ready for tomorrow's survey? Mine's assessing vaccination attitudes. With a lot of antivaxxers, we'll compare two different neighborhoods." Lila pushed outside and they grabbed a bench to rest in the warm but less clammy air under the shade of a towering loblolly pine.

"I've never guided a group before." Maya dribbled water from her bottle over her face. "With an Energizer bunny like Enzo, it's a challenge giving everyone else a chance to contribute. But I'm getting better at it." She set down the bottle and pulled out her iPhone for a photo of the purple coneflowers. "If you rent a car next May for our last conference, can we swing by here again? I'd love to see the azaleas and rhododendrons in all their spring glory."

"Hard to believe our training will be almost over then. Any idea what you'll do after?"

Maya shook her head. "Too many balls in the air. How about you?"

"I know some people in the World Health Organization. Hey, I heard your team is doing *Salmonella.*"

"Can you imagine us knocking on people's doors to ask if they've had one or more loose stools in the last two weeks?"

Lila laughed. "You might get an award for most intrusive questionnaire."

Maya reached up to rub her temple. "In our adjacent states, we'll both work with Enzo. Dr. Bingham's hoping he'll stay beyond the two years of training."

"I can't imagine Enzo will settle for little old Arizona long-term. But he's in your group, so you've had more time to scope him out."

"He took me to dinner for a *Borrelia* discussion, then squeezed my arms to warm me up in the garage. Honestly, the uninvited contact felt too reminiscent of waking up naked with a college boy after over-indulging."

"Girlfriend, do tell."

"About college? Nothing happened, sex-wise, but Enzo's unexpected touching triggered a flashback."

She tugged Lila up from the bench, needing a change in topic. "Let's catch the birds of prey show before we head back to our home away from home."

. . .

Close to noon the next day a sedan marked SECURITY screeched to a stop across from the ivory faux-Colonial on the quiet Atlanta street corner. Midway through an interview on the front porch, Maya glanced over her shoulder but remained focused on her EIS Officers.

"Ma'am, what y'all up to?" Dripping sweat, the rent-a-cop approached with a rolling gait, tan uniform stretched over his paunch.

Maya adjusted her hat and squinted despite the sunglasses. She reached out to shake his hand.

"I'm Dr. Maguire with the CDC. We have five teams in the neighborhood conducting a health study."

Like an aging bloodhound, his cheeks flopped past his jawbone. "Show me ID."

She pulled out her CDC badge. "Is there a problem?"

He waved a pen between hot dog fingers. "This neighborhood has a 'no solicitors' policy. Got a call—someone's knickers are in a knot."

"No one refused to talk." Her breathing rate increased.

His rheumy eyes roamed from her fashionable straw hat to her white blouse stained with perspiration and her tanned toes in sensible black sandals. "Probably an old lady with nothin' better to do than spy on her neighbors. CDC's got a lot of respect in this town, so take your own sweet time, precious."

It was easier to view the encounter as comedy once he roared away and they continued their interviews. She reassured the team and elderly resident on the porch, then headed to the end of the street where Enzo and Keegan checked their clipboards. "You guys trading off the laptop with the old-fashioned paper survey?"

"Yes," Keegan answered. "It's Enzo's turn to go old-school."

"Good. Get familiar with both ways in case technology fails. I'll hang back and observe, but you're on your own."

Enzo pushed ahead and rapped hard on the brass knocker. A teen boy pulled the door open. "Yeah?"

"We're from the CDC and conducting a health survey." Enzo straightened his summer white uniform and flashed his ID. "Can we talk to one of your parents?"

A buzzing noise filtered from the corner of the overhang above

Maya. She swiveled and shouted, "Bees," before several swarmed, stinging her face, neck, and limbs. She fell backward off the porch into the lawn.

Enzo dropped his clipboard and rushed to help her up as the teen yelled, "Ma." A thirtyish woman swung open the screen door and hurried them inside.

"I'm so sorry, we come through the garage. Only noticed those this morning—waiting for my hubby to come home and do something."

Maya dropped to the couch and recited her mantra. *I'm okay, I'm okay.* But the bee stings hurt like hell.

Enzo hovered. "Let me check you over." He pushed up her skirt. She wasn't sure which was worse, his fingers on her thigh or the spreading pulse of pain from the stinger there.

He reached for his wallet. "This black dot means the stinger is still in. It can inject venom for several minutes if I don't remove it."

After pulling out a credit card, he scraped it across the reddened area. "Got it." His eyes dilated as he smiled like a cat with a mouth full of feathers.

She reluctantly accepted his clinical role. Keegan wasn't a physician and couldn't help. With a strained smile, she dropped her head to the couch, overcome by a wave of dizziness. "I thought Lila was the one with emergency experience."

"Ma'am, bring multiple ice packs," Enzo ordered while checking the rest of Maya's body. "Or small bags of frozen vegetables. And washcloths or tea towels to wrap them in."

His fingers held her wrist while he counted her pulse, then watched her chest rise and fall. "Heart and respiratory rates are fast. Any chance you're allergic?"

"No bee stings before." It was panic, just panic. No way was she going into life-threatening anaphylaxis.

"Any nausea?"

She shook her head.

The homeowner returned with ice cubes in plastic bags. Enzo took one and draped it over the inflamed spot on her leg. He put a washcloth in Maya's left hand and pulled her wrist to her leg. "Keep this here."

With firm fingers, he rotated her head on the couch cushion. "One more stinger behind your right ear." He used the credit card to dig it out, then directed her right hand. "Press the ice against this one, too."

"I look like that old Twister game. Stick another ice pack between my toes and I'll hold it on my left ankle to enhance the effect."

Keegan stood from the rocking chair and shuffled his feet. "I wonder if these bees are Africanized. Georgia found some near the Florida border."

Enzo's voice dripped with disdain. "Doesn't make any difference in the treatment but they're more aggressive. Maya, you still doing okay?" He picked up another ice pack and held it to her cheek.

The homeowner draped an arm around her son. "Do you mean those killer bees? Holy crap, what're we gonna do?"

Keegan turned for the kitchen. "I should catch one for analysis. Do you have a paper bag?"

Enzo shoved up from the floor and gripped Keegan's shoulder. "Are you crazy, man? I don't need two patients." He turned to the family. "You all stay away from there. Call your husband and make sure he comes in through the garage."

Keegan lowered back down to the rocker and pulled out his cell phone. "I'll contact CDC. They can help us locate a pest control operator, or someone in charge of monitoring Africanized colonies for the state."

With attention off her for a moment, Maya lay back on the cushions and shifted her legs up to the couch. She was woozy but determined to stay out of another ER. "Could someone hand me a glass of water?"

When the woman brought a cup decorated with a sea creature, Enzo wrapped an arm around Maya while tipping the water to her lips. Then he set the drink on the end table and resumed pressing an ice pack to her cheek.

Maya closed her eyes. It was only panic—she knew how to

handle it. Deep slow breaths. She was safe, in good hands. The cheery octopus on the cup gave her an idea. Her mind escaped again to the Pacific and the graduation vacation trip. Soothing waves washed her skin, reducing the stinging.

"I really am fine." She opened her eyes and caught Enzo studying her. "You guys should complete your survey."

"You've got to be kidding, your health takes priority."

"Response rate is the only thing important to me right now. Our group is aiming for the top one."

"You're the boss. But I'm staying right here in case you feel worse. Keegan, hand me the clipboard. Ma'am, can we start our interview?"

. . .

"You don't need to go up with me," Maya protested as they entered her hotel lobby. "Any bad reaction would have happened by now."

With his hand firmly under her elbow, Enzo pushed the elevator button. "Not a problem. A gentleman always sees the lady safely home."

Maya smiled through her discomfort. The bee stings still hurt. She'd grab more ice from the machine after Enzo left. "It was a memorable training exercise with the bee attack. Nothing this exciting happened during my own course last year."

"I saw you talking to a fatboy in a sedan. What was that about?"

Enzo's disparagement came as no surprise. "Nosy neighbor complained to security. We're lucky CDC has an excellent reputation."

After exiting the elevator, she led him down the corridor and swiped the key card over the lock. When he started to follow her through the door, she raised a hand to his chest. "Enzo, I said I'm fine."

Most of her fieldwork had been with Dave. If he was standing here, she'd allow him to make sure she was recovered enough to be alone. But not Enzo. What was it about him? In the Phoenix restaurant, he elicited flashback to a horror movie. But in the dim light of the hotel corridor, another pair of pale eyes sparked from her memory—Dave's half-brother, Sam Demille. They weren't that similar—Enzo clearly augmented his running with weight training. Not fair to hold against him a few reminders of a fictional clown or a bioterrorist, but still important to be up front about boundaries.

She pushed firmly against his crisp white shirt. "See you at CDC tomorrow. Thanks."

EIGHTEEN

Until the coffee break, Maya's CDC field supervisor lurked in the corner of the Atlanta conference room during the hotwash of the neighborhood survey. "Taking one for the team, Dr. Maguire?"

"Hi, Dr. Jaworski. We're like the post office." Maya glanced at the reddened area on her arm, even more conscious of the swelling on her cheek that makeup couldn't hide. "Neither rain nor snow nor killer bees keep EIS Officers from their rounds."

Keegan joined them. "I reached the state Apiary Inspector. Their morphometrics can identify killer bees, and they can either requeen or destroy the colony."

"Good work, Dr. Williams. My wife and I would love to have you all over on Saturday. Look for an email with details."

As Dr. Jaworski turned to leave, Enzo set down his coffee mug and ran after her. "Could I bother you for your outlook on my assignment later tonight?"

Schmoozing the boss, probably not a bad idea. It relieved Maya's anxiety that his dinner invitation had been anything more than office politics.

After returning with a Cheshire Cat grin, he resumed the survey discussion. "People were amazingly cooperative, weren't they? Keegan and I didn't get any refusals. Of course it probably helped to have a physician on our team."

Keegan appeared to ignore the veiled insult. "It was more challenging persuading the people without diarrhea to participate."

"Sick people are motivated to find out why," Maya answered,

"but healthy people don't have skin in the game." The welt on her arm caught her eye and she smiled at her own joke.

Enzo let out an exasperated sigh. "I don't know why we need a good response rate in the controls. They're not our *Salmonella* cases."

"If doing a descriptive case summary," Maya said, "we wouldn't need the control group. But this is an analytic study."

Ginnie interjected. "I just reviewed a study associating congenital cataracts with global warming. The principles are the same. We're not just summarizing cases, we're doing comparisons to find out what caused them."

Keegan held up a kibble bag. "I'm dropping this at the lab for genetic fingerprinting to see if it matches the owner's *Salmonella* strain."

"Terrific work, all of you." Maya smiled in encouragement but noted Enzo's frown. A bit jealous not being the center of attention? He reinforced the impression by leaping up to toss a red-inked copy of the questionnaire in front of her.

"Some questions were confusing and hard to explain without going off script, which you told us not to do for inter-rater reliability."

"Thanks, Dr. Russo. Pilot tests of your study instrument are important. Achieve consensus on the edits as a team, and we'll head out to a new neighborhood after lunch."

Enzo groaned. "Hotlanta pavement in July. Next we'll get heat stroke."

Maya restrained her laugh, not wanting to aggravate him. He presented himself as uber-confident, and the hot humidity scared him. Wait 'til he got to Phoenix.

"Dr. Russo, the symbol for the Epidemic Intelligence Service has been a shoe with a hole in the sole, ever since we were formed during the Korean War to fight bioterrorism. How is your shoe looking?"

. . .

Before the early evening FaceTime call with Manolo, Maya

studied her appearance in the mirror and hoped makeup from the corner drugstore hid the bee sting on her cheek. She dabbed some on her arm, just in case. With a potential summer storm, temperatures had dropped and she propped open the hotel window to inhale the cooler mist-heavy air.

"Querida, eres hermosa." In one of his longest statements since January, the syllables diffused like a summer breeze through Spanish moss. Maya's mouth dropped open and she held her iPhone closer. He was making exceptional progress with his speech, and she wished she had been a contributor to his healing.

"Mano, I love hearing your voice. The heat's doing me in and my hair's a frizzy mess. So you're thinking I'm beautiful is a balm to my soul."

His father's face emerged from the side, another reminder that they rarely achieved privacy. "Not to put down Phoenix therapists, but here, they're the best. Just saying."

"Sebastian, New Yorkers think they're the center of the universe. Remember, I made it through a couple years of grad school there."

Manolo struggled with another word. "John-n-ny." His dark-haired nephew crawled on his lap while Sebastian pulled the cell phone back for the wider view.

Maya rocked in a pretend hug and blew a kiss. "Hey, Johnny, when I visit again, can you take me back to the gorillas?"

The four-year-old giggled. Did he remember their Thanksgiving excursion? His father's arms scooped Johnny up.

"Hi, Maya, nice to see you," Abdi said. "I need to get this one into his bath."

Ramona took their place, her black hair tracing Manolo's shoulders as she leaned in close. "We're happy the timing worked out, Manolo and Sebastian here at home while you teach at the workshop."

"All for the best," Maya agreed, "as long as they come back to Arizona in August."

Ramona inclined her head to Manolo's. "We could use a breather from NYC craziness. A woman attacked another one on the subway last night, yelling, 'Go back to your country.' So much anti-immigrant rhetoric these days. Abdi's at risk as a Black man, and with his Somali accent, he's doubly damned."

"I can't recommend Phoenix this time of year," Maya said, "but Santa Fe is beautiful."

"Abdi probably can't get time off, anyway. Too hectic with environmental lawsuits."

"Well, you've got an open invitation. Manolo can tell you all the fun things to do there."

There was understanding in his eyes—he wanted to tell the world everything. How could someone so loquacious tolerate speech problems?

Abdi's faint voice drifted from off-camera. "Ramona, can you help wrestle this wildcat?"

Ramona mouthed 'Sorry' and Sebastian moved back in. "Maya, I'll prop the phone and leave you two alone."

"Thanks." Her eyes blinked rapidly. The videochats should be a time to reconnect. But the silences were challenging. They finally conquered them with the nights before the trip, but that was physical connection, not conversation.

She read Manolo's email on her laptop. **Maya, wear are u? 2 far. Famly hugz. Wurk hard. Me 2.** Still spelling errors, but hand coordination improving, stringing sentences together. She suspected his thoughts were more advanced, but he couldn't translate them into words.

"Mano, all our hard work will pay off. You'll see."

She spent a few more minutes describing the *Salmonella* survey, omitting the swarming bees to keep the mood upbeat, then said goodnight. Under the covers, she tried the vibrator, but it didn't work. Damned pills.

· · ·

"Maya and Lila, welcome." As she opened the door, Dr. Jaworski's New York energy was out of synch with the coiling kudzu vines from Atlanta's Hillpine Park smothering the small cottage.

"I'd like you to meet my wife, Roseline Augustin. Rosie, these are two of my best second-year EIS Officers representing New Mexico and California. They're assisting CDC staff with the training course."

Behind Suzanne Jaworski's trim form, her larger spouse glowed in the sultry heat. She curtsied with "Bonjour" and twirled the long multihued skirt.

Lila with her assertive personality beat Maya in greeting their supervisor's wife. "We're not doing any formal lectures, just guiding new officers in field exercises. But it's fun—you learn more while teaching."

"As an academic, I definitely agree with you." Dr. Augustin held Lila's and Maya's hands with both of hers. "But you ladies must promise we won't talk ghastly diseases all night long. Suzie won't make that commitment."

Lila picked up a white wine before dashing through the patio doors to join new officers under the deep boughs of a red oak, everyone escaping the hot Georgia sun. Maya poured a glass of ice water and made a beeline for Keegan as a calico cat brushed against her bare legs. She spotted a second one, a creamy blonde Persian, hunched with a wiggling butt under the glossy foliage of a wax myrtle. When the calico approached, both cats leapt into the air on hind feet and shadowboxed before racing off into the woods.

"Did you see that?" she said to Keegan. "I appreciate any chance for real life beyond the meeting rooms."

"Dr. Augustin was the one who hooked me up with public health." He leaned to sniff a basil plant in the herb garden. "She was my Psych professor at Morehouse and got me into Emory's PhD epi program. Dr. Jaworski gave a guest lecture and recommended EIS."

Maya was pleased with the connection. "We non-physicians should hang together—we're outnumbered. Seriously, I'm glad EIS transitioned to accept more diverse backgrounds."

"You went to vet school in Ft. Collins, right? How's a Southern Baptist Black boy gonna do there?"

"The town's got a mix of lively bars, exceptional scenery, and dedicated scientists."

She knelt to pinch a leaf of thyme, lemony odor wafting to her nose. "Boulder where I did my bachelor's degree is a more progressive town. But the Ft. Collins CDC staff are very sharp, and less bureaucratic than here in Atlanta."

"They encourage us to pick assignments away from our home states, and I'm looking for a big change." He clinked his beer bottle to her water glass. "Maybe we'll work together."

Enzo, towering over both of them, clapped a hand on each shoulder. "Compadres, how are we doing this fine evening? Dr. Maguire, you're looking mighty purty, all healed up from our killer bees."

"Not killer," Keegan said. "Got the analysis back."

"Guess they were attracted to the most fragrant skin." Enzo lifted her hand to his lips and kissed her knuckles.

"Enzo, how many drinks did you have?" She glanced at Keegan, trying to gauge if his reaction was similar.

"I came early to hobnob," Enzo said with a slur. "I lost count. Dr. Augustin's Haitian accent seduced me into a French frame of mind."

Her eyes darted again to Keegan as she prayed he would read her vibe.

"Maya, did you talk to Ginnie yet?" Keegan asked. "She's over there with one of the cats." He took her arm and guided her away from Enzo.

"Thanks," she whispered. "I'm not quick on my feet in social situations."

"He's not my favorite person but he's assigned to the Four Corners region, so we better get used to him."

After spotting the diminutive new officer near their hosts, Maya shook her hand and fingered coral blossoms. "Ginnie, with your Atlanta assignment, you'll be around this vibrant color all the time."

Dr. Jaworski lifted a stem. "Crepe myrtle, isn't it gorgeous? Rosie has the green thumb—we've been here twenty years, and the yard's come a long way. But beating back the kudzu invasion from the park is a challenge."

"Chérie, you epidemiologists are always trying to fight nature. I believe in working with her."

"Speaking of nature," Keegan said, "do you find many ticks in yards like this?"

Like a mama bear cuddling her cub, Dr. Augustin swooshed Ginnie away. "Y'all talk shop. I'm introducing Ginnie to other Atlanta folk so she won't miss Ann Arbor."

"Sorry, didn't mean to scare them away," Keegan said. "But ticks are on our minds, with my placement at Vector-Borne Diseases in Ft. Collins and Maya's *Borrelia* cases."

"No confirmed Lyme from New Mexico last year," Maya said.

"In Georgia, only a handful of cases are reported, after a spike in earlier years," Dr. Jaworski answered. "*Borrelia burgdorferi* appears to be here, including the *Ixodes* ticks that spread it. But we're not a high risk area like northern states, and other ticks not associated with Lyme are more common."

The tall grass glistened with evening dew. Maya glanced to her naked toes in the huarache sandals and bare legs under the vermilion silk skirt. Her mind envisioned the miniscule arachnids leaning out from vegetation and reaching upward to grab the nearest warm body. Tick check before shower.

"Do you have the lone star tick?" Maya asked. "I heard about people developing meat allergies after their bites."

Keegan jumped in. "Alpha-gal syndrome named for a sugar molecule the tick transfers from its last animal meal. Forces you to become a vegetarian. One patient said the smell of meat sends her into shock."

Dr. Jaworski shaded her eyes with her hand. "Back to *Borrelia.* Your report is continuing through clearance, but we're adding cases to it."

With eyebrows raised at the announcement, Maya asked, "Another state?"

"Your same cabin. They thought it was safe following your

cleanup advice, but a cousin's family used it over Fourth of July. They reported fever and rashes this week, no one dying, thank goodness."

Maya wiped moisture beading her forehead. "Dr. Grinwold never contacted me."

"The Jicarillas aren't looping in the state this time. Someone from Keegan's Division is headed down from Colorado for the fieldwork."

"I can't imagine Dr. Grinwold is happy—I need to contact him." She wanted to apologize again to Dr. Jaworski about the diplomatic snafu, but faltered over what to say in front of Keegan.

"Tick remediation can be challenging. Don't feel bad you didn't kill them all."

After saying goodbye to Lila who was cuddling the two cats with Ginnie, Maya hit Keegan up for a ride back to the hotel. She cranked the hot water high and checked as thoroughly as possible for ticks. If only Manolo was with her, he could examine her back. Like anthrax the previous year, she couldn't escape feeling inadequate about *Borrelia*, a thousand miles away from the disease threat she should be battling.

NINETEEN

"Resolve discrepancies in your data—that's your first task. Review any differences in how you recorded answers." After the instruction, Maya sat on a chair in the corner of the meeting room as the trainees went on with their work.

When she called earlier to make sure Dr. Grinwold knew about the additional Dulce *Borrelia* cases, he was frosty. "I could have sent one of the environmental staff like Pam Brown but they're still holding a grudge about the Jicarilla elder."

How long would the horrible accident haunt her? With so many tribal governments in the Southwest, it would be fatal to her career if she could no longer work with them. Keegan's voice penetrated her fog. "Maya, we can't agree on a date."

Enzo stood to the side, arms crossed, looking perturbed. "I typed it directly into the laptop, so I'm right. If he can't read his scribbles, that's his problem."

"Which one?" Maya asked.

Keegan showed her his survey form. "When diarrhea started in a case—I wrote May first, and Enzo has May eleventh."

"The date of fecal specimen collection in lab records could help narrow it down. Do you have patient contact information?"

Enzo slapped at Keegan's form. "Your job, dickass. I'm not going to call someone and admit CDC screwed up."

Maya leapt up in horror. She didn't speak out when Enzo made her uncomfortable, but when he did it to someone else, she was triggered.

Despite the height difference, she laser focused on his smug face. "Your language is totally inappropriate. Resolve it by yourself."

The amber eyes flashed and his body froze, a leopard ready to attack. A moment later, his lips twitched and relaxed into a smile. Like at the party, one hand went to each of their shoulders.

"Sorry, guys, I got carried away. Too compulsive about putting on a good face. I'll take care of it and check back after the break."

As he jogged out of the room, she sank into the chair, nerves shot through with adrenaline.

"I apologize, Keegan, that was appalling."

He rubbed his head. "Not your fault the guy's a jerk."

"The biggest challenge of this job is working with difficult people, and we all need to master it." But Maya was uncertain how well she stuck to her own advice. She didn't recognize the best interpersonal choices until it was too late, like an armadillo frozen in the middle of a road and killing itself by jumping straight up when a car passed over.

"Sometimes I think holing up in a lab to run my own experiment is looking attractive," she added.

"What would you like me to do now?"

"Find out how other teams are handling their data issues."

"Aye, aye, ma'am." He imitated a sloppy salute.

"By the way, why did you choose civilian over Commissioned Corps?"

He glanced in the direction of the other officers in uniform. "Let's just say I have an aversion to regimen."

Maya let the subject drop, not wanting to admit she flunked the Corps medical exam because of her childhood accident. Like Enzo, admitting imperfection was a challenge.

. . .

While eating a grocery store salad in her hotel room, Maya returned a call from Nancy Bingham.

"Thanks for getting back to me. Now that you're halfway done with the training, how's it going?"

Maya hesitated, knowing Nancy's interest in her bonding with Enzo. "Going fine. Interspersed with CDC lectures, this week includes data cleanup and statistical analysis for their reports and presentations."

"Fred told me about the new Jicarilla family with *Borrelia hermsii*. Janey's reporting more *turicatae* cases, too."

"What are the ones in Arizona?"

"From the same abandoned mine. Boards were nailed over the opening, but that can make it more attractive to some. High school kids ripped them out and had a party. Several got rashes and fevers like the original couple. Janey's working on lab confirmation. They might install a metal gate. Some don't like restrictions on public lands, so there's a fight about it."

Maya peeked through the sheer inner curtains to the deepening shadows of the evening. Faint sounds of traffic drifted in. "I wish I was there to help with fieldwork—it used to scare me, but being stuck indoors all day in the city makes me restless."

"And how's our boy doing—Enzo, I mean?"

"He's sharp, a real eager beaver. I caught him reading a novel during one of the talks—he's clearly confident in his knowledge." With Nancy's eagerness for his placement, Maya avoided nitpicking any other complaints.

"Um, okay, I guess that means he's a multitasker."

In Maya's days working at the Arizona health department, she had noted Nancy's tolerance of staff foibles. Once when someone lost their temper over who was responsible for patient follow-up, Nancy said, "No one's working here to get rich, so let's cut each other some slack."

Nancy sounded tired when her aging voice interrupted Maya's memory. "We can use a new hard-charging leader. It's good you're there in Atlanta to vet him, no pun intended."

. . .

On Tuesday morning, Enzo called Maya over to the table. "Here's the descriptive stats we'll include in our *Salmonella* presentation—

number of cases, percentage hospitalized, and percentage younger than five, a higher risk group."

"Did you create an epi curve with number of cases on the y axis and date on the x axis?"

Keegan nodded. "I'm also working on a graph with number of cases in all the age groups."

Enzo twisted in his chair, looking offended by Keegan's mild disagreement, so Maya threw him a bone. "Draft more slides than you need, then practice and pare down because they'll cut you off sharply at ten minutes."

Keegan continued in his calm voice. "On the analysis side, we'll present odds ratios for the association of pig ear treats with illness, because of our case-control study design."

"No," Enzo slammed his folder to the table. "I told you, relative risks are better."

Mindful of Nancy's support for him, Maya again tried to encourage his thought process while correcting. "Enzo, relative risks are preferable. But you didn't collect a sample of the population to compare the proportion ill for those with pig ear treats and those without."

"Without a cohort study," Keegan jumped in, "we have to estimate the association using the odds ratio."

Maya nodded. "Subtle distinctions not necessary for a lay audience, but important to be clear in a presentation for your peers."

Enzo opened his mouth, looking ready to pick another fight, but Lila poked her head into their room. "Hey, Maya, got a minute?"

"Sure. Keep at it, guys. If you don't agree on your slides, work on them separately and then compare notes."

Lila pulled her into the hall. "Your *Borrelia* Epi-X report was released."

Brushing a hand across the back of her neck, Maya wished for more time to review it again. "But several new cases are pending near Tucson."

"A contact from the European Union emailed after seeing the report—they're having a *Borrelia* outbreak too."

"Did they request your help?" Maya's expression was eager for her colleague. "That would be exciting."

"No, he asked for your phone number. He's a physician from Poland, Stefan Duda."

"I remember him—he graduated Columbia a year ahead of me with a PhD."

Lila put a hand behind Maya's back. "Let's head to the cafeteria."

After Maya bought a green tea and Lila coffee, they settled at a table near the window. Lila's finger traced her phone screen. "I just forwarded Stefan's email so you can reply. He's working on a refugee-related outbreak in Oslo."

"I'm not really a *Borrelia* expert but would love to talk to him."

"How are your newbies doing with their slide presentations?"

Maya compulsively wiped up a few drops spilled on the table. "One team's at cross-purposes."

"Which one?"

"Enzo with Keegan. Keegan's easy-going and smart—the problem's on Enzo's side. Remember at Callaway Gardens when I mentioned helping him get oriented? Nancy hasn't had an officer in several years, and is considering him as her replacement when she retires."

"In California, the EIS Officer would never immediately get the job of State Epidemiologist. Of course, we have a deeper bench than Arizona." Lila fluffed her short curls. "Plus Dr. Bingham respects your work. Why wouldn't you be at the top of her list to replace her?"

"Nothing personal," Maya said, "but physicians like you are more often appointed than vets."

"Of course you're right—the clinical docs want to interact with one of their own. So you're concerned about Enzo?"

"He's aggressive, opinionated. Those traits might be helpful when defending public health against other bureaucrats, but something about him makes me uneasy."

Lila swigged her coffee and touched up her lipstick. "What does that mean?"

"I told you he rubbed my arms after dinner. At Dr. Jaworski's party, he said I was pretty and put his arm around my shoulder—but Keegan's too, so maybe nothing. Yesterday he called Keegan a name."

"Well, I'm not attuned to male hormones, if you think he's coming onto you. I'd worry more about the incident with Keegan."

Maya tossed both their cups into the recycle bin. "I'll do what Nancy asked and keep an eye on him, then consider later how much to warn her."

. . .

"Two years since we last talked, eh Maya?" Despite the miles and length of time, she recognized Stefan's friendly voice with the clipped English.

"Yes, I thought you were headed home to Poland when you graduated. What are you doing in Norway?"

He chuckled. "Well, the EU has many opportunities so I'm based in Oslo since last fall. Just picked up my daughter from school, and she's racing down the pathways from statue to statue in Vigeland Park. Some are strange—we just passed a naked angry bald boy. Sculpture, I mean."

"Your email to Lila mentioned refugees. Where are they from?"

"Many originated in Somalia, but they traveled through Sudan, Libya, and Italy on their way here. Ours is *Borrelia recurrentis* spread by lice, not ticks as in your cases. I was particularly interested in your death from JHR, Jarisch-Herxheimer reaction. I have some of those, too."

Maya flashed to Manolo's brother-in-law, Abdi. "There's someone from Somalia who might know if they've had past cases."

"Certainly, consultation will be helpful. But I was hoping you might come over."

With limited international travel experience, Maya's stomach twisted, both in apprehension and anticipation. "You're kidding, when?"

"Your country's been frosty recently with WHO and the EU.

Now might be a chance to bolster those connections. And Oslo's a bit empty, so it's a good time to travel. Everyone's on fellesferie—summer vacation. But a medical detective never takes a break."

"I'm helping with a summer training course, and my boss is sensitive to me being away."

"This collaboration could benefit our understanding of *Borrelia*. I've got to go—my daughter's about to jump into the fountain."

. . .

"Maya, you promised to get back at the end of the month, so why are you even asking?" Dr. Grinwold's growl on the speakerphone filled the small book-lined office.

Tanned wrinkles creased into deep farm-track furrows as Dr. Jaworski sighed. "We were perhaps a bit hasty in our judgment of Dr. Maguire with her car accident. One of her training deliverables is an overseas assignment. I'm authorizing her to travel now, when she would be away from New Mexico anyways."

Maya's mood was boosted by the encouragement.

"I thought you needed her stats expertise in teaching the course. Why would you let her go?"

Dr. Jaworski's Long Island accent thickened, impatience clear on her face. Like Dr. Grinwold, she didn't seem like someone who changed her mind easily. "The work product here is exemplary. Her teams got the award for highest response rate in the field survey. She committed to providing feedback to them by email while she's gone, as they finalize their slides and reports."

Maya searched for additional arguments. "Lila Becker, the EIS Officer from California, promised to evaluate their presentations for me. She'll be Enzo Russo's neighbor, so time spent with him will nurture that important connection. Our group also includes Keegan Williams, the new assignee to Vector-Borne Diseases in Colorado."

The sound of a tapping pen came through. "I'm pleased about the connection with Ft. Collins, since they're the foot in the door with the Jicarillas, after your mess."

Dr. Jaworski's chin dipped in a nod as her expression reflected cautious support. "Maya's our current relapsing fever expert, and we need someone at CDC to get familiar with lice as a source. If LBRF shows up on our doorstep, I want CDC to be prepared."

His loud harrumph echoed among the epidemiology and statistics tomes. "Don't screw this one up, Maya." The caustic admonishment, like from a coach berating his players, rattled her nerves, doing more harm than good.

She counteracted the butterflies in her stomach with a deep breath. A journey of a lifetime or a chance for epic failure, she couldn't guess.

TAKE ADVANTAGE

Hundreds of millions of climate migrants are predicted by midcentury, leading to extreme poverty, overcrowding, and dislocation. In the face of social disruption, civil unrest, and war, basic hygiene is impossible. Risk of an epidemic?

A hundred years ago, lice infected thirteen million residents of Eastern Europe and Russia with *Borrelia* during a five-year period, killing five million. The tan to greyish-white louse vector for transmission is the size of a sesame seed with six legs, hiding out in clothing and feeding on human blood to live.

TWENTY

For the two-hour layover in NYC on her way to Oslo, Maya met Manolo and Sebastian outside the security gate at JFK. Sebastian pushed the wheelchair close to the bench where Maya waited, then left them alone.

She sighed after their deep kiss. "So many weeks since we were together. Sorry I only have a few minutes."

He tugged her to his lap. "Any moments you have, we'll make the most of them."

One of the longest sentences he'd spoken in months—so much progress when they were apart. His breath was hot in her ear as she assured him, "This Norway trip shouldn't take long. It's a CDC-EU goodwill mission to improve ties."

His strong hands clasped her hips, and an unaccustomed but welcome muscle tightened in her pelvis as she felt his response. His thumbs slipped up to caress the back of her neck as his lips bussed each ear and then her eyes.

"Mano, you're driving me crazy, even on the damned Klonopin."

He pointed to a handicapped restroom. "Enough time?"

Unplanned airport sex, so no protection, unless he brought it. In the heat of his taking charge again, she set aside her obsession with being a careful public health professional. "Oh, God, of course, let's try."

Flight announcements and voices outside encouraged a mood of illicit delight. Would Sebastian worry if he couldn't locate them? With the weeks of separation and buildup, only minutes were required for him to pull out a condom and come. It was fine, she assured him when adjusting their clothes, that she didn't have time to climax. With no success in months, her mind was a negative feedback loop of failure.

"Can you do me a favor?" Maya asked Sebastian when he rejoined them after her text message. Her face felt hot—did he guess how they spent their minutes together? "I need to get back through security and make a dash for the gate. Could you contact Abdi and ask him to call me within the hour? The *Borrelia* cases are in Somali immigrants."

"Of course." Sebastian hugged her goodbye. "I'll reach him—don't miss your plane."

"Call from Europe." Manolo held her back.

"My iPhone won't work there. If this were a major emergency, CDC would detail me a phone, but this outbreak isn't big enough. I'm supposed to keep in touch through email."

"I'll write love letters," Manolo whispered when she bent for a final kiss.

She cleared security and reached her gate before boarding started. The timing was perfect as she answered a call from Abdi.

"Sebastian said you're headed across the pond for a health problem in Somali refugees."

"Yes. I realize this is a crazy hour for you guys—trying to get Johnny to bed."

"Ramona's got it covered. Are you actually going there?"

"The outbreak's in Somalis who escaped to Norway. It's louse-borne relapsing fever—LBRF, caused by the body louse, not head lice. Is that something you're familiar with?"

"We were sick with one thing or another during the War a decade ago. I was the only one in my family to survive and make my way to the U.S."

Her stomach turned over, not from the dash through the airport or rushed sex. With only one previous visit to Ramona's over Thanksgiving, she never heard his history.

"Abdi, I can't imagine what you've been through. I never knew my biological family, and it's so much worse to know and love them before losing them."

His voice remained calm. "Thanks, Maya. I remember bloody bug bites as a child, whenever we had to move suddenly. Possibly lice—I don't know."

"I was just curious for a personal perception on louse-borne disease there. Go check on Johnny. I wish I had time to visit." All it took to snap out of feeling sorry for herself and Manolo was to hear someone else's life challenges.

. . .

The Klonopin allowed Maya to relax and sleep on the flights from New York to London and finally Oslo. On the high-speed Flytoget train from Gardermoen Airport to the Sentrum, she reviewed her notes.

Emerging from the station, she looked for the bronze tiger statue where Stefan said they would meet. She spotted him in a blue short-waisted European suit lounging next to the tiger's burnished body.

Relaxed after finding him so easily, she indulged in her hobby of matching him to a media star. A bearded John Krasinski from The Quiet Place, although it was another horror movie she had skipped.

"Stefan, wonderful to see you again." He helped a young blonde girl down from the tiger's back and shook Maya's hand.

"Paula, we'll talk English, like when we were in New York." He turned back to Maya. "You must be exhausted."

"No, I slept well on the planes."

Paula tugged on Maya's blazer. "Our tiger was made by a rich man to celebrate Oslo's one thousandth anniversary. I am six, it was before I was born."

Stefan ruffled Paula's hair. "Oslo's nickname is Tigerstaden. An old poem says the tiger represents the dangerous city. Not so dangerous now."

"Can I take your picture?" Maya reached out to stroke the cold carved head, mouth open in a slight snarl—curious or threatening?

Paula leaned on the outstretched front paw with her head under its chin.

"Paula, do you know that I'm an animal doctor?" Maya turned back to Stefan after snapping the photo. "I hope you didn't wait long."

"I picked her up from barnehage, our kindergarten, open most of the year. We strolled down to the Opera House, then back here. Summers are endless with the sun not setting until after ten."

Maya's lungs inhaled the clean ocean air as she took in the late afternoon light sparkling across the plaza tiles. Stefan grasped the handle of her roller bag and pointed up to the left. "Let's head to our pedestrian street, Karl Johans gate, then catch the Bygdøy ferry home."

"Thanks for letting me stay with you and Kondrat. Hotel prices are high."

"I'm happy we can get back in touch."

Paula caught hold of Maya's hand in a shared goodbye pat of the tiger's head before they strolled for twenty minutes to the ferry, arriving as it loaded. On the boat deck during the cruise, Maya toasted in the warm sun and snapped Oslofjord photos with her phone, until they unloaded within thirty minutes.

Strolling past the Kon Tiki and Fram museums, Stefan said, "Wish we had time to stop in to see the ships from Pacific Ocean and polar exploration history."

"Tempting—was Amundsen first to the South Pole? But I should focus on our investigation. Please tell me about the cases."

He nodded. "After Kondrat takes over kid care—little ears."

Paula made a funny face, and he chased her down the quiet winding lane. When Maya caught up with them, he added, "Wonderful family life here on the peninsula—great schools and close to cultural highlights."

"Folk museum is my favorite—I can pretend I'm a reindeer." Paula twirled and pranced.

"Historic thatched roof buildings were moved to the property. Exhibit on Sami culture is the best."

"Paula, your English is impressive." Maya grabbed the hands of the girl and they circled Stefan. "Did you practice when you lived in America?"

Stefan pushed through a white picket gate and passed under an archway of fragrant vines. "Oslo schools are bilingual. Almost everyone speaks it."

In the house, Paula ran to her second father, a toned young man with copper hair. After Stefan leaned down to his shorter partner and tweaked the tie of his chef's apron, Kondrat guided them to the door and continued to sauté salmon in a pan with onions.

"Go talk microbes on the patio while I finish our dinner. Paula, please clean up."

Maya lowered herself to one of the slotted chairs while Stefan placed his jacket and tie over the back of another. Turning to take in the verdant small garden, she experienced cognitive dissonance. What was she doing in this bucolic setting, peeks of the fjord through the trees—to talk about lice?

Stefan returned with a tray of water glasses, crackers, and orange jam. "A snack until dinner. These are multe—cloud berries—our favorite treat. They're harvested in the wild by the Sami."

After slipping a coated cracker between her lips, she sighed. "This is the best—I can't even describe the flavor."

"We'll pack some to take home. Are you still in contact with your internship mentor, Dr. Simpson?"

She flushed. Things had been so insane, she hadn't called Faye in weeks. "I plan to see her on my way home." She glanced around the garden for the jasmine-like scent. "I don't know how you get any work done during your magical Norwegian summers. Can you brief me on your outbreak?"

"Twenty-three cases of relapsing fever are confirmed in young male refugees from the Horn of Africa, most from Somalia. Itchy rashes, jaundice, abdominal pain, and vomiting. Nine had the JHR reaction that I mentioned on the phone. Three died from multi-organ failure."

"My area's had fewer cases, and only one death, the pregnant woman in my report. I wonder why Norway has such a high JHR rate?"

Stefan took a sip of his water. "Perhaps we're using the wrong antibiotics or too much of them. The patients had varied migration routes, so we're trying to determine when they picked up the lice and infection."

"Ugh, infection, not a word for the table." Kondrat juggled a salad bowl and a tray with the entree. "Bring out the utensils," he called back to Paula.

The investigation discussion was dropped while they devoured the salmon dinner. As a major Norwegian industry, Kondrat said it was served as frequently as hamburgers in the U.S. He shared amusing stories from his job leading tours from the Tiger. With the oil-supported social system, wages and employment conditions, Norwegians often left tip-based jobs to non-citizen residents like Kondrat.

"Although we both grew up in Poland, we first met here at the University at Oslo as undergraduate students," Stefan said. "Tuition is essentially free, and many European students come here."

Maya shook her head. "I was lucky my parents had full-time jobs and set up college savings accounts for me. I saved one year of costs because I finished my bachelor's degree in three years, but expenses still added up."

Stefan cleared the empty plates. "Maya, let me show you our guestroom. You must be tired."

"My body's a bit confused—still afternoon in the States. But I'll take you up on the offer. I need to check email."

After quick notes to Manolo and her supervisors about her arrival, she reviewed draft slides from her teams. Four pairs of EIS officers sent one slide set each, but Keegan and Enzo sent separate ones. Keegan apologized that they didn't have consensus, but Enzo sent a lengthy note about why his slides were superior. She admired passion for a public health cause, but did he edge over to hubris, enough to alert Nancy? A wave of resentment slipped in—why did Nancy put her in this role of evaluating and assisting an alpha male who was older? She knew about Maya's panic disorder—it was too much to ask.

She distracted herself with a short social note to Erika, Stephanie, Janey, and Lila, her closest friends. For a moment, she wondered about all of her friendships being work-related, but brushed it aside. The job of an EIS Officer was all-consuming. She attached a photo of the Oslofjord.

While drafting a separate email to Dr. Simpson, she imagined her mentor still at work—leaning back in her chair, feet on the desk, unperturbed by protocol. She clicked to send the note.

Faye, I'm in Oslo, can you believe it? LBRF, meeting my requirement for an overseas deployment. I'm becoming a *Borrelia* expert, after some TBRF in NM and AZ. Do you remember Stefan, who interned with your EIS Officer while I interned with you? He's my host, working for the EU. Attached is a photo of him and his daughter at an Oslo landmark. I hope to spend a couple days in NYC when I fly home. I could benefit from your insights about a lot of things.

TWENTY-ONE

Thursday morning, a Somali man, younger than Maya, spoke from his couch in the tiny studio apartment a few blocks east of Oslo's Sentrum. "My friend was shot with loaf of bread above head to show not armed." Maya shifted her weight while Stefan sat on the only chair, taking notes on his laptop.

"Women gathered bloody bread around body for children."

As Maya trembled and leaned a hand on Stefan's chair to counteract a wave of dizziness, the man pulled out a sketchpad with charcoal drawings. He flipped through the pages, mostly close-ups of grim faces.

"Excuse me these are sad. Life is different now—do not want to forget those behind."

"I'm sorry to hear about your terrible journey through Libya. You honor all these people with your sketches." She touched Stefan's shoulder. "Is there support here for new artists?"

"Yes—I'll follow up in the office. Bashir, did the clinic help you wash your clothes with hot water to get rid of the lice?" He pointed to the electronic record. "Topical pediculicide wasn't used—lice have developed resistance to most of them."

Maya's skin itched with the discussion of body lice treatment challenges. She admired Stefan's ability to stay in clinical mode. Perhaps he was used to horrible immigration stories.

"No evidence of the JHR reaction," he continued. "Bashir, let's see how your rash is doing."

The young man lifted his shirt to expose purplish scrawls

covering his back, chest, and arms, like tattoos from an artist in a psychedelic dream.

"Erythema multiforme," Stefan said. "See those dark spots on his lips? No specific treatment for this type of rash, and it may reoccur during recovery."

Bashir's fingertips reached to his mouth. "It burns—hard to eat." He picked up the sketchpad again. "Keep me busy."

Maya had clarified with Stefan that she would take the lead on epi questions. "Bashir, when were you in Libya?"

"For a month, camp terrible. Hundreds share mattresses in dirt. Nothing separates us from sky. We escape to sleep under highway in city. Then small raft to Italy, and we fly here."

"When did the rash on your skin start?"

"Itch on plane. We are here now two weeks."

She turned to Stefan. "The average incubation period is a week, so it sounds like the exposure was Libya, not here or Somalia."

He nodded. "Bashir, thank you for your time. Keep in touch with the clinic if your symptoms worsen. There are other medications to reduce the irritation."

After exiting the ground floor residence, Stefan showed her his screen. "His was one of the milder *Borrelia* cases—he was lucky."

Unsure how fortunate he was with the extensive rash and traumatic memories, she hugged her body to counteract shivers. The images of his skin were burned on her brain. "Who's next?"

Curtains were drawn in the second floor room as the door was opened by a middle-aged man wearing a broad white cloth wrapped around his waist and tied over his shoulder. His dark hair draped his forehead and ears in tight ringlets.

"Hallo Mr. Kadafo, may we come in?" Stefan asked. "I understand you've had a Health Assessment. Dr. Maguire and I are following up on LBRF, the louse-borne relapsing fever."

The resident turned on a small light in the corner before sitting at the opposite end of the room. Maya hoped that Stefan could summarize the interview on his laptop because it was too dark for her notebook.

"I apologize," Mr. Kadafo said. "My eye pain is extreme. May I offer you a glass of milk? It is the traditional drink for guests in my country of Eritrea."

Maya usually only had milk with cereal, but thought it would be kind to accept his offer. "Thank you, would you like me to get it?"

He gestured to a small refrigerator. After pouring three glasses, she perched on one of the aluminum kitchen chairs. "When did you come to Norway?"

"I arrived from Libya last week. My illness start day after."

"Do you have a rash?" Stefan continued.

Mr. Kadafo pointed under his arms and at his groin.

Maya sipped the milk. "How long were you in Libya, Mr. Kadafo?"

"Two months. I was journalist, but dictator in Eritrea does not permit free press. My people, the Afar, herd livestock, but many of us mine salt in the Danakil Desert. We are fearless, but perhaps I was reckless. I moved to Asmara, our capital city, where I met my wife. There I investigated government corruption and a friend warned me of arrest warrant. We fled through Khartoum to southern Libya."

"Those marks on your arms," Stefan said, "did they develop with your rash?"

Mr. Kadafo shook his head. "Libya militia demanded five thousand dinars. We gave them what we had, but it was not enough. These are from tool for cattle—branding iron."

Maya reminded herself not to flinch with the repeated dramatic stories. "And your wife, did she also become ill after arrival here?"

His face scrunched and he turned away, words barely audible. "With no ransom, they raped and murdered her. Warning to others."

Maya sank against the hard metal back of the chair. Hearing his story but not knowing him, with only imagination to paint the picture, should have provided sufficient psychic distance. But it didn't. If only she'd seen the deceased wife in the medical record.

"Fra asken til ilden," Stefan said, "like your American expression 'out of the frying pan into the fire.' These immigrants have been through so much. Mr. Kadafo, you had an impossible journey, but you are safe now."

Maya punted. "Stefan, your turn for JHR."

Her colleague's voice was consoling. "Mr. Kadafo, I hope we offered you good care in the hospital."

The man held up his fingers. "Two days, severe pain in head and muscles, very hot. Heart beats very fast. But I am better, except for red skin and eyes."

Stefan closed his laptop and stood. "That sounds like a mild case of the reaction I'm studying. But we will let you rest and I will verify your antibiotic dosages."

Once outside the door, Maya leaned against the building wall. "How about a break? I need to come down after that one. I feel awful for asking about his wife."

"Don't beat yourself up. There's nothing in the records."

"I used to be more hesitant before speaking." Not for the first time, she wondered if Klonopin, or months of overwhelming stress from an incapacitated lover, led to loose lips. "With each accomplishment, did you become more inclined to plunge ahead?"

His laugh was throaty and comforting. "Kondrat says I never lack confidence. We've had a busy morning."

She thought back to the stop at the hospital, a few wrong turns where they couldn't locate *Borrelia* cases, and the two memorable interviews. She knew they should keep working, but badly needed a break. "Could we grab lunch?"

When he nodded, she clarified. "No restaurants. I need to inhale this spectacular Oslo summer day, and get away from imagined lice crawling on my body. Do you know how oppressively hot it would be right now in Atlanta or New York City?"

He shrugged. "Yes, there is some compensation for less than six hours of light in the winter. That's why we put lighted stars in all the windows."

"Enough with the Norwegian traditions, I'm famished. I want sandwiches in a park."

Her impertinent tone clearly amused him. "Let's go to

Slottsparken, grounds of the Royal Palace. From there, I will make some calls. We'll need translators for our next interviews."

. . .

"Oslo must love statues," Maya said as they strolled a narrow shaded path around the multicolored columned palace.

"Only a few here, nothing like the hundreds in Vigelandsparken where we talked on the phone and I invited you to Oslo."

"This is my favorite—so different from a hero on horseback." She gestured toward the bronze woman curled on a white stone with a bronze backpack at her side.

"Dronningdammen, our Queen Sonja. It was installed only two years ago in honor of her eightieth birthday. She's impressive as an artist and a hiker."

They settled on one of the benches near a small pond behind the castle.

"Everywhere I look, there's greenspace." She took a deep breath of the clear cool breeze.

"Oslo is working hard on being a sustainable city, aiming for an emission reduction of ninety-five percent by 2030. Friluftsliv is the Norwegian addiction to open air. Kondrat is fascinated by nature, although not our gross diseases. He's doing a master's degree in biodiversity at the University of Oslo. Not only is it tuition-free, but the class schedule is more sane than American universities."

"I'm surprised he didn't mention it."

"No classes this summer, and our family is his top priority. He fits schoolwork around Paula's timetable, often not possible for me."

Maya paused before plunging ahead. "Would it be rude if I asked you about marriage?"

Stefan chortled. "You're like my mother—she wants us to be husbands."

"I can't figure out the end goal for my relationship. When Manolo was near death last winter, his sister said he wanted to marry me. Now he can't talk as much, and I'm torn up about it."

"We considered marriage." He took a bite of his smørrebrød and recovered a shrimp that fell from its open face to his napkin. "Norway is supportive—the first Scandinavian country to legalize it in 2009. But with a strong support system by the government, younger people have no need of a spouse."

"I was raised Catholic, not allowed to live in sin." She crouched to look for fish in the pond, then turned back with a wink. "Plus, I like the romance of a honeymoon."

On his cell phone, Stefan pulled up photos of sheer snow-draped cliffs falling sharply into the ocean. "Senja Island above the Arctic Circle—an incredible place for the Northern Lights before winter cold sets in. I booked us for October, 2020, when Kondrat is done with his degree. A surprise graduation present and unofficial honeymoon."

"You chose well, it looks spectacular. I appreciate your sharing friluftsliv for lunch." She fingered her final bite of the dense rye bread. "What's this called?"

"Rugbrød."

After swallowing, she stood and reached a hand to help him up, realizing she could postpone the harrowing stories for only so long. "I'm glad Norway has programs to assist the immigrants. We should get back to work, if you don't want to upset Kondrat by getting home late to dinner."

· · ·

Moments snatched in the sunlight for midday replenishment and decompression at night with the bubbly laughter of a child tided them through two full days of interviews, including three patients in the hospital.

As they left the apartment of the final patient on their list, a Somali refugee with only a minor rash, Stefan showed Maya the records on two patients who died from JHR soon after arriving in Oslo.

"I sometimes wonder if medicine does more harm than good," he said. "I need to look at their autopsies for underlying conditions.

I don't know if it was our antibiotics that killed them or treatment somewhere else. All I know is that they died here."

The setting sun peeked through the trees as they headed for the ferry dock. Stefan took a left turn and led Maya up to benches along the edge of a castle, mortared walls built above the shoreline cliff.

"Thank God I'm just an epidemiologist and don't have patient care responsibilities," Maya said. "I couldn't handle the worry over doing something wrong."

"I'm rarely responsible for clinical decision-making, but if I can't figure out the risk factors for JHR, I'm of no help in solving it. Some patients are so sick, they need antibiotics—what's a clinician to do?"

Remembering Manolo's emailed request for historical nuggets, she took a phone photo and asked, "Can you tell me about this fortress?"

He nodded. "This is Akershus Festning, a royal residence for almost a thousand years. Then Nazi occupiers executed members of a resistance group and threw their bodies here in the fjord. After the war, tables were turned. Nazi collaborators were executed here—you've heard of the word quisling that refers to a traitor? Vidkun Quisling—he was one of them."

Maya shuddered at the brutal events near the tranquil harbor. "Norway is held up as a society with everything figured out—we forget how recently it was under threat from a maniac like Hitler."

"What's that phrase in English?" he asked. "One step forward, two steps back. Maybe in Europe, we are complacent. Places like this remind us of a depressing history of invasion."

He tapped the bench and she joined him. "Norway seems to have figured it out. With that cruise ship over there, Oslo's a great melding of old and new. In Santa Fe, we also preserve our history. The buildings are kept humble, particularly on the outside. 'La invidia' means that people shouldn't show off, make themselves grander."

"How ironic, we have the same. Janteloven, being part of the group, not better than others. We are not boastful."

"You could be. I think you know more about JHR than anyone, at this point."

"An unfortunate consequence of our outbreak. If immigrants continue to arrive with *Borrelia recurrentis* infections, we are considering an anti-cytokine drug, but one study found it ineffective. We tried steroids to reduce inflammation."

"Any autopsy results on the pregnant woman from Tanzania who died on the plane?"

He pulled out his phone. "I got a text from the pathologist. The organism is different, *Borrelia duttonii*. That's the one with high mortality during pregnancy."

"Also louse-borne?"

He nodded.

She suddenly recalled that he gave no interviews while they were together. "Is someone else handling press inquiries?"

"The press has modulated news reflecting negatively on our immigrants. Islamophobia is on the increase. You remember Anders Behring Breivik? Hoping to begin a crusade against Islam, he slaughtered more than eighty children at a summer camp eight years ago."

His arm extended in the direction of the docks below. "That building was damaged by Breivik's bomb. Unless relocated, Picasso murals will be destroyed when they tear it down. Some think the building should remain as a reminder that Norwegians also have a capacity for evil."

She'd had more of a close encounter with terrorism than most. "I heard Breivik was in touch with the white supremacist who killed fifty people at New Zealand mosques. This hatred of others is like a contagious disease."

"Stop Islamization of Norway believes multiculturalism is a failure. We are such a privileged society, one of the most stable and happiest in the world. But infected with intolerance, like everyone else."

Maya shivered. There was no completely safe place from those prone to attack anyone different. "I wonder what that group would think of the two of us. Do you think we're acceptable human beings in their value system?"

"I don't care. Living in love and justice is our best defense." Stefan rose to his feet, pulling Maya with him. "Let's go home to my family. It's tacofredag, or taco Friday to you, a recent tradition in Oslo. Kondrat makes ours with fish."

TWENTY-TWO

After a few days in Norway, Maya was fully adapted to the new time zone and woke up energized. Probably the Klonopin helped. Her older parents complained the toughest part of their two trips to China was adjustment of their body clocks.

Someone stirred in the kitchen but she needed to catch up on emails. In a PowerPoint attachment, Enzo provided the final slides for the association of *Salmonella* with dog pig ear treats. He cc'd Keegan and credited his partner's contribution—he was finally learning team skills.

The presentation was an exemplary combination of Keegan's careful statistical analysis and Enzo's flash and polish. Their study reinforced the message that *Salmonella* infections could result from handling contaminated dog treats in addition to more recognized risks like reptiles, poultry, and eggs.

After sending her compliments on the presentation and Lila's good mentoring, she dropped a quick note to Nancy. **I'm learning a lot about louse-borne *Borrelia*. Just reviewed Enzo's *Salmonella* draft—he conveys results with concise but interesting slides. Sorry I missed some time for the oversight I promised, but I'm keeping up with him at a distance.**

"Hei, min venn." Stefan's voice followed his knock, and she swung open the door.

"God dag, Stefan. I'm raring to go for whatever's next on your agenda."

He smoothed the tailored jacket. "I've been asked to help next with a borreliosis investigation in the field and you have more experience than me."

She followed him to the back deck where Paula took the first bite of a heart-shaped waffle smothered in cloudberries.

"God morgen, Maya." Kondrat offered a piece of brown cheese. "Would you like brunost?"

Maya picked up an empty plate and aimed her fork toward Paula. "Can I steal your waffle?"

Paula covered her food as Maya accepted the cheese from Kondrat. "Stefan, you mentioned *Borrelia* fieldwork. What does that mean?"

With a dramatic flourish, Kondrat threw his hands over his ears and Paula copied him.

Laughing, Stefan put his brunost slices on crackers. "I will keep it at the level of polite conversation. Tick-borne *Borrelia hispanica* from Spain and Portugal. Cases are also linked to northern Morocco."

"Oh, kochanie, it sounds exotic." Kondrat flirted. "Can I join you?"

"This new outbreak is associated with pigpens south of Lisbon. Still tempting?"

Kondrat grimaced, but then his face lit up again. "Paula and I can play tourist while you work."

Stefan leaned forward and rested his elbows on his knees. "How about you, Maya, want to join us?"

Her curiosity was piqued but there was much to consider. CDC might support a short stopover to compare approaches with those she used in the Southwest. Hopefully the added days wouldn't eliminate an overnight in NYC on the trip back. Her skin warmed as she recalled the quickie with Manolo in the airport. His typing skills had improved in the emailed descriptions of what they'd do when back in his bed. Soon they'd both be home so she could spend every weekend in Phoenix.

"Let me check with headquarters. If I'm back in Atlanta for the end of the conference and officer presentations, it might be okay."

Kondrat hugged Stefan's neck and cradled Paula's hand. "We are going on vacation—let's pack." His enthusiasm was infectious—she'd try hard to persuade CDC.

. . .

"Stefan, your agency did an amazing job in making these arrangements." Maya unpacked her suitcase in a bedroom of the bright yellow rental apartment with mosaic tile inner walls. Then the four travelers strolled down the lane past Lisbon's massive ornate Mosteiro dos Jerónimos.

"Are you two stopping here?" Maya asked.

"Of course we are," Kondrat answered. "Paula needs to see the burial place of the explorer Vasco da Gama. But not until later. On this gorgeous afternoon, we'll accompany you to the riverside."

The bright red, pink, and purple bougainvilleas overspilled the walls and Maya inhaled the drifting aroma from someone's lunch of grilled sardines.

Kondrat held Paula and Stefan's hands as they ambled down the cobblestones, and leaned his head on Stefan's shoulder. "This is so beautiful, kjæreste. I read about Lisbon on the plane. Next time we should come a month or two earlier for jacarandas blooming."

Stefan sighed. "Meanwhile, Maya and I studied soft leathery ticks that can live seven years without blood meals, just waiting for our sleeping bodies."

Kondrat dropped Stefan's hand and twisted Paula in a pirouette. "We'll cheer you up tonight with our city photos."

At the ancient tower memorial to Portuguese seafarers, Maya and Stefan waved goodbye and hopped the bus.

"Somehow you resolved the crazy unpredictability of a public health career and family life," she observed as the bus headed to the hospital in the city center.

"Kondrat is flexible and enjoys being the linchpin to support my profession."

"Yeah, my USDA friend has two daughters close to Paula's age, and a wife who goes with the flow."

She trailed her fingers through her hair. "My CDC boss in

Atlanta is married to a university professor, and they never had children. It's hard to find role models where both partners have demanding careers and kids."

"You'll figure it out. In Europe, government is more supportive of families. Anybody in mind for this plan, like your physician friend Dr. Miranda?"

"I don't know where we'd be if anthrax hadn't taken him out. I need patience, which is not my strong suit."

The bus slowed as protesters pounded their fists on the windows while holding cardboard signs saying **FASCISTAS IDE-VOS FODER** and **Nazi não te queremil aqui**.

"I can guess some of the words, but can you translate?"

"Fascists fuck you. The other one says Nazi we don't want you here."

A huge black flag with an X'd out swastika blocked her view. "I wonder if this march is a special occasion."

"There's a far-right conference coming up. Earlier this year, cars were torched after a protest against police violence."

"So the U.S. isn't the only place on edge. We're so insular in America that we don't pay attention to other places."

"I like being a citizen of the world." Stefan's tone was proud. "I might jump to WHO at some point to broaden my reach."

Maya spread her fingers on the bus window as if to absorb the energy of the streets. "If all this turmoil gets too much, I escape on a hike."

He nodded. "Us, too. Norway is an amazing place for outdoor activities."

"Once when scrambling hand-over-hand on a Colorado peak, the stones buzzed with electricity—that means lightning's about to strike. The world feels electrified, ready to explode."

"Do you mean politics or our unstable weather?"

"Both. I wonder how cities like Lisbon, Oslo, or New York will cope with rising sea levels."

He led the way off the bus at the next stop.

"I'm an optimist. In five months, a new decade will begin.

Perhaps things will change with your election. Few Europeans like your current President."

Maya let her thoughts drift to the chaos of a demanding job and a new love challenged to the max by both of their disabilities. Often she was unsure of her capacity to cope, especially with the death of Mr. Otole on the New Mexico highway.

But for the few days of the European trip, only focused on work and a new culture, everything had gone fine. What if she retreated permanently to another part of the world, leaving all her troubles behind? But no place avoided threats like *Borrelia* infections in refugees after unimaginable horrors and terrorists using immigrants as an excuse to massacre children.

. . .

The geriatric couple stretched their arms between beds to hold hands in the quiet room at the end of the hospital corridor. They were the only *Borrelia* patients still in hospital, five others having been released and returned home. Maya fantasized about a life-long commitment with Manolo.

Stefan checked medical records. "Typical symptoms of fever, rash, muscle and joint pain, plus severe abdominal distress. Fortunately, no adverse medication reactions."

He gave the records back to the nurse, then turned to the patients. "Olá, I'm Dr. Duda and this is Dr. Maguire."

Maya wasn't sure how many languages Stefan knew, but when there was any doubt, English was the fallback which she appreciated as a language-challenged American.

The woman patted her husband's arm and spoke in slow syllables with a thin, high voice. "Obrigado, doutores, can we help you?"

Stefan turned his hand palm up, tossing the ball to Maya. She gulped and stepped closer.

"Portugal's relapsing fever is associated with pig herds. Do you have pigs?"

The woman nodded. "Sim temos porcos."

The Portuguese words were similar enough to Maya's high

school Spanish that she guessed the answer. "And where do you keep them?"

"Amigos gave us old stone buildings for los porcos in Alentejo."

"That's south of here," Stefan said. "Who cares for them?"

"Minha filha."

Stefan handed the woman his notebook with a pen. "Please write down your daughter's name and how we can reach her."

The woman's eyes darted to her husband. "In Lisboa long time but too much money, need to go home."

Stefan turned to Maya. "Lisbon's been affordable but property investors and speculators take advantage. With increasing rents, thousands live in expensive but squalid apartments, and homelessness explodes."

The old man spit on the tile floor. "Sell parks."

"He's referring to a proposal for selling a popular park to a developer. People protested about losing affordable housing, cafes, and cultural events."

"Malditos imigrantes turistas e estrangieros," the old man yelled, then looked sheepish.

Maya whispered, "I think he said bad foreigners and strange ones. Does that apply to us?"

Stefan took hold of her elbow. "We overstayed our welcome." In a louder voice, he added, "We will visit your daughter. I hope you feel better soon—estar de volta a boa saúde."

At the hospital entrance doors, he pulled out his phone. "Ourique is two hours south on a good highway. Tomorrow, we'll rent a car. For tonight, let's find minha família and enjoy ourselves as malditos turistas."

At the restaurant, Kondrat and Paula shared tales of the Mosteiro dos Jerónimos while they splurged on caracóis, snails in butter-garlic broth.

When Stefan scooped one of the rubbery bodies, Paula covered her eyes and squealed in horror. "Pappa took me to the coffin with a dead person on top."

Kondrat waggled his finger at Paula when Stefan's eyebrows

shot up. "Just a stone statue of the famous explorer, liten jente. I loved the ornate carved arches." He pulled out his phone and shared photos.

They all ordered local specialties. Maya was attracted by the colorful Bacalhau à Brás, with codfish, scrambled eggs, and fried potato dotted with black olives and parsley. Kondrat ordered for Paula a simple, nutritious Cozido, a stew with vegetables. Stefan joked that since they were headed to the Alentejana region for their investigation, he would try the Carne de Porco Alentejana, pork and clams sauteed in white wine.

Maya teased him. "Given the association of pigs with our outbreak, are you sure you want that?"

Kondrat chose Polvo à Lagareiro, grilled octopus with garlic, potatoes, and olive oil. Paula made Stefan change seats so she could sit next to Maya, as far away from the suckers as possible. Then after stuffing themselves with the main courses, they topped it all off with Pastéis de Nata, individual custard tarts inspired by the nuns based in the Mosteiro.

At her first restaurant meal in Europe, Maya was torn between the comfort of her trip with good companions and the hardships of their Oslo and Lisbon patients. Was it possible to enjoy the moment when others were suffering? Manolo's limited conversation before she left and recent emails didn't convey what must be desperation over his lost capabilities.

But she had reasonable health, a loving family, and a job making the world a better place. It was more than a person had a right to expect. Compared with *Borrelia*-infected immigrants, her life was a bed of roses. She took Paula and Kondrat's hands, and smiled at Stefan across the table. "Best meal in my life."

Before turning in for sleep at their rental, Maya emailed Manolo. **I'm counting on everything you promised for a NYC overnight. My colleague's daughter reminds me of Johnny—I miss you all. Give my love to the Mirandas and Abdi. A Miranda by any other name is still as sweet.**

Someday, she might be a Miranda. Before closing the laptop, she spotted a terse email from Enzo complaining that Keegan didn't like his presentation style. He wanted to practice on FaceTime when her iPhone worked again.

Pre-Klonopin, she would have been up all night worrying about the team's disagreement. Maybe Dr. Kim was right and her body was wired to need stress medication permanently.

TWENTY-THREE

After they crossed the Tagus River to drop Kondrat and Paula at the Costa de Caparica for a beach day, the divided highway continued south between low, treed hills. The day was beautiful and already warm, with a few white fluffy clouds spotting the sky.

The landscape reminded Maya of eastern New Mexico, covered with green trees too short to interrupt the brilliant horizon and fields turned golden by the heat. But the town of Ourique was like none she'd ever seen. Most buildings were sparkling white against the blue sky, with red clay tile roofs. A few were splashed on the edges with bright swatches of blue or yellow paint, and others had shutters, a vivid green like the metal balconies. The streets were so narrow, some were one-way.

Stefan pulled over to a petrol stop, then parked next to a café. "Let's grab a snack."

They found a sidewalk table and ordered samosas and rice balls. With the warming temperature, Maya gulped a cold bottle of water while Stefan pulled out his phone.

"I'm calling my contact at the Ricardo Jorge Institute, their equivalent of the CDC. She will bring equipment."

As they finished their meal, sharing stories of classmates and professors at Columbia, a wiry older woman with short gray hair joined them.

"Dr. Barboza." Stefan stood to shake her hand. "This is Dr. Maya Maguire from the CDC."

"Call me Beatriz. Stefan and I met at a meeting in the winter."

She joined them at the table. "I came down last night to locate the pigpens. The acorns from our cork oak forests are their favorite food. Until these cases, we had no relapsing fever since the sixties."

Stefan's lips twisted in a wry smile. "You are very experienced, but I don't think you were working back then."

"Não, still a child, but I dissected insects in my garden." She leaned back, crossing her legs. "We like our independence but everyone is worried. That is the only reason you can work with us."

Stefan nodded. "We will stay one day to learn from your procedures and prepare for this in other areas."

"Norway's relapsing fever is from lice?" Beatriz asked. "Here we have ticks, and a few cases with people exploring caves."

Maya jumped in. "I investigated two infections related to a mine shaft in an area rich with caves."

"We think our *Borrelia* came from Spain," Beatriz explained with a tone of disgust.

"Who are the new cases?" Maya asked.

"The daughter and son-in-law for the hospitalized couple. They helped with the pigs."

Stefan paid the check. "What's the plan?"

"Collect specimens on the family's property, then expand surveillance to other areas in this region tomorrow."

Maya nodded, eager to compare the techniques with her own. "I also had a family infected from ticks in a stone cabin in my state, New Mexico."

"Mexico?" Beatriz asked. "I thought you were American CDC."

Maya chuckled. "One of our fifty is missing—that's our joke. People from farther away don't realize there's a state named New Mexico. Sometimes our mail isn't delivered because it doesn't have international postage."

With thinned lips, Beatriz huffed. "I think we know more about you than vice versa."

After catching Stefan's frown, Maya tried to be self-effacing. "Europeans are so much better at languages. I only speak a few words of Spanish and Mandarin from school classes."

"Southeast Asians pick berries in the greenhouses near the coast," Beatriz said. "Their children learn Portuguese in the schools."

Remembering the Norwegian immigrants, Maya asked, "Do your guest workers get relapsing fever from lice and sanitation problems?"

Beatriz leapt to her feet, grabbing her coffee cup. "You think we are a third world country."

"Dr. Barboza, please forgive me." Maya was more assertive on the Klonopin—was that bad or good?

"The cases from lice in the Norwegian immigrants were so heartbreaking—they're still fresh in my mind. But we're here to be educated on your tick infections."

Stefan guided Maya to their vehicle. "Let's get going. We'll follow you, Beatriz."

As they wound their way out of the town along lanes lined with olive groves, Maya studied Stefan. "Beatriz mentioned children coming to Portugal from Southeast Asia. Can I ask about Paula? Is she your biological daughter or adopted like me?"

"Just before grad school, we adopted her from a Moldovan institution for kids with learning disabilities. Perhaps her family could not care for her."

"Where's Moldova? I guess that's what Beatriz implied about American ignorance."

"Between Ukraine and Romania, independent from the Soviet Union less than thirty years."

"Is she curious about her home country? Whenever I got mad at Mom and Dad, I threatened to run back to mine."

"Not yet." He had a slight smile of satisfaction. "All our adventures in Poland, Norway, and the U.S. keep her entertained."

"My conflicts were mostly with my mother, who wanted me to study harder. I just wanted to play piano."

"I'm the strict parent, like your mother," Stefan smirked. "Kondrat is the nice one, perhaps because he spends more time with her, and that's his nature."

"If she gets curious, you could visit Moldova. But on my trip to China at age twelve, my American privilege glowed like a neon sign."

. . .

When the brake lights turned red on the truck ahead, Stefan slammed on his own. Maya's hand went to the dash and her right foot automatically pressed to the floorboard—responses ingrained from the car accident. He turned off the dirt road to an area with crumbling mud-washed stone buildings and tile roofs dulled to brown. At midday, the heat hit them like a wave when they stepped out of the car to meet their host.

Wind blew dust from the fields in their eyes and Maya instinctively covered her face with a hand. Her home state of Arizona was the epicenter for Valley Fever lung infections from *Coccidioides* fungal spores borne on the wind. But she was in Portugal and needed to focus on *Borrelia*.

"That smoke is a wildfire," Beatriz said. "The largest is northeast of Lisbon, with injuries and homes burned. I'll monitor the news to make sure nothing gets closer. Very bad summer—climate change."

As they reluctantly pulled on coveralls that heated their bodies even more, Maya adjusted her Yankees cap and waved toward the hundreds of dark pigs roaming the hillside. "Free range?"

"Like in your cowboy west, we fence huge areas for our ranches. The pigs spend the day eating cork nuts and resting under shade trees. Their meat is world-renowned for its nutty flavor. At night, they sleep in here."

She gestured to one of the dilapidated buildings. "Most upgraded to better housing for the pigs but those who are poor use these old huts. We set up for tick collection first. Grab those ice chests."

Maya noticed holes drilled in the sides near the bottom. "We didn't use these when I was looking for ticks."

Beatriz nodded. "The chests are set on these metal trays covered with tape, sticky side up. Dry ice in each one releases carbon dioxide, like when we breathe. Ticks are attracted and caught in the tape. Similar idea as a mosquito trap."

"Because ticks feed more at night, do you leave these out until then?" Maya asked.

"Perhaps not. After spreading these through the buildings, we'll set the rodent traps, then come back and check for the ticks."

Maya began pulling the collapsed metal cages out of Beatriz's vehicle. "These are the same kind we use, Waylon and Tomahawk traps. We release the bigger rodents after blood draws—is that your plan?"

Beatriz shook her head. "We bring rodents back to our laboratory for whole blood and organ tissues. Those are inoculated into culture media and examined weekly for spirochetes. In three months, the cultures have DNA extraction for polymerase chain reaction."

After placing traps within the old buildings and surrounding grounds, they checked the metal trays around the coolers. A few ticks gathered, including some swollen with blood.

Stefan was squeamish. "Not something I've done before. This is more appropriate for a veterinarian than a physician. I'll return phone calls in the car."

Maya grabbed his arm and pulled him back in. "No getting off the hook, doctor. If I can talk to human patients, you can handle this."

Beatriz provided them forceps and glass vials for collecting the ticks. "The family slept on cots to monitor for piglet losses. But with no one here now, these engorged ones likely fed on an animal."

They put the samples and coolers back in Beatriz's truck. Stefan fingered the keys for his rental. "Are we done with this location?"

"The daughter and son-in-law will meet us here to collect blood samples from the pigs as they bring them in for the night. Maya can help."

"I don't claim to be an expert but of course I know how. Stefan, now might be a good time for your phone calls. A screaming pig is one of the most horrifying sounds you'll ever hear."

Beatriz chuckled. "You think we are torturing them—just being held is enough to set them off." She handed Maya ear plugs.

As the middle-aged couple pulled up, Stefan verified they were recovered enough from their own *Borrelia* infections to assist in the blood draws. Then he followed Maya's advice and settled into the front seat of his car. "I'll tell Kondrat and Paula to meet us at the apartment."

After driving pigs into smaller pens with sticks, shouts, and the lure of additional food, Maya and Beatriz teamed up with the owners who used a nose snare on each pig as their bodies pinned the animals to a wall.

"Jugular?" Maya asked. Beatriz nodded, then Maya thrust a needle upward beneath the skin of the first pig's neck. She recalled failure to draw blood from a dead sheep. That was her first time feeling inadequate in public health fieldwork. This time, she had more luck, despite the ear-piercing porcine screaming.

A half hour of specimen collection later, Maya found herself flat in the dirt, slammed to the ground by a sow more than three times her weight. Her pieced-together pelvis and fractured thigh throbbed, and she struggled to catch her breath.

"Desculpe." The husband attempted to capture the animal's battering ram head with the nose snare. "My strength is not the same after illness."

Beatriz craned her neck toward Maya on the ground. "Bebê, go back to work. You are veterinarian, não?"

Maya chose public health, not clinical practice. Massaging data on a computer looked appealing on the scorching afternoon far from home. She rotated to her hands and knees, then reached for a clean syringe and needle as the farmer resnared the squealing hog.

After she and Beatriz collected two dozen specimens, Maya peeled off the smelly coveralls. Her back ached from close to two hours of kneeling on the ground and bending under each pig's neck to draw blood as the animal tried to wriggle away. But she wouldn't complain out loud—Dr. Barboza was more than twice her age and still looked spry.

"Beatriz, obrigado. The techniques for tick and pig sampling— these will help in our own investigations. On behalf of CDC, we appreciate the collaboration."

They shook hands after washing them, and Maya thought the woman's shaded brown eyes reflected a more respectful attitude.

"De nada, Maya. Safe travels."

Maya opened the door to Stefan's rental and dropped into the passenger seat. "I'm finally done. Did you have successful calls?"

"I'm happy to report that Portugal, unlike Norway, has no adverse reactions to the antibiotics in its *Borrelia* cases. I need more follow-up on the patients and medical practices to account for the difference." He wrinkled his nose. "You smell a little piggy."

"Sorry about that. Beatriz will contact you with results of today's sampling."

The engine roared to life. "Let's get you back to Lisbon and I will gladly give you first chance at the bath."

TWENTY-FOUR

During a rough night in the Lisbon apartment, Maya failed to find a comfortable position for her pig-battered legs and hips. When joining Stefan for morning tea, she fingered a spot at the base of her scalp.

"Bump on your head from your tumble?"

"I'd appreciate your looking at it." She dropped to a chair and lifted her heavy hair.

"Bad news, you've got a hard tick, not the soft ones we're investigating. And pretty engorged—you didn't feel it when you washed your hair last night?"

Maya's empty stomach dropped. Just a tiny tick—nothing to be afraid of, except for all the diseases it could spread.

On her pre-trip research, she'd focused on relapsing fever from lice, and then the soft ticks during their time in Portugal. What did hard ticks transmit in this part of the world? Too many diseases to count if back in the U.S.—bacterial infections like Lyme disease, anaplasmosis, and ehrlichiosis, viruses like Powassan, Rocky Mountain spotted fever, and Colorado tick fever, and parasites like *Babesia*. The names commingled in her head.

With all her Southwest fieldwork, why did this happen in a country where her resources for follow-up were more limited? Too soon for her morning Klonopin to reduce automatic panic.

"Stefan, just get it the hell off me. Every second it sits there, I imagine pathogens pumping into my bloodstream."

As he murmured about tweezers in the bathroom, she felt its

hard surface again. Why hadn't she detected it in the shower? She'd been exhausted and sleepy—probably picked it up during the hog wrestling.

After he returned and gently pulled out its body and mouth parts embedded in her skin, he dropped it into a glass cup.

"I'll contact Beatriz for tick identification and testing. She got a bit crotchety over our discussion of hygiene and immigrants but I'm sure she doesn't want her guest American epidemiologist dying from some horrible tick-borne disease."

"Stefan, you have a wonderful bedside manner." Maya picked up the jar and studied the tick's swollen brown body.

He spread out Bola de Berlim purchased at a local pastry shop and Maya took a bite. A full stomach offered a natural valium high, as many emotional eaters could confirm. "A doughnut with custard cream and sugar—that should counteract my tick terror. Where are Kondrat and Paula?"

"Sleeping late—they wore themselves out swimming." He placed a hand on Maya's forehead. "Likely too soon for a fever."

"Nothing other than paranoia and aching muscles."

"Our trip has a wrinkle—my office asked us to swing by Morocco for a couple days to consult on a tick study. They're down in resources, and it's the same soft tick and *Borrelia* strain as here in Portugal."

Her throat constricted and the question came out in a higher tone. "Wouldn't they want Beatriz with her decades of experience?" Another country, new relationships to navigate, and more demands to represent CDC.

"She's got her own investigation and doesn't work for the European CDC like me."

Despite a new challenge, an extended work vacation was appealing, escaping all the problems back home. "I promised to bring back as much knowledge as possible." She checked the phone clock. "Four-thirty Atlanta time. Dr. Jaworski's an early bird—she'll see a note within a couple hours."

"That will give me time to make arrangements with Morocco.

Because of recent case increases, they plan to review hospital databases for fever of unknown origin."

"For the FUO cases, have they ruled out other diseases like malaria?"

"That's what I need to verify."

Ideas flitting through her mind like dragonflies, Maya jotted them on her notepad to pin them down. "We can set up tick collection at each FUO residence. If we do that before any further *Borrelia* lab testing on the patients, we'll have a blinded study to avoid biasing the results."

Stefan reached over to shake her hand. "Great suggestions, Dr. Maguire. CDC promised you to me for a week. This might only stretch your assignment a couple of days."

"I just need to be in Atlanta Monday for the end of EIS officer training. Before heading to Morocco, should I start prophylactic antibiotics?"

"Our JHR deaths have been a reminder of the side effects, so I'd hold off until confirmation. Let's check details on our ends, then finalize decisions before noon."

. . .

Except for a few hiccups with Beatriz and the tiny tick from the backbreaking pig work, Maya was satisfied with her overseas fieldwork. Her expertise with *Borrelia* was expanded. She investigated pigs as an intermediate host for infected ticks and learned a new investigative technique using dry ice as a tick attractant. No one else from CDC had a similar opportunity.

Dr. Jaworski replied to her latest email. **Great job, and wonderful reminder of the unique advantages of veterinary epidemiologists. Understanding the relapsing fever life cycle will help with climate change preparedness.**

Adjusting to rapid work changes, using her intellect to mitigate zoonotic risks, and getting affirmation from her bosses—all points of personal pride. She'd been self-assured and calm during her first *Borrelia* field investigation near Dulce. Then the dead Jicarilla elder's face flashed, with her fingers trying over and over to will a pulse.

Maybe she'd been too relaxed and confident. Being hyperalert from anxiety might have given her eyes extra acuity to avoid hitting him. What if he'd still been alive before the blow of her car?

She typed her attorney a note. **Mr. Zielinski, I'm investigating** *Borrelia* **for CDC in Portugal, but anticipate getting home within a week. When can we mail my letter of apology to the Otole family?**

Next, she opened an email from her parents. **Your work sounds exciting. We're relieved you're not on your own. We couldn't afford overseas trips besides China, but happy you can do that now. Travel expands the mind—keeps us from being parochial. Call when you're home.**

Welcome words of support. During the last visit, her mom mentioned that at twenty-six, Maya was at the age when the human brain matured. "Not true," Maya snapped. "Latest studies say the brain doesn't stop developing until thirties or forties." Why were they frequently short with each other? But the data provided a justification for continued insecurities.

With his sense of humor, her dad likely wrote 'parochial.' They never had enough money to travel much, but valued living in multicultural states like Arizona and Colorado. Parochial also referred to Catholic schools, which her mother attended through high school. Was that term still used, given its somewhat negative connotation of being narrow-minded?

Her final email was decidedly not parochial. **Mano, my work here is ending with a few days in Morocco—a final** *Borrelia* **outbreak that Stefan wants my input on. And I'm hoping to contribute a more complex statistical design. Kind of the cherry on top of my overseas accomplishments. Speaking of cherries, I've been passionate for your touch ever since you took mine.**

She felt the heat on her face, embarrassed and inexperienced in writing love letters. Would he be shocked or repelled? She touched herself while clicking back through his provocative emails to her. No, he wouldn't be upset, as she clicked **Send**.

In the kitchen, Kondrat and Paula wolfed down the remaining pastries.

"Tell me about your beach day." Maya eyed the glass with the tiny tick placed high on an open shelf, undetectable from the child's angle.

"It was h-u-g-e." Paula stretched her arms to maximum width. "And soft sand."

Kondrat angled his phone to Maya as she sat between them. "I took this where you dropped us off. The colorful fisherman's huts—aren't they beautiful? And the kite surfers were fun to watch."

Stefan strolled in. "Maya played with the pigs, oink, oink."

Paula's bare feet hit the colorful tile floor and sticky fingers reached around Maya's neck in a frenzied hug. "Oh, can I see them, can I see them?"

Remembering the tick, Maya flinched. But she could barely detect a remaining sensation of its feeding.

"Sorry, sweetie, we won't be at the pig farm again. They were brown from rolling in the dirt. At home, our pigs are pink, like you." She tickled Paula who squealed and dropped back into her chair.

"I hate to spring this on everyone," Stefan said, "but Maya and I need to investigate a few more cases in Morocco."

Kondrat stood to stretch an arm around his partner's waist. "Can't wait to see it for the first time."

Following an awkward pause, Stefan squeezed Kondrat's hand. "Given some uncertainties, it's better for you to head home."

With a sudden sharp movement, Kondrat tugged Paula away to their bedroom.

"Go work out the kinks," Maya said, "and let me know if there's anything I can do to help."

Warm sunrays streamed through bright yellow curtains to gently heat Maya's dark hair, in contrast to sharp male voices and Paula's crying filtering the soundscape.

At the airline gate, Kondrat's downturned lips and angry eyes spoke volumes of his unhappiness. He pried Paula's fingers off Stefan's leg as she sobbed, before Stefan hugged both of his family members goodbye. Maya embraced Kondrat, then stooped to wipe tears from Paula's face with a tissue from her purse.

"I'll never forget seeing you with the big tiger in Oslo. Do you know that cats are my favorite animal? Your tata needs to help me with work for a couple of days, then he'll be home. Okay?"

Kondrat patted Maya on the shoulder, then stalked away to the boarding line, arm stiffly guiding his daughter.

After checking the time, Stefan led the way to their gate. "Paula's very emotional with sudden changes."

"Kondrat seemed upset, too." Maya bit her lip, unsure about comments on their relationship.

"They both love to travel, but having kids complicates a relationship. We used to change plans on a whim, but now need to consider her needs."

Maya dropped to a molded fiberglass chair and plugged her phone into a charger. "Guess it's good I'm nowhere near thinking of children."

Stefan pulled a handkerchief from his pocket to wipe his face, heat from the outside penetrating the concourse windows. "So now I'm in the doghouse. Did you piss anyone off with this Moroccan detour?"

"CDC is used to making decisions on the fly. As long as I'm back in Santa Fe by August first, it should be okay. Can Beatriz help with my tick?"

"She's in Alentejo for her investigation, but promised to send someone to pick it up from the apartment manager. Don't worry, you're traveling with a physician—you'll be fine."

. . .

The sharp light of the setting sun blinded them through the solid glass walls of the Rabat airport, filtered by an ornate geometric framework. On the sidewalk, Stefan shaded his eyes with his hand until pointing to a waiting car. The wan, thin driver with a closely shaven beard and mustache stepped forward. "Bienvenue, docteur Duda. Ça va?" He shook Stefan's hand and touched his heart.

"Dr. Soltani, this is my colleague Dr. Maya Maguire from the American CDC. She doesn't speak French. Perhaps we can use English?"

"Bien sûr, mon bon ami. Stefan and I met at a European Health meeting last year. I understand you both worked this week with Dr. Barboza?"

Maya extended her hand. "Yes, with new cases emerging on multiple continents, it's important to get on top of what's going on."

"Merci, Zouhir, for picking us up," Stefan said.

The carved wooden doors of the hotel were held by a red-uniformed doorman the moment Zouhir's car pulled up between the three-story tall palm trees. He pulled the lever to open his trunk for the attendant.

"After you check in, you will be my guests at dinner."

Stefan shook his head. "You are so kind, but I need to see if my family made it home to Oslo. Can we meet in the morning?"

Zouhir fingered his lapels, then nodded. "Tomorrow, I will pick you up for a meeting at Le Ministère de la Santé. Ten o'clock."

From the front desk, they negotiated the tiled courtyards and hallways arched with carved painted wood to check into their adjoining rooms. Within fifteen minutes, Stefan knocked on the connecting door to coordinate dinner plans. Maya closed her laptop on an email from Enzo complaining about Keegan. Erika had also let her know that their front door camera captured a hooded figure placing another small toy in the mailbox.

"How's Kondrat and Paula?"

"Still in Munich, changing planes. Paula's in meltdown. Kondrat may not forgive me."

Maya flipped through the hotel guide. "I'm wiped out, too. I'll grab something light and eat on the rooftop deck—perhaps take a dip in the pool. Want to escape your worries and join me? I'm sure your family will be fine."

"See you there."

A half hour later at the pool, she sliced through the water and burst to the surface with an exuberant breath. "Beat you," she bragged to her associate who grabbed for the poolside. "You're built like a competitive swimmer. Did you let me win?"

"I used to compete in butterfly years ago. But tonight I had this to slow me down." Stefan ruffled his beard. "In the heat, I should trim it shorter—look dapper like Zouhir."

"Better consult Kondrat first. When Dad shaved his mustache without informing Mom, she blew up. She didn't relish sleeping with a stranger."

Discussion of male facial hair brought her back to the last time she took a dip with Manolo, water glistening from his goatee and mustache. In less than a week, maybe she could do that with him again, and revel in his progress.

Stefan kicked his feet in a slow flutter while holding the edge. "My skin will be pale underneath—not very attractive. Maybe I should shave everything off like Vin Diesel."

"Don't make drastic changes—Zouhir's office should have air conditioning."

She pushed out of the pool and dropped to a lounge chair, hoping the refreshing water had cooled any worries about coming down with a fever from the tick bite. Puffs of pink and purple clouds crowded the sky, clustering above the hillside dotted with white buildings. Lights brightened the city center below and music filtered the air—fast strings, like bluegrass, but other instruments, and haunting singing.

"Do you know Moroccan music?"

Stefan lowered himself to the next chair. "Chaâbi—North African folk music. But Zouhir complained that western rap and pop has taken over."

"Did he tell you the game plan for tomorrow?"

"We'll review records to identify cases and develop the study design. The fieldwork will be collaborative—he mentioned identifying the locations and jointly collecting data."

She pulled up the back of the lounge to sit up straighter. "I'd like to do a case-control study, not just gather data on the patients."

"Let's check with him. I should warn you—this might not be as tame as Portugal, even with its wildfires and rowdy pigs."

"Morocco's well-developed, part of the EU."

"Not technically in the EU. They started talks for a privileged relationship but there's controversy on migrant policies and disputed territory in the Western Sahara. Plus Islamic terrorism, including two Scandinavian girls beheaded while hiking in the Atlas Mountains."

With a shudder, she pulled the towel closer around her shoulders. "I heard someone sent a phone video of the murder to the mother."

"Several attackers were sentenced to death." At the expression on her face, he gathered his towel and room key. "Don't worry, Zouhir is at the top of his game and will keep us totally safe."

Maya was reminded again that she wasn't traveling on her own. She was in experienced, capable hands. Then she felt for the smarting raised area at the back of her neck. "I hope you're right."

TWENTY-FIVE

Zouhir held open one of the ornate iron doors as Maya and Stefan stepped through the marble front of Le Ministère de la Santé. "Thank you again for coming. We've had an explosion of *Borrelia* cases and you each have knowledge to help me determine why this is happening."

As they clustered around a computer, he scrolled the screen. "Here are sixteen confirmed cases from several medical centers serving the northwest coast over the past year, concluding in June. During this period, there were fifty-nine other patients with unexplained fever and no malaria or *Borrelia*."

"What types of *Borrelia* are included here?" Maya asked.

"Same type as Portugal—*hispanica* from *Ornithodoros* soft ticks. But we have others as well, including Lyme disease from hard ticks."

"Were any of the cases JHR, Jarisch-Herxheimer reaction?" Stefan asked. "Both Maya and I had some of those. We're unresolved whether side effects are too severe to risk antibiotic treatment."

Zouhir turned his hands palm up. "I apologize—I did not check. You may remember that my PhD is in Bioagricultural Sciences. So I am more familiar with the vectors."

Maya identified with his embarrassment, not quite fitting in with the physician leadership of public health. "Your expertise with these ticks is invaluable." She wished she'd kept the tick from her neck for Zouhir's identification. "Where did you study?"

"I am a Ram," he said proudly. "Colorado State University, class of 2000."

Her mouth dropped open. "What a small world—my veterinary degree is from there. How did you like Ft. Collins?"

"Colorado gave me my wife who is from Grand Junction. She studied atmospheric science, and is our leading climate scientist."

Reflecting on her own multicultural family, Maya was energized to meet others. "Could she join us for dinner?"

He returned a gracious smile. "I will ask. But let me show you a map of the cases." Pulling it up on the computer, his finger traced the coast. "These are six villages in the Kenitra District where the relapsing fever patients live."

Maya wondered how delicate her diplomacy needed to be. Perhaps with his marriage to an American, he'd be more open to her recommendation.

Nothing ventured, nothing gained. "Portugal focuses on the patients, which provides great information. Please don't take this as a criticism of Dr. Barboza, but a case-control study would offer stronger results."

Zouhir's eyebrows drew together. "Can you be more specific?"

Maya glanced over to Stefan, who gave her a slight smile.

"For each confirmed case and the fever of unknown origin cases," she said, "we should select control households from the same neighborhood for tick collection. The comparison may identify tick bite risk factors using a survey of house type, vegetation, animals, occupation, and recreational activities."

Zouhir squinted. "I will notify the households if you develop the questionnaire."

Stefan pointed to the screen. "Can you grant me access to the medical records so I can look into JHR?"

"Teamwork, I like that. Your assistance with the fieldwork will be much appreciated. I, uh, have some temporary limitations."

In doubt whether it was polite to inquire what he meant, Maya plunged on. "We're pleased to do our part. If there are multiple control households within a mile of the case, we should choose the resident closest in age, ideally within five years. Age-matching will help control for other risk factors."

"Develop your proposals. With luck, we'll finish the plan today."

. . .

In late afternoon, a tiny woman in a long, lightly-striped robe pushed into the room and tugged the pointed hood to her shoulders, revealing thick red curls. "Zouhir, mon mari, have you been a welcoming host? You should all take a break."

He stood to introduce Rebecca, pour tea, and uncover a plate of almond cookies. After a few minutes of niceties, he guided them to the door. "We worked for hours without lunch. If you can show them the Kasbah, I will collect our equipment for tomorrow."

As Rebecca led them to the sidewalk, she pulled her hood up over her hair. "This is a djellaba, but western clothing is also plentiful. With my hair, I don't like to stand out." She flagged down a small blue taxi and climbed in the front with the female driver, then turned to the back seat.

"I will take you to the Mausoleum of Mohammed V, for the ancestors of our king."

After the quick ride, they hopped out of the taxi and Rebecca pulled a dark scarf from her purse for Maya. "A sign of respect for the tombs of our leaders."

A brief rain shower had washed the stone courtyard, leaving the Roman columns reflecting in its shiny surface. The height of the square quieted the traffic noise from the highway below, which paralleled the river flowing to the Atlantic as Maya peered west into sunrays piercing the clouds. A guard in a brilliant red uniform with a white cloak and blue cap stood at the entrance, accommodating tourists who posed for photos with him. On either side, other guards sat on horseback holding green pennants overhead.

After entering the white building with the triangular green tiled roof, a carved balcony allowed them to hover around the tomb floor below. To one side, women clustered in black hijabs covering their bodies and faces. On the other side, teenagers joked quietly in their leather jeans and T-shirts.

"These are our kings." Rebecca gestured to three white stone caskets, the largest centered beneath a dome with floral glass circles. A man in a white robe and red fez hat sat cross-legged at the perimeter, praying quietly from an enormous book. Bright crystal chandeliers reflected in the polished dark stone of the floor.

The reverence of all ages at the tomb brought back her mother's moving story about a high school visit to the gravesite of John F. Kennedy, one of only two presidents buried at Arlington National Cemetery.

As they stepped outside, Rebecca pointed out Zellige geometric mosaic tiles. A breeze from the earlier storm stirred palm tree fronds and cascading red bougainvillea flowers at the plaza's edge. Above all, the red starred flag of Morocco whipped overhead.

"Next on the tour are the beautiful Andalusian Gardens. Let's take le petit taxi bleu again."

Within minutes, they arrived in a verdant area. Surrounded by older clay-colored buildings topped with miniature spiked minarets, the gardens were a quiet oasis penetrated by bird song and light laughter of others enjoying the area. The three found a stone bench and perched in the shade for a rest.

Everywhere Maya looked, cats of multiple hues strolled by, weaving in and out of lofty palms, squat green bushes, and colorful blossoms. Their casual struts were calm with the pedestrian traffic, but they moved away when someone reached to pet. In eastern New Mexico, she'd found dogs with *Borrelia*, and had read a few reports of Lyme disease in cats. If these carried infected ticks, they might play a role in the disease life cycle.

"Rebecca, was it an adjustment moving here from Colorado?"

"I studied French in college. Zouhir first courted me in French, the language of love."

Similar romantic history—Manolo had used Spanish.

"You're also from Colorado?" Rebecca asked.

"I went to high school and college there."

"So you're a western girl like me. Morocco's a cultural adjustment, but cosmopolitan. Zouhir is Muslim so that was the biggest change for me."

"Perhaps you could advise us on important customs," Stefan said.

"Only eat or shake hands with your right—the left is reserved for private tasks."

He nodded. "That one I've heard before."

"Women are often highly educated and valued, but like a New York construction zone, there can be harassment."

"Rebecca, you're such an indispensable Moroccan guide," Maya said. "Such huge life changes for you, yet your climate change job must contribute so much."

"More than half our population and industries are on the coast, so sea-level rise is a problem. The snowpack from our Atlas Mountains is reduced and impacts our drinking water. However, we rank high in preparedness."

"Like Norway, Morocco has committed heavily to renewable energy," Stefan said.

"Ironic that little Morocco is so far ahead of the U.S., n'est-ce pas?"

Maya ignored the gibe. "Like *Borrelia*, many vector-borne diseases increase with population displacement and poverty enhanced by climate change."

Rebecca stood. "A source of continued employment for me and Zouhir. I promised to meet him at six-thirty. Let's get back to your hotel.

· · ·

Zouhir reclined on a couch in the double-story hotel lobby, dominated by a blue wall painted like a psychedelic peacock. When hearing Rebecca call his name, he slowly stood to greet them. "We are ready for our trip north tomorrow. I am sorry for not taking you out to lunch, but perhaps can make up for it now."

"Go freshen up," Rebecca suggested. "We'll wait."

When they returned to the lobby, Zouhir led them down narrow alleyways in the medina between high white-washed walls, some covered with graffiti and others with modern dramatic art. An image on one multistory building dripped water through circular rings of mountains and European-looking villages.

"Jidar," Zouhir said. "An annual street art festival. Some are very dramatic."

Rebecca tugged him to a chair in the shade. "Time for our famous hot mint tea. It seems to cool one off on a warm day."

With a silver teapot in his right hand, the waiter in a black uniform and red fez poured the tea from above his head into the clear glass cups on the silver tray in his left, even stretching dramatically behind his back as he continued to pour.

"That's quite an athletic feat," Maya said.

"An entertaining tradition," Zouhir replied, "and also allows the tea to cool during its journey to the cup."

"I'm happy you're here to help Zouhir study *Borrelia*." Rebecca reached to her husband's hand but didn't touch. "Our family has a personal interest."

Zouhir spoke rapidly to Rebecca in Arabic, but she squared her shoulders. "Mon cher, this has been the most frightening time of our married life. Your pain has been so devastating. Why should you be embarrassed?"

"No one brags about catching a disease they are supposed to eliminate."

Rebecca's lips turned down. "But Maya is new to this work and wants to learn."

"Ma femme, don't frown." He rubbed his sparse beard with one hand, appearing deep in thought. "I have a *Borrelia* complication called Garin-Bujadoux-Bannwarth syndrome, a form of lymphocytic meningoradiculitis."

"Anything like JHR?" Stefan asked.

"It started with his abdomen two months ago. Then he had stroke symptoms with a droopy face and weak arms and legs. The bacteria attacked his nerves."

"Several weeks later they identified *B. garinii* in my spinal fluid. I never was aware of a tick bite—probably complacent after years of work."

Rebecca's smile was provocative with a hint of sorrow in her eyes. "I am quite vigilant at helping him with tick checks now."

Maya couldn't help but worry over her own tick bite, but refocused on Zouhir who had a real health problem from ticks, not hypochondria. "Maybe this isn't the best timing for our joint investigation."

Stefan chimed in. "Maya is right. Zouhir, do you feel sufficiently recovered?"

"They tried, how do you say, the kitchen sink? Antibiotics, steroids, and intravenous immunoglobulins."

"I was frantic and wanted to take him to the States." By the look on Rebecca's face, Maya could tell she wasn't successful. "He still has some abdominal discomfort and hasn't regained muscle strength."

"Enough about me." Zouhir slashed the air with a sharp hand gesture, then softened the mood with a smile. "Your study design was approved and a few families agreed to interviews. Of course we cannot finish while you visit, but we can pilot test the methods."

Maya was gratified she'd pushed her ideas but uncertain how much they'd complete with a partially incapacitated host. It meant her role was even more important.

"Zouhir, I appreciate your considering the control group. Although the work requires more resources, the benefits in knowledge can be tremendous. But don't let me impose a study design that's too ambitious if you're unwell."

"Maya was one of Columbia's top students in statistics when I was there," Stefan added.

Her hands instinctively covered her eyes and she ducked her head. "Please don't talk me up too much—I'll be bound to fail." She didn't think she was spooky or fatalistic, but there were a few elements of their Morocco trip which caused concern.

"If everyone is refreshed, let's stroll la Rue des Consuls, our most popular pedestrian shopping street." Rebecca stood first. "Looks like you're prepared for our occasional pickpockets." Maya wore a small waist pack turned to the front.

The narrow street was lined with colorful masses of carpets on one side and pottery on the other, hung so high that Maya couldn't reach them. "If you see something, bargaining is expected," Rebecca said, "but if not interested, 'la choukran' for no thank you is fine."

Within twenty minutes, Zouhir looked like he was fading from the jostling crowds. "Has everyone worked up an appetite?" When they nodded, he guided them to a favorite restaurant.

"Marhabaan," he greeted the proprietor, who asked about Zouhir's health and his family.

"I didn't know you had children," Stefan said.

"They visited recently—my only benefit of getting ill. But let's order our meal."

The multiple plates included a soup of local vegetables like Paula's in Lisbon, kebabs, stuffed pastries, and savory-sweet pies.

Rebecca pulled out her phone. "Here's Cyndy when she graduated from Stanford in mathematics last year. And Alex is a worldwide utility diver, supporting underwater pipe and cable installations."

"Such demanding jobs." And their son's work sounded hazardous. Maya knew what that felt like, with more than a few sleepless nights over anthrax and *Borrelia*. "How did you juggle work and family?"

Rebecca and Zouhir exchanged glances. "Compromise is essential," he said.

"The culture here has a strong emphasis on family," Rebecca answered. "People care about their work, but family comes first. That makes it easier."

"Make connections—then the inevitable work stresses are minimized." Zouhir caught the attention of the waiter who served new dishes in the middle of the table.

Perhaps Maya's hyperfocus on the task at hand had been a mistake. Slowing down to establish relationships was an unfamiliar concept. Zouhir's close call was a good reminder that a more balanced approach could be healthier and more productive.

Determined to start at once, she replaced *Borrelia* discussion with eating, toasting, and learning about Moroccan life. Despite his recent health scare, Zouhir had arranged for their work with care, and its success didn't require her obsessive worry. Although he limited his consumption to tea and soup, Maya embraced the exotic tastes like she'd done in Lisbon.

TWENTY-SIX

In the car the next morning, Maya's attention drifted between drylands with small trees on the right and bright green irrigated crops on the left. Then Zouhir pulled off the highway. "With your assistance, we can sort out procedures in our farthest site."

The side streets were unpaved and Maya's old injuries flared with the rapid bumps. Tires and trash filled fields, utility boxes rusted, and paint peeled from doorways and one-story buildings. Older vehicles limped along and young people walked aimlessly. Were their TBRF infections exacerbated by a lack of medical care in such a poor area? A donkey pulling a cart loaded with supplies blocked Zouhir's car, already enmeshed in a long line of cargo vans and motorcycles.

After their eventual escape, an alley led to a metal-roofed carport of dirt bricks, reminding Maya of the adobe blocks in the Southwest. The elderly owner met them at the wooden doors to a two-story old building, masses of colorful flowers spilling over high walls.

"Voici Maya Maguire, une vétérinaire américaine," Zouhir said. "Parlez vous anglais?"

The woman held two gnarled fingers close together and answered in a reedy voice. "Un peu."

Maya shook her hand. "Bonjour, Madame."

Their host served highly sugared mint tea on the blue-walled second floor balcony. Stefan asked his medical questions in French while Maya looked over his shoulder to read the notes in English.

Following initial fever, the woman had been hospitalized with life-threatening low blood pressure and severe gastrointestinal signs.

Stefan glanced over to Zouhir. "I'm done, let's make sure she's okay with our setting out tick traps in the carport, garden, and first floor rooms."

Additional traps were disbursed at the homes of two neighbors, including an older man who'd been ill at the same time but never diagnosed. Stefan held his placid dog as Maya drew blood from its front leg.

When they returned to the *Borrelia* patient's house, the woman spread out food on cracked plates in the yard and an assortment of cats gathered, some with dripping eyes or snotty noses. "Can we collect a cat blood sample, too?" Maya asked.

The woman answered in Arabic. "You can try," Zouhir translated, "but these are not pets. They keep the rodents under control."

Maya's neck muscles tightened. The data could be valuable. "Either one of you have experience restraining a cat?"

Zouhir shook his head no, and Stefan shrugged. "How hard can it be? Look how scrawny they are."

Maya borrowed an old towel. "After I throw it over, help me tighten it so the cat can't escape or scratch. Maintain a firm grip on the scruff of its neck so you can control the head and keep it from biting either one of us."

She surveyed the area—no tables for the procedure, and she didn't want to bring a feral animal indoors in case it escaped. "One of your hands controls the head, and the other arm secures the cat against your chest."

Spotting a limping black and white cat with crusts around its eyes, she looked to Stefan. "Ready?" He gave thumbs up.

She dropped the towel on the cat and they knelt quickly to corral it. As Stefan held it close against his knees, Maya rewrapped it to enclose a protruding hind limb. "The claws look like daggers, so don't let go," she warned. As she spread towel folds to unwrap the cat's head, it hissed and growled.

She snapped her fingers in front of the cat's face for distraction and Stefan grabbed the scruff. "Expose the neck now," she instructed.

Eerie yowls filled the small yard when Maya wiped alcohol on the animal's fur. As she palmed a needle and syringe, the cat wriggled. "Number one rule, never let go. You're bigger and stronger—keep that confidence in your attitude."

"I'm an athlete," he joked. "These shoulders are useful for something."

"My life depends on you."

A guttural warning emitted from the cat's throat. As Maya inserted the needle, the legs in the towel exploded. A front paw slashed Maya's arm and Stefan's shifting weight smashed her to the ground. But he kept his grip on the cat's neck as it arched and attempted to grab his arm.

"Drop it," Maya yelled. "Lost cause."

After the cat darted into the bushes, Maya checked on the status of her assistant. "Are you okay?"

He glanced down at both hands. "Bastard missed me. How do you vets do this every day?" Then he looked over to Maya. "Jesus, that doesn't look good."

She followed his eyes to the burning on her right forearm. Blood from multiple lacerations dripped down to her elbow, her pants, and the dirt. When she pulled up her left hand to search for the needle cap, her little finger was numb. Looking more closely, she could see it was bent sharply down at the final joint. But she dug the cap out of the soil and slipped it over the needle and syringe still in her right hand, before dropping them to the ground.

"Getting medical supplies." Zouhir shoved open the garden gate.

Stefan held her bleeding arm. "I don't think these will be too deep, but you may scar. I don't want to apply pressure with anything dirty."

The homeowner hovered and Stefan caught her attention. "Madam, je veux de l'eau s'il vous plait." She nodded and headed toward the kitchen.

He turned back to Maya. "I'm so sorry I didn't keep the hellion under control."

She shook her head. "Restraint can be more difficult than needle sticks. Cats are small but extraordinarily challenging, especially if not tame."

He helped her to an old wicker chair, and the other two returned. Stefan poured water over her arm and Zouhir opened alcohol wipes. "All our government cars carry small medical kits." After Stefan cleaned the area thoroughly, Zouhir unwrapped gauze and handed Stefan strips of adhesive tape.

Maya smiled in gratitude and glanced down to her left hand resting in her lap. "Of more concern to me is this." She raised her hand with the fifth finger at the abnormal angle. "Extreme numbness and a dull ache—not sure which is worse."

"Mallet finger, snapped extensor tendon. A relatively common sports injury. How did that happen?"

"Your big weight," she chastised. "Wish you were a jockey instead of Michael Phelps."

His face drooped. "I feel terrible—I'm a lousy assistant. Zouhir, is there a tongue depressor in your kit?"

Stefan broke it off to match the length of her finger, then taped it lengthwise under her finger to keep it straight. "Zouhir, can you ask for some ice?"

Several minutes later as Maya's finger began to throb, he created a mini icepack on top of her hand. "She needs a better splint, like a padded metal one. Is there a clinic or pharmacy nearby?"

"Non, je suis désolé. But we can return to Rabat."

After several hours working in the heat and the cat explosion, Maya was dizzy, but refused to let her minor wounds interfere with the planned workday. "Let's check our tick traps and go to the next address."

Ticks on an indoor tray and one in the adobe carport were placed into specimen vials and stored in the vehicle trunk. Maya gulped water and appreciated Zouhir's air conditioning as they drove back to the main road.

"Several of the ill young women are back to work at the strawberry farms." Zouhir pulled into a parking area near acres of plastic sheeting in long white lines, punctuated by small red-garbed bodies with covered heads. A foreman came out to greet them and Zouhir negotiated in Arabic. "He will bring over former relapsing fever patients."

Maya jumped in. "Zouhir, you may need to translate for Stefan's interviews. Rebecca will kill us if you have a relapse. So I can set out traps on my own."

"Only if you're sure you're okay," Stefan said.

Maya nodded, grabbing one flattened cage from the back of Zouhir's vehicle with her good hand. Some buildings were modern but older crumbling ruins looked like ideal rodent habitat. Her Yankees cap and water bottle helped her cope with the heat, but Maya moved slowly through the sultry surroundings until her colleagues tracked her down an hour later.

As she panted in the shade against a metal building, Stefan held his hand to her forehead. "I don't remember a thermometer in your medical kit, Zouhir, and I'm concerned that Maya is too warm. It might just be the hot air and humidity, or a reaction to her injuries. Let's call it a day."

She straightened up and protested. "Please don't let me derail our work."

Zouhir shook his head. "I'm exhausted too. This work needs more hands, which I will arrange tomorrow. Let's drive back to Rabat."

Two against one—she gave into the change of plans, no matter how guilty she felt to be the cause of it. Her finger was throbbing and swelling, with no more ice. "Any anti-inflammatories in your first aid kit?"

After she swallowed an aspirin, Zouhir pulled into a petrol station and bought them snacks. Once again on the road, Stefan turned to Maya reclining in the back. "I recommend an x-ray to make sure you didn't break a bone."

"How long for the splint?"

"To make sure the tendon heals, six weeks. You don't play a stringed instrument, do you?"

"No, just the piano. I guess those lower notes aren't so important." She was more concerned about the computer. As her finger unconsciously stretched for an imagined key, she flinched and remembered the letter 'a.' "But it will reattach and heal?"

"Occasionally they require surgery, but that's a last resort."

She leaned back and tried to turn off her brain. The two-and-a-half-hour drive dragged with interminable tedium, but she was too weak to distract with her iPhone solitaire game.

. . .

Just before the clinic closed for the day, Zouhir arranged for an x-ray, which found no fractures. But they fitted her with a metal splint and rebandaged the reddened scratches on her arm. Then Rebecca and Zouhir took them to dinner at a café with soothing jazz.

"So you really think I should head home after one botched day?" she pressed as they completed their meal amid a discussion of next steps.

"Bien sûr," Zouhir answered. "You only committed to help design our study."

"The original plan was to focus on LBRF in our Norwegian refugees," Stefan said. "Then you extended it to TBRF in Portugal and got a tick bite. Now this. I don't want to overdo CDC's willingness to collaborate."

Rebecca waved the waiter down for more tea, and Zouhir continued. "Our initial day identified some weaknesses. If we continue with animal studies, perhaps I should bring a veterinary team with more animal handling experience."

Stefan raised his hands in mock protest. "My ineptitude confirms your wisdom. I'll stick to reviewing medical records and fly to Oslo on the weekend. By then, Kondrat should have forgiven me for his grueling plane trip as a single parent."

Exhaustion and pain from her new wounds spread like an

amoeba throughout Maya's body. She sank back into the cushions. "At least I didn't get beheaded on camera." Within a second, she wanted to swallow the words. Too tired to be diplomatic or her benzos loosening lips?

Zouhir jerked his head from her to Stefan. "Because we're Muslim, you think we're less civilized. Perhaps you forget about threats in your own country, like the far right terrorist who attacked a courthouse in Texas."

Stomach twisting, Maya found her voice. "I'm so sorry—I didn't mean to offend. The challenges from this trip have me overreacting."

Zouhir brushed off Rebecca's hand on his arm. "And in the spring, people were shot at a Pennsylvania synagogue."

Stefan kicked Maya under the table. "Please forgive me and my young American colleague. With a terrorist like Anders Breivik, Norwegians also can't criticize." He paid the bill and they moved out to the street busy with pedestrians and bicycles.

Maya leaned toward Rebecca, hoping for a hug despite the uncomfortable dinner. She had only shared a few hours with her fellow Coloradoan, but felt an instantaneous bond. Rebecca embraced her and kissed both her cheeks.

"I won't see you again," Maya said, "but thanks for your hospitality. Can I keep in touch?"

"I'm available if you need an advisor about work-life balance."

At the hotel, Zouhir pre-ordered an early morning taxi for Maya, then bowed in a frosty farewell.

Maya found herself alone with Stefan. "We should say goodbye now because of my early flight."

"I'll get in touch with the results on the tick from your neck."

She clutched his hands, careful to avoid pressure on the damaged finger. "My work and the brief leisure moments with you have been life-changing. I may not get to work in Europe again, but if I do, I want you by my side, even if you can't control a cat."

He winked and bent to enfold her body. "You're never going to let me forget that. I'll echo Rebecca's support. There's nothing to make your life feel meaningful like a family. You'll find the right time."

Just before midnight in the hotel, Maya sent the Mirandas her JFK arrival time. Enzo had emailed again, worried about the outbreak exercise presentation.

I'll be in Atlanta Monday, she typed, using her ring finger instead of the one in the splint. **But if you want earlier feedback, I'll call on FaceTime tomorrow when back in NYC, and you can rehearse with me.**

Next, she opened an email from Mr. Zielinski. **Let's talk in my office when you're back.**

After packing, she popped an aspirin on top of the Klonopin. Unsure how well she could sleep with the bandaged arm on the right and splinted finger on the left, she nestled into the soft sheets and pulled the duvet up to her chin, air conditioning on high. Photomicrographs of tick species swarmed her brain—she prayed Stefan would contact her soon with news about her own little hitchhiker.

TWENTY-SEVEN

Only ten days since they'd made love in the airport, she scanned the luggage area for Manolo. But with nonstop travel and *Borrelia* challenges in three countries, the time apart felt like a lifetime.

The crowd parted and she spotted them—Manolo pushing his wheelchair by himself, Sebastian hanging behind. Manolo's grin brightened his entire face like the first time they met almost a year earlier at the Phoenix Indian Medical Center.

Gloved hands pushed hard at the wheels and he almost ran her over with his effort. Strong arms yanked her down to his lap and both hands cradled her face before his lips pressed hers. "Maya." Her name settled around them like an afternoon summer mist, and it was repeated again and again as fingers tugged her hair and the kisses brushed her eyes and cheeks.

He pulled on her right forearm covered by the light sweater as he enveloped her in a hug. When she squirmed, he formed the word, "What?" Leaning back, she slipped the fabric up, exposing the gauze bandage. The gesture focused his gaze on the splint, and his eyebrows drew together.

"Cat wars," she joked. "Occupational hazard for a vet. They have big felines in Africa, like lions."

"Lion?" His forehead wrinkled with concern.

She regretted the joke making him worry. "I'm pulling your leg." As her hand brushed his thigh, electricity shot through her nerves. Perhaps separation and anticipation could overcome the damn pills.

"Trouble parking. Sorry to be late."

Her fingers traced his eyebrows. "Not a problem. I'm happy my trip was close to the weekend and we can spend several days together."

. . .

At Ramona's Bronx brownstone, they jockeyed for the remaining pizza slices until Maya's alarm on her iPhone went off. She ruffled Johnny's curly hair. "I promised a call with one of my Atlanta students—back in a few minutes."

She settled in an Adirondack chair outside and caught the blue eyes of a Seal Point Siamese on the fence, framed by the yellowed sky of the clammy early evening. When she started to rise for a closer view, the cat sprung away. After hitting Enzo's number on the FaceTime app, the screen flashed with a rapid moving picture of his naked body as he yelled "Fuck." His phone crashed to the floor pointed upwards for a clear photo of full frontal nudity. Maya turned her cell away to face the rose bushes.

"Sorry, Maya." The casual tone was unconvincing.

"This is the time you told me to call." She held the phone closer but the screen facing the yard.

"Got carried away with the relaxing shower spray. Shitty day— Keegan didn't like one of my calculations."

A headache pounded between her ears. "Are you decent yet?"

"Sure."

She turned her screen to find him perched on the toilet, water glistening off his muscled torso and white towel around his waist.

"Enzo, we scheduled this time to practice your presentation. Get dressed and call me back."

A pigeon flew over and she studied its graceful flight, recalling that some New Yorkers kept them as pets on their rooftops. She hoped the cat would return—anything to distract her brain from the disturbing sight of Enzo's naked body. Images flooded back of the college student after the drunken dorm party. Nudity with the opposite sex only had a negative connotation until Manolo. The phone accident with Enzo was hopefully not intentional.

He called back, fully dressed in a polo shirt and shorts.

"I assume this will not be your costume next Wednesday." She tried to ease the tension with a wisecrack.

His face darkened. "I said I was sorry. Did you look at the final slides?"

After she assured him they were fine, he launched into the verbal part of his talk with the phone resting on a table. His college debating success came through in an engaging performance. He could sell ice to the Eskimos. The latest argument with Keegan was about a statistic, but they had sorted it out with Lila's guidance.

When finished, Maya reflected on other calls. Nancy would want to hear from her, but the report to Enzo's new boss in Arizona could wait until after his presentation. She sent a note to her parents followed by a group email to her work contacts confirming a flight to Atlanta on Sunday and then home on Thursday after the training was over.

As she stepped back into the kitchen, Sebastian said, "I'll run you both over to my place."

"I hate to put you out," Maya answered, but Manolo's broad smile echoed her level of joy.

"Don't worry. Waking up here to my grandson jumping on my chest is a special treat."

Once alone with Manolo, Maya relished the shower's slick contact and warm wet hugs, although awkward with her wounds. He toweled her off and changed the finger splint to a dry one. His legs were strong and coordinated enough to make it from the bathroom to the bedroom on his own without her help or the wheelchair.

Naked under the covers, she succumbed to the fog of the long trip, comforted by Manolo's whisper, "Te adoro."

. . .

The mating howl of an unneutered male cat brought her awake with a start and she turned her head to the open window. Gray light and a whiff of rain drifted in, tarnished by the sour tang of trash. She tiptoed over to slide the upper casement down, hoping to avoid wakening Manolo. She always got up before him, one of their habits formed in only a few weeks of sleeping together at Christmas.

But his dark eyes met hers when she crawled back in. After weeks without sex except for the brief airport rendezvous, she felt shy, still burned by Enzo's phone image. Covering her disquiet, she reached for her iPhone on the end table and opened photos from Europe.

"I was in Paris yesterday for a layover, but no time to see it."

"City of love." The words were slow but strong.

"Next time I go overseas, I want to be with you." She emphasized her determination with a kiss.

"We can love now." He followed his declaration with familiar hands roaming her body. She nestled her back into him, grateful for how they fit together. She was content to be passive, rejoicing in the warmth of their companionship. His fingertips stroked from her face down to her chest and then her belly, tingling her skin. When they drifted lower, she groaned and rotated to face him.

"I'm sorry, I can't climax. It's my damned pills." Dr. Kim was first on her list when back in Santa Fe.

"But don't let that stop you." She rested her hand with the splint against his chest. After using the other to pull a condom from her purse, she guided him into her.

. . .

Manolo was still asleep when she headed out to Long Island City to see her public health vet mentor at the health department. Guilt flickered about leaving as she wrote a note reminding him of her destination. But no one had been such a close professional and personal friend as Dr. Faye Simpson, and they hadn't talked in person since Thanksgiving.

As Maya exited the subway at Queensboro Plaza, Nancy called from Phoenix. She chatted with excitement about Enzo's start date of August fifth. When she inquired about his conference performance, Maya praised his unusual competence as a public speaker. But his distressing personal traits—it wasn't fair to bring those up when her contact with him had been limited since heading to Europe.

At the health department front desk, she phoned Faye who came out to meet her.

"What kind of battle were you in?" The sixtyish woman with a red-gray pixie cut gave Maya a side hug, careful to avoid the long scabbing claw marks and finger splint.

"Our favorite critter, a cat."

"I thought you knew how to handle them."

"I pressured someone inexperienced into service." Chilled by the building's air conditioning, Maya pulled on her light blazer with care to avoid rubbing the aching arm. "But now, whenever someone complains they don't like cats, I'll have permanent reminders that they have a point."

Faye waved toward the front door. "Listen, I've been glued to my desk all morning fielding calls. Join me on an early lunch break."

Once ensconced in a booth at a restaurant around the corner, Maya showed Faye photos from her phone. "Remember Stefan Duda? He interned here during his doctoral dissertation. Now he's with the EU, based in Norway."

"Valuable excursion?"

"Not only did I learn a new soft tick collection method, but I helped Morocco design a more extensive case control study including animal testing. Hence the war wounds."

"It's great to hear you so positive about the job."

Maya felt more energized after the trip. "Do you recall Stefan's partner Kondrat from one of the office parties? With Norway's wonderful child care, the two of them are managing a family and Stefan's heavy travel."

"It can be hard for driven professional women to connect with others on a personal level. I tried once or twice, but it never lasted."

"I met a family in Morocco. The husband's an entomologist and the wife's a climatologist. Somehow they juggled two careers and two kids. But a tick nailed him through work, and *Borrelia* almost killed him. Sober reminder of our occupational hazards."

"Our work is not without its risks." Faye leaned back and pushed her plate of pad thai away. "You know, this might be the year I finally retire. It's been insanely busy. We've got this politically sensitive measles outbreak in an Orthodox Jewish community from vaccination delays and families holding measles parties."

"Faye, you've been talking retirement as long as I've known you, but you love your job. How many other veterinarians get to contribute on such a huge variety of issues?"

"You pegged it, and it's easy to focus on rewarding work if you never marry. My job demands keep me close to home and I only made it overseas once, to London and Saudi Arabia. But I'm yenning for a big trip, maybe to Africa."

"Funny you should say that. Last year, Manolo and I planned an African safari when I finish my EIS assignment next summer."

Faye's sun-wrinkled face turned mournful. "I can't believe what you've been through, with your relationship so new. I wish I had some sage advice."

Maya plastered a deliberate smile. "He's made massive improvement with speaking and writing a few words. We're finally able to reconnect."

"It must be a strain balancing demands of being an EIS officer with a sense of obligation to him."

The remark resonated with the worries tearing Maya up inside. Faye signaled the server for their bill. "I imagine you're out-of-pocket until you get reimbursement from CDC for your travel."

Maya smiled. "Thanks, you do remember what it's like."

"Let's go up to my office—everyone would like to say hello. And I get the feeling there's more we should talk about."

TWENTY-EIGHT

In the cubicles, Maya watched the Columbia University interns frown over their screens. "Proc corr or Proc reg?" one asked another.

She smiled, remembering her first time figuring out the SAS analysis software.

As Faye finished her drink from the restaurant, she assumed her usual posture with feet on the desk amidst the cubicle dividers covered with cat pictures. "You didn't eat much at lunch. Something bothering you?"

"Nancy's enthralled with her new EIS officer. She asked me to mentor him, like you mentored me."

The wrinkles in Faye's plump freckled face deepened. "Not to criticize Nancy, but that seems too much for you, only a year into the program."

Relief flooded. "Thanks, I've struggled with it."

"CDC must respect your abilities to have you guide teams during their summer training."

Maya nodded. "The Arizona EIS Officer, Dr. Russo, is skilled at presentations, but his personal interactions are problematic."

Faye edged closer. "Pardon my prying, but what do you mean?"

Hesitance over her right to judge brought Maya to a halt. Her own emotional intelligence and social skills were inadequate. With all the demands of the past year, she'd become more assertive and accomplished at her job. But since Manolo's impairment and her reliance on the medication, she felt at times out of control and impulsive. Maybe this was not the time and place to bring up her worries about Enzo.

Faye continued. "Whatever you say will be kept in confidence."

Maya deflected her unrest with humor. "What other modern American woman waits until twenty-five to date? My instincts on male-female relationships aren't the best."

"What are you trying to say about Dr. Russo?"

"During a scheduled FaceTime review of his slides, he was in the shower and dropped the phone. I got an eyeful." She ran fingers through her hair. "It's little things he says, and minor physical touches. Enzo knows about my relationship with Manolo, so he can't be coming onto me."

Face contorted like Atlas carrying the weight of the world, Faye exhaled a deep breath. "In my experience, agencies sometimes solve these problems by moving the woman to 'protect her' and minimize her contact with the offender."

That was one outcome Maya hadn't anticipated, and dreaded. Starting over in a new assignment, who knows where, would be disastrous. She stirred her teabag to strengthen the caffeine boost. "His interactions with me are one issue, but he can be a bully, like with his African American teammate."

"Did you say anything to Nancy or his CDC field supervisor?"

"Suzanne Jaworski is my supervisor, too." Maya was still unclear on Dr. Jaworski's level of respect for her judgment after two problematic legal issues.

They were interrupted by the Assistant Commissioner, and Maya said goodbye. "I'd better head out. Took me an hour to get here by subway from the Bronx."

In the lobby, Faye put an arm around Maya's shoulders. "Sharing a supervisor may complicate bringing up these issues, but if Enzo's behavior affects the work environment, you should do it. If you need an outside sounding board, don't hesitate to reach out."

. . .

Repeated phone calls and text messages to Manolo went

unanswered, so she texted Sebastian offering to pick up soup and dessert. His answer was confusing. **Will be at Ramona's, giving you time alone to sort things out.**

Manolo might be unhappy at the day-long abandonment. Using Sebastian's key, she unlocked the brownstone front door and unloaded her daypack in the kitchen. Barely visible among the crammed bookshelves, Manolo's body was illuminated by a small tube TV as he reclined on the overstuffed couch. He didn't look in her direction.

Remembering his use of Spanish to seduce her, she tried the same. "Mi corazón, ¿qué tal? Sorry to be out so long, but you've got me now—no emails, phone calls, or anything except a focus on you."

Still no acknowledgment of her presence, and when she knelt down for a kiss, he leaned away. Before his illness, he was always in passionate seduction mode, so she was spoiled—he had acted like she could do no wrong.

During the past few months of anthrax recovery, the neurologic damage made him distant, but he'd made progress. Sensations from the early morning seeped in. His cognitive or emotional levels couldn't regress in just a few hours. She reached out to stroke his cheek, and he knocked her hand away. His rejection could mean he no longer recognized her. She dropped back to her heels on the braided rug and scrubbed her head, confused and despairing.

"Manolo, are you all right?"

"No." The word was forceful. If he'd declined in function, he might not have answered. A glimmer of hope—maybe he was angry. Only once before had she glimpsed it aimed her way, after her drunken El Día de los Muertos rejection of him over his secret marriage separation. Being pissed off—much better than a drop back to the deep dark.

"I told you last night that I needed to see Faye. You'll be back in Phoenix soon and we can spend most weekends together, right?"

"Soon."

Monosyllabic answers—she needed to research whether his

recovery might include relapses. "I brought dinner. Let's eat and I'll show you more pictures of my trip." At Christmas they dreamed of future vacations, and her European visit without him might be a reminder of his disability. She set the iPhone aside.

"Can I have a kiss before we eat?" This time when she bent toward him, he didn't stop her, and she imagined a slight response from his lips. Before anthrax, he tended toward optimistic cheer, an emotional salve for her own zigzags. But now the shoe was on the other foot.

. . .

In bed, Manolo slept with his back to her and didn't respond to her caress. Despite a night of tossing and turning, she awoke early to pour a bowl of cereal. After he stumbled into the kitchen for breakfast, she joined him on the couch, draped with a black throw covered with an image of the Puerto Rican flag.

"I know your Dad is proud of your heritage. How does he come down on statehood versus independence?"

"We are Americans. State."

"He came here as a student, so NYC is your home."

He nodded.

Something about his attitude disturbed her. She asked a question fraught with hazard. "But you'll return to Arizona?"

He nodded again and she burst into tears, relief dousing her skin like a summer monsoon. Her words were hushed, floating on the charged current between them. "I don't want to be separated from you."

"Phoenix is now my home."

Maya dropped her head to her hands. "I wish you lived with me, so I could help you." Then she grabbed his arms with a flush of excitement. "What if you moved to Santa Fe?"

She had accepted their separations from living in neighboring states, and moving in together before the end of her two-year training was a new thought. Her blood raced with anticipation, but also trepidation. What was she offering to take on?

His face fierce, a hand reached out to trace her cheek. "No burden. Want to work again."

"Your same job—infectious disease specialist at the Phoenix Indian Medical Center?"

He nodded. "My goal."

She studied his eyes, now alive with purpose, unlike the crypt orbs before their Taos trip in early May. "Did you talk to them?"

A whipped puppy, he frowned and curled inward. "Not yet."

Too soon—she shouldn't have asked. He might not recover to function as a competent physician, or IHS might not reinstate him. She knew the pressures of trying to prove oneself.

"Take your time. You know I'll wait for you. But my flight to Atlanta is tomorrow. Any ideas what to do with our final day?"

"Museum with Johnny."

She recalled taking his nephew to the zoo at Thanksgiving. "Which one?"

"Natural history—you love animals."

Leaning her head on his shoulder, she scrunched closer to the warmth of his chest. "I'll call Ramona. Any kid would have a ball there."

. . .

Manolo quickly tired with Johnny at the museum and Maya realized she'd been overly optimistic. Sebastian had dropped them off and left them alone to appreciate kid energy in the *Hall of Biodiversity*. Maya loved the *Spectrum of Life* with its display of microbes, her medical detective focus. But the wall exhibit with its hundreds of specimens was too busy for a small child.

Despite residual soreness in her scratched arm and snapped finger, Maya pushed the wheelchair to the dinosaurs. Johnny rode on Manolo's lap, clutching the plastic triceratops she bought in the gift shop. They didn't stay long in the exhibits. The four-year-old's lips trembled and he hid his head in Manolo's shirt when the sound effects frightened him. So they finished in the Discovery room with the giant African baobab tree and its puzzles, skulls, and books.

Manolo dozed as Maya read to Johnny about the extinct saber-toothed tiger, and when Johnny yawned too, she phoned Sebastian to pick them up.

During an after-dinner couch cuddle with a DVD of the *Les Misérables* twenty-fifth anniversary concert, Manolo fell asleep. They were both fans of Broadway music and the singing was spectacular, but there was too much death.

One Day More—a dramatic song from the musical about destiny and being parted. Being in control relieved her anxiety when life with Manolo was uncertain. The path from paralysis and reduced cognitive performance to a fully-functioning physician and husband was clouded. Juggling a career and a meaningful personal relationship was too challenging. Could she navigate all their needs, or was their bond a victim of fate?

TWENTY-NINE

Manolo remained asleep when she caressed him in bed, so she headed to the shower alone before Sebastian dropped her at LaGuardia. But he usually slept later than her, so she didn't know how to interpret his lack of response. His words had emphasized working, not their personal futures.

When the plane landed at Hartsfield-Jackson airport, Lila met her at the luggage carousel.

"You're a gem to brave the Atlanta highways to get me." Maya reached up to hug her taller colleague. "Having help with my bag is wonderful with both arms slightly out of commission."

Lila gently rotated Maya's bandaged right arm, then eyed her left finger in the splint. "Did these slow down your hot weekend in the Big Apple?"

"Hot and cold. Started out wonderful but ended a bit crosswise. Everything's up in the air."

"Volatility is normal with neuro healing. This final week of the EIS course is jam-packed, so it'll distract you from the home front."

"Thanks again for mentoring my teams. I owe you big-time."

Lila shrugged. "I played hooky last weekend for Chattooga River rafting. Almost as exciting as Enzo-Keegan tension."

Maya's mind slipped back to the Rio Chama. She almost lost her life rafting there, and on the road, the Jicarilla elder lost his. Although she didn't bear responsibility, her guilt remained, not fully scrubbed clean by travels to another world.

After grabbing Maya's bag, they headed for the parking lot. "I don't know what's up with the Enzo and Keegan team," Maya said. "Do you have any clues?"

"As a lesbian of middle-eastern origin, my radar for prejudice is on high."

Lila's sardonic tone was matched by her ruby-red grin. When they hit the sunlight, the lenses of her blue-framed glasses darkened to hide her kohl-outlined eyes. "Enzo's not said anything specific against African Americans, but he seemed to pick fights once or twice with Keegan and no one else."

Perspiring in the late afternoon heat, Maya swept her hair up into a quick ponytail. "How has Enzo been with you?"

"I'm invisible like wallpaper—nothing positive or negative."

Maya thought about what to say as they climbed into the rental. His full-frontal video exposure getting out of the shower must have been an accident. "I mention Manolo at every opportunity, so he's aware not to expect anything. Besides, after our final three days of training, he'll be in Arizona—equal opportunity to annoy both our states."

. . .

While the trainees sat through lectures on leadership and ethics, Maya didn't spend much time with Enzo. His face lit up when he saw her across the room, but they didn't cross paths. With such important topics, Maya didn't mind the refresher. But when the talk turned to the Core Activities of Learning, she took the opportunity to absent herself and meet with Dr. Jaworski on her own CAL fulfillment.

Maya settled in the chair on the other side of the desk from her supervisor. She admired framed photography portraits interspersed on the walls with Dr. Jaworski's professional credentials. "Are those yours? Manolo—Dr. Miranda—does black and white western landscapes, like Weston and Adams."

"I can't claim a creative bone—these are Rosie's. As a psych professor, she's more interested in people than I am."

Her thin fingers traced along the brown hair, clipped so short it was almost shaved. "That came out wrong." She glanced at Maya's finger splint. "What's that from?"

For the first time, Maya wondered if Dr. Jaworski was revealing challenges in personal interactions, too. "Minor incident with a cat." Her red blazer covered the claw marks.

In a typical brusque manner, the subject was dropped and Dr. Jaworski opened her computer to Maya's EIS record. "At the halfway point of your two-year training, I'm glad we can meet in person to review your progress. Some of your CALs are still unfinished."

Maya nodded. Between the Atlanta course, Manolo's instability, and the European *Borrelia* trip, fulfilling CALs were at the bottom of her priority list. Thinking of her EIS program coming to an end next summer brought a rush of blood to her head.

"You did well with the May anthrax talk, but we need to determine a topic and venue for a longer in-depth presentation."

Her least favorite activity, speaking in front of big groups.

"And you need to write a scientific manuscript for a peer-reviewed journal. My preference is for you as first author."

"I took the lead on the MMWR drum report last year."

Dr. Jaworski studied the screen. "But those weekly reports don't count. Are your current investigations far enough along to summarize? Given the number of individuals and agencies involved, it will be a challenge to coordinate."

Like *Hamlet*'s Ophelia, Maya's clothes weighted her arms and legs into the depths. "I haven't a clue where to start."

"I told you Fred likes to write. He's published a lot and can help you identify scientific journals. Are you back in his good graces?"

Maya pasted a fake smile. "I think so. He had no objections when we extended the *Borrelia* investigation in Europe." That was putting the most positive spin on it. His cryptic responses to her email updates during the past few weeks indicated he might not be in the best mood about her being out of the office.

· · ·

At one o'clock, she entered the classroom set aside for her team's final presentation preparation. She was greeted by applause and a few shouts of "Welcome back" from the ten officers. Enzo was on his feet within seconds and leaned down for an uncomfortable bear hug. Feeling the eyes of other trainees boring into her spine, she shoved him away and waved the finger splint in the air to defuse the awkward moment with humor.

"Cat got the better of me. Very embarrassing for a vet, so please don't rub it in."

Enzo took her hand to look more closely. "Is it mallet finger? How does a cat do that?"

"Clumsy male assistant who couldn't hold it." Regret coursed through her veins. The indirect insult to Enzo and his gender didn't reflect how she truly felt toward Stefan.

"Don't brush us all with the same stroke. Some of us know how to be gentle." He squeezed her right forearm, the one with the hidden scratches, and she recoiled.

Keegan called from the table. "Maya, could you check my calculations one more time?"

She turned from Enzo, grateful for the interruption. Seeing him in uniform didn't erase her memory of him naked.

After a busy afternoon of practice presentations, the group broke up to make dinner plans. Enzo again cornered her.

"I'm headed out for a run. I'd ask you to join me, but I know you don't do that. I'll pick you up for dinner around seven."

Maya spotted Keegan gathering his notes. "Sorry, but I have other things to complete." Enzo's eyes narrowed before she spun away to approach the table. "Keegan, with your vector-borne disease assignment in Ft. Collins, I want to touch base on *Borrelia* in Europe."

As he answered, "Sure," Enzo pushed his way back into their conversation.

"We have *Borrelia* in Arizona, so I should join you after my run."

"Not tonight," she said firmly. "I'm exhausted and plan to turn in early. I know how important keeping fit is for you. I'll see you tomorrow."

After Enzo stormed off, Keegan gave Maya a ride to his apartment for dinner. "Hope you don't mind a mixed salad. I'm trying to empty the refrigerator before the movers pick up my stuff."

She perched on an empty chair. "Atlanta's your home town, right?"

"My family thinks Colorado will be cowboys and Indians. They don't understand my choice."

While reaching for the salad dressing, she adopted her best imitation cowboy drawl. "Well, I hunkered down there for nine years. So you can tell 'em we have a few longhorns with the herefords."

He sat down across the table. "I need to get up to speed. My knowledge of *Borrelia* is limited to Lyme disease. No one but you knows about the other species like *hermsii* and *turicatae*."

She followed his lead into science mode. "About thirty thousand Lyme cases are reported each year and the real number is probably ten times that. So relapsing fever feels kind of unimportant."

"We've never had lice cases—tell me about your overseas work."

As Keegan lingered over his salad, Maya summarized the Norway study. "My trip finished in Portugal and Morocco with ticks."

"You should visit our program to talk about it. Have you been back since vet school?"

She shook her head. "It was a great place for four years. My favorite activity, when I got time off from studying, was hiking along the Poudre River."

"Once I get my bearings, let me talk to my supervisors about inviting you."

Remembering her meeting earlier in the day, she perked up. "Dr. Jaworski said one of the CALs is a longer presentation. If I prepared a detailed summary of all my *Borrelia* outbreaks, I could share it with your staff. They might be a friendly audience."

"Sounds like a good plan, unless Enzo insists on joining us."

"Yeah, what's going on with him?"

"I was kind of kidding." Keegan cleared their plates into the sink. "If the Arizona EIS Officer wants to stop by, he'd be welcome, either at the same time as your visit or a different one."

"Sometimes he's downright rude with you."

Keegan shrugged. "He's obnoxious with everyone at times, but I'm not female. You should see the way he flirts."

"Thank goodness it's not just me." Maya stood to grab the dish detergent and kicked herself for the comment. Like a kite in the wind, she wafted between relief she wasn't Enzo's only focus and concern about a bigger pattern. But lots of guys had hormones on overload. When did it crossover to something requiring a report to Nancy or CDC?

"Keep me updated, Keegan, on any problematic interactions. Nancy's grooming him for her own job and wants my feedback. She's got me between a rock and a hard place. I'm supposed to encourage him to bond with Arizona. But I also feel an obligation not to let her get a pig in a poke." The casual clichés blanketed her angst about the troubling dilemma.

THIRTY

On Tuesday morning, Dr. Jaworski offered Maya a CDC office and phone to check in with Stefan.

"How's everything in the Land of the Midnight Sun?"

"Things are going swimmingly, to use an American expression. We're in a Lofoten Islands cabin near our northern lights trip planned for next year. Majestic in summer, too, and our family can relax. Hopefully, Kondrat can forgive me for all my time away."

"I envy you. I slipped in a NYC weekend before returning to Atlanta."

"How's your boyfriend doing?"

Maya swiveled in the chair. She had a great working relationship with Stefan and considered him a friend, but hadn't unburdened herself of all the issues with Manolo. Simple answer was best.

"He's recovering his neurologic function."

"I'd love to meet him some day. When I'm back from holiday, I'll write up our outbreak for *Eurosurveillance*, one of the leading European journals. You can be a co-author if CDC allows you to stay involved during data analysis, write-up, and the long process of clearance and peer review."

His timing was perfect. "Sounds great—EIS Officers need to complete certain deliverables, including publication."

The line was quiet for a moment. "Last time I checked, Beatriz was territorial about her work, particularly after you compared lice-infested Norwegian refugees to Portuguese immigrants."

Maya spun one of her bear claw earrings. "I'm not the most

tactful person, and I've put my foot in it more lately. I'll contact her with my apologies and offer to help with analyses. Did she mention results on the tick that bit me?"

"It was *Ixodes ricinus*, castor bean tick. That species is linked with Lyme disease, but with the small number of cases there, I'm not sure you should take prophylactic antibiotics. Lizards are the reservoir host."

For an epidemiologist, the low risk was comforting. But as a person with anxiety disorder, Maya wished Beatriz had completed the lab work. They probably batched up ticks for periodic testing as part of scientific studies.

"I removed your tick last week. That's the average time for the erythema migrans rash to show up, although it could take a month. Is there someone who can look at the back of your neck?"

Maya flashed to Lila. "I got it covered. For the Moroccan study, do you think Zouhir will allow me to stay involved?"

"Not fully recovered from his own *Borrelia* infection, he was a bit temperamental about our discussing the two beheaded Scandinavian girls."

"Yeah, I hope I didn't jeopardize good relations with my stupid comments." She remembered the unsettled issue with the Jicarillas, and dropped her head to the desk. "Perhaps I should stay behind the computer and away from anything with people."

"Maya, don't overreact. These conflicts happen every day. You've seen footage of animals fighting. I think we're not far removed from all those basic instincts of us versus them. People can be prickly, just waiting for a bruised ego."

She pulled a small brush from her purse and adjusted her hair. He was right—she was too sensitive. Or maybe not sensitive enough to other people's feelings. First priority when back in Santa Fe—meet with Dr. Kim and restart the group therapy, plus discuss the problematic meds.

"Stefan, if you tire of data analysis, you should go into the diplomatic corps. You always find the right words to smooth things over."

Maya ditched another dinner offer from Enzo in favor of joining Lila. But in the parking lot, they were greeted by a flat tire on Lila's rental. "Oh well, we'll need to replace it. Good thing we don't have a reservation and didn't dress up. Ever done one of these?"

Maya shook her head. Lila opened the rear hatch and lifted the floor panel to pull out the lug wrench. She loosened the first lug nut. "Thank God they didn't overtighten these or we'd have to find someone with muscles like Enzo to help." She guided Maya through every step. "I'm returning this tomorrow so it will be safe to drive on the spare until then."

Looking at her blackened hands, Maya suggested cleanup in their hotel rooms, then they were filling their plates from the Chinese buffet within thirty minutes.

"Keegan says Enzo's a flirt," she confided to Lila. "Did your work with Enzo confirm that?"

"I'm out and proud so I doubt he'd be interested. With other women, he's full of bonhomie, although I didn't pay particular attention."

Maya took a bite of her eggroll. "Sometimes he comes across as patronizing."

"He's definitely the life of the party, and you're right, he has a healthy ego."

"Nancy's request to mentor him is a burden. She was invaluable to me during Manolo's illness, and I should pay her back. But riding herd on Enzo is challenging."

Lila shrugged. "She's expecting too much. He'll either succeed or fail on his own—not your responsibility." Then she cracked open the fortune cookie. "Nothing is impossible to a willing heart." She twirled the thin slip of paper through her fingers. "Unlike you, I didn't meet the love of my life during the first EIS year. However, I'm going to save this one—it might be good luck for year two. What does yours say?"

With trepidation, Maya opened it. "Your road to glory will be rocky, but fulfilling."

"Glory, huh?" Lila waved for the check and smiled in

encouragement. "With our teams doing their final presentations tomorrow morning, that sounds very auspicious."

. . .

Upon returning to the hotel, Lila verified no rash at the back of Maya's neck. Combined with the promising fortune, Maya fell asleep in an upbeat mood. The next day at the Emory Conference Center, she was impressed with her five teams and their summaries of the *Salmonella* from pig ear dog treats. Her own performance from the previous year paled in comparison.

Enzo was the most comfortable, modulating his voice like an accomplished thespian. For his part, Keegan was serious and quiet with no mistakes, but didn't wow the audience with his statistics. The team had made the smart decision for Enzo to wrap it all up.

Lila cornered Maya for lunch. "Embarrassing to admit, but I think they did better than our group last year."

"Must be the incredible training you provided since I was AWOL half the time."

Enzo raced up and pulled them into a three-way hug. "Ladies, that was fun."

"You did a fantastic job," Maya said with genuine enthusiasm. "A credit to your debate training."

"A few trophies clutter my mother's mantel."

Maya unwrapped from his embrace. "Your partner did well, too. He mentioned his family coming for the closing remarks, so I'm going to meet them."

She hurried back to her room and finished packing, then checked out. As she waited to store her luggage, Keegan came in the front door with a female entourage.

"Maya, are you leaving already? I want to introduce you to my family."

She shook all their hands. "It's wonderful to meet Keegan's rooting section. I'd love to join you for the final ceremony."

Both grandmothers, his mother, and two sisters filled a row along with Maya. She discovered that Keegan's father, career Army, had been killed in the first Iraq war. The lone male in the group was his younger brother, a recent high school graduate.

"We were overjoyed at Keegan's university graduations," his mother whispered before the session started. "Especially at Emory for his doctoral degree. No one else in our family attended college." Then she turned to his brother. "But Kevin's following in Keegan's footsteps at Morehouse in the fall."

The CDC Director closed out the month-long training with an exhortation to emulate the example of EIS founder Dr. Alex Langmuir with a life-long commitment to learning epidemiology in the field. "Like Dr. Langmuir, when competent persons are thrust into challenging circumstances with supportive supervision, excellent results are certain."

The EIS Director expanded on the remarks. "Dr. Phil Brachman was the second EIS Director after Dr. Langmuir. Dr. Brachman described Dr. Langmuir as visionary, clairvoyant, tenacious, well-prepared, scientifically honest, and optimistic. That's what I'm expecting from the EIS class of 2019 as you head off to your assignments. Be a good civil servant and work to benefit the public."

Keegan's family led the audience in a standing ovation, and Maya saw him duck his eyes at their exuberance. One of his grandmothers tugged on Maya's sleeve.

"The Centers for Disease Control and Prevention. Can you imagine our Keegan being part of all this?"

Maya smiled, sharing their excitement. "I'm psyched to have Keegan posted close to me."

"So far away," his mother said. "I wish he matched with an Atlanta assignment."

"We're encouraged to go somewhere new," Maya answered, "to expand our network and become a respected colleague, not just another student."

Keegan joined them. "Are you all worrying about Colorado, again? Maya lived there, and she recommends it highly."

She nodded. "For someone in vector-borne diseases, CDC's Ft.

Collins office is ideal. I can't wait to work with him—he's done you proud and is well-prepared to do an outstanding job."

Lila joined their celebratory group. "If we don't leave, Maya's going to miss her flight."

When they arrived at Hartsfield and Lila dropped her at the departures curb, Maya leaned in for a final hug. "I'm so happy Keegan's family could come. It reminds us of what we've accomplished already."

"I hope you remember that. Sometimes I think you're too hard on yourself. Power of positive thinking—everything will look up from here."

Wondering whether to believe Lila, Maya recalled her discussion with Faye. Things were on an upward trajectory only if her Enzo concerns weren't addressed with her re-assignment.

HEATING UP

Record heat, historic droughts, devastating wildfires—those are the obvious effects of climate change. But the spread of disease agents and vector species is an invisible threat.

The spirochete first discovered in Japan migrated worldwide, and continues to surprise in new places.

Ixodes is the hard-bodied superhero of ticks. Transmitter of Lyme disease, babesiosis, anaplasmosis, Powassan encephalitis, and relapsing fever.

How does one arachnid do it all? If the planet keeps warming, they'll be the only ones left behind.

THIRTY-ONE

A sparkling starscape with crisp clear air was the boost Maya needed to perk up. Also refreshing was Dave's tanned open face and wide grin at the Sunport arrivals curb as he tossed her bag into the back of the pickup. He glanced at her metal splint before pulling onto the highway. "Girl, you need to stay here in the Wild West to avoid encounters with unruly critters."

"I should wear a billboard—STUPID WITH CATS."

He tousled his wheat brown hair, streaked with blond highlights from summer work outside. "Meow—someone's a bit short-tempered."

"Yeah, my body clock reads almost two in the morning."

"We're happy you're staying the night. Everyone's looking forward to seeing you at breakfast."

She rolled down her window to revel in low humidity. "God, I miss this weather. You working the Bernalillo County Fair?"

"Yup. Tomorrow there's an awards dinner. I'm getting a plaque in thanks for my service, can you believe it?"

"Pay anyone off?" She made a fist and punched his bicep. "Seriously, I'm glad someone's recognizing their ornery cowboy. Wish I could be there but Dr. Grinwold's holding me to my promised return of August first."

"Well, you'll need some Zs before crossing that deadline off your to-do list."

. . . .

Golden rays of sun illuminated powder blue morning glories drooping outside the kitchen bay window. At the counter, Maya cut up strawberries to garnish the waffles Emilia poured onto the griddle. As the horses whinnied from the barn, Dave pushed out the back door clutching a cup of coffee.

"Are you guys going to the county fair?" Maya asked.

"The girls had baked goods in the competition on Saturday."

"He mentioned an award tonight."

Emilia moved the first waffle to a plate. "We're all excited. He partnered with the university on coloring books about animal care and vaccination. Take a couple from the sideboard."

Maya flipped past a page with a puppy wagging its tail as a vet injected a rabies vaccination. "Wish I could stay."

Turning back to the sink, Emilia rinsed the blueberries. "I do too. I'm worried. Twice last week when I got home from my evening shift at the restaurant, he had one too many. The girls were asleep, but still."

Maya rested a hand on her friend's broad back. "I'm so sorry. Is that aborted attempt to see his mother still weighing on him?"

"He tried letters and packages but they all came back."

Maya noted Emilia's dark lashes glistening with moisture. "Earlier this summer, I told him I was seeing a psychiatrist and taking meds for my issues. I recommended he talk to someone."

"Stubborn bastard. It's tearing me apart, and we keep fighting. He hasn't followed your advice, but we'll get through it." Emilia headed down the hall to wake up her daughters.

After Maya entertained the table with her tale of the exploding Portuguese cat, Dave dropped her at the Rail Runner train stop in Bernalillo. She anguished how to remind him about the benefits of counseling but hadn't resolved her own questions about managing stress without medication. Now was not the time before his big night.

"I'm proud of you. You deserve this award." She hugged him goodbye. "Ask Emilia to send photos."

In Santa Fe, she walked the block from the rail station to the health department, pulling her suitcase behind. First stop was Dr. Grinwold.

"Almost on time." He glanced at his watch. "Dr. Jaworski called and said they were grateful for your assistance with the summer course and overseas *Borrelia*. No one's worked on so many relapsing fever cases. Your pulling that off reflects well on how Nancy and I trained you."

Nodding, she plopped into his guest chair. "With my overseas requirement done, you can keep me for the remaining year."

"Nancy's excited about Enzo Russo starting Monday. I gather he did well at the course."

Dr. Grinwold wasn't in Enzo's supervision chain and Faye's warning made Maya reluctant to stir a hornet's nest. "He'll be a good contrast with me—he loves public speaking."

His short nails clicked against the coffee cup. "Thank goodness I can turn her down when she wants to borrow you. CDC Ft. Collins completed investigation of the new Dulce *Borrelia* infections. They want the publication to include all the cases."

"I'll check with Janey about her latest ones from the mine shaft."

"A good report will alert clinicians and motivate tick control."

She nodded. "With Lyme disease, people are more diligent about tick checks in New York."

"Speaking of diseases affected by climate change, we had a heat wave while you were gone. You worked with NYC on analyses of heat-related morbidity and mortality. Let's do that here."

Pleased that he remembered her Columbia internship, she rolled her bag down the hall, poking her head into Erika's office.

"You're turning into Robo-Vet." Erika lifted Maya's hand with the metal splint, then turned her other bare forearm to expose the reddened long welts. "Either that, or you've been in a war zone."

"Embarrassing for someone who grew up with cats. But enough about me. How are things on the home front?"

"Gifts in the mailbox stopped when we installed security cameras. Thanks for suggesting it. Bit of a lull here on disease reports, so you can recover from your eventful trip."

"Dr. Grinwold wants a report on deaths and illnesses from heat. Think broadly, including heart and other chronic impacts."

Erika woke up her computer screen with a mouse jiggle. "Look at you, already in tight with the boss. Where's this fire coming from?"

Maya blushed and shook her head. "Believe it or not, I had to supervise new EIS Officers. First time for everything. I can't say it was entirely comfortable."

Erika saluted. "Yes, ma'am, send me your marching orders, then join us tonight for dinner."

. . .

The offices were empty at six when Maya called an Uber to get home. After shifting her suitcase to her car, she drove to the faux adobe on the west side and parked behind Erika's minivan in the driveway.

Kyle somersaulted on the grass as Erika turned from the front door, key in hand. "We stopped at the park to burn off energy but it didn't work."

From the Prius back seat, Maya unzipped her bag. "Kyle, is there something in here with your name on it?"

"What, what, what?" He squealed with glee as she handed him the six-inch Norwegian troll doll with a blond braided beard, knitted green cap, and cheerful blue eyes.

Maya followed Kyle into the living room. "Many of the trolls were scary, but this guy was soft and cuddly."

Erika kicked off her flats as she rubbed a pale eyebrow. "Yeah, we had enough alarm this summer."

"Rolf working late at Tax and Rev?"

"No, Minneapolis. His grandfather has kidney disease and might need dialysis."

"That's rough. I've already lost three of my four grandparents, so I treasure my Tucson grandma."

A thump drew her gaze to the living room where Kyle bounced on and off the couch. "I'm hungry," he yelled.

From her purse, she pulled out a gleaming cheese slicer wrapped in tissue paper. "My gift for you—it's an ostehøvel from Lillehammer where they had the 1994 winter Olympics."

"Good timing." Erika opened the refrigerator door and reached into a drawer. "Before leaving, Rolf picked up Bergenost—a Norwegian-style butter cheese from New York."

The cheese and crackers lured Kyle to the table. Erika zapped leftover carrots and served them with a tuna pasta salad for the main part of the meal.

As she loaded the last plate into the dishwasher, Erika said, "Let's stretch our legs. We spend too much time hunched over computers."

While Maya and Erika strolled the paved street, Kyle darted from yard to yard, checking out any child with toys on the grass.

"Mom, can we look for lizards?"

Maya's feet thudded to a stop at the mention of lizards, host for the *Borrelia*-infected ticks in Portugal. "Erika, see any bull's-eye rash on my neck?"

"You're clear. You know we don't have evidence of local Lyme transmission."

"Got a tick bite in Portugal. A Moroccan colleague had neurologic complications when bitten on the job. Kyle, what kind of lizards are we looking for?"

Erika steered them to the rocky arroyo behind the homes. "He loves black-and-yellow striped whiptails."

"I've seen those," Maya said. "All females—the embryo develops from an unfertilized egg. No males needed."

"Now there's a thought."

"Rolf leaves for a few days and you forget you need him," Maya said with a chuckle.

"Speaking of needing men, what's up with yours?"

Maya adjusted her cap to block the sharp glare of the setting sun. "Making great progress on his recovery without me. But he's headed to Arizona soon, so we can get together on weekends."

"Mom, can I paint too?"

Kyle tugged on Erika as they approached the back gate.

"Oh God." Erika raced to the fence, Maya and Kyle trailing. S-L-U-T was sprayed in dripping blood-red letters.

Maya glanced at Kyle who didn't seem to understand, then threw her arms around Erika.

"Can't cry," Erika whispered. "Don't want Kyle to know anything's wrong."

"Would your backyard camera have captured who did it?"

"Won't see behind the fence."

"You need another camera." Maya took Kyle's hand. "I bet you can find a whiptail under one of those rocks." Turning back to Erika, she added, "Call la policía." She hoped using Spanish would keep Kyle from understanding.

He ran after a lizard but it raced for a hole in the embankment. Within ten minutes, Erika joined them at the arroyo's lip. "Not to worry—they reported an epidemic of gang tagging. Recommendation is to paint it over. I called Rolf and he'll take care of it when he gets home tomorrow."

"I assume you reminded the cops of the previous incidents with the mailbox and birthday party." Maya glanced at the time on her iPhone. "I can get to the hardware store before they close. Let me at least cover it up, then Rolf can do the whole fence again to make it look nice."

Erika embraced Maya. "Thanks, you're wonderful."

. . .

Maya tightened her robe after the quick shower. FaceTime chimed and she grabbed the iPhone with excitement. Both Miranda faces filled the screen. "Maya, we're happy you're home," Sebastian said while Manolo gave a thumbs up.

Her heart thumped in hope. "Are you back in Phoenix? When can I visit?"

Sebastian squeezed his son's shoulder and Manolo said, "Staying here."

She froze, skin chilled by the breeze drifting through the open window. "I don't understand."

"Another month," Sebastian said. "Things are going well with Mano's therapy and I'm handling Johnny's child care until pre-K starts."

With the unexpected news, she plastered on a weak smile, shunting aside thoughts about taking a larger role in Manolo's care. The NYC therapists were helping him—that was the important point.

"No problem, Dr. Grinwold has me busy as usual." She took a step to the window and cranked it closed. "Can Manolo and I talk for a minute?"

Alone on the screen, Manolo's smile widened—not as broad as when they first met the previous August, but appealing nonetheless.

"Mano, are we okay?"

"Por supuesto." *Of course.* A relaxed and easy answer, so maybe nothing to worry about.

She plugged the iPhone into the charger after their short chat. No one ever postponed their EIS training program for personal reasons, so another month focused on her career was advisable. She was grateful for her scheduled appointment with Dr. Kim, a chance to solve all her problems.

. . .

After Maya's update, Dr. Kim turned from her keyboard. "How long did you date Dr. Miranda before his infection?"

"About a month, but we worked together for several months before that."

"And you feel guilty about not arranging for him to live with you. Does that seem out of whack? You're a sensible scientist, and waited a long time before starting that type of relationship. Would you compromise your job, or make that level of commitment, if he didn't become ill?"

"Of course not, we agreed to take it slow. But his illness is our new reality, and he could use my help."

"Based on his decision to stay in NYC, perhaps he wants to stand on his own feet."

Maya nodded. "It's out of my hands, but there's another issue to discuss, something we disagreed about before."

Dr. Kim's severe dark eyebrows raised and Maya took it as a signal to go on. "I haven't had an orgasm since February. It's terribly frustrating for me and Manolo. Sometimes my brain feels cloudy, I'm forgetful, and speak more often without thinking."

"But you've had no suicidal thoughts and don't feel at risk with activities like driving."

"No, I'm never clinically depressed, only panicky. Klonopin reduces fear but also removes a filter—words go from my brain to my mouth more quickly. Diplomacy is a major job requirement and I'd prefer to manage my anxiety with your cognitive therapy group."

"You had a highly successful month—I don't want to see you lose ground."

Maya squirmed on the chair. "I'm not sure if my confidence is due to work accomplishments or the drug. My boss has me in the office and Manolo's out of town. This might be a good time to taper."

"As I said in June, we can try a different prescription."

Maya forced her courage to the point of announcing, "I found a benzo group on the internet, and they have very specific guidance about tapering."

"You'll follow online advice over a board-certified psychiatrist?" With spidery fingers, Dr. Kim slammed the laptop closed. "Good luck with that."

"Before my trip, you said I could just stop my small dose. So tapering won't be a problem."

"Benzo brain—that's what the zealots call it. Misplaced hysteria. You had that nasty reaction the last time you discontinued it. Let's try another med with fewer side effects."

When Maya shook her head, Dr. Kim stood up. "My next patient is probably in the waiting room. The slow taper schemes are no risk, if your body can adjust to being without medication. But schedule all the group sessions and weekly appointments to monitor your progress."

Back at home, Maya searched the scientific articles and support groups again. Benzo brain—alterations lasting years. It was challenging to sort out effects of the original condition from those associated with benzo long-term use, and easy to draw erroneous conclusions.

Klonopin had been helpful along with Ativan during her few crises. But she managed *Borrelia* in three countries, a snapped tendon, separation from Manolo, and a presumptuous trainee. August seemed a magical month in Santa Fe—spectacular weather and tourists in a good mood. Why not make it the month for more personal growth?

Tapering would help her body adjust to a reduced dosage. Mind made up, she placed online orders—mortar and pestle for grinding the tablet to a powder, graduated cylinder and distilled water for precise mixing into a measured liquid, and syringe for drawing up a dose to squirt in her morning juice. Using an Excel spreadsheet, she created a schedule with calculated daily reductions, starting off by one percent. A small amount—unlikely to trigger any major panic.

THIRTY-TWO

Reducing the Klonopin dose wasn't as easy as Maya hoped. Confusion and nightmares ruled August, but she got through it. Shakes, visions of leaping in front of buses—her body's sensitivity to such tiny reductions from the tapered dose was astonishing. But the mood instability reinforced her conviction that an abrupt reduction or switch in medication would be worse.

At the first meeting after Maya was clean, Dr. Kim showed skepticism about the tapering scheme. "What you described concerns me. Are you experiencing suicidal ideation?"

"Those were momentary images, and I'm feeling more stable. Your group therapy has really refined my coping skills."

Thinking back to sessions where she explored her challenges of working with difficult people, others had their own asshole stories. She hadn't seen Enzo since Atlanta, and Nancy was happy with his initial weeks of work in Phoenix.

To meet her training requirement of first authorship, Nancy and Janey offered Maya the lead on the Tucson *Borrelia turicatae* outbreak. Enzo complained it was his state. But Nancy assured him that during his two years in Arizona, he'd be in charge of many other outbreaks.

When Maya informed her attorney's office of her return, Mr. Zielinski scheduled an appointment. Her nerves flared at the potential reasons for him wanting to meet, but she understood that her fears were often worse than reality.

The secretary ushered her in.

"Good to see you again," he said, his bulk crammed into a wheelchair.

"You had crutches in May. Have you had a setback?"

"Spinal fusion didn't go as well as it should have." His eyes crinkled. "Think I should sue someone?"

Once again, she was impressed by his humor in terrible circumstances. Given his obvious wealth, she could have stereotyped him as a shark. But he'd been gracious and kind. His name was listed on ads for the upcoming Indian Market as one of the major sponsors.

She dropped to the leather couch and locked on his warm dark eyes, trying to reduce her breathing rate. "I emailed you about my letter to Mr. Otole's family."

"We need to hold onto it. I'm concerned about civil litigation."

"What do you mean?" As blood pounded in her head, her body yearned for Klonopin.

"Anyone can bring a civil complaint. After a Native American holding a cell phone was shot to death by law enforcement, the town reached a half-million dollar settlement with the family."

"But my situation isn't anything like that."

"Has the tribe or the Otoles contacted your health agencies?"

"The Jicarillas are bypassing the state health department on new *Borrelia* cases."

His fingers stroked dark hair gleaming in sunlight slanting through a multipane window. "If there's a lawsuit, I'll introduce your letter as evidence of your true sorrow. With the medical examiner concluding Mr. Otole was already deceased, we have evidence of your innocence. Don't worry, you're in my capable care."

Something about his masculine assurance in the face of disability, so similar to Manolo's, soothed her soul.

. . .

Maya's extra month without Manolo was filled with responses to disease reports, analyses of heat-associated illnesses, and edits of the *Borrelia* draft. After Rolf repainted his adobe back fence to blend in Maya's quick coverup, he installed another camera on the roofline angled to catch any more activity.

"Our home is like an armed camp," Erika joked to Maya. "But with no new problems, we only occasionally review footage. Can't let it take over our lives."

Stephanie invited Maya to Zozobra for the Friday night of Labor Day weekend. Maya had missed the iconic Santa Fe tradition last year, and it might be her only chance depending on her next job at the end of her training.

"Home by the end of the week," Manolo promised on their FaceTime call.

The grin on his face matched her level of joy. "Come to Santa Fe. Zozobra's a fifty-foot paper-stuffed statue. His bad deeds inflate his huge ego, and the citizens band together to roast him. We can banish all of last year's despair."

A few days later, Maya picked up the Mirandas at the Sunport. Her jaw dropped as Manolo walked out of security with hand crutches. Sebastian carried a small luggage bag.

"No wheelchair?" She kissed Manolo hello and hugged his father. "I can't believe you surprised me like this, but it's wonderful."

Manolo's hand cupped hers with the splint. "Your cat wounds?"

"I'm doing great with you here. Losing this annoying contraption soon—it's been challenging to type."

Driving north from Albuquerque, Maya focused on La Bajada's steep hill, tackling it for the first time since she stopped the Klonopin. Manolo in the front passenger seat inserted a few words into his father's narration of August activities with Johnny. Maya smiled shyly at Manolo's piercing gaze. He knew this road made her nervous, and the hand squeezing her leg confirmed his support.

At her apartment, Maya filled several water bottles. "Traffic will be insane, but if you have a placard, we can find handicapped parking near Fort Marcy."

Manolo opted for the bus. As throngs pushed into the park, Maya scanned the lawn for Erika's family. After texting Stephanie, she spotted her friends eating enchiladas on a plaid blanket. Greeting the group, Sebastian was his usual gregarious self, the way Manolo used to be.

Two rowdy teenagers palming beer cans stumbled close to Kyle and Erika leapt to her feet. "Watch out," she yelled, and stood guard until they left. "Family event—not supposed to have alcohol." Rolf drew Kyle closer and Erika collapsed to the blanket. "Sorry—irresponsible teens are a sore spot." But Maya admired her friend's mama-bear courage.

"Gloom collector here." Stephanie handed out slips of paper and pens. "When you're ready, I'll take them up to the box at Zozobra's base and we'll burn them for happier hopes."

Elated to share the celebration with Manolo, Maya could only think of one gloom—a civil lawsuit. She could guess what was written on the slip of paper Erika handed over.

Stephanie regaled Sebastian with Santa Fe stories and Manolo ate slowly as they relaxed with music and food. When Kyle returned with his parents from exploring the park, he showed off a small Zozobra marionette.

The wind picked up strength during the sunset and Zozobra's long white arms eerily streaked the sky. Mournful moans emanated from the loudspeakers. Kids twirled while blowing bubbles and everyone shouted, "Burn him, burn him." A red Fire Spirit dancer with a huge headdress gyrated at the base brandishing two flame torches. The angry moans grew louder, terrifying. Erika slipped plugs into Kyle's ears, and he cuddled in his dad's lap.

Most of the crowd was on its feet in a roaring frenzy. Maya remained on the blanket, warm and secure between Manolo's legs as his arms held her close, near Kyle and Rolf. Sebastian, Stephanie, and Erika surrounded them, a garrison against more reeling strangers.

A small flame erupted from the base, lit by the fire dancer. Zozobra's red lips and green eyes glowed as flames slipped upward and audience screams intensified.

"Heat's strong," Rolf shouted and hugged Kyle tighter, even though they were well back from the secure stage area. Waves of white fireworks cascaded in long lines down both sides as Zozobra disintegrated, with bursts of color painting the sky and mariachi music overpowering final lamentations. Then the festive recording switched to Queen and Bohemian Rhapsody.

Lights on utility poles sparked on and broke the magic spell as the crowd collected their belongings and headed to the gate. A brisk wind blew the acrid smell of fireworks and burning wood away as Rolf carried Kyle on his back and the women gathered supplies.

"You're not a real Santa Fean until you've done Zozobra," Maya said to Manolo and Sebastian on the bus. "Thanks for sharing it with me."

. . .

After their flights earlier in the day and the evening's revelry, the Mirandas were yawning back at Maya's apartment. She folded down the couch for Sebastian with towels set on the chair. In her room, Manolo snoozed naked in her bed, his clothes dropped on the floor. The sights and sounds of the festival lingered as she laid her head on the pillow, until sunlight dappled her eyelids.

She squirmed in tight to Manolo's back and reached an arm around to caress his chest and stomach, then detected his arousal. Before she had a chance to complete a first stroke, he spiraled in her arms and kissed her ear. "I'm stinky."

She nuzzled closer and said, "Earthy," but he stretched his legs for the floor and headed slowly for her bathroom. She darted after him and locked the door behind her. "We have a tradition of making love in the shower."

"Big fan of tradition."

After scrubbing every inch of each other's bodies, they luxuriated on the bed with limbs entwined. The only thought niggling in the back of her mind was her oral contraceptive. She discontinued its use at her February gynecology checkup, and they used condoms during their sexual reunion in the summer. But in the fuzziness of the Klonopin withdrawal, she forgot to verify need for additional protection during the days of restarting the pill.

None of that mattered when she was able to climax, body quivering and muffled moans. "Too long, way too long," she whispered as his breathing slowed and he adjusted his weight to her side. Then his fingers brought her over the precipice a second time. She'd been right—there was nothing wrong with her or their physical relationship. It was just a benzo side effect.

A half hour later, she helped him to a kitchen chair, then opened a note with their names on it. "Headed to Starbucks for coffee and paper. See you late morning."

She cradled Manolo's head to her chest. "I appreciate your dad leaving us alone. Maybe next time you can travel by yourself. Should I cook something?"

"Cereal is fine. What are we doing today?"

"You and your Dad are artistic." She thought back to the brief rest stop at the Georgia O'Keefe home on her way to Dulce. "Want to see the O'Keefe museum near the Plaza?"

She recalled with a jolt that she never told him about the accident on that trip. But it made no sense to bring it up now.

When he looked up after a spoonful of granola, he leaned over to kiss her cheek, and she giggled.

"I can't tell you how wonderful this feels." She returned his kiss with arms wrapped tight around his neck.

Her iPhone on the table rang, and she reluctantly let go of the embrace. "I'm on emergency call this weekend and there's a *Salmonella* outbreak in Cruces, so I have to check this." As she reached for the phone, **Mr. Zielinski** flashed on the screen.

"Attorney?" Manolo asked.

The authoritative middle-aged voice blared in her ear as she held the phone. "Maya, sorry to bother you on a Saturday, but I have some important information."

"Hang on a second." She touched Manolo's hand. "I need to take this." Out on the patio, she leaned against the back gate. As her anxiety ramped up, she grabbed for a lawn chair and let her knees buckle. "What is it?"

"I talked to Mr. Otole's family."

"You what?"

"Your instinct to reach out gnawed at me. A civil lawsuit would be unbearable, and you wanted to express sorrow at his death. But your letter was too much an admission of guilt. I sounded out their current state of mind, and conveyed your concerns without implicating you in any errors."

She pulled her knees close to her chest and wrapped one arm around them, the other clutching the phone. With the winds from last night ushering in a cold snap, she regretted wearing only shorts. "What did they say?"

"Although enraged initially, their attitude softened with the autopsy and lab reports. They no longer hold a grudge, just regret he didn't have a peaceful death, surrounded by family members. But he was doing what he loved, fishing the Rio Chama. They acknowledged he liked to get a buzz on."

Tears leaked from her eyes and she lifted her shirt to brush them. "Like a choir from heaven—you don't know what this means to me. Thank you for checking with them."

"It's good we can close out our business on such a positive note."

When she pushed open the kitchen door, Manolo's gaze dropped from her moistened eyes to the damp T-shirt. "What's wrong?"

Her first instinct was to say nothing, but Manolo knew Mr. Zielinski from the anthrax accusations. He might worry that FBI suspicion had raised its ugly head. "Nothing new from last year." She sat down next to him and held his hands. "I had a car accident and there were legal questions."

"When?"

She hesitated and glanced away. "In May." When she turned back, his face contorted. He was upset at the end of July when she spent a day visiting Faye. But he'd looked nothing like this.

"What happened?" The question was ground out between gritted teeth.

She owed him the truth. "As I drove home from my first *Borrelia* investigation, the weather was atrocious and I sideswiped a Jicarilla elder in the road." Her words stuck in the back of her throat. "But he died of exposure before my car hit him, and the sheriff didn't arrest me. Mr. Zielinski called with the good news that the family isn't considering civil charges."

Manolo pulled his hands away and wiped them over his face, muscles still rigid. "El Día de los Muertos."

Day after Halloween. "I broke off our relationship because you didn't tell me about your marriage and days-old divorce."

"Promised future honesty. Thought you did too."

They had pledged complete transparency, not wanting to repeat early missteps. Why didn't she tell him about the accident? She was mortified by what happened, and living in different states minimized their time together. But in truth, she had thought of him as 'less than' with his brain damage.

"You don't need me. Don't trust me to share your troubles." Frustration and shame creased his face.

"I was only trying to shield you from additional stress." She was proud of her ability to maneuver job and life on her own, but she'd gone too far, cutting him out because of his disability. "I'm sorry, this was different and I need you to forgive me, like I did for you last year."

The apology seemed inadequate and forced an answer he might not be ready to give. He struggled so hard to regain his life and her lack of faith likely reminded him of miles to go. Those insights flooded her mind too late. Sebastian strolled in and froze at the sight of their faces. Manolo stood up and ordered, "Call cab. Need time alone—figure us out."

Tears that began with joy at the attorney's news now burst into sobs, with no medication to dull the panic blow. Once again, another holiday weekend was cut short because one of them kept things too close to the vest. But this was worse, she reflected in a soggy heap on the couch. In the fall, the relationship was early, built on work camaraderie and attraction. Now, they were committed to each other, even if not married, and she hadn't realized the full extent of what such a bond required.

THIRTY-THREE

As Maya drove south from Santa Fe, aspens enameled an orange streak against the forest green of the Sangre de Cristo ski valley and splattered the Sandias when she arrived in Albuquerque. She'd admitted to Dave that her personal life was screwed up again. Like a magician, he was redirecting her focus with the meeting at his USDA office.

After settling on where to submit their paper about the New Mexico dogs and rodents, she suggested a writing plan. "We can start with the reason for the study in the introduction."

"The results drive everything. Let's finalize tables and graphs."

She made a mock bow. "You're first author, so I defer to you, fearless leader."

When Emilia texted that she was starting dinner, Maya followed him home to the ranch.

"You timed this overnight visit because you know how much I love the bosque in the fall," she said, stepping out of the Prius. She spun in a slow circle, arms opened wide to the golden groves of trees, a tint of mauve in the west as the sun dropped behind the adobe house.

As Dave stopped by the horse barn, Emilia came outside, black hair plaited in a single French braid interwoven with a white ribbon. Maya circled her, admiring the technique. "That's pretty. I tried one of those but my hair isn't long enough."

"Mi esposo has many talents." Emilia swung open the screen door. "Did he tell you our family is expanding?"

Maya dropped her eyes and grasped Emilia's hands. "Are you expecting?"

"So he didn't say anything—you guys are very work-obsessed." She directed Maya's gaze to the kitchen and a gangly kid, face covered in pimples. "This is Braxton Farnsworth, Dave's brother. Say hello to Dr. Maya Maguire, veterinary epidemiologist extraordinaire."

Braxton's hair and eyes were lighter than Dave's. As he extended his hand in slow motion, eyes to the floor, he more closely resembled Sam DeMille, Dave's deceased half-brother. The vision of Sam's bloody, hateful lips at his death twisted Maya's stomach.

"Braxton came to visit and we're hoping to make it permanent." Dave joined them and cuffed the kid's buzz cut. "Let's go help the girls with the ponies while the ladies make us dinner."

Emilia swatted her husband on the rear as they pushed out the door, then headed to the refrigerator. "Dave should have given you a heads up. He's helping groups that support lost boys, those kicked out of the sect. Braxton's only twelve but got uppity with the elders—smoking, drinking. So like Sam, he was expelled from church and home, another casualty of polygamy."

"Sam's diaries didn't mention a younger brother, other than Jacob being killed in that construction accident."

"Braxton was born after Sam's expulsion."

Maya tore up lettuce for the salad bowl. "This is a lot for you to take on, an almost teen son."

Emilia nodded. "We're not taking the responsibility lightly, and Dave's stepping up to the plate. He's haunted by family he can't connect with. In the week Braxton's been here, Dave hasn't had a drink or snuck a cigarette. He's trying to set a good example—a good loving one instead of scary God-fearing punishment."

"I feel guilty I didn't say more to him about his drinking issues." She'd mentioned therapy but never brought up Alcoholics Anonymous or similar programs.

After reducing the flame under the hamburger meat, Emilia gave Maya a quick embrace. "Nine months since Sam DeMille's death and you both are still dealing with it."

"Speaking of nine months," Maya said, "I thought you were pregnant."

Emilia's face darkened. "We tried. Dave adores the girls but also wanted a son, like a lot of guys. I've got uterine fibroids, so it might not be possible."

Maya carried the salad bowl to the table and lowered to one of the chairs. "I'm sorry to hear that. For a moment, I imagined you and me going through pregnancy together."

"Hermana, not you?"

Maya shrugged. "Only a few days late. I restarted the pill so we didn't use condoms. It shouldn't be a problem but you never know."

Emilia turned off the stove and joined Maya at the table. "Want to pick up a rapid test kit from the drugstore?"

Unused to such intimate talk with a friend, Maya blushed. "I'll check with my doctor."

"Dave said Manolo hasn't been in touch since Labor Day." Emilia flashed a supportive smile. "But that's only a couple of weeks. You guys exploded last fall when he admitted romancing you before his divorce. Just two major fights in a year—not bad odds."

"We'll work it out." Maya's forced thin smile conveyed more confidence than she felt.

"The offer stands." Emilia went to the back door and yelled to the corral. "Tacos are ready."

With the eager expression of a growing boy, Braxton plopped down at the table but Dave grabbed him by the collar. "We wash up before dinner, right, girls? Braxton, use this faucet so we can dive in sooner."

When the girls came back down the hall, they gathered around the long wooden table. Dave picked up Emilia's and Braxton's hands, and the others followed his example. Maya didn't remember them saying grace at other meals, but Dave proceeded.

"Bless us, Lord, for family, no matter how it's constituted." He winked at Maya and pushed the tub of sour cream toward her, knowing her favorite Mexican food topping. "Now let's dig in." Teresa and Lydia dueled over control of the shredded cheese.

After a dessert of churros, Maya accompanied Dave and Bo, their old Labrador retriever, on a final walk of the property. A series of short whistled hoots floated from the barn as they checked the horses. "Screech-owl's joined our tribe."

"I think you were also including me as family in your blessing. Thank you."

"Only a bit more than a year since we met, but feels like longer, doesn't it?"

She nodded and kicked at a clod of dirt. "A lot of time, not enough personal progress."

Dave stopped her pacing with a hand on her arm. "So what's he done this time? His lie of omission last year was corrected before you got close—only a venial sin, in my book. I gave you advice back then to forgive the guy. Need it again?"

She leaned on a pine split fence rail and gave up her soul to the almost full moon glistening over the northern foothills of the Sandias. "I'm the one who needs Confession. Not his fault, this time. It was mine."

. . .

Maya woke Tuesday morning at sunrise, feeling renewed by the nature sounds of the ranch. After piling her bedding on the washer, she opened the front screen door to let Bo lumber after the roosters and relieve himself. Newspaper from the front porch in hand, she headed to the kitchen and handed it to Dave.

He pulled a box of tea from the cupboard. "Help yourself." Then he sipped his coffee. "I know you won't drink this poison."

Emilia joined them and accepted Dave's second cup. "Maya, should we swing by the store as we discussed?"

"You still haven't clarified what's going on with Manolo." His curiosity could have been piqued by Emilia's question. But finding out whether she was pregnant wasn't a process she wanted to share despite mentioning it to Emilia. As a fan of wedded bliss, Dave might be overprotective and push marriage on Manolo.

"I need to finish mocking up data tables with your husband."

Emilia turned for the hall. "Okay, Maya, it was nice to see you. I'm dropping the girls at school, then enrolling Braxton."

Dave gave her a kiss. "If he gives you any trouble . . ."

After a long, collegial morning in Dave's office, Maya headed back north to beat the late afternoon rush hour. As she pulled into the health department parking lot, she felt a familiar twinge in her belly and headed for the restroom.

Menstrual cramps. No reason for concern, after all. A Chihuahua-sized part of her was sad—it would be incredible to have Manolo's child. But the Great Dane in the rest of her body was relieved for an irregular cycle as she adjusted back to the oral hormones. Not the time to be pregnant—high-pressured job, estranged from Manolo, and him still struggling for a functional life.

As she passed Dr. Grinwold's office, he called out. "How did the manuscript drafting go with Dr. Schwartz?" Scientific publication was one good connection with Dr. Grinwold. He was an expert and she didn't begrudge his passion for it.

"Extremely productive. We worked out an initial proposal for authorship, possible journals, a writing schedule, and a mockup of the results including the additional sampling Dave did while I was in Europe. Would you like to see it?"

"Not at the moment. Nancy asked us to call. There's something new with *Borrelia* in Arizona." He tapped out the number and clicked the desk phone to speaker. "Nancy, whatever it is, you don't need Maya now that you have Dr. Russo."

"Fred, several members of the Havasupai Tribe in the Grand Canyon are infected with *Borrelia*, according to the CDC lab. But a new type for us, *miyamotoi.*"

Enzo's assertive voice came on the line. "It's transmitted by hard-bodied ticks, not the ones Maya worked on in Dulce and Tucson. We suspect *Ixodes pacificus*, the western blacklegged tick, documented previously in Hualapai Mountain Park near the Havasupai reservation."

"When we were in Atlanta, Lila mentioned Northern California having that tick, plus the spirochete."

Enzo answered. "One California survey found cross-reactivity between the different types. Some human and tick samples also tested positive for *burgdorferi*."

Why did he always try to be the smartest guy in the room? But she damped her irritation and gave a calm response. "Dual infection with Lyme disease—that's complicated. How serious is the illness in the Supai cases?"

"One patient reported ten separate fever episodes this summer," Nancy said. "And his parents are both hospitalized at Phoenix Indian Medical Center with meningoencephalitis. Their brain and nerve damage manifested through gradual onset of trouble with walking and cognition."

"Any bad reactions to antibiotic treatment, like JHR?" Maya asked. "Dr. Duda found an unusual number of those in the Norwegian immigrants."

"You mentioned Manolo moving back to Phoenix," Nancy said. "If he's working at PIMC again, he could review their records."

Maya paused and flushed, grateful for a reason to interact with him. They always connected on a work level, even when their personal relationship got thorny. "I, ah, I'll call him tonight and find out if they can do that."

"Nancy, this is all very interesting," Dr. Grinwold said, "but I go back to my initial question. Why are you involving New Mexico?"

Nancy's voice changed in tone, almost begging. "I know I promised not to borrow Maya. Enzo is quite competent and could do the investigation alone in normal circumstances. We're thrilled to have him on board."

Enzo's voice broke in. "I can handle it."

Nancy's placating words continued. "But this requires a long hike down to where the *Borrelia* cases live. Supplies need to be transported by pack mules. The trip isn't without risk so a team is needed for backup. Maya's hiked in the Grand Canyon and is familiar with the hazards of death from falling or heat stroke."

"Perhaps someone from vector control?" Dr. Grinwold asked.

"Despite the brilliance and eagerness of my new EIS Officer,

I want Maya's expertise. No one's more accomplished in *Borrelia* fieldwork. She's collected hard and soft ticks plus animal specimens in multiple environments. The European CDC said her contributions were quite valuable."

The thought of hiking and working with Enzo was not appealing, and Maya searched for other solutions. "Given Lila's knowledge of *B. miyamotoi* in California, perhaps she'd be a reliable partner for Enzo."

"Lila headed up that *E. coli* gastroenteritis investigation from romaine lettuce last fall," Nancy answered. "California has some new cases, including kidney failure, so she's tied up."

Maya's relationship with Dr. Grinwold had been cordial since her return from Europe—no more grumpy boss dead set against sharing her. She glanced at her healed left baby finger, tendon repaired on its own after splinting, with only occasional residual twinges. Hardly an excuse for avoiding fieldwork.

Once again, she wondered about withholding her Enzo misgivings. He was flirtatious with her and some other female officers, while abrupt with his African American teammate during the training. Not sufficient reasons to refuse the assignment, but she tried one more time for an alternative, partly to test Enzo's flexibility. "CDC's new EIS Officer in their Ft. Collins office, Keegan Williams, was Enzo's partner this summer. I bet he'd love the opportunity and—"

"He knows less about this than me," Enzo interrupted with a barely muted growl.

"They sent Dr. Williams to Alaska for the month." Nancy's voice remained conciliatory. "He's sorting out if their Lyme cases are indigenous or imported. Ft. Collins suggested using Maya on this *miyamotoi* outbreak."

"Will my previous work with native nations be an issue?" She glanced at Dr. Grinwold, not wanting Enzo to hear about her association with the Jicarilla elder's death.

"The Hualapai Tribe mentioned no concerns when I provided your names as our possible team members," Nancy answered.

"Fred, are we okay with this? Maya's been in your office for six weeks. I'm sure a few days away won't break you."

He peered at Maya. "With a long stretch behind a computer, she deserves getting out again. I'll update the assignments for our daily consult calls here."

After they hung up, Maya slogged back to her office. She wished Dr. Grinwold had asked her opinion before acquiescing to her assistance on the new Arizona *Borrelia*. But his hardly hidden personal relationship with Nancy likely influenced his agreement. As soon as she dropped to the chair, her cell screen lit up. Enzo Russo.

THIRTY-FOUR

Enzo's voice was best-buddies-reuniting enthusiastic. "Maya, I hope you didn't take my comments as reluctance to work with you. You know how eager I am to prove myself."

No one with eyes or ears could miss that. A year earlier, she was in the same boat. "New EIS Officers have a lot of performance pressure."

"Will your mallet finger allow some fieldwork? Can you fly to Phoenix tonight?"

"I just drove sixty-five miles up from Albuquerque and I'm tired. How about I wrap things up at home tonight, then come tomorrow morning?"

"The drive to Hualapi Hilltop is four hours, followed by an eight mile hike to Supai Village. I reserved mules for late morning to carry duffel bags of our equipment and sleeping bags."

Maya released a deep sigh. "They don't have lodging?" Then she remembered the refreshing breezes, faint coyote calls, and brilliant Milky Way from her high school camping trip. There were some rewards for giving up a soft bed and shelter.

"The lodge is fully booked. This is prime time for hikers."

With a free hand, she gathered her laptop and daypack. "They should find someplace for us to stay if we're investigating their illnesses."

Not an appropriate diplomatic attitude to model for her new colleague. Perhaps it was the mixed emotions from the pregnancy unease and estrangement with Manolo. She regretted promising to contact him about patient antibiotic use, although work might compel him to talk again. Time to wrap up the call and hit the road. "Okay, I'll be there tonight. Do you have the equipment?"

"When you described all your *Borrelia* studies here and overseas, I paid attention. Everything's already loaded."

"I'm counting on you. I realize outbreak responses often need to be organized in a hurry, but you're not giving me time to think and provide input."

Once at home, she located a duffel bag in the closet and collected hiking boots, jeans, and a flannel shirt. Recalling the heat deeper in the canyon, she tossed in shorts, a T-shirt, and her swimsuit. The high school backpacking trip had revealed hidden canyons with places to cool off.

She placed a call to Erika. "Do you have a sleeping bag I can borrow? My next *Borrelia* investigation in Arizona requires camping, and the last time I did that, I had Manolo's."

"Not an outdoorswoman, I'm afraid. If you're headed to Arizona, can you use his?"

"Probably. I need to check with him anyways about these illnesses."

To avoid the highway jammed with Albuquerque residents speeding home from their state government jobs in Santa Fe, she planned to take the airport shuttle. Having a few moments with Erika would foster bravery for upcoming personal and work expectations.

"If it won't put you out with dinner plans, can you drop me by the shuttle? I'm too tired to drive to the Sunport."

"Sure. Rolf can do kid duty and you can tell me about this latest outbreak."

After hanging up, Maya called Sebastian—Manolo had been ignoring her calls.

"Maya, good to hear from you." He didn't sound angry although he'd be protective of his son's feelings. She assumed Manolo had shared the reason for their latest breakup.

"How are you both doing?" She kept her tone amiable.

"Hanging in, thanks. Mano is consulting with the Indian Health Service from home on his computer. He's threatening to boot me back to NYC."

So she wasn't the only one tangling with Manolo over his struggle for independence. Having more alone time without his father could renew their relationship. Then she regretted wishing Sebastian away. "Amazingly great news, but I'll miss you being close by."

"What's up with you, hija?"

"Another *Borrelia* outbreak in Arizona. Can I catch a few hours of sleep at your place and borrow one of Mano's sleeping bags? I could use his help with these latest patients."

"Hang on while I check—"

"Just a second," Maya interrupted. "We were in a rough place on Labor Day weekend and he's not picking up my calls. You probably heard it's my fault. I can find other options, if he's still too upset to talk."

Sebastian's voice had an edge of impatience. "Let me check with him and I'll call you back."

Through her living room window, Maya spotted Erika pulling up. If staying with them required discussion, Manolo could keep nursing his grievances. "Don't put yourself out." Maya hung up, immediately sorry for the snark.

On the short drive to the shuttle stop, Erika devoured the latest news. "I can't imagine Dave with a twelve-year-old half-brother."

"Family's everything to him. His mother refuses to connect, so this is a way to restart some kind of healing."

"And Manolo—hope you can fix that. I think you're reading too much into what Sebastian said." Erika braked by the curb as the bus began boarding.

The shuttle was almost to Corrales with the setting sun bathing the Sandias in a coral glow before her phone rang with the call from Sebastian. "Hija, you can stay the night. Send your flight info and I'll meet you at baggage claim."

"Thanks, Sebastian. Please try to forget how I spoke earlier— too much happening at once."

Within three hours, she retrieved her duffel from the Sky Harbor conveyor belt and texted Manolo's address to Enzo for the morning pickup. As she turned to look for her ride, Sebastian strolled up, arms spread wide for an affectionate fatherly embrace.

"No roller bag this time?" he asked.

"A pack mule's carrying my stuff into the Grand Canyon, so it needs to be soft-sided."

"You can update us at the apartment. Glad you can visit."

. . .

Manolo stood to greet her as she pushed in the front door, Sebastian behind with her bag over his shoulder. Manolo smiled and accepted her hug, but didn't linger for a kiss, so she didn't either.

"Tell me about your trip." Using both hands on the arm rests, he carefully lowered to the chair, while Maya sat on the couch with Sebastian.

Summarizing the investigation plans, her voice was deliberately friendly and professional. "Nancy would appreciate your checking with IHS for any adverse reactions after antibiotic treatment for *Borrelia* infections."

"Happy to help." His tone sounded genuine. Maybe it brought him as much joy to work together as she was feeling at this moment. They'd been a good medical detective team, even before it was personal.

"Would you like anything to eat?" Sebastian pushed his loose gray hair back from his forehead and headed for the kitchen.

"I'm drained. My colleague is picking me up at five tomorrow—I can let myself out."

"All right," Sebastian said. "I cleaned up my bedroom for you."

Her eyes skipped to Manolo, who didn't blink. So that's how it was going to be. "I hate to inconvenience you with my leaving so early."

Manolo remained silent and Sebastian responded. "You have a demanding trip. One night on the couch is not a problem for me. Have a good rest."

Maya headed to the guestroom, not bothering to shower. From behind the closed door, she could hear indistinct sounds of both men turning in. A single tear slipped out as she tossed and turned. Work leading to a personal reconnection had been too much to hope for. Exhaustion won out and she fell asleep.

. . .

Her iPhone alarm went off at 4:20 and she dragged herself into the bathroom. By 4:50, she waited inside the front door as Sebastian snored on the couch and Manolo came out to join her.

"It means so much to me that you're working with IHS again," she whispered.

His smile was crooked but proud. "Me, too."

A brisk early morning gust rippled her damp hair as she pulled the duffel to the porch. Manolo retrieved his sleeping bag from the floor and joined her. She was tempted to breach the psychological distance, but there was no time. "I think we'll be in the Canyon a couple of days. When we're done, can I stay here before flying home?"

"Of course."

After the jeep pulled up and the driver's door opened, Enzo loped up to the porch. "You must be Dr. Miranda." His shadowed height loomed over both of them as he extended his hand to Manolo.

"Dr. Russo, welcome to Arizona." Did the clipped words and tone reflect his residual neurologic damage or something else?

Maya handed Enzo her duffle, and Manolo pushed the sleeping bag into her arms.

"I hoped this would be us." His voice was soft, full of regret and recrimination.

Surprised, she spun away with moisture welling in her eyes, then opened the vehicle and chucked the bag in the back. As they pulled away from the curb, she glimpsed Manolo in the passenger side mirror, illuminated by a flickering porch light. No hand was raised in a goodbye wave. Like an octopus shifting colors to adapt to its environment, he offered no reliable indicators of his interest in reconciliation.

She rubbed her temples to clear the cobwebs and leave the personal behind. "So tell me about your first six weeks in the Grand Canyon State." Enzo obliged with lengthy observations about interesting consult cases, lamenting that Arizona didn't measure up to Boston, Harvard, and the east coast in general.

In less than two hours, the sun was up and they were at the outskirts of Prescott. Maya asked for a quick drink and restroom break at the Circle K. After glancing at the time on her iPhone, she persuaded him to let her take the wheel. Tight timetables were a panic trigger, and taking control to meet them was infinitely preferable to being a passive passenger with someone else's aggressive driving

"Come back here when you have a chance." She turned off the AC and rolled down her window. "Just the right elevation to avoid nasty southern Arizona heat, but not so high in altitude to get slammed by Flagstaff's big snowstorms."

Passing a store selling western gear, he joked, "Think I should become a cowboy?"

"The Victorian homes here might appeal to you and you like academic settings. Prescott College is held in high regard."

He adjusted his Boston scally cap. "Why do you think so many gays go into public health?"

Maya glared at him before refocusing on the two-lane highway. "What does that mean?"

"Well, Dr. Jaworski, Lila, and Keegan."

"Dr. Jaworski and Lila, yes. However, we know nothing about Keegan's personal life." His comment swelled her mental cache of concerns about his maturity. She paused to tap the brakes for a speeding truck to pass. "Public health is about making the world a better place through prevention. Conservative people work in it, but the workforce probably skews progressive."

As he dug into a pocket for his phone, his tone was ingratiating. "I'm just commenting."

She toyed with her sunglasses and slipped in one more glance, adopting an instructional attitude. "We're on the front lines so we need to work with everyone. I find personal interactions and public health communication are more challenging than the science."

"Hmm," he said as he flipped through his phone messages.

"Enzo, you're naturally talented on the communication front if you keep an open mind to the diverse groups we work with."

He swiveled to give her his full focus. "Why Dr. Maguire, you ain't going sweet on me?"

The inappropriate flirtation stunned her into silence. But the arduous trip ahead couldn't be avoided, and she needed to cut him some slack. After an hour and a half calmed by classical music, she pulled up to the Roadkill Café perched next to an imitation western town with a log-framed jail and a Wells Fargo Stage & Freight storefront. As they entered the restaurant, a buzzard with a fork loomed overhead, and inside, taxidermy cluttered the wooden walls.

"What have you gotten me into?" Enzo pointed to the 'Swirl of Squirrel' and 'Splatter Platter' on the menu.

"I had no idea this was here," she defended herself. "You said we have ten miles of hiking, so we better fill up."

They ordered breakfast burritos to go. As they waited for their food, Maya explored the small gift shop for tchotchkes. "Sure you don't want to pick up a souvenir?" She dangled a silver key chain with **Get Your Kicks on Route 66**.

Back at the jeep, she continued to drive. "For me, a cold breakfast is better than being a nervous passenger if you were eating and driving. And this way, you can appreciate the scenery."

With the sparsely-vegetated mounded hills, he looked in all directions and shrugged. "Not much to see—I don't understand the fuss about Route 66."

"Maybe it'll grow on you." At the small sign for Frazier Well and Supai, Maya took the right on Indian Road 18 and pulled off. "You take over. I need a glucose infusion."

First stop was a security checkpoint where they reviewed Enzo's permit and verified no weapons or alcohol. Then he carted out a duffle with their sampling equipment and dropped it in the area for lodge delivery. After stashing their two personal duffels in the spot marked campground, he shoved their sleeping bags and a tent into another bag for the campground pile.

She forced the dilemma of one tent from her mind to focus on immediate issues. The trip had been arranged in haste, and sudden changes made her head spin. "Sorry I didn't help with organization. Is this anything you've done before?"

"No, have you?"

"I've backpacked in the Grand Canyon. Thanks for arranging mules to carry our gear. For our tick collection, I assume we won't have access to dry ice, so we'll be tick dragging."

He led her back to the jeep. "Vector Control lent us these adjustable hiking poles. We can use them with the white fabric in the supplies. I tried them out last night in a field near my place."

"You have thought this through." Always compulsively prepared, her own lack of planning unsettled her stomach, or maybe it was the hastily consumed burrito. But it was too late to back out. She filled her daypack with three water bottles and snack bars. The mood among the other hikers was hyena-level hyped. The chirpy exchanges emphasized their good fortune to overnight in one of the natural wonders of the world.

His expression unusually tentative, Enzo locked the vehicle and racewalked to the cliff edge. "Off on our grand adventure. If we keep ahead of the mule train, it will be a lot less smelly. And thank God it's downhill."

THIRTY-FIVE

Rainfall risk was reduced in September and Maya was grateful. The trail which switchbacked steeply below the canyon wall was rough but not slick, and started out wide. On the mesa flat, they moved aside for the second mule train ascending the canyon.

After that, they had to watch their feet more closely for steaming scat. With a morning temperature in the high seventies, the odor was tolerable. Once in the lower canyon, the walls closed in, offering more opportunity for shade. Around one corner, a lone mare and foal munched the chamisa.

For four hours, Enzo bragged about his running regimen getting him in peak shape for this type of work. He effused about his Harvard professors and quizzed her about those at Columbia. He seemed genuinely interested in every detail of the overseas investigations and Stefan's position with the European CDC. "After EIS, international health could be a good fit for me."

Maya recalled Nancy hoping that he'd stay in Arizona permanently. At some point during his two-year training program, Nancy would have to work out plans for his future role, and it would be inappropriate for Maya to reveal them.

Between gulps of water and keeping up her end of the conversation, she stewed about the single tent. She could ask if there was a second one hidden in the collection supplies. Enzo had told her she only needed appropriate clothing and her personal sleeping bag. Why didn't she verify all this? But she'd been too anxious about seeing Manolo to double-check Enzo's plans.

They had miles to go and she didn't want to insert conflict before it was necessary. Surely someone in the village would offer a couch if she really needed it to avoid a shared tent. She focused on the hike and her surroundings for distraction. The canyon walls reddened, the sky seemed a deeper blue, and the vegetation thickened as the trail wove through the rocky arroyos. The striking scenery drove home her luck to be in the area. If traveling for recreation and not work, the hiking permits were hard to obtain and luggage transport by mule was costly.

Like a rainbow after a thunderstorm, the solution to the problem beamed. She had camped under the stars on the high school trip. Not a cloud on the horizon, and the autumn temperature was comfortable. No need to sleep close to Enzo.

. . .

By midafternoon, they crossed a plank bridge over the stream among towering trees with trembling golden leaves, and passed mules penned by leaning fences. One roamed the trail, unattended, and Enzo gave it a wide berth. After reaching the small village of Supai and checking in at the tourist office, they stopped to calorie load with hamburgers before locating their bags deposited by the descending mule train. Then they poked their heads into the post office to find out about the households with infected family members.

"September's been so hot." The clerk wiped his neck. "Ninety degrees already. Here's a map to help you locate the sick people. Also, some hikers stopped by here on their way back up. They spent a week in the campground and showed me rashes on their arms."

"We didn't hear about them," Enzo said. "Any other details?"

"Two men in their twenties, up from Tucson last week—can't remember any more. By the way, one of the Council Members wants you to stop by her home first, marked here."

"Thanks." Maya and Enzo laughed at their simultaneous single-word answer. "You're very helpful," Maya added.

With a village of only a couple hundred people, the map was easy to follow. The Council Member shut off the hose in her garden and guided them inside to her kitchen table. She scrubbed her leathered hands in the sink, then poured ice tea. "Please review your plans."

"On the properties that provide permission," Enzo said, "we'll drag for ticks and set out small stainless steel rodent traps. Tomorrow we'll check the traps and take specimens. That includes blood and ear biopsies."

Her wrinkled face pinched with concern.

"The traps will be hidden to avoid discovery by kids," he added, "and our suits will prevent infection when processing animals."

"What rodents will you catch?"

"Lots of deer mice," he answered, "although this would be the first study to find them with *Borrelia miyamotoi*, the spirochete infecting the people. The white-footed mouse is a reservoir for the organism in the northeast but apparently not found in the Grand Canyon."

"So why are you catching them?" The elder's expression remained skeptical.

Enzo rose to hover over them and leaned his fingers on the table. "Not much is known about which animal species maintain the disease in nature. This could be a real breakthrough if we identify a new one."

The Council Member stood up and took their tea glasses. "You may check for ticks but no moon suits for an experiment that might bring notoriety. No rodent trapping."

Enzo followed her to the kitchen sink. "But my boss—that was the agreement. We hauled all the equipment down to the canyon."

Maya stepped behind him and touched his arm. "Ma'am, we respect your concerns. Could we set the rodent traps after dark and remove them before dawn, to avoid any public alarm about the activity?"

"The Chairman approved your plan without full consensus from the Council." She put the rinsed glasses in the cupboard and slammed the door. "We need more time to consider the optics of rodent trapping."

"Checking pets won't require moon suits," Maya said. "Can we do that with the families' permission? Dogs may be a good indicator species, providing important information to the families."

The elder escorted them to the door. "If they agree."

Outside on the road, Enzo let loose with a barrage of profanity. "Nancy's going to have my head. How can I fail my first big assignment?"

"She's not that way—keeping good tribal relations is more important."

They passed the church nestled close to the canyon wall, and Maya stopped to admire it. She wanted to snap a photo but it wasn't allowed. The structure had walls of uneven stones, a red and black painted door with a cross in the middle, crowned by a curved gray metal roof and swamp box. Attached to the left was a rock wall bell tower topped with a white wooden cross. As a lapsed Catholic, she was drawn toward a brief time for reverence and reflection, but the door was locked.

A few feet away, they ascended a small set of wooden steps leading to the grass-green home with a sloping dark roof. The young couple who answered the door reported fevers, headaches and rashes earlier in the month, and out of concern for their young daughter, sought medical attention. They gave permission for checking their dog penned behind the home, and Maya drew blood from the jugular vein as the wife held the squirming midsized mutt's neck.

"We're more worried about the uranium mine up canyon. That could pollute our water supply. Can you do anything about that?"

Enzo promised to find out more as Maya placed the blood tube in her pack. "This needs refrigeration until spun down for serum to check antibodies."

"I really did some planning," he answered in a huff. "The Supai Health Station's laboratory promised to process any blood samples and transport them by helicopter to the state laboratory."

After they dropped off the specimen, a middle-aged woman met them at the door of the next home near the helicopter landing strip. "My husband's with his parents at the Phoenix Indian Medical Center." Maya took notes as Enzo asked questions and the daughter-in-law unloaded her anguish for her family's recovery.

The final yellow-planked home housed a young woman alone with an infant. Her husband, shopping in Seligman, was another patient with intermittent fevers. They obtained final approvals for sampling.

Back at their duffel next to the two-story lodge, Enzo forced the rodent traps aside and cursed again. A teenage girl stopped and stared, then moved on.

"Enzo, cool your jets." Maya pulled out the table-sized white fabric. "Fieldwork often requires improvisation. Let's do the tick dragging."

After inserting her hiking staff into the folded pouch on one end, she ordered, "Grab forceps and those small plastic containers." At the first home, she yanked her white socks over her jeans. "You'll avoid ticks crawling up your legs if you do this."

With a hand hooked around the white twine attached to the fabric end with the pole, she began a systematic sweep dragging the ground. After each pass, she turned the fabric over and Enzo picked off ticks for the containers in his daypack.

"Can you tell what kind they are?" He held up one clear vial to the light.

"A few are engorged with blood. We'll need a microscope to verify."

"Besides the *Ixodes* we suspect for relapsing fever, we could find the Brown Dog tick or the Rocky Mountain wood tick, linked to Rocky Mountain Spotted Fever."

"Glad you're considering all the possibilities, Dr. Russo."

For the next pass, they reversed roles. After collecting behind each of the three homes, they went back to their equipment bag, tailed by a small group of nosy kids. Maya took out one of the vials and showed the tick to them. "If you ever see one of these on yourself or your pets, let your family or another adult know. Removing it quickly can keep you from getting sick."

"You guys head on home." Enzo shooed the gang away. "Sunset's around six-thirty, so we better grab something to eat and head down the trail to the campsite." At the café, they chose chicken sandwiches for their packs. Back to a lighter mood, he offered to carry the tick dragger and handed her his walking pole for the remaining two-mile hike.

Shadows deepened as they rounded a corner and Havasu Falls dropped off to their right. It was tall and delicate, white spray cascading into a brilliant turquoise pond below.

"Color's from dissolved calcium carbonate and magnesium," Enzo said.

"You read up. I'd give anything to join those swimmers right now."

"We can probably squeeze in time tomorrow."

"Only if we finish our work first," she reminded him.

Upon reaching the campground, they dropped their bags in the dirt under a cottonwood intermixing a few gold leaves with the green. All the spots with picnic tables were taken, but they could do without.

"Too bad we don't know where that Tucson couple stayed." She glanced up at the purpling sky through the trees. "Let's wait for more tick dragging until the morning."

Dropping to a flat rock extended over the bubbly blue creek, they pulled out water and sandwiches. "You mentioned never doing a hike like this before. How's that runner's body of yours holding up, Dr. Russo?"

"Not a care in the world. How about you?"

"Hiking down is hard on the knees, but I'm fine." She pressed on the muscles of her lower back, tight from hours carrying the daypack.

With the sky barely bright enough to climb back to the campsite, they retrieved flashlights and rummaged through the duffel with the sleeping bags. It was time to get the discussion over. "Do we have only one tent?"

"Minimizing weight—it's big enough for two."

She pulled off her ponytail tie and shook out her hair. "Sorry, not something I'm comfortable with." Then she unrolled Manolo's sleeping bag onto its ground cloth.

Enzo lifted his eyebrows in surprise. "I hope at this point we're good friends and colleagues."

She flattened her bag, removing a few rocks underneath. "I slept without a tent in the Grand Canyon during high school. At the café, they said it's going down to sixty-five tonight. Perfect sleeping weather, plus I love the stars."

His lean face transformed with childish petulance. "I don't know why you're so stubborn. I'm not an experienced camper but I could let you have the tent by yourself." He didn't look eager for that outcome.

"No, Enzo, I enjoy the fresh air. Maybe I'll hear an owl. Want any help assembling it?"

He turned his back. "I practiced that last night."

She formed her clothes stuff sack into a pillow and crawled into her bag, flashlight at her side.

"We were up early," she told him while he finished erecting the tent. "See you tomorrow."

After Enzo's movements settled down and the breeze picked up, she rubbed her hands over bare arms draped on the sleeping bag. Her fingers bumped something firm on her elbow—probably a scratch from the vegetation except it felt unusually smooth. She grabbed the flashlight and twisted her arm for a clear view. A scab?

If camping with anyone else, she might have called for help. But not Enzo—her feelings and impression of him were too scattered. Although the memory was several months old, she had no desire to repeat the sensation of his hands on her skin as he removed bee stingers.

She scoured her pack for tweezers. Then, unable to hold the flashlight, she gently pulled at the small protrusion by feel. When the tugging released, she picked up the light and shone it on the tweezers held close to her eyes. In the faint beam, the tiny legs struggled for purchase, body fully engorged with her blood. Must have been feeding for hours. She dropped the torch again to grab a vial.

After Stefan removed a tick from her hairline in Portugal, she should have detected this one sooner. And Zouhir became deathly ill from his tick bite in Morocco. Not surprising to be at risk after so much field time searching for ticks. Dying for a methodical check, she stroked her fingers over all accessible skin. Despite the brilliance of the Milky Way, the flashlight was inadequate. Every tiny mole set off a mini-alarm. A more thorough personal inspection could wait until dawn. Requesting Enzo's help was not an option.

THIRTY-SIX

The bag was too warm, but leaving it unzipped for more ticks or a larger critter was too big a bogeyman. The pinch of every sharp rock conjured chelicerae, the tick's mouth parts that cut through the host's skin. Her eyes popped open to interrupt the unwelcome sensation of creepy crawlies. She hadn't seen such a blanket of stars since her pre-Christmas car camp with Manolo at Chaco Canyon. The faint haze from the warm afternoon didn't block the billion bright holes burning through the fabric of dark space.

Enzo shifted around in his tent and the sound of laughter glided over from other campsites. Leaves rustling in the gentle breeze provided a soothing backdrop. Before Manolo's hospitalization, they planned another camping trip. Her heart ached with his absence. For most of the day, the work load and stunning area that few ever experienced had blocked out her personal problems.

His body might never again tolerate long hikes like this one. Thoughts drifted to Gabby Giffords, the Tucson congresswoman who made a partial recovery after a terrorist's gunshot. Her brain injury prevented resumption of duties in Washington. Manolo was making progress but his neurologic impairment might forever limit his speech and physical abilities. Could his brain process the clinical analyses required for his job?

When he abruptly fled Santa Fe on Labor Day weekend, she was sure his rejection would reverse itself. She'd hidden the horrible car accident, but in the end, it had no long-term consequences on her life beyond increased vehicle-associated anxiety. So why was he so upset at being out of the loop? She imagined him hiding something awful—it would diminish their relationship, make it feel shallow. But these were special circumstances, and maybe that bothered him the most. She had treated him differently because of his illness.

She needed to talk all this over with him, apologize, and encourage him to vent his feelings. Clearly it wasn't something minor because of the way he acted at his apartment, shutting her out of his bedroom. Despite the late hour, she pulled out her iPhone, tempted to call. No signal. Patience, that's what was called for. With the disrupted rodent sampling, Enzo said they could finish tomorrow and hike out on Saturday. Time enough to formulate a strategy for winning back Manolo.

. . .

At sunrise, she awoke to the cooOO-oo-oo-oo of the mourning doves. During the winter camping with Manolo, few bird sounds had greeted them. Dove coos were at the top of her list for comforting notes, so she lay still for a few more minutes as the light slowly brightened the golden leaves. Then she headed to the small campground bathroom with composting toilets, eager for a better tick check, as much as she could accomplish on her own. When she returned, Enzo crawled out, wearing white boxer shorts and no shirt.

"Oppressive in the tent last night. Maybe you had the right idea."

"Enzo, get some clothes on, I'm hungry."

In response, he dropped to her sleeping bag and performed twenty-five rapid pushups. "Let me use the facilities and then we'll head to Supai Village."

After he dressed and they hiked the two miles back, Maya rummaged for supplies in the duffel at the post office.

"I need to visit that dog where we got the blood sample." She held up the vial with the nighttime tick. "Found this on my elbow and want to make sure I didn't miss any on the puppy."

"Whoa, maybe we should check each other over." His reaction was no surprise.

"I think we can manage by ourselves, thanks. Let's get back to the first house."

With the help of the owner, Maya thoroughly combed her fingers through the animal's fur, finding a new engorged tick in one ear which she deposited in Enzo's container. Hot air radiated from the sunlit canyon walls to her skin. Her head spun and her stomach rumbled.

She yanked on her ponytail to make it tighter, elevating the hair off her neck. "We should have eaten first." They purchased bean burritos and perched on a rock.

"Without rodent trapping, our workload's tremendously lightened," she said. "Wish we could do more. Keegan mentioned discussions with North Carolina State University about urine tests with more sensitivity in picking up infection."

"Now, who's getting ahead of herself?" Enzo snickered. "Human specimens aren't part of the protocol. Sounds like the tribal leaders are at odds about the study, and we can't spring something new on them."

"I know, just trying to make lemonade out of lemons."

"After we tick drag the campground, I insist we carve out some downtime at the waterfalls. Did you bring a swimsuit?"

Every inch grimy from two days of sweaty work, a quick dip would be hard to pass up, even if the thought of less clothing around him was discomfiting. "That's what people come for—I'm prepared."

He leapt up and reached down to help her stand. "Let's get this show on the road."

. . .

Because of the possible campground cases, they spent hours tick dragging the campsites. Almost everyone had headed for the falls or up the trail for a long climb out of the canyon. But a few laggards eating breakfast asked about their work, and Maya provided fact sheets from the health department about preventing and recognizing tick-borne diseases.

In the early afternoon, Enzo mused about heading to the village for lunch. Maya shook her head. "We've hiked back and forth so many times, always passing Havasu Falls—I'm dying to jump into it. I'll be fine with an energy bar."

She took her red suit to the restroom and changed, adding tan shorts and a paisley T-shirt. At the campsite, she found him almost naked, wearing only black swim briefs. A dip into cold water washing away two days of muck would overpower any awkwardness. As they approached the falls, the helicopter flew over carrying locals, tourists, and their single dog serologic specimen up to the canyon rim. With a strenuous hike on the docket for the next day, the metal hardware in her leg lobbied for absorbing the exorbitant flight cost. But the refreshing pools would invigorate her aching muscles.

After discarding her outer clothes and boots, she let out an involuntary yip when exposing her body to the azure icy pool. Enzo raced ahead and jumped in, barely pausing to remove his footwear. As he swam with a rapid crawl to the falls, she turned on her side to join him at a more leisurely pace. Each stroke changed the geometric puzzle view of magnificent red rock walls projecting between blue sky and water. Approaching the base of the hundred-foot drop of water, she stayed back while Enzo stroked through a narrow gap behind the falls.

"Whew, all that power, what a rush." He shook his head rapidly to spray the water from his thick brown hair like a Chesapeake Bay retriever. "You should try it."

"No thanks, I'm in heaven already."

"I want to check out Mooney Falls—twice as tall as this one."

Maya swam to the flat area where she entered, Enzo performing a perfect breaststroke behind. Climbing out to the warm rock next to her clothes, she sprawled in the sun. "I'll pass on that other waterfall. You have to go through caves and down slippery steps clinging to chains."

He gave her one last splash from the pool before leaping out to slip on his thick wool socks and boots. "Chicken. See you tonight."

The quiet sounds of nature, interrupted by occasional shouts from other revelers, lulled her into total relaxation. She appreciated the time alone after Enzo headed off. No matter how hard she tried, she couldn't get a handle on him. He had brilliance, enthusiasm, and compelling confidence. On the other hand, he was egocentric and impatient, with hints of prejudice toward people who were different.

But no one was all positive or negative. Her own contradictions were frustrating as hell. Who was she to judge another imperfect human? As the sun lowered behind a cliff face and shadows moved across her rock, she slipped on her clothes and boots. Not looking forward to another hike to Supai for dinner, she blessed her good luck when discovering a fry bread hut along the trail.

From an outcrop near the campground, she was dangling her legs above the creek when Enzo jogged back, sweat glistening on the wide expanse of bronzed skin. She maintained her focus on his face to avoid the revealing swim briefs.

"Hey, we've only been separated a few hours." He pointed to her arm as he lowered himself next to her. "Do you tan that fast?"

"Dozed off next to the falls—Chinese don't burn easily."

He twisted his torso to peer behind his shoulder. "A lot of Italians don't burn either, and the sun is less intense this time of year."

"Was Mooney Falls worth the effort?"

"Hell yeah, you should have come. I would have talked you down the scary parts."

Maya was reminded of Manolo easing her descent on the steep Bandelier National Monument ladders. But camper descriptions of the Mooney Falls trail increased the fear factor. Unwilling to appear vulnerable with Enzo, her decision to snooze at Havasu Falls brought no regrets.

She noticed him eyeing the food remnants clumped in a greasy paper towel on her daypack. "Have you ever tried fry bread? Some call it pillows of doughy happiness. A small stand's selling it along the trail. I'm not sure when they close so you better go."

"I'll do that now." He pushed himself up and leaned against the cottonwood. "We should hit the trail at six tomorrow to leave our gear for the mule train before seven."

She lifted her legs from the rock edge. As she reached down before standing, he hoisted her up by her armpits. She jerked away from his damp hands, almost tripping over a tree root and catapulting into the creek. Had it been her imagination that his fingertips lingered for a moment on the sides of her breasts?

"Get out of here," she chided, hoping to break the tension. "I don't want to be responsible for a starving Harvard doc."

He patted his exposed six-pack midsection. "Don't worry, nobody comes between this guy and a meal. I'll work it off tomorrow."

"Okay, I'm turning in early. My phone alarm is set at 5:30 to help you break down the tent."

"Suit yourself. Hope it won't be as hot as last night."

. . .

She dozed in spurts, fretting about the long climb. But she had managed the hike out of the Grand Canyon on the school trip. At three thousand feet of ascent in only six miles, that had been much steeper than the two thousand feet and ten miles ahead of them. When the moonlight filtered through the cottonwoods, she tugged out her phone and checked the time. Midnight. She adjusted her stuff-sack pillow and turned over onto her stomach.

Something brushed her ear and she awoke with a start, memories flooding back of the wild burros sniffing her face on that earlier trip. Then a heavy weight compressed her spine and rib cage. She gasped for breath and thrashed to dislodge the frightening burden.

"What the f—"

A hand muffled her mouth. She was trapped in her sleeping bag and couldn't move.

"Maya, it's me. Settle down."

She recognized Enzo's voice, close to her ear.

"Don't wake up the campground. This is our last night—come join me in the tent."

His fingers around her lips started to relax.

"Get off me and we'll discuss it." Her words seethed at whisper level. What the hell was he thinking? When he slipped to her side, she rotated toward him. His eyes glinted in the moonlight. She tried to speak but his hand again covered her mouth.

"We're great together. You're on the outs with Dr. Miranda— that was obvious the other morning. We're not working at the same health department, so none of those stupid prohibitions."

His hands moved to unzip her sleeping bag. "All cleaned up— let's enjoy ourselves before hiking back to the real world."

She clutched for his hand to stop him. "This isn't going to happen. It doesn't matter what's going on with Manolo—I'm not available to you."

"Your hot body in that red swimsuit sent a different message." Grabbing the back of her neck, he leaned in for a deep kiss, his mouth tasting of mint toothpaste. She squirmed and pushed at his shoulders, her body still trapped in the bag. When her short fingernails dug into his cheek, he came up for air and she wiped her lips.

"Enzo, I said no. Go back to your tent before this gets a hell of a lot worse."

He rolled away and crawled to his knees, then reached out to stroke her hair. "Your loss." His tone was casual and she was relieved he didn't lose his temper.

With the zip of the tent confirming she was again alone, she punched the makeshift pillow, frustrated at feeling any gratitude that he accepted her rejection. She drank water to dilute his taste, then checked the time on her phone. Four o'clock and no cell coverage. With less than two hours until they had to pack, additional sleep might not be possible.

She took several more deep breaths. There was no real danger— lots of other campers were in earshot if she yelled loud enough. It was probably just his stupid ego, thinking he was God's gift to women. Had anyone ever turned him down?

After resuming a facedown position on her stomach, she pulled the end of the clothes bag over her head, trying to shut out the world. But it didn't work. Her hamster brain rewound Enzo's advance, over and over, searching for a quicker, less invasive ending.

THIRTY-SEVEN

They packed up without speaking as the predawn sky lightened. Sounds of other groups doing the same floated over. After dropping the personal duffels at the campground pickup site for the ascending pack mule train, they hit the trail. At the village, staff had moved their sampling equipment bag to the pile for lodge pickup. So they purchased pan dulce and headed out as sunlight sparkled off the steep canyon walls, not yet warming the interior.

Within two hours, Maya paused to rest on a boulder and gulped her water, turning tepid with the heat on her daypack.

"How long for the silent treatment?" Enzo asked.

The water bottle smacked the rock face as she dropped it and faced him. "Can you guess why I'm upset? That stunt you pulled last night was borderline assault. I gave no signal that I wanted you to come onto me."

He took a swig from his own water supply. "My interpretation is different. I took you to a fancy dinner in Atlanta and rescued you from killer bees. You've gone out of your way to welcome me to the EIS Program. No one could have been nicer."

She retrieved the bottle to verify it was intact. None of the precious drops had spilled. "Nancy asked me to help you transition to the Southwest. My being professionally friendly during the past few months was not an invitation to anything more, let alone forcing a kiss. Let's get the hell out of this canyon."

When they finally topped the mesa, Maya checked her phone. One o'clock, six hours. Fast pace, strong motivation. The mule train had passed them just before the last switchbacks, and their bags were in a pile to be sorted through. After they loaded the back of the jeep, Maya held out her hand for the keys. "I'm driving."

His right hand twirled the braided leather key chain and the other stroked his left cheek with the scratches. Darkening of his chin and upper lip indicated he hadn't shaved, so without access to a real bathroom, he likely didn't get a good look. Her stomach tightened anticipating his reaction once he did.

Then he gave her an oblique smile and handed the keys over. Once in the passenger seat, he fell asleep, periodic snores emitting from his full open lips. A flutter of pride swept from her heart to her head as she glanced again at the marks on his face from her nails. What kind of explanation would he give in the office for them? Probably something about diligent tick dragging through the underbrush.

All of her supervisors' admonitions flooded back. To accomplish the mission, get along with difficult people no matter what it cost. But those instructions didn't include what Enzo had done. Was it serious enough to report, putting a stain on his career? Or only miscommunication, as he implied.

Nancy's request to mentor him had always seemed doomed in advance. She hoped her initial prejudice against him didn't have any impact on the results. Maybe he sensed her antipathy and relished a challenge.

. . .

After a brief rest stop in Prescott, she switched places with Enzo and kept her eyes closed as they approached Phoenix. If she couldn't see other vehicles, they couldn't elevate her heart rate any more than it was already pounding from outrage over Enzo and trepidation about Manolo.

She had texted from Prescott that she would join the Mirandas for dinner if staying another night was okay. Manolo answered **Yes.** Blunt and to the point, similar to his minimal communications in recent weeks. Still likely upset with her.

As Enzo pulled into the small subdivision of apartments, the setting sun dusted the top of South Mountain Park where Maya watched the sunset with Manolo in mid-May, the evening they made love for the first time since New Year's. Four months later, and their relationship had gone backward, despite his neurologic progress.

After bringing her bag to the doorstep, Enzo floundered, words finally contrite. "Maya, I regret upsetting you. I'll wait here until you're sure they're home."

Based in neighboring states, working together was unavoidable but she wasn't ready to accept his apology. "Manolo is here. You can go."

She rang the bell and Enzo headed to the state vehicle. Sebastian opened the door and she didn't look back.

Local TV news with the latest shooting didn't help her mindset. Manolo, reclining on the couch, picked up the remote and shut the TV off, then rose to hug her. "Glad you made it back okay."

"Thanks, trip was a mixed bag." Glancing down, she was embarrassed by the canyon dust and dabs of mule manure on her boots and lower legs beneath the shorts cuff. The fragrant pinewood scent from the rosemary Sebastian chopped at the counter didn't counteract her own odor. "Mind if I use your shower?"

Manolo's eyes tracked her head to toe. Did her squirrely edginess from Enzo show through? "Be my guest."

"We planned salmon, parmesan couscous, olive-oil sautéed broccoli, and salad," Sebastian said. "All right with you?"

"Sounds heavenly. Couldn't beat the spectacular setting, but civilization is definitely welcome. I never had a chance for a full shower or sit-down meal."

Once in the bathroom, she luxuriated in the warm spray. The cool temperature of the waterfall had been refreshing, but soap scrubbed away grime and stupor of interrupted slumber. Footsteps filtered under the door jamb although no one stopped or entered. The door was unlocked just in case. Making love with Manolo would help counteract Enzo's invasion, but he didn't join her.

After slipping on a casual yellow smock and toweling her hair, she dug through the smallest pocket on her daypack for the bear claw earrings Manolo gave her on Halloween.

In the kitchen, he handed her the salad bowls and removed the salmon from the countertop oven. Then he sliced it in three pieces and put it on plates. She hadn't seen him prepare food in months. Another step toward independence.

Dinner discussion was one-sided about the magnificent canyon. After Sebastian cleaned up the dishes, he brought bedding and set it on the arm chair, then headed down the hall to the guest bedroom. It was clear they determined she'd sleep in the living room—a painful flush prickled her skin to imagine that conversation. But with the chair piled high, Manolo joined her on the couch. She curled her legs up underneath and rested her arm across the back.

"One patient with JHR." He broke the silence with the carefully spaced words.

Gratified they were communicating for work, she smiled in delight, although not at the medical news. "Did you tell Nancy? Are the clinical signs like my pregnant lady in Albuquerque?"

"Yes, but no death."

Her fingers stretched to trace a faint scar on his forearm. "Thank you, I hope they're on the road to recovery." She yearned to initiate foreplay, but feared his response.

He reached up to stop her hand's movement. "We are good colleagues."

His skin was warm and she shifted closer. "Manolo, we've had no time to talk since you left New Mexico three weeks ago. I should have told you about my car accident. It may seem I didn't trust you to handle the information, or to be my rock."

He touched his fingers to her lips. Her mouth opened with a sharp inhale as erotic lightning shot through her limbs. But with her reaction, his hand shifted to the pillow.

"Last fall, you wanted slow." His dark eyes darted away, then refocused on her own. "I need to be equal partner. No pity sex."

She was about to justify her late spring omission—not wanting to impede his recovery with the weight of her accident and legal jeopardy when his cognitive functions were limited—but his final words shocked her into numb silence. He was so wrong—she ached to make love again, free of the Klonopin side effects, and pity had nothing to do with it.

When he stood and turned for the hall, she followed and hugged his back. Resting her cheek on his shoulder, she whispered, "You tell me when you're ready."

. . .

On Sunday morning, the conversation was light and tension lessened. Manolo no longer appeared upset, just reserved, and she was grateful for the change in tone. She understood where he was coming from, and could adjust to it. Being flexible wasn't her strongest quality, but one she was working on.

In Santa Fe by airport shuttle in the late afternoon, feeling too dependent on her friends and needing time alone, she called an Uber for a ride home. Then she lay on the couch with the heating pad under her lower back and phoned her family for a tourist travelogue of the sights. Despite having lived most of their lives in Arizona, none of them had been to Supai.

Within a few minutes of her arrival to the office the next morning, Dr. Grinwold knocked on her door. "Welcome back, find any spirochetes?"

"I don't know yet, but our tick collection was very successful, including one on my arm."

Dr. Grinwold's face took on an unaccustomed concern. "You need to report any risks on the job."

Did that include amorous teammates? She hadn't figured out what to do about Enzo, but Dr. Grinwold wasn't first on her list for help. "The tick on my arm was submitted along with the other specimens from the village. It wasn't attached long and the Southwest's not endemic for Lyme disease, so I'm not taking antibiotics."

Perhaps she learned a lesson with Manolo about her poor judgment on what to share. "I also removed an *Ixodes* in Portugal, but no symptoms of Lyme or relapsing fever. Even checked my temp a few times to make sure. Tick test is pending."

"All right, I'll bug Nancy for rapid processing of this latest one." His lips turned up in a rare smirk—had he finally made a joke?

"Thanks, I'll sleep better if you can find out the results." Maya followed him to his office.

Nancy's voice was more terse than Maya remembered from recent months. "Enzo's here on speaker. Maya, why didn't you back him up when he tried to convince the Council Member to allow rodent sampling?"

Dr. Grinwold's heavy face drooped and Maya jumped in. "That's not entirely true. She didn't want to be part of an experimental study because *B. miyamotoi* hasn't been found before in Grand Canyon mouse species. And she was worried that our protective suits might cause alarm."

"We came all the way with the appropriate equipment." Enzo's tone had a practiced polish. "We could have overruled her."

Maya had to acknowledge his political dexterity. He was trying to undermine her, probably because she rebuffed him, but he managed to keep any petulant whine from his complaint.

"I disagree. In light of recent delicate situations with native nations—"

She hesitated, certain she didn't want Enzo knowing about the flare-up with the Jicarillas. "I recommended diplomacy, respecting their sovereignty. Depending on initial results, the study can be extended." She deliberately avoided offering to help again.

"Sounds like a challenge and an understandable difference," Nancy said. "We'll be in touch so Maya can work with Enzo to write up a summary."

After requesting expedited handling of Maya's tick specimen, Dr. Grinwold ended the call and rounded the desk to face her. "You didn't inform me about this dustup over the rodent sampling. Perhaps next time they'll handle it on their own. Get in touch with Pima County to finish your draft paper by next week."

Back in her office, Maya toyed with her phone. Should she

contact the county first, or Enzo? A call to him might reinforce his sense of power, that he could get her worried. Dr. Grinwold and Nancy didn't sound as upset as she might have expected. The usual interpersonal and interagency jockeying—it should blow over.

Janey thanked Maya for the call. "County supervisors want rapid publication to justify stricter control over the caves and mines. I envy your Havasupai trip. With my leg healed, I could persuade Óscar to take off work and apply for a winter permit."

"Janey, can you check for Tucson campers who had rashes?"

"We don't have any new *Borrelia* reports in Pima County."

"Coordinate with Enzo Russo, your new EIS Officer. An outreach to Tucson dermatologists may identify patients who consulted on a rash without diagnostic testing."

Maya doodled on her notepad after hanging up. Did other women like Janey deserve a warning about Enzo? But Óscar was an alpha-male boyfriend, and Janey might think Maya was overreacting to one unwelcome kiss. Enzo's advances in the canyon could have been precipitated by the closeness of their fieldwork instead of a pattern.

He was slick and could fight back. She didn't want to be accused of being a hysterical recent virgin. Shit, did she ever let Enzo know that? And she had no appetite for wrecking his public health career. She knew what that felt like, after legal investigations of her involvement with anthrax and Mr. Otole's death. Did swimming in the falls give him the wrong idea—was it her fault she wasn't clear with him?

Let it slide, there was nothing to be gained by making a scene. Enzo was full of himself and impetuous. She shut him down, and that was the end of it.

TRANSITIONS

All biological organisms undergo transitions through life cycles. Eggs of the body louse, *Pediculus humanus humanus*, hatch to release nymphs, which mature after three molts into adults. They're gourmets, dependent on human blood for survival—animals are no substitute.

Tick larvae hatch from eggs, then molt to nymphs, which molt to adults, sucking blood at every stage to survive. They have a larger zoonotic circle of life, including pets, livestock, rodents, birds, and other wildlife species, depending on the tick. But despite all those available sources of sustenance, the female dies after giving birth.

Species longevity requires sacrifice, especially on the distaff side.

THIRTY-EIGHT

On November 4, Maya hunkered at the back of the darkened meeting room in the Atlanta hotel and evaluated Enzo's talk. Headquarters had recognized him in July as an accomplished communicator, so he was invited to present his *Borrelia miyamotoi* investigation as the "Communicating with Confidence" example at the surveillance course. She tried to ignore his subtle dig when describing their abortive attempt to collect rodent samples.

Their paths didn't cross after the September trip to Supai. He kept her in the loop when *Borrelia* was confirmed in some of their collected ticks and the two campers from Tucson after Janey tracked them down. But she lucked out, the tick from her elbow was negative. When rodent trapping was finally approved, he went back down the canyon with an Arizona vector control specialist.

His final slide projected, the lights came up. Her name was absent from the author list or acknowledgments, and she was surprised Nancy approved her being left off. But her name had been included on an initial draft of his paper for journal submission, so there was little to complain about.

Maya's role at the week-long training session was to assist in the surveillance system workshops. With his work on relapsing fever, Enzo had developed a proposal for improved reporting of rash illness, but she arranged to mentor another officer team.

In the afternoon, she headed over to Dr. Jaworski's office. The entrance was blocked by a throng of demonstrators. Signs with **Lyme detected = Lives saved** and **Stop the pandemic** waved in the air. Someone pushed a brochure at her. After clearing security inside the building and waiting for an elevator, she reviewed the pamphlet's summary of concerns about the quality of Lyme disease testing and neglect of chronic patients.

In her CDC supervisor's office, she dropped to the guest chair. "Sorry to be a few minutes late. How long's the demonstration been going on?"

Dr. Jaworski brushed her buzz cut. "Since this morning. Good thing they don't know you're an expert on *Borrelia.*"

"My experience with *burgdorferi* is limited. We have so few Lyme patients in the Southwest, and they're usually traced to states with lots of *Ixodes* ticks."

"You found a few of those at Havasupai?"

"Enzo said most ticks were other species, and none had *burgdorferi.* The patients had relapsing fever, not signs compatible with Lyme."

Dr. Jaworski pulled up notes on her computer screen. "I notice you still haven't fulfilled your requirement for a lengthier presentation."

Maya tapped her foot, searching for a solution. "Keegan Williams, the new vector-borne officer in Ft. Collins, invited me to provide a *Borrelia* overview there. I'm overwhelmed by my commitments to all these different investigations."

"Remind me what's pending, and I can prioritize."

"I'm lead author for the Arizona cases from the abandoned mine, coordinating with Pima County and the state health department. Draft's been approved by local supervisors and should be ready next week for CDC and public information officer clearance."

"That's important for your requirement of one journal submission. What else?"

Maya ticked off her fingers. "I'm co-author on multiple reports—Dr. Russo's for Havasupai, the eastern New Mexico dogs with USDA, and the overseas investigations which aren't done yet."

"You're only assisting, so the timelines will sort themselves out. But if anyone demands an unreasonable turnaround, I'll mediate."

Leaning back in the chair and trying to relax, Maya continued. "There's the usual on-call rotation during the day and some nights and weekends. Without a state public health veterinarian, Dr. Grinwold has me taking a leading role on zoonotic diseases like plague, hanta, and rabies. State staff assist, but it keeps my head spinning."

"You're also handling food and waterborne outbreaks plus communicable diseases like flu and measles."

Maya nodded. "Not alone, of course. New Mexico has a good team. But that's the advantage of working in an area with fewer resources. I'm learning about everything."

Dr. Jaworski glanced at her office clock. "I have another appointment in five minutes. With your assignment done in June, Fred will be recruiting your replacement at the May EIS conference. To help him, you need to give a stellar presentation, reflecting on the quality of the New Mexico training."

After pulling out her notepad, Maya wrote a reminder. "Time's getting away from me. I assume you'll need an abstract by the end of the year?"

Dr. Jaworski nodded and Maya recognized a new trainee poking her head in the crack of the partially open door.

"Anything else?" Dr. Jaworski asked.

Her supervisor was entitled to know if there was a real problem with Enzo. But it wasn't illegal for him to make a pass at the campground, and he stopped when she said no. Not immediately, but without dramatic calls for help. The incident was weeks behind her, and thinking about it now was counterproductive. The first-year EIS officer opened the door wider, and Maya offered her chair.

. . .

After leaving Dr. Jaworski's office and crossing the street to the hotel, Maya passed through the demonstration again. She almost collided with an older woman who thrust a sign in her face and shouted "Chronicity recognized means patients heard!" She remembered some scientists asserted that the over-representation of women in chronic Lyme sufferers meant it was just due to hysteria.

She recalled her own body contradicting the experts. After her initial attempt to stop the Klonopin landed her in the hospital, Dr. Kim had been adamant that she should stay on a benzodiazepine. She'd also disagreed with Maya's dose tapering for slowly weaning off benzos, but Maya was convinced it helped her body adjust.

So despite her respect for authority and dedication to the scientific method, she acknowledged that much was still unknown, and couldn't dismiss the protestors' concerns. A text came in from Erika as Maya climbed the stairs to the second floor of the hotel. Maya returned it using FaceTime.

Erika's usual resolute face was contorted with tears. "Someone jumped me as I climbed into my car in the driveway. He tried to choke me, yelling 'Puta,' but I managed to hit the car horn with my hand. Rolf ran out and chased the guy away."

"Are you hurt? Did you call the police?"

Erika tilted her chin to show Maya the neck abrasions. "Rolf took me to the urgent care. Doc said I'll have bruises but nothing serious. I'm at home for the rest of the day."

"That's awful, I wish there was something I could do to help. Any idea who it was?"

Rolf poked his head in. "Our front door camera didn't pick up anything, other than his build and height. He had on a dark hoodie. But the police are checking our neighbors' cameras."

Erika's phone chimed. "Sorry, Maya, I need to take this other call."

"Okay, keep me posted, and stay safe. I'll be in Santa Fe late Friday and can help catch up on work you've missed, or babysit Kyle, even on the weekend."

After Erika disconnected, Maya wiped her face with a cold wet washcloth. She was fed up with feeling vulnerable all the time. When walking alone, most men didn't fear the possibility of an attack. Some countries required women to be accompanied by men, but threats also loomed in more progressive places. Always looking over one's shoulder, scoping out who was approaching. Anticipating rapid footsteps coming up on her, bad intent headed her way.

Only once had she worked totally alone, when interviewing men who attended a feast of anthrax-infected antelope. That experience had been harrowing. If Dave or Manolo had done the interviews, it wouldn't have crossed their minds to worry about it. Some women with full-time fieldwork might carry a weapon, or accept the risk and assume it wouldn't happen to them, hoping for a cell phone signal to reach help in time.

Appetite gone, she settled for an apple while watching the Atlanta evening news, including coverage of the Lyme protests. It sounded like they planned to picket CDC all week, wanting to force revised guidelines. Then her FaceTime chirped and Maya saw Erika's face again, this time more outraged than tearful.

"It was that guy who got fired for the porn story. A neighbor's camera caught his license plate. But no clear shots of him."

"God, Erika, I'm so useless all the way across the country. Are you safe there? You could stay in my apartment."

"We'll be fine. The police will maintain surveillance and this might be over quickly."

"Any links to earlier incidents—toys in the mailbox, the party destruction, or the spray paint?"

Erika shrugged. "Too early to say, but I'd bet on it. I shouldn't rush to judgment, but I always found myself uneasy around him."

. . .

Maya tried to distract herself from freaking out about Erika by reading emails on her laptop. Janey had a wording change from the county public information officer for their *Borrelia* paper, who wanted the phrase **need for further relapsing fever surveillance** replaced by **need to look for more relapsing fever cases**. The PIO thought surveillance had too negative a connotation. Maya understood that science was a group effort. But the paper was intended for a medical journal where surveillance had a specific meaning. Its importance was emphasized by the meeting she attended.

Please see if they will change their minds, she typed. **Surveillance is the most appropriate word.**

Her stomach growled—the apple wasn't enough. A knock on the door drew her attention. Many of the out-of-state EIS Officers were staying at the same hotel and she assumed it was one of them. When she opened the door, Enzo's pale eyes glimmered with the last rays of the setting sun slicing in from the window at the end of the hall. A hand behind his back thrust forward a bouquet of pink roses before he closed the door and leaned against it.

"Figured I needed to get back in good graces with my sweet China doll. You avoided me all week."

Typical Enzo, always keeping her off guard. "I don't know what to say, or where to put these."

He stepped to the dresser and seized the ice bucket. "Sorry, should have bought you a vase. Go get some water from the bathroom."

As she tilted the bucket under the faucet, her mind swam with options. Since his forced kiss and criticism of her work to Nancy, he'd been professional and courteous in their phone and email contacts. But her skin still crawled with memories of his disrespect for her personal boundaries.

When she emerged from the bathroom, he took the bucket and arranged the flowers before setting it on the desk. Maya rearranged the flowers and moved it to the coffee table.

"Enzo, you might think it's a compliment, but Chinese women don't appreciate being referred to as China dolls. And I'm not your anything. Are you clear about that?"

His gleaming smile vanished. "If we're sharing complaints, why didn't you congratulate me after my presentation today?"

The abrasive tone gave her chills, but she knew it was wise to defuse him.

"You always give polished presentations. No other first-year was invited to give two talks—Dr. Jaworski recognizes your skill."

He smirked. "Yes, but your support would have been appreciated."

"You didn't list me as a co-author." The minute the words left her lips, she regretted them. She hated pettiness, especially at work.

"They asked me to speak, not you."

Deflect. "I'm a lousy speaker. So they definitely made the right decision." Her tone attempted to mask the sarcasm.

His patted his stomach. "I'm starved, want to grab dinner? We can go over our *Borrelia* draft report."

"Skipping it tonight. I got bad news from a colleague and I'm in a foul mood."

He took a step toward her. "So let me take your mind off it." His body blocked the door.

"Enzo, you're so kind to think of me." She picked up her mental rapier and thrust with a clear, firm parry. "But I said I'm not up for it. Don't let me keep you—check out one of the Atlanta nightclubs."

A hand slipped behind her neck under her hairline. "We haven't been together in weeks."

"Based on your sniping to Nancy about our rodent sampling, I didn't think you liked working with me." She hoped a reminder of his irritation would trigger his exit.

But then his left hand moved to her shoulder, tugging her close. She raised her hands in protest, careful to avoid contact. Like a lion toying with an antelope downed by one swipe, his hand tightened as he bent at the waist to breathe in her ear.

"Two months and Nancy's reported no visits. You used to check in with her when you came to Phoenix. So you and Miranda aren't back together."

He was right. They talked on FaceTime—Manolo wanted to ease back into things as friends. His work hours increased to half-days, and his verbal aptitude exploded. Sebastian planned a return home to NYC by Thanksgiving, and Manolo was adamant about caring for himself. It was a test he self-imposed, to determine he was back to full-speed.

"Enzo, this has nothing to do with any other relationship. I don't want one with you."

He shoved her hard and she fell back on the bed, his body falling with her and pinning her down.

"You're a beautiful woman. You deserve to be loved."

With his right hand restraining both her wrists over her head, he groped with his left hand under the hem of her skirt. His weight was heavy on her legs and she couldn't free a knee. The more she wriggled, the more she sensed his arousal. She stopped moving, hoping to talk him down before fighting back.

"Enzo, this can't happen. You don't want the consequences."

He locked eyes. "Unlike the camping trip, we're totally alone. No one needs to know anything, if that's what you're worried about."

She carefully pronounced each word. "Unless you leave now, the police will know about it."

His left hand continued roaming, slipping to the front of her underwear. "You're kidding. We're two healthy single adults, why should anyone care about us making love?"

"I said no six weeks ago and nothing has changed."

"My need for you has grown. We could be a splendid team, professionally and personally."

So working together was important to him. He wouldn't rape her. This was his overweening attempt at a seduction. His hand began to stroke on the outside of her underwear, trying to get her excited. She maintained a steady voice to mask her fear of him escalating. "If you want any chance of preserving our professional relationship and your career, you'll get out of my hotel room now."

Making threats might not be the wisest decision—she was vulnerable to his displeasure and strength. But she had one last thread of hope he'd see the wisdom of stopping before she fought back and yelled for help, not that anyone might hear.

His lips drifted from her own to the pulse at her throat. "Your increased heart rate says to me desire." His fingers slipped under her panties and she trembled at the warmth of his skin.

"It also means anxiety and anger." She raised her voice to shouting level, hoping to scare him. "STOP NOW—YOU'RE HURTING ME!"

One of her hands twisted free and she grabbed his arm before he achieved penetration. He ceased exploration and rolled to his feet. "I don't understand, you're missing a good thing. Presumably you're out of practice."

She squirmed off the bed, pulled down her skirt, and raced to the door, flinging it open. "GET OUT."

He halted in the doorway, suddenly submissive and pleading. "Maya, you misinterpreted my passion. We just need to spend more time figuring out what turns us each on."

"Enzo, one more second before this hall is filled with a bloodcurdling scream."

He bowed at the waist, then sauntered past her. "I'll follow your advice and find a nightclub. Goodnight, Maya."

THIRTY-NINE

In the shower, Maya scrubbed her skin with the washcloth until it was red. Flashbacks swarmed of the college incident, her first time imbibing alcohol, too drunk to remember who took off her clothes. Even though the health center found no evidence of sexual activity, the sense memories had stuck, clouding the initial weeks of Manolo's flirtation.

But now she'd been sober, and Enzo too. No taste of alcohol on his lips, and no excuse of impairment to argue lack of consent. He knew what he was doing, but given his supreme confidence with women, he'd never view it as assault. She'd experienced how he shaded the truth about their disagreement with the Hualapai council member. His version of events or hers—which would hold more weight?

She slipped on her robe and curled up on the upholstered chair. Erika had reported sexual harassment at the health department, and her former coworker tried to strangle her.

The iPhone chimed and Erika cried out, "They got him, the guy from Chronic."

Maya pushed aside her own indecision. "I was so worried about your attack. Have you recovered?"

"Yes, I'm thankful to put this behind us. I can't believe how long it's taken to stop the harassment."

Apprehension about Enzo didn't equate with what Erika went through. The focus needed to stay on her friend. "He's in jail now?"

"Yes, but the cops warned he's eligible for bail."

"That can't be true."

"First arrest, no criminal record."

Movement from the chair to the bed reflected Maya's frustration. "But it was a life-threatening assault. Call my attorney, I'll text his number. He won't let you down."

"Thanks, Maya, I really appreciate your support. I never imagined my own #MeToo moment escalating so far."

After Maya hung up and sent Mr. Zielinski's number to Erika, she sheltered under the covers. Erika said Me Too. Enzo's aggressions at the canyon and hotel violated her mental and physical autonomy, but he didn't physically hurt her. He was so confident of his sexual attraction, she needed to say no repeatedly. No woman should be vulnerable to unwelcome touch, but it wasn't rape. She couldn't think of a thing that led him on. Being collegial wasn't an invitation.

Did his actions justify reporting it? Her word against his—there was no evidence. She desperately needed a confidential sounding board, with no potential consequences, until the full implications were clear. She could talk to Erika when back home, but Erika was strident about those issues, even before the attack in her driveway. She might tell Dr. Grinwold without Maya's permission.

Her cognitive therapy group? Patients met with the understanding of confidentiality, but something could leak out. Lila was an option—she worked with Enzo on investigations that crossed Arizona-California boundaries and Maya had shared earlier concerns. But she was another one who could bring it to higher authorities, not what Maya was ready for.

Dr. Kim was the best choice. A regular appointment was already scheduled for Monday when she was home in Santa Fe, soon enough.

. . .

Enzo's devil-may-care pose, like nothing happened, was getting to her. During the instructional talks Wednesday afternoon at the conference center, he kept glancing at her. Thursday's scientific writing session and work on her assigned group's presentations refocused her. Friday morning, Enzo was first to present his rash reporting system.

Every moment of his talk, she wished she was anywhere else. But her job was to give feedback, and she couldn't duck it. She tried to look away, but his self-possession was mesmerizing. No other first-year had his aplomb. The cocksure attitude could get him in trouble with work relationships, as well as the extreme discomfort he gave her. Dr. Jaworski's office was nearby—this was the last chance to officially report his actions in person before flying home.

Each day, the Lyme demonstration grew in size and volume. With issues so long-standing, and patients believing their lives were at stake, emotions were raw. As she zigzagged through the protestors on the south side of Clifton Road, Maya was relieved that she wasn't in a Public Health Service uniform.

Ringed by the police, the crowd swirled and compressed like a baitball of fish threatened by predators. She ducked to avoid a waving wooden sign, then almost tripped over a child in a tick costume holding hands with a young woman, probably her mother. Just as she glimpsed the **CDC SAVING LIVES** sign on the black fence, a deafening boom and bright light flashed, pain coursed her body, and she lost consciousness.

. . .

When her eyes fluttered open, she caught a glimpse of sunlight from the window. Then a voice floated through a deep tunnel.

"Maya."

Not Manolo—he was in Phoenix. Despite a loud buzzing noise, she heard another familiar voice.

"Doctor, she's waking up." Sebastian, too? But the words were so distant.

Her head turned and she opened her eyes to find Manolo's hands on her shoulder and Sebastian at the door with a doctor in a white coat.

"Maya, you're in the hospital again." Manolo's face was close but the words were indistinct. The buzzing, or maybe ringing, dominated the room no matter how she twisted.

She felt pressure on her head and her fingers detected the texture of gauze wrap. Then pain from her left hand began to radiate, and she peered down to find it bandaged. Her left thigh burned, but she couldn't see it through the sheet.

"What happened?" She formed the words but they echoed in her head with the ringing in her ears.

The doctor hovered into closer view. "A flash-bang grenade was tossed at the demonstration."

"Puñeta, using those deadly weapons for crowd control." Sebastian spun away and knocked his fist into the wall, then swore again.

"Police said they didn't do it," Manolo answered.

"What's wrong with me?"

"We think the grenade landed near your feet," the doctor said. "Many are designed to emit light and noise only, but sometimes they fragment, or cause rocks or pavement to disintegrate into shrapnel. Your skirt was lit on fire, so there's burns on your outer thigh. Shrapnel hit your hand and skull. There's some hearing loss, which might be temporary."

"I need to use the bathroom." She tried to push up from the bed with her right hand, but the room started spinning and she sank back down.

"Let me find a nurse to help," the doctor said. "The injury to your inner ear causes dizziness."

The young woman in scrubs helped her to the toilet, keeping an arm around her waist as everything danced in front of her eyes. When back in bed, she raised her left arm again.

"My hand is numb, but more pain than my run-in with the cat."

The doctor looked up from a review of his computer tablet, then nodded to Manolo, who stroked her arm. "You lost your finger." His face was taut with grief.

"Shit, and it just healed from mallet finger. Glad I'm right-handed." She was proud of her ability to joke—perhaps it was the realization that her situation could have been much worse. Or maybe it was the warm buzz from a line the nurse had hooked back up. "What time is it?"

"Noon Saturday," Manolo said.

"We flew in from Phoenix last night," Sebastian added.

"Thank you." Her eyes darted to both of them.

"I intended to fly back to NYC, so it was on the way."

Sebastian's smile contradicted deep lines crowding his forehead. "Your supervisor, Dr. Jaworski, stopped in after the accident, and we met her this morning. Several of your colleagues swung by on their way to the airport—a striking young woman from California and a very worried young man headed to Ft. Collins."

He removed a card from some roses. "Another doc left this beautiful bouquet. *Maya, get well soon so we can work together again. Enzo.*"

Manolo frowned but lifted his phone. "I got calls—Nancy, Dr. Grinwold, Stephanie, Erika."

"There were no evening flights from Flagstaff," Sebastian said. "Your folks will be in tonight."

"Dave?" she asked.

"Our third Musketeer," Manolo answered. "I texted him."

She glanced over at the fluids entering her right arm.

"I ordered a morphine drip," the doctor said. "There's no problem of interaction with your past benzo meds."

Visual images began to recede along with the audio, and Manolo kissed her forehead. "Get some rest—we'll be here to keep an eye on you."

· · ·

The rest of the weekend was a blur of visitors and increased pain as she insisted on dialing back the morphine dose. On early Sunday, her mom was almost hysterical.

"I always worried about this fieldwork. You're good with computers—you should stay there."

"Mom, this wasn't fieldwork. I was in the wrong place at the wrong time."

When her mom went to the cafeteria, Maya asked her dad, "Did they figure out who threw the flash-bang?"

"Each side is pointing to the other. Those stun grenades are a controversial form of crowd control, but police are close-mouthed about their use. Still claiming it was a demonstrator. A little girl had something fly into her face and she's hospitalized here. But they say she'll be okay."

In her groggy state, Maya didn't realize the bomb had injured anyone else. "Dad, can you walk me over to see her?"

"I'll ask the doctor."

When he returned, a nurse pushed into the room with a wheelchair. "Dr. Maguire, we have to use this. Let me disconnect the drip."

Once down the hall, her dad said, "I'll find Mom in the cafeteria. Manolo and Sebastian are at the hotel sleeping late—they were awake all Friday night with you."

Other than the lighter complexion, the blonde girl asleep in the bed looked like Dave's youngest—five years old, at the most. Her cheek was bandaged, and a haggard woman held her hand.

Maya's dizziness had abated enough that she could hold her head up, but she was still grateful for the wheelchair. "I'm Maya Maguire. I was hurt with the flash-bomb, too. How's your daughter doing?"

A tear dripped from the woman's puffy eyes. "I'm scared. Livvie's gone deaf."

A cold cloud dulled Maya's vision as she struggled to provide reassurance. "My hearing has improved—I'm praying for the same for Livvie. Did they say if she can go home soon?"

"Tomorrow, after a checkup from the specialist to give us a path going forward."

"Good for you. Not sure when I'm getting sprung."

The woman squeezed her daughter's hand. "My husband hasn't been able to work our farm in Vermont since he got chronic Lyme."

She looked up with an apologetic expression. "I heard you're with CDC and we're protesting CDC policies. But we didn't throw the bomb—we wouldn't do that with our children there."

Maya maneuvered her chair closer and reached out her right hand to cover both of theirs. "Thankfully no one was killed. With Thanksgiving coming up, our families have a lot to be grateful for."

Her mom and dad met them in the corridor as the nurse wheeled her back to the room. After restarting the pain medication, Maya asked for the iPhone.

"Do you mind giving me some privacy?" They looked a bit dejected, but acquiesced. She hit Dave's number with her thumb and cranked up the phone's volume.

"About time you called," he chided. "High on those meds?"

No one else shared her dry, barely visible, sense of humor. "Fat chance. How's your family doing, including its newest member?"

"Everyone's fine, including Braxton. He never attended a real school, so we worried about his adjustment. But he's taken to it like a duck to water." Dave exuded pride through the soundwaves.

"With any luck, he's got your brains."

"Considering all the darker qualities running through our family, I can only hope."

Penetrating the ringing in her ears, Maya heard a clamor of cheerful barks. "Is Bo saying hi to me?"

"You betcha. Hey, this damned *Borrelia* finally took you out."

"What do you mean?"

"Well, you got injured in a Lyme disease protest."

Maya tried to laugh, but it made her head hurt. "Quite a stretch."

"Seriously, should I fly out? How long are they going to keep you? You're a western girl, you belong back here. One of my kids might let you ride her pony."

"Dave, I appreciate the offer, but I'm full up on visitors. Stay there and cherish your kinfolk. I'll be home as soon as I can."

When she clicked off the call, her parents stuck their heads back in. "We need to figure out where you'll recover." Mom, taking charge as usual.

She dropped her phone and leaned back into the pillows. "Can we talk later? I think I'm done in." Maybe for once she could give into others making decisions for her.

FORTY

In the battle over caretakers, Manolo won—they flew to Phoenix on November 12. Her parents accepted the plan because they were only a few hours away in Flagstaff and could hardly argue with their daughter having her own personal physician.

"Don't worry about coming back until after Thanksgiving," Dr. Grinwold said on a call before she left Atlanta. "You haven't used many days of vacation since last winter. If you're up to writing papers on the laptop, keep track of those hours toward work time. But don't push it."

Sebastian flew back to NYC. Although he offered assistance, Manolo insisted he fly home to see his grandson. In Maya's hospital room, Manolo had promised, "I can drive, I can cook. I want to take care of Maya."

By the time Manolo pulled into his carport in Phoenix, Maya was exhausted but ecstatic. "I can't do anything without more sleep."

He climbed out of the driver's seat. "Wait one second, let me grab my wheelchair. Guess it was good I hung onto it." After helping her inside, he maneuvered her to his bedroom.

"Manolo, are you sure you want to take care of me? You were still pissed at me last time I was here."

He pulled back the bedcovers and leaned over for a brief kiss. "It feels good to be needed. You okay with sharing my bedroom?" As she nodded, he began to undress her. "I'm on cloud nine we're both recovered for this."

Her pulse pounded with his touch. "Last year I battled a killer disease and never got infected. All the damage was to you. I didn't think life could get any worse."

After he joined her under the covers, she stroked his arm with her good hand. "This year, I'm hit with one thing after another. Dr. Grinwold called me Joe Btfsplk, the world's worst jinx." Her eyes closed and her voice faded. "Wish I didn't need to get into this much trouble to show how much I value you."

The next morning, lying on the right to ease pressure on her flaming hot left thigh, she awoke to strong fingers kneading her back. "How are you doing?" he asked.

"In bad need of a shower. Can you help?"

"One of our favorite places." In the bathroom, he removed her bandages and examined her wounds.

"Stitches are healing fine, no redness for infection. Burn looks good, but we'll keep the temperature cool."

"I'm astonished at your speech progress, and with everything else. Guess our two months mostly separated was good for something."

"But no more time apart, okay?"

She nodded, then pretended to pout. "I don't want to give up hot showers."

"I'll get you clean." He hung both their robes on the door hook and her skin dimpled with the cool air. After he pulled in the stool and sat her down on it, he adjusted the rain shower so the spray was diffuse over her head. He took his time with baby shampoo, avoiding the three-inch wound. Hyacinth body wash cleaned her face and he traced carefully over her left hand.

When his hands and cloth moved over her breasts, she sucked in a deep breath, aroused despite her intention to remain relaxed. He didn't touch the burn but stroked her legs, pausing to kiss the childhood scar on the inside of her right thigh.

At her feet, his fingers slowly massaged each toe with the bubbly body wash, and she leaned against the tiles, nerves tingling again. Tugging her away from the wall to lean her head on his shoulder, he scrubbed her back. Then he pulled her upright into his arms and used his bare hand to caress with provocative thoroughness her last remaining areas. As her knees weakened, he let her drop to the stool and picked up the washcloth to quickly bathe himself. She reached out to touch him.

"Haven't tried this with only one hand," she whispered.

"Let's wait, no rush." He turned off the faucet and guided her to the rug, then toweled her off and redressed her wounds. "We'll have a clinic recheck later."

As he helped her lower back into the bed, she answered. "I trust you with my life."

He leaned over for a kiss. "It's not going to come to that."

Within a half hour, he carried a breakfast tray with scrambled eggs and cactus jelly toast.

She winced while trying to shift upward against the carved pine headboard, despite the raft of pillows behind her. "Can I have an ibuprofen? Shower was refreshing, but also woke up some pain cells."

"I'll keep track of what you take." He brought a glass of apple juice and the pill. "Can you manage breakfast on your own?"

Not wanting to be totally reliant on his personal and doctor skills, she nodded.

Dark eyes squinted as he caressed her cheek, then he turned for the door. "I'm working from home today. Call if you need something."

Her eyes eased open when he returned, clock showing noon. He removed the untouched breakfast tray and came back with a smoothie. "All quiet on the western front, to quote Dave." He dropped his bathrobe and crawled in naked next to her. "Want to cuddle and watch an old movie?"

"Your choice." She gulped the drink and drifted off.

When she awoke, the TV was off and she could smell spaghetti sauce. Hanging onto the bed, she pulled a brand-new red negligee from the back of the chair and slipped it on. Did he go shopping?

The rest of her clothes were clean and neatly folded on the dresser. Hugging the wall, she joined Manolo in the kitchen.

"That looks even better on you than the store mannequin." He set down the spoon and drew her into a hug. With his hand, he stroked her head. "Not too dizzy? You can use my crutches."

"Thank you." She fingered the silk, barely covering her rear end. "This is wonderfully soft on my tender skin, but you need to be closer for me to hear you well." With her right hand, she pulled him in, tongues flirting. Both of his arms circled to keep her from falling. When she leaned away, he helped her sit at the table.

"Remember the first time I made spaghetti for you?" he asked.

"Sure, last fall, after spending the afternoon at the pow wow."

"We're having it again to celebrate your homecoming."

After dinner and cleaning up, they retired to his bedroom and crawled under the covers. He clicked the remote. "I found a romance called *Holiday in the Wild*. It takes place in Africa. We're headed there when EIS is over, right?"

For the first time since his infection in January, she felt like they were back to where they'd been before.

. . .

For the next week and a half, they fell into a routine. They showered together and he changed her dressings before breakfast. At PIMC, he worked a few hours before coming home for lunch. She talked to her colleagues by phone and edited the numerous *Borrelia* papers on her laptop, except for afternoon naps when Manolo scheduled his speech and physical therapy.

Enzo was one of the first incoming calls. "Dr. Maguire, my next draft of our Grand Canyon *Borrelia miyamotoi* manuscript is ready for your review. But I'm sure you're still recovering so perhaps I should just take it over on my own."

No mention of the Atlanta hotel. Should she share that she was on her way to discuss him with Dr. Jaworski when taken out by the flash-bang? The pain, vertigo, and tinnitus were still too strong to focus on the optimal way to deal with Enzo. But she'd be damned if he cut her out of the study.

"I'm sure Nancy would agree this is not time-sensitive. So email your draft and I'll work on it when I can." She hung up abruptly to put him out of her mind.

Erika called on Saturday. Her voice was jubilant with more verve than Maya had heard in months. "Good news! They're keeping him locked up. Turns out he assaulted another woman eleven years ago in Oklahoma. So no bail."

"That's fantastic. All I could think about was your perp lurking around every corner, breaking into your backyard again, even your house. Oh, I'm sorry, Erika, I shouldn't even mention such terrible possibilities."

"I appreciate hearing someone else is as freaked as me. I've gotten a lot of empty stares and muted responses in the office. It seems like people want to pretend it didn't happen. Everything he did, smarmy comments and unwelcome touches followed by the porn story, mailbox toys, Kyle's party, and his almost choking me to death—it's looping like a gruesome movie trailer in my brain."

Maya remembered the call scheduled with their mutual psychiatrist to replace the cancelled in–person appointment. "Erika, do you still see Dr. Kim?"

"Sure, but I don't think she relates. She's never had that creepy male attention."

"What do you mean?"

"Well, she's not the most appealing female on the planet—too tall, acne scars. She reminds me of Morticia from that movie The Addams Family. Plus she's gay."

More than a year earlier on the bus home from the Santa Fe Indian Market, Erika had said being attractive in the Southwest was a curse. Did she really think men only wanted to demonstrate their power over pretty straight girls?

"I don't understand why men assault women, Erika, but I don't think being nice-looking or heterosexual is the full answer."

"Maybe for some, bees buzzing to the most colorful flower." A burst of child screams and cries interrupted. "Gotta go, Kyle just somersaulted the couch and Rolf's at the market."

Erika didn't know Maya had been attacked too, although the

circumstances didn't compare. Erika's choking required medical follow-up, and Maya only had unwanted sexual advances. Not in the same ballpark. Erika still operated from raw emotion and fear— clear advice about Enzo wouldn't come from that quarter.

Manolo knocked on the bedroom door and entered with a cup of yogurt and berries. "Not interrupting, I hope?"

"No, Erika had to deal with little boy rambunctiousness."

"After breakfast, can you handle that from a big boy?"

The brief discussion of toxic masculinity with her friend slammed her desire with a fly swatter. "Can we put a pin in it? I'd love to escape from the house."

"How about the Musical Instrument Museum? Thousands of instruments from around the world." Then he drew back, stricken look crossing his long face. "I mean, if that's not a terrible reminder of your hand injury."

She patted the bed as an invitation to join her and took an enthusiastic spoonful of yogurt. "Music always soothes the savage beast, even one as tame as me. The museum sounds wonderful."

The only shadow over their day out was finding the Corvette windshield smashed, so they postponed the museum visit until early afternoon after the glass repair company stopped by to replace it.

. . .

November was Maya's least favorite month, overcast and gloomy no matter where she lived, with little snow to play in. A year earlier, she and Manolo had started and ended their personal relationship, then restarted it again.

But during the flash-bomb healing, the brilliant blue sky pierced by saguaros and palm trees was cheery. Some businesses even wrapped tree trunks with white lights in preparation for the holidays.

Monday morning, she verified Manolo had left for PIMC and propped herself in bed with pillows before placing the FaceTime call to Dr. Kim. When the psychiatrist's face popped up on the screen, Maya reflected that Erika was right. The narrow severe face and dramatic dark hair was dour like Morticia Addams, although she never noticed the acne scars before. But Dr. Kim smiled and pulled her Irish Setter into the frame.

"Not sure how to make use of a therapy animal over the phone, but thought that Psy's sweet noggin might be beneficial. Any animals to cuddle in Phoenix?"

"Unfortunately, no, although my Tucson grandma has a gorgeous sable Persian."

The dog darted out of the picture. "How are you doing?"

"Manolo brought me to a checkup. Everything's healing on schedule, no infections, just need tincture of time."

"Maya, when we're wounded with a traumatic event, mental health is critically important. You should restart group therapy, although we've never done it remotely."

"I'll contact you when I'm back in Santa Fe. I'm worried about sleeping alone because my nightmares have increased. Whenever I wake up from one in Phoenix, Manolo is here to comfort me."

Dr. Kim pushed the long dark strands out of her eyes and adjusted her rimless glasses. "We'll work on techniques for you to soothe yourself. It's not healthy to rely on others for our sanity."

Maya's eyes darted out through the lace curtains of the bedroom window to the squirrel racing along the top rail of the wooden fence. Like the rodent, Maya was frantic, with more to consider than the Lyme disease demonstration. Enzo could go fuck himself—the last person she wanted to focus on. But a reasoned sounding board would be wonderful, before she blew up his career.

"Uh, I need to ask about the definition of sexual assault."

The glasses fell away and Dr. Kim's eyes bored through the screen. "Maya, are you safe? Do you need someone to help you get away from Dr. Miranda?"

"No, no, someone else I worked with. I wasn't raped, but I'm uncertain of the boundary for reporting."

"Is the threat still imminent, for you or anyone else?"

"I don't think so. Nobody I'm in direct contact with now." Maya glanced at the bedroom door with Manolo's robe hanging from a hook on the back. It was too early for his return. "It's a he said, she said thing. He crossed a boundary with me but he's not a predator."

"All right, if you're sure this can wait, we'll talk about it when you're home. My priority is making sure you're handling it psychologically, and I can provide emotional support for any legal decisions. If not rape, I'm guessing it's a misdemeanor. As usual, anything you tell me will be confidential. In New Mexico, I'm only required to inform law enforcement about abuse of children, the elderly, or disabled."

After they hung up, Maya walked slowly to the empty kitchen. With Manolo's occasional temper, she couldn't trust what he'd do to Enzo. Better to sort it out in person with Dr. Kim before letting more people in. She had little solid evidence of Enzo crossing a line, other than his swearing at Keegan and her discussions of concerns with Lila and Faye. The revelation could tarnish their careers with controversy. But could it happen again if she didn't do something? Still disquieted, at least she'd taken active steps to figuring out a resolution. Knowledge was power.

During the May lunch with Nancy and Enzo in Phoenix, he reminded her of the horror clown from *It*. But Enzo was smoother and more ingratiating, like the Richard Gere character Dennis Peck in her favorite noir movie *Internal Affairs*. A team spent the whole film trying to nail the duplicitous vice cop for multiple murders, and almost didn't succeed because of Peck's charm and connections. Enzo wasn't evil like Dennis Peck, just entitled and racist. He touched her intimately without permission. If Manolo ever knew, the blow-up would be unimaginable, perhaps with a dangerous confrontation. A chance she couldn't take.

FORTY-ONE

With global news of the CDC EIS Officer and little girl injured in a violent Atlanta Lyme disease protest, Stefan called from Oslo and Rebecca Skyped from Rabat. Janey and Óscar gave Maya's grandmother a ride up from Tucson on Saturday and cooked them a Salvadoran dish before heading back south. Her parents drove down from Flagstaff on November 19. While Manolo worked, they brought her to the downtown Phoenix library to browse the stacks and read newspapers.

Maya and Manolo still hadn't made love, beyond his bedtime backrubs and arousing body washes in the shower. She wanted to ask why they were waiting, but had some guesses. It would take more weeks for her wounds to heal. She needed ibuprofen and was still doing everything one-handed. When she inadvertently turned over onto her left side in her sleep, the healing burn jerked her awake. And their relationship had been tested, in multiple ways.

On the Saturday before Thanksgiving, he asked if she felt up to an evening out. "The Phoenix ZooLights are a huge attraction. Animals plus Christmas lights—can you think of a more magical combination?"

After parking, they joined the crowds crossing a bridge strewn with lights including automated monkeys swinging overhead. Kids squealed on the camel ride and Manolo asked, "Tempted?"

"In healthier circumstances, but tonight, I'm just pleased to be ambulatory."

Huge multicolored lighted butterflies flitted between the trees, and branches glowed purple and red. The illuminated animatronic tortoise extended his neck and the tiger waved his tail. One exhibit had a TV with a live stream of baby ferrets. Although more electric animals than real ones were out, the eyes of a lion reflected from its enclosure and its deep-throated roar was eerie.

Finding a bench overlooking the lagoon surrounded by lights flashing and reflecting in the water, Manolo suggested they stop for a rest. Earlier in the day, the temperature had been in the seventies, and they had lunch on his small back patio. But after dark it was dropping into the sixties. With gentle fingers, Manolo zipped up her jacket.

"Last year, you came to join my family in NYC for Thanksgiving." He leaned close. "This year, I want to announce something special when your parents join us."

"Our Africa trip."

"No, something longer." From his pocket, he pulled out a platinum ring nestling a small square diamond. "When Mom died, Dad set her ring aside for one of us. Ramona didn't need it—when Abdi proposed, he gave her an African amethyst."

"Mano, what are you saying?"

"Will you marry me, Maya? I want to make a real commitment, to head off any more misunderstandings of what we mean to each other."

She squirmed in embarrassed discomfort. "Did your first wife wear it? It may seem petty, but that would bother me."

He shook his head. "I didn't ask for it. I probably knew it wouldn't last."

But it lasted eight years, she wanted to say. How could she know if she'd do any better?

A light breeze stirred her hair, and she brushed it out of her face. In January, with his life-threatening cardiac arrest, his family let slip that Manolo had been thinking marriage. It had been eleven long months of wondering if he'd be functional enough to talk about it. She should be out-of-this-world with joy, but instead, weighted down by reality.

"How do we manage it? You work in Phoenix and I'm in New Mexico. I don't know if either of us have recovered enough."

"I might not be up for full-time employment and you're always going to be short a finger." He kissed her cheek to soften the joke. "But your training is done in seven months. Next spring, we can figure out where to work and live, together."

She looked down to her damaged left hand, a ghastly dark scar where her fifth finger used to be. "I can't wear your exquisite ring."

His fingers went to her chin and his lips brushed hers. "No rush to put it on until you heal."

She glared at the hand again. "I was so self-conscious, Chinese with an Irish last name and keloid scars from the bike accident. Now burns on the other leg and slashes like a horror movie on my arm. But nothing compares to a ring bringing focus to a missing digit."

He lifted her left palm and kissed it. "I love your missing finger—a reminder I could have lost you. Shook me out of my stubborn preoccupation with getting you to respect me as a partner."

His lips moved to her right palm. "But who says we need to follow other people's rules? Wear it on your right hand."

She wrapped her hand around the back of his neck and bussed both of his eyes. "I've been on edge all year with your prognosis up in the air. The logistical unknowns were more than I could handle."

"Are you still fixated on all those uncertainties?"

"Yes and no. I want to be your wife and have a family. Let me think how to say this. Sí, mi amor, quiero estar contigo para siempre."

"Very nicely said." His lips came close to hers. "I want to be with you forever, also."

. . .

At home in bed, they held each other. Maya made the ring snug on her right finger with a bit of tape. She stroked his cheek. "If we're talking about marriage, why aren't we making love?"

He leaned over to sprinkle kisses on her throat. "I want you to feel better, physically and emotionally. We've gone through so much."

"But I miss you, having all of you."

"Remember when we talked at Halloween last year about us both wanting kids?"

She nodded. "That's something I want to give you that you didn't get before. I fantasize about little Lin-Manuels."

He groaned but smiled. "Him again. Someday you need to admit if you fantasize about him when we make love." He softened his words with another kiss. "Given our careers, it will take a village to help us expand our family. Before we move back to that level of intimacy, I'd like to wait until Thanksgiving."

Her fingers danced over his abdomen but refrained from stroking lower at his request. She breathed into his lips. "You're going to drive me nuts with this, aren't you?" After pulling away, she lay with her good hand behind her head. "But I agree on making sure we're ready. I was a few days late after we made love on Labor Day weekend, and wondered if I was pregnant. Both the excitement and the fear were strong, and we were estranged—couldn't share it. I don't want to go through that again."

Her body twitched and she covered her eyes. "One other thing. Sam Demille in his diary said I should focus on being a good Mother. Am I buying into his beliefs if I want to be one? Before I met you, I used to think I'd wait longer before a commitment."

Tugging on her hand, he pulled her to face him. "Nothing from that dead fanatic should influence us. Let's do everything right this time—no chance for mistakes."

She smiled and feathered his lips using the hand glittering with the engagement ring.

· · ·

On Thanksgiving, they cuddled on the couch watching the Macy's parade on TV, recalling it in person a year earlier in Central Park. Maya's parents were busy making stuffing and loading the turkey into the oven. In midafternoon they phoned Maya's grandmother who was sharing dinner with her church community in Tucson. Then Maya set the table while Manolo helped her parents transfer the food into serving platters and bowls.

Once gathered around, her mom led them in a personal prayer. "The scientist in me praises doctors like Manolo for bringing our daughter safely home to us. But my Catholic faith believes in the destiny of good people like this young couple. Thank God for your recovery and reunion."

Manolo smiled. "I'm glad you said that, Barbara. There's some plans we'd like your blessing on."

Maya's dad clapped a hand on Manolo's shoulder. "Son, I like the sound of that. What do you have in mind?"

Maya pulled out the diamond from her pocket. "My CDC training is winding up and I'll start job applications this winter. Late June would be a perfect time for a wedding and a honeymoon to Africa."

Her mom squealed and leapt up, face colored to match her pulled-up pile of red hair. "The best news—let me see that ring. I want to help plan, if that's okay with you."

Maya reached out her right hand to hold Manolo's. "The only thing we've determined is the day for the ceremony, June 20."

Manolo leaned over for a kiss before he sat back, beaming. "After decades of marriage, when we're old and gray, we thought that would be a date to remember. 6/20/20."

Maya reveled in the happiness radiating from everyone's faces. She had no anxiety or doubts. Remembering back to her first *Borrelia* patient in May, she stroked her belly. "And if blessed by the animal gods in Africa, a year after that you could cuddle a grandchild."

Maya's parents drove home to Flagstaff in the late afternoon. After reaching Manolo's family on a FaceTime call, Maya waved the diamond on her right hand. "We'll size it for my left hand when I'm healed."

"So you finally put a ring on it," Sebastian joked. "Don't let this girl get away."

Manolo gave a thumbs up and Maya stumbled over her words,

overwhelmed with emotion. "Your family is an inspiration. I want what you have with Johnny, ever since we borrowed him for the zoo last Thanksgiving."

"We might fight for the wedding here," Ramona responded.

A trace of stubborn resolve crossed Manolo's face. "We'll see, hermana. Date's set, but location's still up in the air. If you bring Johnny out here, we'll make a real cowboy out of him."

Late at night, they sealed their commitment by making love for hours. Using fingers and lips, they became reacquainted with every inch of each other's bodies. No vibrator was needed for multiple orgasms. Perhaps passion postponed was ecstasy enhanced.

FORTY-TWO

The next morning, Manolo strolled naked into the bedroom juggling a breakfast tray with one hand and his open laptop in the other. "I have a wonderful surprise. At least, I hope you think so."

As he set the computer on the bed, he angled the screen toward Maya, displaying the iconic red rock towers of Sedona. "I envied your hot tub with your friends in Santa Fe. Let's celebrate our momentous decision at a spa." He scrolled to a photo of a resort at the base of the cliffs.

She lifted up on one elbow, skin covered with a sheen from the earlier romp. "I've been there but never overnight. You're treating me like a queen. Should I adopt a British accent?"

"Save it for tonight." He tugged her out of bed. "You can pretend to be one of those Singapore princesses who attends a British boarding school."

She picked up the sheet from the floor to avoid tripping and grabbed her suitcase. "Can't wait to indulge all your fantasies."

. . .

By midday, they checked into a room with soothing earth tones and a balcony framing jagged multicolored peaks textured by a light morning snowfall. "One of the IHS staff recommended the Red Rock Café for lunch," he said.

In homage to their earlier discussion, she dropped into a deep, deliberately clumsy curtsy. "I'm eager to follow your lead, master."

Nestled in the café's casual booth and starving from an

inadequate breakfast, they were happy to find it served all day. Maya chose blue corn huervos rancheros and Manolo banana blueberry walnut French toast. After inhaling the fruity fragrance from his plate, she helped herself to a few bites.

"This last year has been impossibly rough," he said between mouthfuls. "But everything's finally falling into place."

"I just need to finish my commitment to CDC and figure out my next job so we can balance work and family."

"Is that all? But I can be flexible too. There may be other positions in IHS outside Phoenix."

"Faye thinks I'll have my pick of jobs based on my broad experiences."

"Including conquering anthrax and *Borrelia*." He held her hand and twirled her ring, sparkling in the slanting early afternoon rays. "Before Thanksgiving, we briefly talked about kids."

Maya couldn't avoid the image of Bina Lucero in the ICU before she lost her baby boy and her life, leaving her daughter without a mother. Standing next to Bina's mom, Maya had absorbed the intensity of parent-child bonds and the existential fear of losing them. She often wondered if her biological family in China shattered over their need to give her up under the one-child policy.

Her memory flashed with her family's return to Anhui Province when she was twelve. As holiday fireworks lit the Hefei sky, she'd studied the display from the motel room window and announced, "It's my biological family. They know I'm all right." Her adult brain couldn't imagine where that insight had come from.

Manolo reached out a hand to brush her hair out of her eyes. "You're awfully quiet. Maybe I put the cart before the horse."

Her fingers stroked the back of his hand. "No, the choice of kids has to influence our decisions."

She had the advantage of role models within their own families—her parents and grandparents, Ramona and Abdi. And other couples like Dave and Emilia, Erika and Rolf to offer close-to-home inspiration and advice. Then she recalled Stefan and Kondrat, Zouhir and Rebecca. "But other countries sure make it easier."

"Well, as we ponder these weighty decisions, my IHS friend had another suggestion. Ever heard of sound healing?"

"No, but it 'sounds' intriguing."

"Sedona is a spiritual center. People worldwide are attracted to its special energy."

She laughed. "And a hotbed for UFO sightings. Aliens have been dogging me all year, first Dulce, then Roswell, and now here."

He shrugged. "Just an explanation for things we can't understand."

She pulled out her credit card for the waiter. "I'm wading courageously into new journeys, so let's take the next step."

. . .

In the darkened room, windows heavily shaded to bar the sharp Sedona light, Maya and Manolo lay on yoga mats for the private session. As the faint fragrance of incense filtered, candles glowed from every table and shelf in front of a rainbow of crystals. A dark-skinned older man wore a wool shawl with a cowl around his neck. "We'll begin with silent meditation," he said with a slight accent she couldn't identify, "to focus our energies and access the Divine."

Maya never found meditation successful, brain too much on overdrive. But she made a conscious effort as the shaman guided them in relaxing all their muscles. Warmed by a thin furry blanket and arms stretched to her sides, her fingers were millimeters away from Manolo's, energy transferred without touching.

Picking up two mallets, the man stroked glowing purple vases, each one vibrating with a different tone. With the tranquilizing sound waves, Maya was surprised to fade deeply into a trance, untroubled by her past injuries or any unresolved decisions. One of the shaman's hands maintained a deep singing tone on a huge white vase at her feet while the other transferred the oscillations to four golden bowls he rested on her body. As her skin and muscles trembled, he lit a stump of sage in a seashell placed on her groin. She receded once again into a pleasant torpor, and the shaman transferred the bowls to Manolo.

At some point, a quiet thrum sounded and she opened her eyes to eight bronze gongs mounted to the wall being struck in turn. "As we transition back into the world, these drums represent the chakras including the heart, throat, and third eye."

Staccato pulses from a rattle made out of a turtle shell alternated with tempered thumps on a drum. A few words Maya didn't recognize were uttered, and she was helped to sit up by the shaman. "Rest there for a moment before you stand. I'll leave you alone and meet you at the reception desk."

She reached out her arms and Manolo pulled her into a hug. "Quite an otherworldly experience," she said.

"Worth doing?" He kneaded her back with his fingers.

"Definitely. I need to lock these sounds and vibrations into my brain and draw on them when I'm stressed."

. . .

On the way back from dinner, Maya asked Manolo to swing by a grocery store. He glanced from his dark suit to her short red dress with its plunging neckline. "I think we're overdressed. What's on your shopping list?"

"Strawberries, chocolate syrup, honey, and whipped cream." She tucked her arm around his waist and led him inside.

Like a Fourth of July sparkler, a grin transformed the angular planes of his face. "Are we making dessert?"

She leaned full into a hug, breasts pressed against his chest, lips meeting his with desire. "Something like that."

A rough voice interrupted from the end of the aisle. "Hey buddy, whatcha do to get that one?"

Maya's fingers on Manolo's back froze in place. He stiffened but planted a smile as he turned to the middle-aged man in a black leather jacket. "Just lucky, I guess."

After they completed their purchases, Manolo carried them to his Corvette. "Sorry about that."

"Why should you apologize?" Maya lowered into her seat, then waited for him to take the wheel, her breath steadier after safely avoiding a confrontation. "You're not responsible for all rude males."

Face distorted, he abruptly twisted in his seat. "If it hadn't been in public, it might have ended differently. I get triggered when people objectify you, especially guys. I know how hard it is, always feeling like people are looking at you, drawing conclusions, thinking you're out of place."

Maya stopped him from turning the key. One of the longest strands of thought he'd expressed during his recovery—she was blown back by the forcefulness of his emotions. But what the guy said was mild compared to what others had done, like Enzo.

"Manolo, it's not the first time a guy's come onto me. You gonna kill them all?" With her left hand, she stroked his frown.

He nuzzled her hand, gentle over her scar. "You work with a lot of men and travel for work. I can only imagine how often something happens. Thank God I don't have to know about it."

She withdrew her fingers and studied both hands in her lap. If ever there was a golden opportunity . . . . But this magical weekend was the celebration of their commitment, with only one tiny interruption. Important to keep singly focused on the two of them.

. . .

Back in their room, Maya took the grocery bag from his arms and set it on the chair. When he reached to caress her, she shook her head. "Nope, you can't help. This is all on me." She removed his suit coat and tossed it on the bed, followed by his tie and white shirt, carefully setting the silver cufflinks, tie tack, and her ring on the end table. Retrieving the smoke-grey tie, she bound his wrists together in his lap.

His eyebrows went up. "What's this? Not that I'm complaining."

She pressed her lips to his and widened them into a deeper kiss. "No talking either, or I'll have to find another tie."

As she shoved him down to the bed, he nodded, breaking into a grin. She eased off each shoe and sock, fingernails feathering his feet into tiny twitches. Tugging him by his tied wrists back to his feet, she loosened his belt and unzipped his pants. As she dropped them to the floor, his arousal was already fully developed. Her hand brushed with the lightest of touches, promising but not delivering. Removing his blue boxer briefs, she left him exposed.

He aimed his hands to lift her skirt, but she swatted him away and sat him back on the edge of the bed. Starting at her feet, she pulled off the black sandals and trailed her fingers slowly up her right leg. Grabbing the bottom of the red silk, she gradually worked it over her head, tossing it on the bed to join his clothes. She lifted his hands toward the front clasp of the black lace bra. "You can unhook this."

With some difficulty, his fingers separated the two halves and lingered over her breasts before she slipped it off. His hands lowered to her lace panties. For a few moments, she gave into the languid strokes, her arousal lighting up like the candles at the sound healing. Then she whipped off her final piece of clothing and grabbed the loose ends of the tie, leading him to the bathroom.

After guiding him down to the navy rug on the floor, she turned back for the bag. "Not the bubbly spa you wanted." She gestured to the claw-foot tub. "But I'll track one down for you tomorrow night. This will do for cleanup."

One finger on her iPhone started Kehlani's mixtape *While We Wait*. With the sultry lyrics and throbbing beat, she danced slowly over his prone figure before lowering to the floor.

She adjusted his arms so they supported his head, washed the strawberries in the sink, and squirted them with chocolate in the ice bucket. As she offered the first one to him, his tongue circled it, sucking off the chocolate, before taking a bite. The second one was for her, followed by a creamy kiss.

He reflexively flinched as she sprayed the whipped cream all down his front. "Let me warm you up," she whispered. Her lips brought him to a rapid climax and she loosened the tie. "Too quick," she chided, "but now it's your turn. Or should I say mine."

They reversed positions on the rug. Holding up the honey jar and the whipped cream, he asked, "Any preference?" She pointed to the honey and her breasts, then the cream for lower parts. Her fulfillment was more languid but neither of them minded, and he was ready again when laughingly scrubbing each other clean in the warm bath.

. . .

After a night of deep sleep, they awoke to crystal clear skies and temperatures in the forties, snow all melted. "You surprised me last night," Manolo whispered in her ear.

"Surprised myself." Maya rolled tight into his arms. "Was it worth it?"

"Oh, yeah. Let's try some of that again, without the extra food sources."

An hour later, he unlatched the door to retrieve a tray of croissants and drinks. He drew open the outer curtains, allowing light to filter through the sheers. "With this glorious weather, we should get outside." He fed her a bite of flaky pastry. "Many people come here seeking Sedona vortexes."

"Which are?"

"Sacred sites that foster healing and enlightenment."

"Sounds intriguing, but I have my heart set on Devil's Bridge. I picked up a map from the lobby. Less than two miles one way, relatively flat."

"Last year, you led me on a hike in Bandelier Monument on El Día de los Muertos. You might have a proclivity toward the macabre."

"Not at all. I get enough spookiness from the mysterious microbes. And I've never sat through a single horror movie. But the view from this trail is supposed to be the best."

A half-hour north of Sedona, they passed a sign for their destination. Then a long tawny shape leapt from an arroyo on the right, landing in the middle of the road. In one jump it vanished into the junipers and pines. Manolo slammed his brakes. "Cougar. I've never seen one in the wild."

"Same here, and I grew up in Arizona."

He swerved over to a wide spot and turned off the engine. "Whew, I'm still shaking. One second faster and we would have collided."

She placed a hand on his chest to slow his breathing. "Mountain lions occasionally kill people on trails but this felt more exciting than threatening."

Manolo adjusted his cap and brushed away tiny drops of sweat from his forehead. "The Navajos and Pueblo tribes view mountain lions as protectors. Maybe it's a 'face your fears' kind of thing."

By the time they reached the small parking area, foreboding anvil clouds diminished the intensity of the sun. On the wide trail, Maya's tennis shoes quickly matched the red color of the lower cliffs. Her eyes darted between the bushes, alert to any large animal movement. As they approached the top of the large sandstone arch, the trail steepened with a series of rock stairs.

Maya tugged Manolo down to catch their breaths and re-energize with water and granola. She eyed the natural bridge which couldn't have been more than ten feet thick at its narrowest point fifty feet above the canyon below. Around them, jagged pinnacles, too steep for trees or ground cover, pierced the darkening sky. She took photos of other hikers venturing across the bridge. Surely she could do it too.

A text from her mom lit up the iPhone. **Tornadoes near the National Memorial Cemetery and Phoenix Mountain Park, not far from you. You okay?**

We're fine, she texted back. **In Sedona, not Phoenix. We'll call when back home.**

She showed the phone to Manolo. "Hopefully we'll have a home to return to," he joked. "I'd worry more if we'd heard the cougar growl. The Apache believe it's a harbinger of death."

"I'll go with the Navajo and Hopi belief in protection." Shivering, she steeled her nerves. "If we're going to do this, we better do it now before that bad weather reaches this area."

Inhaling a deep breath, she marveled at her change in luck, or maybe sense of accomplishment. *Borrelia* was under control with expanded tick education, including another children's coloring book planned with Dave. Despite some unresolved issues and the handicap of one less finger, she was thankful for her recovery from flash-bang wounds and benzo dependence.

She stood up and offered Manolo a hand. "I keep thinking about the cougar. It's so adaptable, they're increasing in the west."

He cuddled her close. "Adaptable—good word for what we've gone through this past year."

Tracing his emerging goatee with her lips, she smiled. "I learned bravery and persistence from you." His face beamed with the compliment.

With a wave of Sedona sagacity, she suddenly appreciated her growth from the challenges of the cursed past year. Before anthrax, Manolo took the lead on their relationship, but since then, she had grown into the driver's seat. He was always there, even when the path was murky, supporting her evolution.

Maya's musings were interrupted by the whoop of a teenage girl making ballet leaps for her boyfriend's video. Inspired by the girl's exuberance, Maya took her first step. With Manolo next to her when the bridge narrowed to five feet, vertigo kicked in as she was forced uncomfortably close to the sheer drop-off.

She locked her eyes on the large bush improbably growing from the top of the arch and stepped ahead of him on the rough surface, wobbly on loose rocks as the winds picked up. Her damaged hand stayed locked in his until he settled his fingers on either side of her waist, steadying both of them in the comfortable middle lane. When her left foot moved forward, his followed, and they continued their synchronous dance until safely back on solid ground, just before the storm clouds broke.

CODA

Some zoonotic microorganisms, capable of spreading from animals to people, primarily hug to one species. Their sole focus is transforming cells into deadly factories. But when they make the leap, humans are not prepared.

(This new story continues in MayaVerse Book 3, Corona: A Microbial Mystery).

Author Notes

The MayaVerse at https://drmayamaguire.com/ offers entertaining, educational, and enlightening insights into the mysteries and threats of microbes from animal hosts (zoonoses). **Please join the Reader List** to keep updated on other publications beyond "*Borrelia*: A Microbial Mystery."

Links are available to previous novels in the series and short stories, including prequels or side stories to the novels. The alphabetical MayaVerse novels are published wide, which means the ebook, paperback, large print, and hardcover formats are available from multiple retailers. Most of these links are available at https://books2read.com/millicenteidson/. Audiobook versions are still in development; check the MayaVerse for updates.

COVID-19 has made the work and challenges of the Centers for Disease Control and Prevention (CDC) more visible. However, its seventy-year training program for disease detectives still flies under the radar (https://www.cdc.gov/eis/about/history.html).

My own training as an EIS Officer formed life-long relationships and a dedication to excellence in epidemiology. I treasure the support from my two other veterinary colleagues in the class of 1983, Drs. Faye Sorhage and Marguerite Pappiaoanou.

Several veterinary EIS Officers from the class of 2019 provided substantive information for *Borrelia*: Drs. Grace Vahey, Joseph Hicks, and Allison James.

The MayaVerse continues to benefit from my family team of Lian Henderson, inspiration for and feedback on the Maya Maguire character, and Tom Henderson, audio and visual media advisor for Maya Maguire Media.

Borrelia was initially drafted in November, 2021 with support from NaNoWriMo (https://nanowrimo.org/). The novel was then critiqued in its entirety by Vermont author Liz Teuber. Writing groups providing critiques of individual chapters include The Burlington Writers Workshop (https://burlingtonwritersworkshop.com/), which I proudly serve as its Secretary. BWW reviews were contributed through its Fiction Novel workshop (Dick Matheson and Mike Magluilo, co-hosts) and its Romance workshop (Vicky Phillips and Millie Eidson, co-hosts). The Open Genre Discussion of the Green Mountain Writers Group (https://greenmountainwriters.com/) has been a constant source of inspiration (Stephen Kastner, coordinator). Finally, *Borrelia* has benefited from feedback through the Sisters in Crime (https://www.sistersincrime.org/) Murder, Mystery & Mayhem Critique Group, and from instructors and students at Champlain College and the University of Vermont.

Additional organizations and authors have provided support. None of us could find our readers without mentions on blogs and newsletters from other authors. Important groups include two Sisters in Crime chapters: Grand Canyon Writers (https://grandcanyonwriters.com/) and Tucson Old Pueblo Chapter (https://www.tucsonsistersincrime.org/). The Alliance of Independent Authors is a valuable organization (https://www.allianceindependentauthors.org/) .

Provision of information by agency employees or workshop participants does not imply endorsement by those individuals or groups. Scientific nomenclature including when to italicize organism names can be confusing. For more information, see: https://wwwnc.cdc.gov/eid/page/scientific-nomenclature.

Although *Borrelia* is informed by fact, it is a work of fiction. Descriptions of events, locations, agencies, or Native American Nation staff and functions are intended to anchor the stories in public health science and the larger world, but do not represent specific activities of real people or institutions.

Borrelia Discussion Questions

Book groups interested in discussions with the author should email <u>drmayamaguire@gmail.com</u>.

Borrelia crosses genres, with multiple themes in the framework of a zoonotic disease. The following questions may help in thinking about and discussing the novel.

1. The genre elements include mystery, women's fiction, and romantic suspense. How do each of these elements contribute to the overall arc and your enjoyment of the story?
2. The main character is a young Chinese American woman adopted as an infant by an Irish-heritage family living in the Southwest. What elements of the character's background enrich the story?
3. What are some biological, regional, cultural, and religious influences on our perceptions of 'the other'?
4. How does the 'me too' theme impact the story? How do you define sexual harassment? What do you think of the decisions the characters take in response to it?
5. The Southwest is intended as a character in itself. How does geography and history influence the story?
6. Maya's perceptions are enlarged by her work in other countries. In what ways do you think exposure to other cultures and ways of life impact us?
7. What are current challenges in balancing work and personal obligations? Are there different roadblocks to achieving this for men and women?

8. This story takes place in 2019, just prior to the coronavirus pandemic. Although the story is fiction, what elements of the story will likely change in 2020?

9. How should public health policy balance the needs of society versus those of individual patients, especially in the face of different perspectives?

10. Zoonotic diseases are those in common between humans and non-human animals. How are transmission, investigation, prevention, and control more complex for zoonotic diseases than those infecting only humans?

11. What is the role of climate change in the story and for zoonotic diseases?

12. How can someone with a veterinary medical degree contribute to disease investigations?

13. For authenticity, writers often rely on personal experience, while protecting privacy of those sharing life events with the author. Writers also use research and close consultation with others to create characters, plot events, and settings not their own. As a reader, do you have a preferred balance of work informed by an author's imagination, research, and representation of their background?

About the Author

MILLICENT EIDSON is the author of the alphabetical Maya Maguire microbial mysteries. The MayaVerse at https://drmayamaguire.com/ includes prequels, "El Chinche" in *Danse Macabre* and "What's Within" in *Fiction on the Web*, and a side story, "Pérdida" in *El Portal Literary Journal*. Awards include Best Play in *Synkroniciti* and Honorable Mention from the Arizona Mystery Writers.

Dr. Eidson's work as a public health veterinarian and epidemiologist began as an EIS Officer with the Centers for Disease Control and Prevention and continued at the New Mexico and New York state health departments. She has authored over a hundred scientific papers, articles, and book chapters. Currently, she is a public health faculty member at the University at Albany and the University of Vermont, and teaches a UVM course on zoonoses and climate change in its Larner College of Medicine.

With formative years in the Southwest, Millie enjoys reconnecting with Arizona family, heritage trips to Norway, Ireland, and China, and wider travel worldwide. In retirement from full-time public health work, she has settled in Vermont with her husband Tom Henderson and daughter Lian Henderson, inspiration for Maya Maguire.

Other interests are photography (website and book cover photos are primarily the author's), painting, hiking, and bicycling along the beautiful Burlington, Vermont waterfront.

Social media links:
www.linkedin.com/in/eidsonmillicent
Maya Maguire Media | Facebook
Millicent Eidson (@EidsonMillicent) / Twitter
Millie Eidson (@drmayamaguire) • Instagram photos and videos